About the au

Colin Farrington was born in Teesside in 1954 and spent his formative years living in the shadow of the best of playgrounds — a slag-tip. His occasional attendance at Eston Grammar School led to his struggling with Latin but excelling at sport, particularly football. Subsequently he joined the Army and travelled extensively, experiencing holiday-fun camping in the path of an army of ants in Kenya and in snow at minus 30 degrees in Norway. He played chess in San Ignacio on the Belizean border with Guatemala.

In addition to Colin's two published novels, another significant achievement was to cross the Pyrenees and then trek with his tent 500 miles across Spain to Santiago de Compostella, thereby expiating his sins and obtaining a certificate granting entry into Heaven. Not wishing to be premature, however, he is working on a fourth novel. Colin has two sons and lives with his partner Sarah.

KALANGBA JUNCTION

To

Andy and
Lynn
Best wishes

Colin Yarrington

26th Nov,
2022

COLIN FARRINGTON

KALANGBA JUNCTION

Vanguard Press

A CIP catalogue record for this title is
available from the British Library.

ISBN 978 1 80016 288 4

*Vanguard Press is an imprint of
Pegasus Elliot MacKenzie Publishers Ltd.*
www.pegasuspublishers.com

First Published in 2022

**Vanguard Press
Sheraton House Castle Park
Cambridge England**

Printed & Bound in Great Britain

Dedication

I dedicate this book to my partner, Sarah Horne. Her love and practical support enabled me to write it.

Also by Colin Farrington

In the Shadow of the Kestrel

Five Masts in the Bay

Coming soon

The Nemesis Man

Chapter One
Welcome to Sierra Leone

The cherry-red canvas bag nestled between Neffie Goodwin's knees as she occupied a seat on the upper deck of the ferry making slow progress across the mouth of the Sierra Leone River was testimony to her considerable travelling experience. Visually reassuring, in these circumstances the bag which was her only luggage was also comforting to touch. More than once she had, without thinking, gently squeezed her knees into the fabric until she met with the firm resistance provided by the clothes within. It was as if she were gaining tactile pleasure from the bag just being there.

The woman sitting to her left on the bench kept looking at her watch. The man sitting on Neffie's right nearest the gangway was known to her, but she had made his acquaintance less than three hours previously. The most striking aspect of his appearance wasn't that he was black, or that he had a broad, flattish nose, or that his black hair was short and wiry — this after all was Sierra Leone — but that he was wearing glasses the lenses of which were the largest she had ever seen, and consequently magnified the limpid brown eyes they assisted. If Neffie had been wearing a red hood she might have been tempted to say, "My, what big eyes you have." It wouldn't have been true. On this, the first occasion that the man took off his glasses in front of Neffie to wipe them clean, which he did with an apparently unused white handkerchief, she noted that his eyes were smaller than she had expected them to be. They had the look of belonging to a short-sighted man in need of help. No sooner had the man returned the spectacles to balance on the features they were designed for than he regained an appearance of fashion-conscious intelligence. Their magnification renewed, Neffie didn't feel that they posed a vulpine threat.

"You must think we're so inefficient," said the man, turning his head slightly towards Neffie, but keeping his eyes, as if he were trying to divine the contents, focused on the cherry-red bag between her knees. He was referring to the chaos they had experienced on the Lungi side of the river behind them, and the ensuing delay.

Neffie was about to tell her companion that she had learned to be philosophical when travelling in Africa, but before she was able to express that thought, and back it up by recounting some of the encounters she had had, the man rose to his full height of five feet eight, and, without saying where he was going, said simply, "Excuse me, I'll leave you to enjoy your holiday alone for a few minutes."

That word 'holiday' irritated Neffie. Despoiling her self-image, it made her idea of having come to Sierra Leone to do voluntary work frivolous. Hardly an echo, but a sentiment expressed frequently enough at irregular intervals to have made her meaning unequivocal, back home, stretching way back in time, Neffie had made it public knowledge that she would have loved to have been an anthropologist. For her, even though she was presently employed as a teacher at a primary school located in one of the more salubrious suburbs of Ferrousby, there could be no better job than living with and studying people whose way of life was in marked contrast to her own. The reason she hadn't embarked upon arguably the more adventurous professional role at the outset of her working life was one of simple expedience, for having trained to become a teacher she had felt bound to teach; besides, the thirteen weeks paid holiday per annum concomitant with the pedagogic life, and the opportunities for travel which they allow, are second to none.

It was little wonder, therefore, that Neffie took her travelling seriously. Over an adult lifetime to date of thirty years she had undertaken a number of trips that were memorable for being as daring as this, her latest African adventure. More than a decade ago she had locked the front door of her terraced house in the North Yorkshire village of Yatton behind her and set off on a journey the ultimate destination of which, before she returned home that is, was Vladivostok, the Russian port overlooking Golden Horn Bay in the Sea of Japan. Notwithstanding the prospect of travelling alone by train several thousand miles across Siberia, Neffie's greatest worry prior to shutting that same front door was that she would miss the bus timed to take her the eight miles into Ferrousby in time to catch her first train. Following such a calamity, down the line a chaos of transport timings would ensue. The journey by train from Moscow would take seven nights; a week of discovery, of her inner self, and, as an amateur anthropologist, of the citizens of Mother Russia.

In a general sense a similar pattern of soul-searching within to match her worldly explorations without can be discerned in her more recent expeditions. Take the one she had set about five years ago. After handing in her notice to take a year off from teaching she boarded a truck in London and headed south across the channel. Then it was onward through France and Spain, eventually to trundle across the Sahara Desert, and much more of the African continent. At least on that expedition she was travelling with like-minded people. It has to be said, however, that there isn't necessarily safety in numbers. On a similar trip the previous year the Bedford truck had been held up by bandits, and though the female members of the group had been allowed to continue on their way, all the men were shot.

To give just one more example of Neffie's intrepid nature when it comes to exploring our planet we shall venture into the Karakorum Mountains, there to imagine ourselves sitting on the back of a yak following the teacher in question's lead. The beast's broad back is swaying alarmingly as it places one sure foot in front of the other on its heart-stopping trek — heart-stopping for its passenger that is — along a narrow, precipitous path, a sheer rock face to the left, a scary thousand feet drop to the right. There's no turning back.

Yes, there had been many such expeditions and adventures on every continent save the coldest, and it was woe betide the thoughtless or dangerously provocative individual who dared to equate Neffie's concept of travelling with mere tourism. This was a mistake which Sebastian Forrest, Neffie's partner in life and love, had made at an early stage in their relationship of five years duration, but it was an error of judgement he hadn't repeated since, and this despite the fact that as a former member of the Special Air Service Sebastian had sufficient confidence in his own ability to survive in difficult circumstances, and enough audacity to rib his partner in other ways, but primarily for being a 'meek and feeble woman'. Presently Sebastian enjoyed working as a freelance journalist. He supplemented the pittance he received per line from that rewarding occupation with the more substantial remuneration he earned working as a security officer on a building site. In that role it was a case of needs must. For the simple reasons that Seb was neither unemployed nor a school teacher who has a six-week long break in the summer, he had been unable to accompany his partner on her journeys into the unknown. Another compelling reason for him to stay at home was that he was often financially embarrassed, and had become adept at juggling: needless to say, it wasn't with balls.

Back on the Sierra Leone River Miss Nefertiti Goodwin was aware that as the only white person within her field of vision she attracted several studious looks, mainly from children. She returned their curiosity with a disarming smile that was quickly reciprocated. To a man, and a woman, the adults whose expressions she read were no less friendly. Somewhat disconcertingly however, to judge by the intensity of his gaze a young man of about twenty appeared to be entranced by her. It wasn't that she felt threatened by his scrutiny, but she did feel herself blush as she turned her head askance to focus on the scene in the vicinity of Freetown Harbour, specifically the cabins along the shore and the more impressive red-roofed, white-stucco buildings behind; at the tall palms which, leaning in the same direction at a slight angle to the perpendicular, provided shade and made for a pleasing aspect, and at the dwellings amid the dense vegetation covering the slopes of the hills which served as backdrop to the city. Neffie was used to being the centre of attention in class, but this was different. This was stimulating.

Deep down Neffie hoped that her lover was pining away with longing in the house they shared back in Yatton, that he was missing her just as much as she would miss him, and perhaps her first little weep would be, when alone at last in her hotel bed, as soon as tonight. If everything were to go according to plan, six weeks hence she would cross the threshold in Yatton, drop her bag on the coconut mat behind the door, and attempt to match Seb's bear-like hug. From past experience she could easily imagine, because one thing usually led to another, that soon after she would be carried upstairs to bed. If everything were to go according to plan, on the morning following her return she would be back at school in charge of her class, none of whom was older than four. Aboard the ferry steering placidly towards Freetown Neffie smiled to herself as she thought on how far away that world of ordered regularity and excitable children was, and not just in miles.

The vacant seat beside her was once again taken by the man whom she had only recently met. His name was Samuel Massequoi. By virtue of contacts, she had made a week prior to her departure, the weary teacher — she had been travelling for the best part of twenty-four hours — had been met by him at the airport. Conceived and put into effect back home in England this arrangement had gone according to plan, though she wouldn't have included in that plan the considerable apprehension she had felt as she descended from the plane to make for the terminal buildings, all the while thinking of a contingency plan if Samuel were to have proved unreliable.

Aware without stating the obvious as to where her companion cum escort had been, Neffie turned toward Samuel and, smiling, questioned with one word, "Comfortable?"

Samuel stretched out his legs into the gangway and, crossing his right ankle to rest on his left, said, "I am now."

The movement of Samuel's lower limb drew Neffie's attention to the hole in the side of his baseball boot, just behind the toe-cap. It was significant.

Before she had cast eyes on Mr Massequoi in person Neffie had a good mental image of what he looked like. It had been provided by the photograph of him which she carried in her money-belt. It hadn't taken Neffie long to discover that her apprehension as to whether he would turn up was unfounded. No sooner had she presented her passport and visa at the immigration control desk than she was led off by a man who was remarkably conspicuous for his pristine white shirt. Miss Goodwin had been escorted to where Samuel was waiting. Evidently Mr Massequoi was considered by the immigration official to be an important person, and perhaps that was because he was, and in all probability still is, a teacher. Far from wishing to depreciate Samuel's status, Neffie did, however, consider an alternative explanation: simply that people were always this helpful in Sierra Leone.

The distance from Lungi Airport to the capital is just over eighteen miles, and two hours after setting off in a taxi the pair were still a few miles from the hotel which for the foreign visitor was to be that day's final destination. The delay which Samuel had been embarrassed by was caused by a problem loading vehicles on to the ferry. A lorry carrying sacks of rice had caused mayhem by breaking down on the loading ramp. Judging by the number of dilapidated vehicles discarded by the side of the road en route to the ferry, Neffie had concluded that mechanical breakdown was a commonplace occurrence and spare parts to effect a repair difficult to obtain. Evidently in many a case breaking down had proved terminal.

Neffie's fatigue from travelling was compounded by the heat and high humidity. The air temperature even at this hour — it was six-thirty in the evening — was twenty-nine degrees centigrade, and although our intrepid teacher had no idea as to what the temperature had been when she had boarded her last flight of the day and journey at Schiphol, it had been immediately apparent that the difference in thermometer readings between Holland and here was marked.

This being August it was the height of the rainy season, and hardly a day passed without a heavy downpour of that warm rain which is so typical of the tropics. Neffie had arrived too late in the country to have to evade or be soaked by that day's deluge, but the sky all around was a brooding mass of dark nimbus. The lugubrious clouds weren't ubiquitous, for here and there patches of clear blue yonder were visible, and the vaporous accumulation aligned with the setting sun was tinged with a silvery luminescence. It added to Neffie's sense of awe and mystery as to what she would encounter in the days and weeks ahead.

"So what can you tell me about Freetown?" enquired Neffie, demonstrating fortitude in her willingness to communicate when what she really wanted to do was rest her head on Samuel's shoulder and go to sleep. For being fleshy the upper arm of the lady to her left would have been more comfortable.

"Well," began Samuel, "it's the city where I live and work, one of just over a million souls trying, as anywhere, to make their way in life, some more successfully than others, some more honestly than others. If there's one fact which I can tell you as accurately as you would expect to hear from a tour guide it's that the city was founded on March 11th, 1792, by Lieutenant John Clarkson, and as you probably know it quickly became a haven for freed slaves, hence the name."

Samuel had begun recounting the city's history enthusiastically, but, being a man of considerable empathy and perception, he soon realised, despite Neffie having posed the question, that even the small amount of information he had imparted thus far was failing to properly register: his interlocutor's face looked glazed.

"But there's no need for me to burden you with a welter of boring facts this evening, exhausting you further unnecessarily. I'll tell you all you want to know about the glorious deeds of our colonial masters tomorrow, after you've rested."

Neffie wasn't too glazed over to be able to detect the heavy sarcasm in Mr Massequoi's reference to the British. The phrase 'our colonial masters' was one which she would hear several times in Samuel's company.

Taking Samuel's advice, because she really was too tired to hold much of a conversation with the new acquaintance seated beside her, and to give her thoughts free rein, she let her eyes float over the faces of the people seated nearby, and then take in the greater number crowded as pedestrians on the vehicle deck below. The man whom she believed had been staring at her, somewhat lasciviously in Neffie's view, was nowhere to be seen, and Miss Goodwin imagined that it had been when Samuel had returned to take up his seat beside her that the individual in question had left the scene.

Neffie noted that a great many of her fellow passengers, but particularly the women, were dressed in clothes of vibrant colour, attire which she recognised as being typical of Africa. No doubt the passengers that had congregated near the ship's bows were hoping to make a quick getaway once the ferry had berthed. The anticipation plainly visible in the crowd below certainly gave the impression that the skipper of the Fourah Bay was only too willing to cooperate with his passengers' wishes in this regard. It had been to Neffie's surprise and initial consternation that the Fourah Bay had left Tagrin Point on the Lungi side of the estuary with her ramp lowered and her bow doors open. They had remained thus for the entire voyage. A little way out from her point of embarkation Neffie had wondered whether the crew had simply forgotten to make the ship seaworthy. On that possibly being the case she now wondered whether it was just good fortune that the Fourah Bay hadn't been swamped. She could easily imagine the consequence of a sudden inrush of water, for in her mind she was able to picture with perfect clarity the Herald of Free Enterprise lying on her side in relatively shallow water barely a mile from Zeebrugge. Occurring just over four years previously, in March 1987, the cause of the tragedy in which one hundred and ninety-three people lost their lives was negligence. The boatswain, the person responsible for closing the bow doors, had been asleep in his cabin when he shouldn't have been. Neffie wondered whether the consequences of a man being asleep on duty had ever been so dire.

In a similar vein she knew full well that ferries capsizing and then sinking as they churned the waters of Africa's great rivers were not uncommon incidents, and like the tragedy of Zeebrugge, there was often great loss of life. A recurring factor in 'accidents' of this kind was that the owners and skippers put profit before safety and packed in as many fare paying passengers as possible, so that the craft became grossly overcrowded; although it also has to be said that the ire of people that may have to wait days for the next ferry when the ship in front of their eyes is about to depart would, understandably, be considerable. The Fourah Bay wasn't overcrowded, a fact which was obvious as Neffie studied the throng say of a hundred people waiting patiently below. A ship the size of the Fourah Bay could accommodate that number easily.

Even though titles such as the Wilder Shores of Love by Lesley Blanch and A Vindication of the Rights of Woman by Mary Wollstonecraft counted amongst the many books she had read, Miss Nefertiti Goodwin didn't consider herself to be an ardent feminist. She wouldn't have been able to put up with Sebastian if she had been. Nonetheless, she couldn't help but notice that it was mainly the women amongst the throng standing that were burdened by heavy loads. Some carried children on their backs. A few, perhaps thinking that the most arduous part of their labours was in raising and lowering their heavy loads — be an individual burden a bunch of plantains or a sack of rice, a five-gallon water container or a bundle of clothes — kept their respective goods atop their heads. Several sacks of rice were in evidence. No doubt to save their strength for some onerous task to come, the men, most wearing jeans, t-shirts and trainers, carried very little. Neffie did happen to notice that two young men several yards apart were in charge of tyres, the man nearest the front of the throng being in possession of four of the vulcanised rubber rings stacked in a wheelbarrow, whilst the individual standing towards the rear with only one tyre to look after controlled it effortlessly with long, slender fingers.

Just as Neffie was about to return her attention to the structures along the slowly approaching shore, most prominent of which was a lighthouse to warn ships about the wrecking rocks on which it stood, her musings were interrupted by Mr Massequoi's mellow voice as, evidently forgetful of his earlier solicitude with regard to Neffie's energy levels, he proceeded to furnish his fellow teacher with a few additional facts.

"It may interest you to know, Miss Goodwin, that this ferry was provided by the Italian Government in anticipation of the African summit in 1980, and not, as you might have imagined, by our former colonial masters."

She noted that at least Samuel was smiling broadly when he made the comment. "I thought it looked in quite good condition…" She had been about to say 'for Africa' but thought better of it. There was no point, she thought, in exchanging jibes. In keeping with the stilted tone of Samuel's delivery Neffie found the snippet dull. Nevertheless, she decided to try to make amends for any obvious lack of interest on her part, even if her reticence, born of fatigue, was making life — that part of it taken up by the river crossing — difficult for her guide.

"The Italians would appear to make excellent ships if this one is anything to go by, but tell me, Mr Massequoi…"

At this point Miss Goodwin determined to resolve another matter, and that was that she could no longer put up with being addressed so formally. For her to be called 'Miss Goodwin' by someone who was more or less the same age as her, and with whom she was likely to spend some time, reminded her of school, and this being the August holiday that was the last place she wanted to bring to mind. Rather than voice her concerns about the ferry they were on being open to the river therefore, as she had intended, she chose to be amiable instead. "If you don't mind, Samuel, I really would prefer it if you would call me Neffie. In fact I'll go further than that and say I'll be annoyed if you don't."

Revealing two rows of small even white teeth Samuel beamed his acquiescence. The look in a pair of brown eyes partially obscured by the way the light entered through the lens of his glasses was further confirmation that he had no intention of annoying Neffie, but having grown accustomed to making formal pronouncements he had to check himself when next he spoke. "I'm sorry, Miss Good... I mean Neffie... it's just that you speak English so beautifully, and your manners are so..." There was a short pause as the speaker struggled to find the right word.

"Impeccable?" suggested Neffie, not taking herself too seriously.

"I was going to say gracious," Samuel responded. "Anyway they remind me of all those fine ladies alighting from carriages and attending balls in search of a suitable husband in the novels I have to read for my degree course."

"It sounds like Jane Austen world to me," Neffie responded, raising her eyebrows questioningly even though she was fairly confident that her supposition was correct.

"I do admire her novels, don't you... Neffie?" Samuel emphasised her name as if it were a word he had only just learned to say, which in one sense it was. "I have yet to read Mansfield Park but my favourite Austen novel so far is Sense and Sensibility. I love the gradually diminishing inheritance on offer to the Dashwood girls at the beginning."

"I'm afraid she's not really my cup of tea," said Neffie, puckering up her face, thereby adding visual expression to her verbal statement of disdain.

"Not my cup of tea... such a lovely English expression... so refreshing... yet so redolent of our colonial masters it could be straight out of a Jane Austen novel," said Samuel.

Miss Goodwin, though she didn't see herself in a bonnet and had never alighted from a horse drawn carriage in her life, and because she wasn't particularly looking for a husband either rich or poor, was charmed by Samuel's comparison nonetheless. She found it odd that her interlocutor was so impressed by the novels of an eighteenth century female English author whose world and subject matter couldn't have been more different from Samuel's own, yet at the same time, judging by his comments about the British thus far, could be somewhat scathing of Miss Austen's countrymen and the culture they had tried to impose on Sierra Leone.

It wasn't that Samuel's echoing taunt was spoken with venom, but it was undoubtedly sardonic. It led Neffie to conclude that Samuel desired to let it be known that the children had now grown up and no longer needed their foster parents to wipe their noses, as it were. The refined English lady, though undoubtedly charmed by Mr Massequoi's accolades, was surprised by them nonetheless. Hitherto the conversation had been perfunctory, and even though the tea Neffie would have loved a few sips of wasn't to be had for love or money, she did feel refreshed a little, and being invigorated was more inclined to talk. Two factors encouraged her loquacity. Arguably the most important was that for the first time in Samuel's company she felt as if the ice was broken, as if an invisible barrier to free and easy conversation had been removed. She now felt as if she was speaking to a friend rather than to a complete stranger.

The other influence working its magic, albeit indirectly, upon Neffie's vocal cords, was the weather. Now that the sun was sinking beneath the horizon the temperature was palpably lower, and whereas up until a few moments ago for Neffie the air had been stifling for being so sultry, presently an offshore breeze rippled the water and cooled the skin.

Aware weeks before she had set out from home that Sierra Leone is predominantly a Muslim country, and not wishing to offend religious sensibilities was reason enough for Neffie to dress in a style which she considered to be appropriate. The only parts of her body visible to the world were her face, hands and certain parts of her feet. Her two corporeal soles were supported by sandals. The sudden drop in temperature had prompted Samuel to put on and zip up a smart, navy-blue jerkin he had been carrying. He suggested to Neffie that if she was feeling the sea-breeze too keenly they could give up their seats on the exposed upper deck and try to obtain similar perches on the deck below, where they could shelter behind windows. Neffie dismissed the idea in an instant, informing that she hadn't been as comfortable since getting off the plane. Thinking that the thin material of his jacket wasn't going to be warm enough to suit, Mr Massequoi was momentarily disappointed. It didn't, however, take him long to recover his spirits and reveal his normal far from downcast expression. He took pleasure in believing that once they were alongside the quay, in about twenty minutes judging by their present speed and distance from shore, the chilling effect of the breeze borne on the Atlantic would have dissipated. The thought occurred to him, and it was a sympathetic one, that it must be dreadful to have to contend with the winters where Neffie lived, and farther north than that. This thought, rather than the sea-breeze, made him shiver.

For a man who had never been near the place Samuel knew a great deal about the part of England where Neffie lived. He was the father of a teenage boy called James and the former husband of a woman from Freetown called Linda. Mother and son were now domiciled in Britain and lived in a terraced house in Luxborough, a sizeable town of approximately fourteen thousand souls four miles from Yatton. Whether from love or expedience Linda had remarried. Her second husband was an Englishman called Peter. The couple who were now, Mr and Mrs Hind, had met when Peter had been posted to Sierra Leone, as a voluntary service overseas worker, to perform his voluntary tasks. It was through Samuel's estranged family that Neffie had learned about him, and it was from them that she had obtained his photograph. Apart from a few bare facts about James' schooling, that about summed up the extent of Neffie's knowledge of Samuel Massequoi and his family ties.

Soon after having shaken hands for the first time at the airport, Neffie, acting as a courier on Linda's behalf, had handed Samuel a letter. He had secured this epistle in the zipped inside pocket of his jacket, from where, as far as Neffie was aware, it had yet to surface to be read. She presumed that Samuel was prepared to wait for a time when he could be alone to savour the pleasure or came to terms with the disappointment regarding the progress or otherwise of his son. Miss Goodwin's knowledge of Samuel Massequoi's former marital situation might have been scant, but she knew nothing about his present personal circumstances. She had a yen to know whether he had found a replacement for Linda. From what he had said thus far she was able to determine those aspects of his life and personality that he was keen to project, if only obliquely. They were that he was an intelligent, well-read, university-educated individual, and as such could be considered eligible.

Neffie studied her companion's physiognomy as if eligibility in the mating-game wasn't out of the question, even though it probably was. She did this in a way that any young heterosexual woman might look at an attractive member of the opposite sex, in a way that even if she was happily married, and married she certainly wasn't, would be perfectly natural. Neffie had earlier noted that the chest, when it was covered only by his shirt, was compact and lissom.

The perfectly natural appraisal of another's appearance wasn't only one way. Just as Neffie had studied Samuel's physical attributes he had studied her. What had struck him above all else about this evidently refined English woman with the mellifluous voice wasn't that on average she was several inches shorter than the women he was accustomed to seeing in the streets of Freetown, nor the apparent softness of her unblemished white skin, but rather, when compared to the simplicity of local styles, her freaky hair. Protruding one and a half to two inches above the forehead, the thick crop of mouse-coloured hair resembled, though for being too rigid not exactly, the thatch forming the roof that overhangs the walls of a village dwelling. Back from the overhang the style was less severe, so that the hair rounded the back of the head to end a little lower than her shirt collar. With a little imagination the style could be said to have been modelled on a helmet of the type worn by soldiers in Cromwell's New Model Army. Given Neffie's pacifist views however, to describe her hair in such terms to her face would be ill advised.

Samuel had noted that in the main Neffie's eyes sparkled with exuberant life, but that on the rare occasion when her mood became a little sombre and they temporarily lost their diamond lustre, they turned into, as it were, deep pools of translucent water wherein a man might drown. Alternatively, but equally bewitching when they sought to implore, her eyes were able to project the pleading look of an orphaned puppy, one seeking a home: as yet this appealing look was alien to Samuel. Judging solely on the basis of her ocular expressiveness, for Neffie there was the tiniest fulcrum of time between joy and sadness, sadness and joy. Her response to events, comments, or the mental observations she made, was instinctive and usually immediate. It was her good fortune, and the good fortune of the people that she chanced to meet, that her joyful expression was the one that usually prevailed. Despite having just travelled a significant distance across the globe Neffie's eyes retained their life-affirming radiance in which Samuel also detected a glint of playful mischief. Taking her face in the round, and with mischief in mind, all that Neffie needed to appear truly elfin was a small upturned nose, but this she lacked. The teenager that Neffie had been just over a decade ago, upon looking into the mirror at her maturing face and developing breasts, had wanted her nose to have been smaller, her lips to have been fuller, and her breasts to grow larger. Apart from the latter, which had grown as she would have wished, like any individual who isn't a paragon of beauty, she had had to come to terms with the shortcomings, as she had perceived them to be, of her genetic inheritance. The mature, professional woman that the anxious teenager had become was perfectly at ease with the features the combining of her parents' genes had formed. She had determined long ago that she would change nothing about the way she looked, save, perhaps, for her hair. More than once, and primarily for school's sake, she had resisted the temptation to dye it a shocking colour.

"Perhaps we should make our way down to the car deck," said Samuel as soon as it was obvious that disembarkation was only minutes away.

The woman sitting to Neffie's left, in obeisance to Samuel's suggestion as if it were a command, rose to her feet and with a downward sweep of her hand straightened out her bright yellow dress. "About time too," she muttered aloud, looking directly ahead, her frustration was aimed at no one in particular.

It took a few moments for Neffie to realise that the woman who was a stranger to her was a stranger to Samuel too, and that the synchronised action of vacating their seats to stand was either coincidence or a case of auto-suggestion. Similarly, acting with the degree of coordination one would expect of dancers in a well-choreographed ballet, other people seated in the vicinity of the two teachers neither led nor followed Samuel as they arose.

By this time, it was dark. The moon and the vast majority of stars were hidden by cloud, but like an old blanket gnawed by rats to reveal gaping holes, through them could be seen the odd twinkle from a distant constellation. Unlike the illumination visible ashore, where it appeared that the main source was a number of strategically placed oil lamps, the Fourah Bay was brightly lit, and the passengers that had been seated on the same deck as Neffie and Samuel were clearly visible as they gathered their luggage and other items. Then languidly, nonchalantly, these same passengers filled the gangway to wait their turn to descend the stairs to the vehicle deck.

Samuel was amongst this throng. The woman behind who was closest to him even had the temerity, albeit of a friendly kind, to give him a gentle push in the back as he stopped and turned to beckon Neffie with a look and a simple gesture of his hand. The signals were for her to come and push into the space he had left between him and the teenage girl in front. Miss Goodwin, although she would have liked to have responded positively to Samuel's offer, did what she always did when exiting a crowded place, whether it be the Theatre Royal in Newcastle after a performance by the Royal Shakespeare Company, or upon leaving a venue in any one of several cities at the end of a Bob Dylan concert, and that was to remain seated until the multitude had cleared. She found the process of leaving less stressful that way. Consequently, rather than her being compliant with Samuel's wishes, she beckoned him to sit and wait. Not wishing, at this juncture, to become separated from the woman he already felt some responsibility for, he did as he was effectively told.

Waiting until last was a strange experience for Samuel, and now sitting a few rows ahead of Neffie, he did his best to hide his impatience.

"Why is it so dark everywhere but here?" she enquired, scanning the shore where the larger buildings were eerily dark and the street lights, if there were any, were invisible.

Her question was genuine in that she wanted to know the reason why, but it also served a secondary purpose of providing a distraction to pass the time.

Samuel hadn't been looking at Neffie as she spoke, but even with the back of his head to her he couldn't fail to recognise her voice. Turning his head to look over his shoulder he replied, "The bane of living in Freetown at present is that there are regular power cuts. There is electricity only three days in seven. You've come on an off-day."

Eventually, once the ferry had docked and the cars, a bus, and a number of trucks had been driven off, and most of the pedestrians had also departed to disappear into the African night, Neffie suggested to Samuel that now would be a good time to go. She had no objection to his carrying her bag. She was eager to demonstrate trust in her new companion. Samuel led the way down the loading ramp onto terra firma without being jostled or hindered in any way. The experience, was satisfying. He had no difficulty in finding a stationary taxi, although he was fortunate in that it was the only one waiting at the rank. Their destination was to be the Sussex Hotel. Located in the city centre, as a place for a young woman travelling alone to stay Samuel considered it to be of a standard likely to be in keeping with Miss Goodwin's needs, whether as the tourist she would rather not be described as, or as a volunteer eager to salve her conscience by working to redress the imbalance between the affluent countries of Europe and their impoverished erstwhile colonies. Information as to the suitability of the proposed accommodation he had gleaned from reading the hotel's literature: it wasn't derived from having stayed there himself (why would he?) or from the recommendation of a friend or colleague. He knew it to be the most expensive hotel in the city.

The taxi-driver's facial features were difficult to discern in the shadows. Leaning against the door of an old Austin Cambridge he greeted Samuel as the teacher approached. Mindful of this being the only taxi presently available Samuel didn't want to lose it to someone getting in before him. He had, therefore, quickened his pace upon leaving the ferry, so was a good twenty to thirty yards ahead of Neffie when he returned the taxi-driver's greeting. For being English of a kind the words that the two men exchanged weren't totally unfamiliar to Miss Goodwin, but they sounded sufficiently quirky to bring a smile to her face as she drew closer to where Samuel and the driver stood chatting.

"Aw di bohdi?" enquired Mr Massequoi.

"No bad, bohdi fine," replied the driver.

It took a few moments for Neffie to work out the meaning of what had been said, and when she had she was prompted to consider the differences between regional accents at home, of what it must be like for a person from Kent, for example, hearing the broad speech of Northumberland for the first time.

There followed a further exchange between the driver and Samuel, also, as Neffie learned, conducted in Krio. This manner of speaking widely used in Freetown is based on an archaic form of English. The conversation Neffie was privy to from a few yards distance, and could broadly interpret, resulted in the fare being agreed and the driver getting into the car. Unfortunately, there was an error of judgement to put right. He had mistakenly assumed that Samuel was to be his only passenger, and would, therefore, want to sit in the front passenger seat. Upon realising Samuel's association with the white woman now standing by the rear door with one hand on the handle as if she were intending to go somewhere soon, the taxi-driver proved capitalist to a fault and raised the fare from 300 to 3,000 leones. He assumed that the bag which the local man was carrying belonged to the relatively rich foreigner who had just arrived in the country, and as we know his assumptions weren't wide of the mark. There followed a few minutes hard bargaining in respect of how much Miss Goodwin would have to pay. Eventually the men shook hands having agreed a sum which Mr Massequoi considered to be acceptable. Moments later, when Samuel and Neffie were seated in the backseat together, but with the cherry-red holdall between them, in hushed tones the wheeler-dealing teacher explained that he had beaten the driver down to 1,000 leones. In sterling it amounted to just over £3. Miss Goodwin was grateful.

Sitting comfortably as they pulled away from the rank, without indication it was noted, Neffie was thinking of the occasions she had negotiated fares in various cities, at home and abroad. For being a case of the taxi-driver trying to fleece a naive tourist she thought it prudent not to mention the incidence in Grenada. The similarities between then and now were only too evident, and she didn't want to upset anybody. Instead, she simply smiled to herself in the knowledge that on that occasion the passenger in question wasn't as naive as the Spanish driver had thought.

Neffie didn't think it imprudent however to mention the time she had taken a taxi from Benito Juarez Airport to travel into the Mexican capital. "When I took a taxi into Mexico City," she began to explain, "the

25

little Volkswagen Beetle I had opted for was fitted with a meter. I couldn't take my eyes off the infernal machine as it whizzed round at an alarming rate. Just as disconcerting was the fact that the numbers were so high… I mean to say in the tens of thousands."

"That would have been tens of thousands of pesos I presume," interjected Samuel, eager to reveal the range of his knowledge.

On either side, as they drove slowly past, figures emerged from the shadows and then evanesced back into the night.

"Fortunately," Neffie continued, "when the time came to pay I discovered that the damage to my finances wasn't going to be as nearly as bad as I had imagined."

"Why was that?" inquired Samuel, inadvertently placing his left hand on top of Miss Goodwin's where it rested on her bag.

This tactile contact was unintentional, and Samuel couldn't have reacted faster in returning the hand, offensive in respect of his own sense of propriety, to rest on his thigh. "Terribly sorry," he said. He was obviously genuinely embarrassed.

In response Neffie made a dismissive gesture with the hand which had been sandwiched and continued with her story.

"Well, the Mexican Government had drastically devalued the currency, but the meter in the car I was in hadn't been altered accordingly. It amused the driver when he saw the look of relief on my face when instead of the 30,000 showing on the meter he asked me for a mere… I think it was 30 new pesos."

"That's an improvement on 30,000!" commented Samuel.

Some of the pedestrians they passed emerged eerily out of the inky blackness to be momentarily silhouetted in the car headlamps. Neffie noted that several people walking in the same direction as the taxi were likely to turn their heads to scrutinise the slowly approaching vehicle, and then the bright lights reflected the questions posed by the whites of each onlooker's eyes. Appearing like welcoming oases amid the surrounding gloom, there were a small number of brightly lit establishments along the way, bars mainly, each having the facility to generate its own electricity.

Above the soothing tones of Chris Rea singing about being home for Christmas, and between the intermittent exclamations of the driver berating a cyclist for taking up too much of the road on a bicycle showing no lights, or a foolish pedestrian stepping out to cross the street, Samuel apologised yet again for the lack of centrally-generated power. He admitted that the cut in the supply wasn't a problem for which he could blame the country's former colonial masters.

Twenty minutes later, the taxi pulled up outside the gate of the Sussex Hotel. At last Miss Nefertiti Goodwin had arrived at the place where she was to lay her head.

Chapter Two
Early Doubts, Early Fears

After Neffie had handed Samuel the exact amount to pay the fare, and he in turn had completed their business with the taxi-driver, the vehicle drove off in the opposite direction to the way they had come. Presumably, and primarily because the ferry which the teachers had crossed the river on was the last of the day, for the remainder of the evening the fares to be had at the quayside would more than likely be few and far between. On leaving the vehicle Neffie was gratified to see that the Sussex Hotel was brightly lit for having its own generator. The prospect of spending her first night in Sierra Leone fumbling about in the dark, or at best gauging the layout of her room by torchlight, wasn't one she had relished.

Situated at the corner of Lightfoot Boston Street and Wilberforce Street, and built in a style which owed more to French influence than the actual colonial power, the Sussex, its fenestrated, ground floor illumination designed to tempt all that drew near, appeared like a constellation of comfort and hope in the surrounding gloom. The wrought iron gate that separated the three-storey building and its garden from the outside world, and which was set in a wall that was imposing for being almost twice Neffie's height, had been opened electronically once Samuel had stated who they were and what they were about: he did so by speaking into the adjacent intercom.

Once inside the building Neffie noted that the foyer was far from ornate. Designed to be cool rather than plush, the open space in front of the custom-made main desk was remarkable for its chessboard floor. Following one behind the other, the receptionist leading the way and Mr Massequoi bringing up the rear, it was a trio of two men and one woman that climbed the stairs leading to Neffie's room. Miss Goodwin noted that the two photographs they passed on the staircase were hardly a matching pair, one being an image of Queen Elizabeth II attired in queenly regalia, and the other a portrait of Sir Bobby Charlton when he was a player. Neffie, having great respect for the queen but no interest in football, came to the conclusion that she would have rather seen photographs of worthy people from Sierra Leone than familiar faces from home. No sooner had the three playing follow-my-leader arrived at the designated door than the receptionist inserted a key with a large wooden fob attached into the lock to let in the Sussex Hotel's latest patron.

All the while the generator had been purring audibly but unobtrusively in the background. That it powered the globes which illuminated the garden paths, and the lights in the vestibule, and on the stairs and landing, and not forgetting the solitary lamp by the side of the bed, was clearly evident. What it didn't power, as was proved by the hotel worker when he pulled the cord which acted as a switch, was the large fan above Neffie's head. It remained motionless in the centre of the ceiling.

This was unfortunate, for here in the city centre the air had lost the pleasing freshness Miss Goodwin had experienced on the ferry. Indeed, so stifling was it that the new arrival wondered whether she would be able to sleep. Observing her grimace at his failure to waft, the receptionist, who was called Josh, and who, having recently arrived from the Banana Islands, hadn't been in the capital for much longer than Neffie, strode towards the window with the intention of opening the outer shutters; but not before switching off the lights. The last clear image Neffie beheld before the room was once again plunged into darkness was Josh's concerned expression.

Neither of the teachers moved, and the near silence of their stillness was in stark contrast to the clatter Josh made as he went about his work. He thought a little elucidation wouldn't be amiss.

He said, "Lights attract the bugs, and we don't want to do that do we, Miss?"

Not for the first time since she had arrived in Sierra Leone, being referred to as 'Miss' reminded her of school.

It sounded as if Josh was experiencing some difficulty in opening the shutters because the others heard him mutter a few words under his breath, words that were indiscernible other than for the general sense of frustration they expressed. Eventually, however, and probably in less time than it seemed to take, the shutters were flung open and the lighter shade of darkness that was the sky above Freetown and beyond was revealed. After closing the window behind him, to keep out the bugs, Josh returned to switch on the bedside lamp. The air in the room was no less stifling than it had been prior to the plan to compensate for the fan's inertia being put into action.

Switching on lights as he went about his business, Josh showed Neffie the en suite facilities. It was a matter of pride to him that the toilet flushed and the shower produced hot water seconds after it had been switched on, and who would argue that his sense of pride wasn't justified, for he knew, as did Samuel, what the majority of people in Freetown had to contend with when performing their ablutions, and to some extent Josh was also aware of the poor to mediocre facilities on offer in less agreeable hotels.

Neither unduly impressed nor disappointed, Neffie tried her best not to let her lack of enthusiasm show. She noted the absence of towels, shampoo, soap, items most women would consider essential for making life bearable in a sticky climate. Satisfied that he had done his utmost to make the hotel's guest feel welcome, the man from the Banana Islands hovered. The look on his face was as legible as a neon sign above a cinema's doors. It expressed his expectation of an ex gratia payment. Notwithstanding Joshua's apparent fluency in the subtle art of silent communication, Neffie chose not to respond in the way in which the hospitality worker had hoped. Not yet attuned to local customs and manners, she left it to Samuel to deal with the matter on her behalf.

Speaking plain English he did so politely but firmly. "What game are you playing, man?" he said, and without waiting for an answer he added, "You've done your job for now so you can go. Please shut the door behind you."

To Neffie's surprise Joshua left the room with a broad grin on his face and a shrug of his shoulders, as if to say, "You can't blame a man for trying."

Once he had gone Neffie felt really mean, but she took heart in having further confirmation that Samuel was on her side, though now it was his turn to linger as if he hadn't anywhere else to go and nothing else to do. His motive for loitering with intent was anything but selfish. His forehead still glistening with the perspiration exuded from having carried Neffie's bag up two flights of stairs, he sought to assist the English woman further by enquiring if there was anything, anything at all that she needed. Neffie had no doubt that if she had given Samuel a list as long as her arm, he would have done his utmost to obtain the items on it immediately, and those which he couldn't obtain as early as this evening, he would make every effort to bring the next morning.

To make it easy for her to get at her belongings Neffie moved her bag from the one and only chair in the room, whereupon Samuel had unceremoniously dumped it, onto a blanket which was neatly folded atop the foot of the bed. More than likely the blanket would be superfluous to requirement. When Neffie opened her bag to reveal two halves packed with consummate care and skill, packed using restraining straps to keep clothes, toiletries and prophylactics against nasty diseases, securely in place, Samuel was amazed to see how much stuff it contained. "You really must be an expert traveller to be able to get everything you need for… how long did you say you intend to stay?" Samuel observed and then enquired.

"Five weeks," said Neffie.

"And to think that you were able to take it on the plane as hand luggage… I'm impressed."

"Thanks. I do think I've refined my packing to almost a fine art," she beamed.

Neffie was about to extract a towel but thought better of it for the simple reason that she didn't want to give a man whom she had known for only a few hours the opportunity to see her more intimate items of clothing, specifically her bras and knickers. Her alternative course of action was to squeeze between Samuel and the bed in order to open the door. The invitation by gesture was for Samuel to exit without further delay.

After confirming that it would be fine for him to come back at ten the next morning, as had already been arranged between them in the taxi, Samuel made to do as he was bid. "Ah gladi fa mit yu, a de go," he said as he was about to step into the corridor.

"I'm sorry," Neffie replied, not so much by way of an apology, but as a request for linguistic elucidation.

"I was speaking Krio," responded Samuel. "English is the official language of Sierra Leone, but in the streets and markets people speak mainly Krio. I shall teach you some if you wish. What I said was nice to meet you, goodbye."

"Ah gladi fa mit yu, a de go," repeated Neffie, falteringly.

Like Joshua before him Samuel left with a smile on his face, but unlike Joshua his expression of delight was derived from the knowledge that in accordance with her wishes he couldn't have done more to assist Miss Goodwin than he had, and that he had proved himself to be a good ambassador for his country, albeit one who hadn't left its shores.

Following Mr Massequoi's departure Neffie showered in silence, and then emerged from the cubicle to put on her sarong and flip-flops. She preferred not to wander around hotel rooms in unfamiliar cities completely naked, and her sarong, a garment which she had bought in Thailand a few years back for less than a pound, was a treasured possession, one which was ideal for a tropical climate. Her plan was to go straight to bed. She hadn't eaten anything substantial since lunch-time, but as she wasn't feeling the slightest bit hungry she decided to do without supper. She did, however, feel an urgent need to slake her thirst. This she did by almost draining her water-bottle. When travelling, particularly in hot countries, Neffie made a point of not becoming dehydrated, and so carried two cylindrical water-bottles with her wherever she went. She considered them to be essential items of equipment in that they enabled her to drink in places where the water deemed safe to drink was in reality suspect. She was able to drink from one bottle whilst sterilising tablets extracted from her store of prophylactics did their work in the other. The last thing she wanted to go down with was amoebic dysentery.

Included also in her plastic container of preventatives, along with more mundane but no less essential medical items, was her supply of chloroquine tablets. Neffie had suffered from the debilitating effects of malaria on her previous trip to West Africa, and didn't want to experience the same again. Sitting on the side of the bed she carefully removed one of these tablets from the foil strip securing the remainder and popped it into her mouth. Gulping the last mouthful of water taken from a tap in Holland she washed the pill down without tasting it. Demonstrating methodical composure, she returned the foil to its plastic container and the container to its bag: everything had to be put back in its proper place. She knew from experience, more from having witnessed the 'bad luck' which had befallen others than from being inconvenienced herself, that to be anything other than methodical would more than likely lead to chaos.

The chloroquine consumed, she took two sterilising tablets and the empty water bottle to the wash-basin, and she filled the bottle with water from the cold-water tap. At this point she discovered that even in the dark it would have been impossible to have made a mistake by replenishing from the hot-water tap because it didn't work. It didn't perturb her in the slightest that Joshua's pride in the hotel's plumbing would appear to be misplaced. The water that flowed from the cold-water tap was tepid. The tablets which Neffie dropped into the bottle were reputed to kill every harmful organism. The instructions on the packet had informed Neffie that the water would be sterilised, and therefore safe to drink, after half an hour, but she liked to allow longer — at least an hour — for the chemicals to do their job. Even though Mr Massequoi had told Neffie, and she was convinced he had told her a truth, that if there was one aspect of Freetown's infrastructure which worked reasonably well it was the water supply, with time on her hands she was taking no chances.

When she had done all that was necessary for the continuance of good health the teacher in search of adventure decided it really was time for bed. It was a little after nine. Despite having dried herself thoroughly after exiting the shower, Neffie soon began to feel the effects of the heat and humidity as salty globules once again moistened her skin. The sensation told her beyond doubt that she would have no need of the blanket, and after first stowing her bag — now zipped up securely under the bed, she removed the unwanted bed-cover. It was then that she saw it, the creature, the cockroach, the largest she had ever seen — and she had seen a few on her travels — run across the sheet as it sought the cover of darkness.

Miss Nefertiti Goodwin wasn't the sort of woman to scream, but she was startled by the insect's sudden appearance and subsequent rapid movement to the extent that she dropped the blanket. It didn't hinder let alone kill the loathsome creature, this creature that disgusted her, and the little scavenger disappeared, to she knew not where. Once she had regained her composure, however, Neffie sought a suitable weapon, and unquestionably the most suitable to hand was a flip-flop. Either of the pair she was wearing would do, but being better able to maintain her balance by reaching down with her right hand to stretch across her body, it was from her left foot that she removed the flimsy item of footwear. Armed and primed to kill, for several seconds, the weapon raised menacingly above her head, the pacifist with regard to human conflict stood ready to do battle. She knew from encounters in the past, which had led in turn to a little light desultory reading, that she would have to strike hard to kill a creature which had existed as a species for around two hundred and eighty million years, and whose body could survive for a week following decapitation.

The cockroach chose not to reappear. Neffie's high degree of readiness looked as if it would be ineffectual. She realised that she was probably wasting her time in maintaining such a blatantly threatening yet, for being motionless, essentially passive posture, and decided to go on the offensive, to become proactive in her desire to end the insect's life. Demonstrating the agility of a cat, flip-flop in hand she pounced onto the bed and rolled across the mattress to the side where the lamp was, its base positioned atop a bedside cabinet. Even in these moments of energised activity Neffie noted that the mattress barely yielded beneath her weight. Grabbing hold of the lamp as she dropped to the floor, she directed its illumination to search under the bed. The light-bulb's revelation was that the linoleum covering the few square yards of floor directly beneath the bed was cleaned less often that the rest of the room. Evidence was provided by a considerable amount of dust and fluff, a discarded comb, and a glossy magazine. The elusive cockroach was nowhere in sight.

Thinking that the items which she had discovered were best left alone, Neffie made no attempt to move them from where they lay. Upon returning the lamp to its normal resting place, she surveyed the room one last time whilst feeling for the switch. Her immediate environment and the objects within it didn't impress her. In addition to the items already mentioned the furniture consisted of a dressing-table positioned against the wall at a right angle to the bed-head, and in front of that a rickety chair. Both were of a style and condition that in Britain would more often be seen in a skip than a shop or a hotel bedroom. From a pole above the window hung thin violet curtains. Joshua had drawn them. Neffie had no idea how long she would be in Freetown, but she was relieved that she had booked into the Sussex Hotel for one night only. Far from happy with the utilitarian dinginess of her accommodation, she wanted to be elsewhere, somewhere where the plaster wasn't crumbling so obviously, where the floor space beneath the bed was clean, and where the window-frame wasn't so obviously rotten. Most importantly she wanted to be where the air was fresher, either naturally or as the result of it being agitated by a rotating fan. The possibility of there being air-conditioning in Sierra Leone she didn't consider. She found it, as a means of staying cool, to be too excessive. Consequently, it wasn't on her wish list.

By touch alone Neffie switched off the bedside lamp. This enabled her to appreciate the crepuscular quality of the light cast by the garden globes and then filtered by the curtains, a faint patterning which hadn't registered with her earlier. This was probably because she wasn't lying on her back gazing up at the ceiling when Joshua had sought to keep the insects at bay. The remarkable effect of the global emanations was the creation of small and large concentric circles and ellipses, the most expansive reaching to the centre to form an ellipse around the useless fan. This feeble luminescence was silvery, and gave Neffie the impression that she would soon be going to sleep beneath the light reflected by several moons.

Neffie hadn't wanted to wander naked around the room, but, having removed her sarong and placing it between her two pillows, she chose to sleep naked. At least the sheet under which she stretched her legs felt and smelt freshly laundered, as did the pillow-case. Despite being so tired she didn't immediately drop off to sleep, but lay awake for a while staring up at the shapes depicted on the ceiling. She succumbed to dark thoughts. She wondered whether she really was in love with Seb, and more worryingly, she wondered if Seb was really in love with her. What if at this very moment he was propping up the bar of a Ferrousby nightclub, hoping to find solace in the arms of another woman, a woman with predation in mind. To her surprise she discovered that merely thinking of the possibility of such an eventuality made her jealous. Consequently, as a tear trickled from her left eye and a bead of perspiration ran down her right cheek, she realised that she really did love the man she had left behind. It had been her choice, and though glad to have made it, she comforted herself with the thought that the five to six weeks apart would soon pass.

No sooner had she dispelled her dark imaginings regarding Sebastian however, than other concerns popped into her head to cause disquiet. What if she were to succumb to any one of a number of dreadful diseases prevalent in sub-Saharan Africa: diseases such as dengue fever, bilharzia, Weil's disease and cholera to name but a few? More debilitating for possibly being fatal, what if she were to be bitten by a venomous snake or spider? She knew that green mambas and puff adders abound in the regions she intended to visit; and of course she had heard of the black widow spider. Her fear didn't last long. She knew from experience that such drastic eventualities, though undoubtedly possible, were unlikely to befall a 'sensible girl' like her. The last image to come to mind before she drifted off to sleep was that of the fleeing cockroach. Where could it have got to? she wondered.

Neffie awoke. She didn't know precisely how long it had been since she had drifted off to sleep, but she sensed that she hadn't been in the land of nod for long. She awoke to hear the sound of legs scurrying across the wall above and behind her head. The staccato sound was particularly disturbing for the fact that she had awoken from a nightmare in which the loathsome creature that had escaped death by flip-flop had returned to enter her right ear, where it had proceeded to burrow into her brain. To ensure it was clear of invaders, with her finger she poked inside the organ on the side of her head. Naturally she was relieved to find the auditory cavern empty of invasive life-forms.

For a while she was still, her eyes focused upon the fan's three motionless blades, her ears pricked in anticipation of the slightest sound. The scurrying on the wall behind her had stopped. It was as if whatever had been making the noise had sensed that its movements were being detected and targeted. Needful of fresh air she got out of bed, put on her sarong, and went to open the window, all without switching on a light. Once the window was open, she could hear crickets chirruping in the flowerless bushes. Still wearing her sarong, she clambered back onto the bed and pulled the sheet up over her. In addition to the chirruping outside she could now hear a swishing sound. The image it brought to mind was of a person sweeping a path with a bristle brush. Presumably the path in question was the one which led through the hotel garden. The person involved in what was either a nocturnal leisure activity or a job to do was evidently in no great hurry to finish.

The creature on the wall must, by whatever nerve impulses were at its disposal, have come to a decision that at long last it was safe to proceed, for Neffie heard it once again: on the move. To her consternation it seemed to be approaching her right ear. The approaching menace was too much to bear. She threw back the sheet and forsook the mattress with the alacrity of a woman who has just realised that she could be about to share her bed with a scavenger only a fraction of her size, perhaps not even a thousandth. Careless of the open window she switched on the lamp and caught sight of the same villain, she was certain of it, that she had espied earlier. The cockroach didn't hang around for long, but scuttled down the wall to disappear behind the headboard. Being a teacher of small children Miss Goodwin wasn't accustomed to resorting to bad language, but at that moment a number of words cathartic in nature popped into her head. Neffie's training and perhaps old-fashioned sense of propriety were such, however, that none of the expletives escaped her mouth. Instead, she scanned the floor to ascertain where she had left her flip-flops. Their heels protruding from under the bed, she was about to stoop and pick one up when she heard footsteps approaching on the stairs.

Neffie felt at least two cool rivulets of perspiration trickle down her back as she turned her attention from the now insignificant insect and stared in anticipation at the door. She realised that in the confusion of her arrival, when she was more than a little disoriented, she had omitted to obtain the key to her temporary sanctuary, and that the door remained unlocked. She didn't feel totally insecure however, for there were two small bolts at her disposal, one six inches from the top of the door, the other a similar distance from the floor. She deftly secured them both.

Stepping back to inspect her handiwork left her feeling only a modicum safer. It would have been naive of her to think that these bolts would have kept out a determined assailant: a shove by a hefty shoulder would send screws, bolts and splinters flying. She was glad to be wearing her sarong rather than wandering about naked, but even in that garment she felt a little undressed.

It was then that Neffie's consternation reached a new level. She could only look on in mute horror as, barely perceptibly, barely audibly, the door-knob turned. It was obvious that this was being done as surreptitiously as possible, for barely a sound emanated from the other side of the door. The sudden realisation that very soon she could be in mortal danger caused Miss Goodwin to gasp for breath, and she was sure that her deep exhalation and subsequent inhalation were clearly audible to the potential intruder. A second involuntary reaction was that she felt the hairs on the back of her head and neck stand upon end as if they were electrically charged; a third was the proverbial cold shiver that ran down her spine.

Neffie couldn't be absolutely certain that pressure was being applied to push the door open, but she sensed that it was. When the door failed to budge, whoever was trying to gain entry allowed the door-knob to return to its original position. There followed an interval in which nothing happened. To Neffie it seemed to last for as long as a minute, but in reality the suspense lasted no longer than a fraction of that time, possibly no more than ten seconds. It was Neffie who broke the spellbound inactivity, and thinking that there was indeed something more she could do to strengthen the barrier between herself and her likely nemesis, she made a beeline for the room's only chair.

It is said that the shortest distance between two points is always a straight line, and though that statement may or may not be true (bearing in mind that we are also told that the fabric of space is curved), the shortest route may not be the most efficacious. It certainly wasn't in this instance. In her haste bordering on panic Miss Goodwin caught her thigh on the corner of the bed. At the moment of impact Neffie's training and decorum were completely forgotten as she voiced an expletive worthy of a soldier in barracks when he (or she) has just been told that leave is cancelled.

The pain Neffie experienced was sharp and short-lived rather than protracted, and therefore didn't hinder her progress for long. Without her injured leg giving way beneath her in two strides she was able to pick up the chair. She discovered that it was heavier and less rickety than she had imagined or perceived it to be, but apart from having to carry it as far as the door that was no bad thing seeing as she intended to secure it at an angle between the floor and the door knob. To accomplish this, she tilted the chair back over so that it rested on two legs, thus enabling the top of the chair back to be wedged into position.

If asked Neffie would probably have been unable to identify the film, but she undoubtedly got the idea from having seen the same being enacted, either at the cinema or on television, back home.

She was, by now, careless of maintaining any illusion regarding her presence, and even went so far as to accentuate the noise she was making, her frame of mind being such that although she didn't yet have the courage to open the door and confront the stranger, she was certainly in no mood for pussyfooting.

A few paces removed from where she had expected the stranger to be, the creak of a floorboard gave Neffie the impression that the creepy and unwelcome visitor, by leaving the vicinity of her door, had given up on his dubious quest. To all intents and purposes this supposition was confirmed moments later when Miss Goodwin heard a second creak; it came from halfway down the stairs.

Sensing that the threat, certainly to her equanimity if not with the same degree of certainty to her person, was over, Neffie took measures to regulate her breathing and slow down her beating heart. After all, she hadn't practised yoga for most of her adult life not to be able to call upon its wisdom in the form of esoteric exercises when it was needed. It was certainly needed now.

In relation to how much her fear had receded, Neffie's breathing and heart rate began to normalise. During these restorative minutes she remained standing as if transfixed, her eyes fixated on the door knob. Gradually, as the minutes passed, her thoughts and feelings regarding recent events mellowed until they became quite positive, so that eventually she convinced herself that she had never been in imminent danger of being raped or murdered, or both, and that the entire episode had been a mistake, a misunderstanding too silly for words.

The man at the door, so Miss Goodwin now imagined, was probably a bit tipsy and had climbed one flight of stairs too many in his search for his solitary bed. Yes; that was probably the real reason for the nocturnal goings-on. Neffie's rationalisation could be considered naive, but on the other hand, as a means of reconstituting her frayed psyche, it was undoubtedly helpful. Indeed, so helpful was it that latterly she was able to smile to herself at what she had come to believe had been her over-reaction. That said, she climbed into bed still wearing her sarong and without having removed her hastily improvised defence, namely the chair. Resting on the side of her body that was least comfortable to her as a sleeping position, she kept her face, and therefore her eyes, turned towards the door. She hadn't switched off the lamp, but she had remembered to close the window. Her knees bent so that her legs were drawn up into a foetal position, eventually she drifted off into a dreamless sleep, dreamless as far as she could tell when she next awoke.

Just after eight the next morning there was a determined knock on the door that from inside the room was no longer under close observation. Neffie had been awake for all of five minutes when she heard the rap on the door repeated thrice over. Bright sunlight filtered through the curtains, but only intermittently, so that it seemed as if the sun and clouds were working in conjunction to create heavenly semaphore. The silent transmission projected no danger therefore contained no warning.

To the recipient lying on her back still coming to terms with the world that was greeting her slowly waking psyche the message read simply 'rise and shine'. Clearly by this time the dark thoughts which Neffie had succumbed to the night before had dissipated, and it was with a note of cheerful optimism that she spoke. "Who is it?" she enquired.

"The police, Miss Goodwin," a male voice replied.

Perhaps it was simply because her view of the world had changed considerably overnight, or as recently as since it had become suffused with bright sunlight, that she entertained no doubts as to the sincerity of the reply. Alternatively, perhaps it was the immediacy and straight-forwardness of the response that convinced her. That said, however, Miss Goodwin was far from willing to let a man — or men — into her room in her present state of undress.

After giving the matter some thought she said, "I'm not dressed. Would you mind coming back in quarter of an hour so I can make myself presentable?"

"Would half an hour be better?" a second but no less amenable male voice replied. "We don't want to rush you into making yourself presentable."

Neffie detected a hint of wicked playfulness in the tone. She had wondered if there were more than one individual waiting upon her convenience, and now she knew.

"That would be perfect," she replied.

She heard the policemen departing, the sound of their footsteps slowly diminishing prior to Neffie becoming as if deaf to them altogether. These sounds near at hand were replaced by a more general volubility emanating from the street below. The English woman's senses were now alert for being fully awake. Even as she imagined the brightly coloured scene in the street below, she gave some thought as to why it was that the police had chosen to call at such an early hour. From her visitors' tone she sensed that the visit was either routine, or enquiries were in progress regarding the failed attempt to gain entry into her sanctum. She certainly didn't believe that she was about to be arrested.

The thought crossed Miss Goodwin's mind that a villain might already have been arrested for having perpetrated a hideous crime on some other innocent and unsuspecting woman who would otherwise have remained unmolested had she, Nefertiti Goodwin, not done what she had. The thought disturbed her more than a little. Her most recent appraisal as to the motives of the nocturnal prowler, when she had convinced herself that he was no more than a little boy lost, as it were, were clearly subject to revision. After five minutes had elapsed Neffie made a move to get out of bed and commence her ablutions. Five minutes before the triple knock reoccurred she was ready to receive visitors.

The two men that Neffie opened the door to and then allowed to enter were remarkable in that they looked alike, and the similarity wasn't on the rather spurious basis that to a white person all black people look the same. For the reason that they not only looked alike physically, but dressed in a similar style, Neffie gained the impression that the policemen were brothers. Their close-cropped, black hair had been cut in such a way that it wouldn't have surprised Neffie if they had gone to the same barber together and that whoever was second had followed whoever was first into the chair, each to ask for a number one, or two, or

41

three, or whatever number was deemed appropriate. To all appearances the climate and the cut were perfectly matched.

In apparent contradiction to their sensible styles up top, however, Tweedledum and Tweedledee each sported the first traces of a beard and a moustache. There being little facial hair on display as yet, it wasn't inconceivable that for want of something better to do the two plain-clothes members of Freetown's constabulary had instigated a wager between themselves, the evidence suggested that it couldn't have been more than two days previously, to see who would be able to grow the most impressive full-set, within a month say. Not yet hirsute the faces confronting Neffie were perfect ovals, revealing small, barely perceptible ears when viewed full frontal. Accentuated by their short hair both men possessed high foreheads, whereupon the ebony skin was perfectly smooth. In Miss Goodwin's eyes the first aspect of their physiognomy indicated intelligence and the second, the absence of furrows, was revealing of youth. Each wearing a sports jacket over a casual shirt of colour and pattern chosen by the detectives to demonstrate a modicum of individuality, the manner of the two men was unthreatening, pleasant in fact.

Neffie had deliberated as to whether or not she should ask to see some identification. No sooner had she decided, somewhat naively perhaps, to take these self-proclaimed officers of the law at their word than they took out their badges and held them at arm's length for Miss Goodwin to inspect.

The detectives introduced themselves. "This is Detective Constable Charles Conteh, and I'm Detective Constable Julius Kallon," the policeman, who for being a fraction of an inch taller than his colleague by the same measure repudiated the Tweedledum and Tweedledee epithet, informed her.

Neffie estimated Constable Kallon's height to be about five feet ten inches; his brother officer's — though evidently the pair weren't brothers — to be half an inch less.

"How may I be of help?" enquired Neffie, helpfully.

"We apologise for disturbing you like this on your first morning in Freetown, Miss Goodwin, but we like to get the formalities out of the way as soon as possible. We would like please to check your visa and

42

passport," stated the Constable firmly, and then, perhaps thinking that his manner had been too overbearing, he added deferentially, "This really is just a formality I assure you."

Neffie turned the focus of her attention from the speaker to the hitherto silent policeman, who smiled reassuringly as her eyes met his. "Excuse me, gentlemen," said Neffie prior to turning her back on the detectives in order to raise the front of her shirt, as discreetly as possible, in order to extract the requisite documents from the pocket of the cloth money-belt fastened around her waist. Exposing even a couple of inches of bare midriff to the view of strangers she deemed inappropriate. She handed the navy-blue booklet to Constable Kallon. Like a reader of a who-did-it crime novel intent on finding out who had committed the murder in the hotel bedroom without having to plough through the evidence and numerous red herrings to make the discovery, the constable turned immediately to the back page, the page containing the holder's photograph and personal details. After checking the image with reality and finding that they were a perfect match, he handed the passport to his colleague to search for the visa: it was one amongst many.

"Nefertiti... that's an unusual name," commented Constable Kallon in a tone which invited response.

Miss Nefertiti Goodwin could tell by the hint of a smile on Mr Kallon's face that he thought her name amusing. Conscious of the fact that the sound of the six syllables also brought a smile to the face of Constable Conteh, the teacher proceeded to explain. "Yes... it is an unusual name, isn't it?" she replied, emphasising the confirmation rather than the question, the latter being unquestionably rhetorical. "I have my father to thank for bestowing it on me. Of course at the christening font I was totally oblivious of what I was about to be named, but I came home from my first day at school in tears because some of my peers had laughed out loud when the teacher called the register. It was then that my mother told me that it had been my dad's idea, and it didn't matter what she thought about it because his word was law in our household. Dad's a builder by profession, and when he's not putting up joists or laying bricks, he spends his free time reading books about ancient Egypt. He could probably tell you as much as a university professor who lectures

43

on the subject about the sphinx... the pyramids... pharaohs... all that kind of stuff."

The expressions on the faces she beheld told Nefertiti that some further explanation was required.

"Nefertiti was Akhenaten's queen... you know... the pharaoh who lived in the fourteenth century... BC that is... and reorganised the order of worship."

On becoming apprised of this knowledge the policemen glanced at each other with raised eyebrows, a communication which, though wordless, stated quite clearly that they were contending with yet another example of British eccentricity, as if it were a frequent occurrence.

"I haven't met anyone named Nefertiti before..." began Constable Kallon. He was about to expand on this statement when he was cut short by his colleague.

"Nor I," interjected Constable Conteh forcefully. "It's wondrously strange don't you think, Miss Goodwin," he continued, charming Nefertiti by his eloquence, "that we as citizens of Sierra Leone spend a great deal of time in our formative years learning about British culture and the British Empire, and yet it would seem that you... the British that is... look to a dead civilisation for your inspiration."

Neffie wasn't of the opinion that the pharaohs and their consorts had had a significant influence on the people of Britain as a whole. "We're much more up to date these days," said Neffie, mindful of the influence of ancient Greece and Rome on the language they were speaking. Choosing not to complicate matters further, however, she thought better of bringing her scant knowledge of the classics into the conversation and said simply, "Not everyone in Britain is like my dad and interested in ancient history. After a moment's pause for thought she added, "Though lots of people are named after..." she searched for the right word, "characters in the Bible. Anyway, Nefertiti was the name my parents gave me, and even though I may not be stuck with it, as I've grown up with it, from the age of five I've grown to like it. Now I wouldn't be without it."

"I think it a pleasant name," said Kallon.

44

"If my wife and I are blessed with another daughter I shall suggest that we call her Nefertiti," added Constable Conteh, "after the Egyptian queen and in honour of your visit."

"Well, I love being called Neffie," said Neffie, "so maybe the daughter you hope to have would come to thank you for your choice of name."

These words gave the unmarried and presently unattached Constable Kallon sufficient grounds to address the teacher as 'Neffie' as he enquired as to the purpose of her visit.

Chapter Three
The Home Front

Seb Forrest didn't hear the two pistol shots that were fired as a signal for the occupants of the unmarked car to take evasive action, but that didn't mean he was deaf, out of earshot, or dead. It simply meant that the action unfolding nowhere but inside his head had begun the moment after the report of the second of the two shots had died away. By this time Archie, Seb's comrade-in- arms, had slammed on the brakes of the covert Vauxhall Cavalier. Needing no further prompting, and demonstrating the sense of urgency required if the soldiers were to have a chance of surviving the ambush, Seb opened the front passenger door and, careless of how hard the landing, dived out of the vehicle.

In his mind's eye Seb saw himself roll over the uneven ground adjacent to the track they had driven along. He rolled over three or four times, stopping belly down only when he judged himself to be far enough from the car not to present an easy target, at which point he brought his Walther up into the aim. In the meantime, so as to keep the bad guys' heads down while allowing time for Seb to take up a firing position, Archie had already fired a double tap through the Vauxhall's windscreen. Or at least he would have if this had been a genuine ambush by terrorists whose aim was to kill or capture the soldiers, but as Seb's recollection of the action had been a training exercise he had been involved in a decade previously, for obvious reasons, and no matter how many times the exercise was repeated, the windscreen remained intact.

Rather than shatter the glass Archie had opened the driver's door and, having crouched down in the apex of space created when the door was slightly ajar, thereby using the body of the vehicle as cover, he fired at least one double-tap in the direction of what in this instance was a colourful target, specifically a party balloon dangling from a length of string tied to a post about fifty yards distant. By the time it was Seb's turn to provide covering fire and it was Archie's turn to move, the balloon as yet remained inflated; but not for much longer. In the next instant after Seb squeezed the trigger to shoot the first of his two successive rounds on its way, the yellow balloon popped out of useful existence. The memory brought a smile to Seb Forrest's face.

For the reason that a considerable length of time had passed since Sebastian's recollections had been for real, and because in his fond memories he imagined himself as a fast-draw gunslinger like the Sundance Kid, it was a sequence of events he had reprised, as it were, many times. To him that shot was as satisfying as a hole-in-one must be to a golfer, or riding the winner in the Grand National must be to a jockey. Usually, and it was certainly the case in this instance, it was whenever Seb's brain failed to function as he would have wished in the present that he allowed his mind to wander back in time and savour his balloon-popping talent of yore. Imaginatively it was only after he had burst the same balloon with the same bullet twice or thrice over that he was able to reconnect mind and body in the here and now.

Together again at last, mind and body were back at his desk. Seb sat facing the wall that was at a right-angle to the sash-window of the back bedroom of his and Neffie's Yatton home. The wall in question was adorned with what to Seb's perception were the strangely distorted shapes of countries: some being elongated; others compressed. The map, known as Peters Projection, is the work of the German historian Arno Peters. His aim was to provide a more realistic representation of the world rather than a Eurocentric depiction. There was no bed in the bedroom. To save space that item of furniture had been replaced by a futon which was presently serving as a settee. At times Seb was waiting, hence his mind's dreamy drift back to 1980 and the so-called 'troubles' in Northern Ireland, for inspiration's lightning bolt to strike, and at other times, by thinking hard, he did his utmost to come up with an idea, a good one if possible, a mediocre one if it wasn't. His mental powers, or lack of them, oscillated between the two states of mind. He was tempted to lie down on the futon and stare up at the ceiling to find inspiration, but resisted for the reason that he would probably nod off to sleep.

The task he had set himself this Wednesday lunchtime was to write a feature of one thousand words. Assuming that eventually he would conjure up an interesting topic to write about, the piece would appear in the next edition of the Luxborough Times, a weekly regional newspaper which appeared on Fridays. A copy of last week's edition was lying on the floor within easy reach.

Being merely a 'stringer' Seb wasn't paid much for his verbal toil, but he undoubtedly enjoyed the kudos he gained from seeing his name in print, and that was more of a motivation than money. He knew himself well enough to realise that his ego required recognition, and that had to be for his writing, in whichever form it appeared. This was understandable given that his wish was to climb the ladder, to ascend from the lower rungs of this weekly undertaking. His hope was that one day his journalistic output would lead to greater things. How that 'greatness' would manifest itself as yet remained unclear. Perhaps, he had mused in moments of self-indulgent fancy, his perspicacity would be recognised in high places, and consequently his talents would be put to good use, in politics for example, at the national level. Or, alternatively, perhaps the ladder he climbed would reach the top of Mount Parnassus.

Back on planet Earth Sebastian earned the bulk of his money from working night-shifts as a security officer on a building site across town, the shifts in question being from five p.m. to eight a.m. the following morning. A weekend shift lasted twenty-four hours. It wasn't the hourly rate of pay that provided him with a reasonable wage, but the considerable number of hours he spent on site. It was on this, one of two days off from that job that he had to conjure up a feature length article on a subject which would be of interest to the twenty thousand or so citizens of Luxborough and its environs. This being his fourth week as a hack, it was proving to be no easy task.

A number of factors had combined to compound the difficulty and add to his sense of being under pressure. Naturally the aspiring man of parts sought to eliminate these obtrusions, but before he could do so he first had to identify them. Not in order on the scale of severity were the following detrimental points.

First, Seb had been awake on duty for most of the previous night, and hadn't slept well that morning. In Forrest's opinion the most debilitating aspect of working when most people are asleep, and trying to sleep when most people are awake, was that he was a light sleeper. It only needed a voice to rise from the street as the speaker bade a neighbour or a stranger passing by 'good morning', or the unmistakeable clang of ladders being raised and then lowered as the cheery window-cleaner went about his business, to wake him. Subsequently, because he had already slept for a few hours and therefore removed the pressing need he had felt on getting into bed, what an almost impossible undertaking it was for him to regain oblivion.

Probably the most bothersome cause of Seb not being able to get back to sleep once he had been wakened was Neffie's absence. Jealous thoughts pervaded his psyche. This jealousy wasn't primarily sexual in nature, though there were occasions when he let his imagination wander into the realms of carnal knowledge. Then his disquiet was that much greater, and he tossed and turned all the more as a consequence. At some point, however, he would rein in his vivid imaginings with the thought that since they had been living together Neffie hadn't given him cause to be jealous in the ways of the flesh.

More often than not Seb's jealousy took a different form, and was based simply on the fact that Neffie had chosen to spend what he thought was a considerable length of time in a place far removed from where he was. Of course he knew that the disquiet he suffered stemmed from his being possessive, selfish even, but that realisation was of no help to him, at least in the short term, in overcoming his visceral ordeal. He remained jealous of the fact that Neffie would be involved in social intercourse on a daily basis with people whom he didn't know, and in all probability would never meet.

The emotions Seb had to contend with consequent upon Neffie's physical separation from him were clearly not new, but to date their familiarity provided little comfort. He hadn't become desensitised to what he believed were feelings akin to grief. For Seb the only difference between mourning the permanent loss of a loved one and the hiatus he had to endure was one of degree.

The transitional phases in his grieving process weren't difficult to identify. First there were the days and nights when the overriding sensation was numbness. His world was then a limbo devoid of emotional pain, and joy. He realised that Neffie's absence allowed him greater freedom of course, but whether this freedom to do as he pleased manifested itself in watching football on television of an evening without his having to bargain, persuade, or, and this would be most unlikely, cajole, or whether it was apparent in the choice of food on his plate, these were poor compensations for the numerous consultations and compromises two people living together have to make, if the relationship is to be harmonious, on a daily basis. It usually took three or four days for the work of the unseen anaesthetist, as it were, to wear off, after which there followed a more turbulent phase, a phase which could last for several weeks as Seb tried to come to terms with the removal of his rib.

Throughout this second phase the former soldier saw himself as a doughty sailor cast adrift on a lonely ocean, and his foremost task was to steer his little raft, through the maelstroms of his own making, towards reunification. Life at this time became a test of Seb's emotional strength in the face of the many temptations his freewill, in a mind inclined to be hedonistic, could muster. He knew that were he not to succeed, he would fail miserably.

An aspect of Sebastian's ordeal by separation which he considered less than it was perhaps wise so to do, was that he wasn't necessarily the only person suffering as a consequence of Neffie being in foreign parts. During these all too rare moments of self-negation he pondered the possibility that Neffie's parents would also be concerned for the safety of their intrepid daughter; and then there was her elder sister to consider. Being a tried and tested globe-trotter herself, Seb knew that she would be the most phlegmatic of the family, and with regard to her 'little' sister would work on the basis that no bad news is good news.

Insofar as Seb's glazed-eyed ruminations were able to take into account Neffie's feelings, his hope was that she would be missing him as much as he was missing her, and his fear, a fear which he was reluctant to admit to himself let alone the world at large, was that no sooner was he out of sight than the distancing effect of travel would expunge him from her mind. Furthermore, he doubted whether it was possible for the itinerant teacher to feel the piquancy of separation as strongly as he did. If she were to, he concluded, he would have felt a somewhat wicked combination of pity and delight. After giving careful consideration as to the nature of his perturbations at this time, Seb was able to justify his depth of feeling by reasoning that the turbulence he endured was testament to his love.

It was perhaps significant that Seb didn't give much thought for Neffie's safety and physical well-being. He took it for granted that she would return home unscathed. His apparent lack of concern in this regard didn't derive from a canker of callousness within his soul, but stemmed from an appreciation of his partner's survivability. His confidence in Neffie's ability to emerge from situations most would find threatening couldn't have been more positive, knowing as he did, that she could bring a calming, pacifying ingredient to almost any volatile human brew. He ascribed this ability in part to her experience of dealing with up to twenty-six unruly three- and four-years old children morning and afternoon five days a week during term time. Anyway, he didn't doubt that he would see his beloved again either on, or, if flights were to prove problematic, soon after the appointed day.

It's not difficult to appreciate why Seb was presently unable to put pen to paper, why it was that he was unable to focus his mind sharply enough to be able to come up with a single idea. Not for the first time, after laying down the pen which he had held poised between thumb and fingers for the past quarter of an hour, Seb turned his head to take in the view through the small rectangular panes of glass that made up the sash window. The scene which greeted his eyes was different from the scene he had gazed out upon five minutes ago. Proceeding from being overcast, the sun's brilliance was now pervasive, and although the movement of the trees and bushes adorning the back gardens of the terraced rows indicated a change in pressure, it was as a consequence of the breeze which had just risen that the last vestige of cloud cloaking the orb had been driven away.

To Seb sunshine could be a mixed blessing. The thought crossed his mind that an improvement in the weather would encourage his widowed next-door neighbour to venture out of doors to sit in the yard cum garden, an eventuality which either by chance, or, following a telephone call or two, wittingly, tended to encourage her friends to call. No matter how the little coterie of women came to be there, however, a cacophony of thought-disturbing chatter would ensue.

There are undoubtedly occasions when living in close proximity to neighbours has advantages, but there are also disadvantages to contend with: none more so than the exceptional noise Seb's and Neffie's bedsprings made during lovemaking.

In point of fact, nobody from the adjacent house did emerge as Seb sat ruminating on whether he was just as much an annoyance to his neighbour as she could be to him. In particular he was thinking of his efforts at music-making whenever he sat al fresco strumming or plucking the strings of his Spanish guitar. Even though he thought he sang and played quite well, well enough to serenade Neffie like a troubadour, a minstrel who has given up on wandering, he didn't fail to consider that the back-yard audience, when the only chance to escape the assault on their ears was to retreat into the house, may not appreciate his recitals as much as he did.

Wandering in thought if not in body, the minstrel's ruminations were interrupted by the shrill, repetitive tones of the telephone ringing. The only landline apparatus in the house was located on the bottom step of the stairs. Its positioning wasn't ideal, but it was better since Seb had drilled a hole in the bottom corner of the living room door. He had done so to enable him to feed the line from the handset into the socket on the living room wall, and, subsequent to his handiwork, be able to close the door fully. In a draughty house that small hole led to no small achievement. One of the draughts in question could still be felt when either member of the household was speaking or listening on the telephone. It emanated from the gap around the front door and wafted down the passage to where Seb would usually be sitting on the third step up, Neffie, perhaps because she was shorter, on the second. Strange as it may seem, and despite the draught, both found the foot of the stairs a relaxing place to hold a conversation with an interlocutor far removed.

Summoned from his as yet fruitless cogitations, Seb jumped to his feet. Normally when sitting at his desk he wore carpet-slippers, but in this instance, having unwittingly discarded his left slipper he knew not where, his footwear was definitely singular. The shrill summons calling for haste, Seb was able to make only a cursory search for the missing item, and it was to no avail. Consequently, it was an unbalanced figure that made his way down the stairs. Seb felt strangely lop-sided. Upon surviving the descent, he was gratified to pick up the receiver before the caller lost patience. In response to his greeting and identifying who he was, the journalist in search of a story was surprised to hear a mellifluous voice which, though immediately identifiable for being familiar, he hadn't heard in ages. The voice belonged to Liz Humble. Seb often referred to this friend of Neffie's as Humble Liz.

Chapter Four
A Meeting of Minds

There are people we meet during the course of our lives whose influence is out of all proportion to the time spent in that person's company. If asked Seb could have come up with the names of several individuals who came into that category, but possibly the most influential person in his life was the SAS corporal whose name he had either not learned or couldn't remember. The NCO in question was Seb's instructor and mentor whilst the unit he was a part of was on exercise in Kenya. Not being able to cite the corporal's name didn't prevent Seb from being deeply impressed by the man's relaxed style of conducting a lesson: on what bits of kit to keep where in case of having to crash out of a location in a hurry; on bush craft in general and tracking in particular. Arguably the most important lesson of all, however, was the advice he gave, and that was always to do, whenever one found oneself in a tricky situation, what the enemy least expected. This wisdom, wisdom which as soldier and civilian Seb had acted upon two or three times over the years, had proved invaluable.

In contrast to the anonymous hero from his past, whichever way round Seb pronounced the name of the person at the other end of the line, it was a name which he remembered easily. This was hardly surprising seeing as she was a friendly acquaintance as well as being a member of the influential clique. Seb had met Liz on only two previous occasions, but he believed that she had some mystical power over him in a way not dissimilar to the influence brought to bear on a luckless hero of ancient Greece by the goddess Athena, or Hera, in the face of hostility from no less a deity than Zeus himself.

Their telephone conversation was the first of its kind between the two and lasted a couple of minutes. If Liz had been talking to Neffie the duration would have been half an hour at least, but being mindful of the bill Seb was disinclined to chat, and therefore kept his conversations succinct, even terse. Despite the brevity of the call, however, for Seb its import must have been inspirational, for as soon as he replaced the receiver he limped back up the stairs with, if it's not a contradiction in terms, a spring in his step.

His first concern upon re-entering the back bedroom that served as an office was to regain his sense of balance. It staggered him to have to walk with one side of his body a mere fraction of an inch farther from the carpet than the other. Consequently, he set about searching for his missing slipper in earnest. Eventually, having got down on his hands and knees to search under the desk thoroughly, he caught a glimpse of a squashed heel peeking out from where it was almost hidden by the cover draped over the futon. What a relief it was for him not to feel lop-sided.

Definitely inspired, it soon became evident that Seb's mental powers had also been restored. Athena, or Hera, had no doubt been at work to cast out their protégé's inertia. Both feet firmly in place he sat down at his desk and began to write. Almost effortlessly he composed the factual article that had previously been such a problem. It wasn't a literary masterpiece, but that didn't matter: what newspaper article ever is? He wrote about the journey he had taken by train from Yatton to Eskmouth the previous summer, a scenic route across the moors of approximately twenty-five miles. He sought to improve on the undoubted banality of the piece with humour.

If further proof were needed that he, or the goddesses, had succeeded in overcoming the torpor cast over him by Zeus, it was evident in the enthusiasm with which he made the telephone call to the number just given to him by Liz Humble, and the decisiveness he displayed in arranging to meet the woman who was a total stranger to him.

For the fact that Liz had provided Seb with more than the stranger's number, certain aspects of the stranger's life past and present were known to him as he drove up the narrow lane leading from the outskirts of Luxborough to the single row of terraced houses overlooking the town. The dwellings in question had been the homes of miners and their families in a previous era, and the hill which the terrace backed onto was riddled with defunct shafts and workings. The iron ore which these toughest of men had toiled to extract for use in the nearby steel works had become exhausted decades ago, and the houses in which they had lived were now privately owned by the likes of first-time buyers — single or coupled. Amongst the many young families were a few retired folk.

From a quarter of a mile away Seb cast his eyes along the terrace that was his destination and estimated that twenty properties made up the row. The address he was looking for was number twenty-two, Hillside Terrace. He noted that without exception the properties were well kept, many of the houses having white-washed walls. Nearly all the windows were double-glazed. Satellite dishes were much in evidence.

Notwithstanding their industrial foundations, the contiguous dwellings had a cottage charm about them, a bucolic ambiance which was further enhanced by the row's setting amid farmland, where gently sloping pasture provided nourishment for cattle and sheep.

A blot on the landscape in respect of the view from the bedroom window of any one of the properties in question — assuming that the roofs belonging to the market town of Luxborough spread out on a contour line below are anything but — is the council refuse collection centre situated halfway between Hillside Terrace and the town. The site which Seb had driven past in his Renault Clio less than a minute earlier gave the impression that it was much more than it really was. Enclosed by twelve feet high, three-pronged metal fencing, each prong piercingly sharp, the facility could conceivably be mistaken for a detention centre where the main concern being security the perimeter is patrolled by armed guards leading fierce dogs. It didn't look the sort of place where the local populace is able to deposit empty wine bottles and plastic containers to be recycled.

The woman whom Seb had come to visit at twenty-two Hillside Terrace was Shirley Margai, a radio journalist from Sierra Leone who had come to Britain to visit her mother. How Miss Margai's mother came to be living within a stone's throw of Luxborough Seb as yet had no idea. Liz Humble's knowledge of Seb's impending African connection, at least that which she had imparted to him, had amounted to Miss Margai's name, occupation, country of origin, and the reason for her visit to these shores. It was obvious, if he was at all interested in Miss Margai's story, that he would have much to learn. Given that his own circumstances were presently closely connected with Sierra Leone, at the very least he was bound to be interested in gleaning information about the country at first hand. There was also another obvious common denominator between the two journalists, and that was it —they were both in the same line of work. This had been a significant factor in their having arranged to meet in the first instance. The tools of their trade might well have been different, and though there might also have been a divergence in their reasons for so doing, they shared a desire to communicate with the public at large. Whatever the course of events about to unfold, Seb was ever mindful that he was calling upon Miss Margai at the behest of the irrepressible Liz Humble acting as humble impresario, and it was testament to her influence that he was about to take the radio journalist to lunch.

To Seb there was nothing unusual about the row of houses he drove past as he searched for the number he had in mind. There were several terraces of this kind in the area, a single row standing out on a limb from all other human habitation. To people from foreign parts and other counties however, the fact that the public road separated each house from its front garden could be thought strange. The majority of the well-tended gardens Seb drove past were replete with vegetables mainly, neat rows of cabbages and cauliflowers, and the spindly leaves that revealed where onion sets were growing, and though it was obvious that cultivation of the land for food took precedence, gaudy flower heads suitable for cutting as decoration for window-ledges and the dining table were easily discernible. Just as discernible, but for paintwork designed to be recognised by their occupants rather than any natural colouring, were two pigeon lofts. Letting the car crawl along at a few miles per hour, for a moment Seb craned his neck forward so that his chin almost rested on the top of the steering wheel. He was searching for a flock of pigeons wheeling in flight overhead. He saw nothing of the kind.

His attention thus focused elsewhere, Seb had unwittingly driven past the house he had come to visit, but that didn't matter in the slightest. There being only one road in and the same road out of Hillside Terrace, his plan was to drive to the end of the row and turn around so as to be facing in the right direction to go for lunch. That manoeuvre completed and now heading back the way he had come, Seb set about searching for numbers above the doors. The fact that no two doors were alike was yet another indication of private ownership, and that the people that unlocked and locked them as they came and went were individuals with individual tastes.

Seb noticed that there were no odd numbers, and that explained why the numbering was so high atop the first door he surveyed. It turned out that the house he was looking for was situated more or less midway along the terrace. It was perhaps a hangover from his army days, specifically his second tour of duty in Northern Ireland, impelling Seb to drive slowly past the house rather than stop directly outside where there was parking space available. It was as if he needed to make a reconnaissance of the target before committing himself.

It was so far so good, when in the next few moments, Seb discovered that the address he was looking for exists, and with regard to that singular fact, he hadn't been sent on a wild goose chase. He also discovered that he didn't much like the colour scheme of the house he now scrutinised. The door was a shade of green which doesn't exist in nature, and to match it the window frames were painted in the same unnatural and, in Mr Sebastian Forrest's opinion, distasteful colour. There were lace curtains at the downstairs window, and though Seb caught only a glimpse as he passed, he was certain that the curtain had moved, and consequently he was certain that someone behind the curtain had been giving him the once over.

After passing a couple of parked cars the journalist with a nose for a story pulled into the kerb. About twenty yards further on two girls were playing hopscotch on the pavement, although they paused in their play to watch the stranger get out of the car. In the end garden an elderly man wearing a cloth cap, a shirt rolled up at the sleeves, and trousers held up by braces, was filling a carrier-bag with the fruits of his labour: in this instance vegetables. The thought crossed Seb's mind that the old-timer was possibly a former miner long since retired from extracting rock from beneath the ground on which his house was standing, and upon which he and Seb were going about their business. After further consideration, however, Seb realised that he had made an anachronism, and so invented an alternative history for the gaffer in his garden. In the new version Seb imagined that this old-timer had spent his working life in the steelworks, or in the shipyard. Both industries had thrived along the banks of the river flowing into the sea a couple of miles the far side of Luxborough Hill, and the blast furnaces and cranes would have been clearly visible from the hilltop vantage point behind the terrace; but like the Colossus of Rhodes, or the Hanging Gardens of Babylon, such sights hadn't been seen for years, not since the area's heavy industry had declined.

Seb smiled at the girls and then nodded his head as an indication of the direction he was about to take. In effect he was telling them that they had no reason to interrupt their game for his sake. To the gardener he raised his hand in a friendly gesture of greeting, one which was reciprocated in a similar manner. Nonetheless, upon turning his back he felt that three pairs of eyes were following his every move, at least until eventually unmistakeable sounds told him that the game had indeed been resumed.

Seb had been correct in his assumption that his arrival hadn't gone unnoticed by at least one of the residents in the house he intended to visit. Unbeknown to him it had been Miss Margai who had ruffled the curtain. Consequently, just as he was about to rap his knuckles on the door, he was pre-empted as the door opened to reveal the woman who was to be his lunch-date.

Standing behind her, an inch or two taller, and, judging by her mien, definitely curious as to the appearance of this expected visitor, was the person whom Seb presumed to be Shirley's mother.

"Forrest… Sebastian Forrest," introduced Seb, trying, as if he were the world's most famous secret agent on a mission, to imbue an air of mystery into his identity.

Shirley smiled at him without a word of reply, and without a valedictory word to her mother stepped across the threshold into the street. In the mind of her visitor all the mystery was with her at the moment. Just as he was indicating to Shirley, with a gesture of his hand, the way to travel, he beheld the penetrating look in the eyes of her mother as by her unseen hand the door was closed.

"Mine is the green Renault Clio," he advised as they approached the girls playing hopscotch. Seb pressed the remote to open the doors and could tell from the way that the vehicle lights flashed that he had omitted to lock them. To get the right result he had to press the remote again.

Under normal circumstances the former soldier would have opened the front passenger door for his guest and stood aside to close it after she had got in. On this occasion, however, Miss Margai was one step ahead and took it upon herself to open the door, get in, and make that same self, comfortable. Seb got in beside her, and thinking that some acceptable physical contact may be of use in breaking the ice, so to speak, held out his hand to his guest in welcome. The assertiveness of this gesture, conducted in the spatial bubble that Seb was lord and master of, caused Shirley some confusion for catching her in two minds. She had been about to fasten her seat-belt, but paused in the act of clunk-click every trip in order to shake, rather tentatively, the proffered hand. Seb couldn't help but notice his passenger's nervousness. It made him think that all her actions in his presence thus far had been a front, and that she was trying to bluff him. This observation enabled him to gain, in principle not unlike two children playing on a see-saw and as one goes up the other drops toward the ground, correspondingly greater confidence, one may even go so far as to say the upper hand.

In point of fact Seb's aim wasn't to achieve supremacy in any sort of power game with Miss Margai, but merely to be in a position which allowed him to be generous in putting his guest at ease, just as with any reasonably balanced see-saw, the time would come when she would be in a position to put him at ease.

His confidence high, Seb put the car into first gear and was about to move off when he caught sight of Miss Margai looking over her shoulder and focusing her attention on the newspaper folded in half on the back seat. He had consciously placed it in the position and at the angle it was so that the person sitting adjacent to him, were she to turn around for an instant, would be able to read the headlines at a glance. Of course he was aware that his name and photograph were on the front page of the copy he had placed to be so conspicuous.

Following on from her fleeting look behind Shirley turned to Seb and, in a tone which suggested that she already knew the answer, enquired, "Is that the newspaper you write for?"

For having pulled away from the kerb but for not yet being fully aligned with the road, Seb checked in his wing mirror to ensure that a vehicle hadn't crept up on them otherwise unawares. After confirming that the road in front and behind was clear he allowed himself a reassuring glance at the object which had caught Miss Margai's eye. No;

it hadn't transmogrified into The Guardian, Times, or Telegraph. In that fleeting look, as he had turned his head through almost one hundred and eighty degrees, Seb had noted that Shirley's mother's head had replaced her daughter's at the window, and not covertly, to watch their departure; and that the woman sitting beside him was of striking appearance. By this time she had regained at least the semblance of composure.

The crowning glory of Shirley's impressive appearance couldn't have been anything other than her hair. It was of a style Seb thought was redolent of one of those seemingly manufactured boy bands he had viewed, prior to hurriedly switching channels, on television. In more avant-garde, metropolitan circles the style in question would probably be described as unisex, and therefore normal. Boyish blond hair framing a black face certainly made for an interesting combination.

There being no time for in-depth study in the driver's fleeting appraisal, we must perforce be neglectful of that part of a human-being's physiognomy which is most revealing of the inner being, other than to say that Shirley's eyes were brown and oval.

More obviously discernible to a fleeting look was Shirley's apparel. Seb noted that his new acquaintance was dressed as if for a cool day in spring or autumn rather than for the warm day in summer which it was. He attributed this to the African lady being susceptible to the cold, and that although the temperature was high enough for an Englishman to tend to his plot in shirt sleeves, Seb wondered if Miss Margai thought differently about it.

Despite this Saturday in August being mainly cloudy, the sun seemed to be trying hard to put in a longer than brief bright appearance, but was repeatedly thwarted in its supposed ambition. In conjunction with the sun the weather gods were sending messages of variable heat to the people of northern Britain, and the changes in temperature corresponded perfectly with the dappled light that came and went.

Miss Margai was smartly dressed. Her attire consisted of an off-white, almost cream, woollen outfit noteworthy for the ruff-neck which became compressed like a concertina each time the wearer lowered her head. The dress contrasted markedly with Miss Margai's dark skin. On her legs she was wearing black tights; on her feet black brogues. Once Seb had assimilated the superficial aspects of his companion's demeanour, each time he turned his head slightly to look at her, of course while keeping one eye on the road, he was able to add to the mental picture of the face he had been inwardly painting since they met.

From the gallery of facial expressions he had integrated over years, Seb was of the opinion that Miss Margai's disposition was sunny, her smile being bright and broad enough to dispel the darkest of clouds threatening her home town of Freetown at the height of the rainy season. In addition to the smile that frequently parted her mouth to reveal teeth that were enviably white and even, an equally remarkable feature of Miss Margai's face was her furrowed brow. It gave the impression that her corrugators had been working overtime to belie Shirley's otherwise natural radiance. Seb had imagined that he and his guest were the same age, give or take a year or two either way, but her worry lines made her look older, and caused Seb to conclude that she had had a hard time of late. He wondered if Liz Humble's intimation that Shirley had an interesting story to tell was in part revealed by the African lady's forehead.

Shirley's appearance, particularly the smartness of her attire, caused Seb to change his plan. Instead of taking her to a nearby pub where an adequate lunch could be had, usually in the company of old-age pensioners with time on their hands and a little money to spare for leisure, for a modest outlay, he thought that it would be more appropriate to go to the more up-market venue that was the restaurant in his own village.

The interval between his nodding affirmatively to the question about his contribution to the newspaper lying on the back seat and any further conversation was protracted, but no sooner had Seb made up his mind about where to go in preference to his former plan than he returned to the topic which Shirley had initiated. "Yes," he said, somewhat belatedly. "I write features for the Luxborough Times and that is the Luxborough Times. I focus mainly on subjects that are likely to be of interest to people that live and work in the town... not forgetting the large number of residents that have retired after decades working in one of Ferrousby's heavy industries. You know the sort of thing... local issues of interest to local people. My remit also includes writing about prominent personalities that have a connection to the area... local boy... or girl... makes good. Look at that so-and-so!"

The imperative interjection he made as his right foot applied enough pressure to the brake to allow a couple of young tearaways on bicycles to make a sharp right-angled turn and cross in front of the car unscathed. The only indication that the boys were about to do what they did was a quick glance over the right shoulder in each case. Evidently the young teenagers thought the telepathy achieved by the merest eye-contact would be as effective as a proper hand signal, and was therefore communication enough. Once the human hazards had cleared, presumably to be the cause of mayhem elsewhere, Seb increased speed up to the legal limit.

He also returned to trying to impress Shirley with his story. "I struggled to come up with something to write about for this week's edition," he resumed as he steered through the acres of new housing that had sprung up on the outskirts of Luxborough, "but eventually I came up with the goods… a thousand words to good effect. I don't mind telling you that I was chuffed to bits to see my piece highlighted on the front page… along with my photograph. I don't know if you noticed."

"Chuffed to bits?" echoed Miss Margai interrogatively as once again she turned to look at the newspaper in question.

"It's an expression people use in this part of the world when they're really pleased with something, or delighted at a result," Sebastian explained prior to returning to his former vainglorious theme. "Please feel free to take a closer look," he invited.

It was becoming increasingly apparent to Miss Margai that she was sitting next to a man who was of an age, and at a stage in his life, when it was necessary for his ego to prove its worth by drawing attention to its small achievements. She thought this desire to project power and influence was a peculiarly masculine trait. A couple of men she had worked with back in Freetown, males of a similar age to Sebastian, had behaved in a similar fashion when in her company. Miss Margai had learned to be tolerant.

Accepting the invitation Shirley reached behind for the folded broadsheet. Being careful not to impede the driver, she spread the newspaper across, but an inch above, her knees. Seb observed that Shirley was meticulous in holding the newspaper at its edges, and because she didn't allow the underside to make contact with her dress, he concluded that she was wary of becoming a victim of newsprint in the form of smudges, stains and smears.

Seb eagerly awaited comment as he pulled on the handbrake after stopping at a temporary set of traffic-lights preceding a lengthy stretch of road works. A tall, rangy figure of a man with a suntanned face, and wearing a yellow jacket and a white safety helmet, climbed into an excavator. The machine he set in motion looked like a large toy rather than a practical piece of construction equipment; yet it obviously did serve a practical purpose, and that was to excavate a trench in which to lay a pipe.

"That's really impressive," Miss Margai commented, raising her head from the piece she had merely scanned to observe the activity taking place beyond the windscreen. She wasn't being disingenuous in her comment. "I won't read it now," she added, folding the newspaper she didn't intend to part with, for the time being at least. "Reading in the car makes me feel sickly," she explained before adding, "but I would like to borrow this if I may."

The implication of this request didn't fail to register with Sebastian: it would seem that there was to be a second meeting.

"Have you always been interested in trains?" enquired Miss Margai, referring to the subject matter of Sebastian's article.

Seb failed to notice the mischievous glint in her eye as she spoke, but he did detect the tone of an aunt asking a question of a teenage nephew whom she hasn't seen in years, and who has just been given a train set for Christmas. Responding to a gentle toot of the horn from the possibly helpful, perhaps impatient, driver of the car directly behind, he delayed his reply until he had moved off to drive on the wrong side of the road past a long line of red and white bollards.

"Not particularly," said Seb, without the slightest intonation that he had been irked for thinking he was being patronised, "but as the train that runs across the moors from Ferrousby to the seaside town of Eskmouth stops at Luxborough, and because hordes of people make the trip to the coast by car... I thought I would remind my readers that there's an easier way to travel."

Seb paused in his explanation of why he had written the article in question to consider the accuracy of what he had just said.

"Actually," he continued, "it's not the journey that's so bad, it's the fact that parking in Eskmouth is horrendous… particularly at this time of year."

Shirley smiled, and this time, out of the corner of his eye, Seb couldn't fail to notice the hint of superciliousness briefly on display. It was as if the recipient of the information was amused slightly, perhaps charmed, by the gravitas of the subject. On the basis that in this one regard he was able to read Miss Margai's thoughts, Seb decided that the wisest course was to be more self-effacing.

"I know this must seem trivial fare to a journalist of your experience," Seb proclaimed.

His proclamation was a shot in the dark. In reality he had no idea whether Shirley's work was any less 'trivial' than his own, or whether she was well-practised at interviewing certain African leaders about why war was ravaging the countries they led. He had no idea how high up the scale of scoops she had climbed.

"But you would have to agree that transport is an important issue for every country, and when the country in question is as small and as densely populated as this it's even more so. My greatest concern is that within my lifetime England's once green and pleasant land will be almost completely covered with tarmac and housing estates, and that the green bits in between become permanently littered with cans and other detritus thrown by careless people from out of their cars, and that our children come to believe… if they don't already… that carrier bags make for attractive appendages to our hedgerows. I suppose you've interviewed the great and the good of your country, and perhaps even farther afield," he concluded, turning the spotlight, as it were, on Shirley suddenly.

Seb hadn't intended to broach or go anywhere near the sensitive subjects that are immigration and population density, but as a consequence of the comments he had just made he was happy for Miss Margai to have her say on the subject if she so chose, he was happy to allow her to rise on the see-saw of their acquaintanceship whilst he dropped to the ground.

"Well… now that you mention it," responded Miss Margai as she returned the newspaper to the back seat, thereby giving Seb the impression that she had thought twice about wanting to borrow it, "I suppose that I've interviewed a number of famous people… famous in Freetown that is… but whether I would describe them as being either great or good is debatable."

Once again Miss Margai flashed her brilliant white teeth in Seb's direction as she brought to mind some of the characters she had had to work with: this time her smile transmitted not a hint of condescension.

"And besides," the radio-reporter continued, "it must be great to live in a country where features about trains and people going to the seaside to spend an entire day on leisure are highlighted on the front page rather than having to read about diamond-smuggling, political unrest, corruption, and…" Shirley paused for a moment as she considered whether to add to her trilogy of bad happenings, but notwithstanding her wish for lunch to be a pleasant occasion, she decided not to hold back, and with a sheepish look and a hesitant voice that together communicated her sense of shame she added, "… and mutilations."

"Are things that bad over there?" enquired Seb. Naturally he thought of Neffie and wondered what she was doing at that very moment.

"The country has been in turmoil for years," Shirley replied. "It's not just in high places that corruption is rife, as you would probably expect of a West African country, but it permeates every stratum of society. You better believe it to be true when I tell you that the government under President Momoh actually saved money by increasing the salaries of its employees… in some cases by up to seventy per cent."

Her excitement at the significance of this revelation was clearly evident in Shirley's voice, as was an unmistakeable African intonation.

"How was that possible?" asked the incredulous driver. It wasn't that he doubted Shirley's sincerity in communicating the intelligence he had just heard, it was simply a matter of his not being able to rationalise the logical absurdity of it. It seemed more improbable than quantum theory.

"By eliminating so-called 'ghost-workers' from the payroll… you'll know the sort of thing I mean… a situation in which wages are paid to people that don't exist. Does that sort of thing happen here? I don't suppose it does. Here everything seems so well-ordered and efficient," commented Miss Margai as she observed the smooth flow of traffic arriving from several directions at a roundabout half a mile out of town.

"When I was in the army I did hear of a paymaster who created a fictitious regiment of several hundred men, all of whom were then paid, as far as the army was concerned, on a regular basis. I presume that the money went directly into a bank account... or bank accounts... for which only he... the paymaster... had access. I suppose the fact that we're so dependent on computers these days allows that sort of thing to be done more easily." Seb was eager to let it be known that corruption involving the misappropriation of funds isn't a uniquely African phenomenon.

"Did he get away with it?" Shirley enquired matter-of-factly, as if it was the one question she was bound to ask.

Her countenance, indeed her entire body language, clearly indicated that she was presently more at ease than she had been hitherto in Sebastian Forrest's company. The see-saw that was their platonic relationship thus far had attained a point of perfect equilibrium.

"For a time," Seb replied, "but he must have been caught in the end or I wouldn't have got to hear about it."

He paused for thought for a moment. "I think there must be a kind of psychological imperative at work that compels some people to commit acts of fraud to such a degree that even though they expect to be caught in the end, they aim to have one hell of a time beforehand. I've read of people... and they come from all walks of life... accountants... school secretaries... charity commissioners... that have spent tens of thousands of pounds... money that didn't belong to them... on holidays, upmarket cars, expensive clothes, visits to top restaurants... you name it. If, on the other hand, they had thought that they could get away with leading such an exorbitant lifestyle indefinitely they must be mad."

Shirley nodded in silent recognition of the validity of Seb's statement. He slowed down prior to overtaking a horse and rider, his intention being to cause as little harassment to both as possible. In view of the bends in the road ahead the road markings prohibited overtaking. Seb realised it was a risky business, but on the basis that the oncoming traffic had hitherto been light, with a car or van approaching only intermittently, he made his move. He completed the manoeuvre safely as it turned out.

"I did interview Siaka Stevens, our former leader, before he died, but I have yet to meet President Momoh," said Shirley as soon as she became aware of the straight stretch of road ahead and that the driver had become more relaxed. "As for what's going to happen in the future, I fear that the political unrest so much in evidence at present will soon descend into civil war. There have already been several killings and mutilations in Kono District."

"Killings and mutilations in Kono District," echoed Seb. "That's terrible!" The thought crossed his mind that Neffie might not have made the wisest of choices in travelling to Sierra Leone for the school holiday.

"It's not uncommon for rebels in the east of the country to cut off the hand... both hands in some cases... of people they don't like the look of, or that have committed what in this country would be considered a petty crime."

The teller of these hideous tidings couldn't fail to notice the look of concern on her interlocutor's face. The transformation that had come over him was like a dark cloud crossing the face of the sun.

"Didn't you know that such things are going on in my country, that there are people capable of committing such atrocities, and not only on men, but on women and children too?"

Seb declined to answer the question directly, but responded by asking a question of his own. "Did Liz Humble tell you that my partner... Neffie she's called... it's short for Nefertiti... flew to Freetown just over a week ago, her plan being to spend the summer holiday doing voluntary work of one sort or another?"

"Liz didn't tell me anything about your personal life," Shirley replied.

"Well now you know at least one important snippet, and in the light of what you've just told me you can imagine my concern... for Neffie's safety I mean."

"I'm sure she'll be fine as long as she doesn't travel to Kono. That's where all the trouble is at present."

Seb realised that he wasn't sure where Neffie intended to go once she had arrived in Freetown. Up until now this hadn't been a concern, primarily because he knew that she would always want to be flexible in her travel arrangements once she had arrived in the country. For knowing that in Africa it was not unknown for people to wait days for a bus or a ferry he believed that it was the sensible attitude to have.

He was about to enquire further about the instability in Kono District, but Miss Margai spoke first. "That's impressive," she said, pointing with her finger at the pinnacle they were passing on the left.

Seb made a mental note that describing something as 'impressive' was a word Shirley liked to use when offering praise. The local man prepared to take on the role of tourist guide as he followed the finger pointing at a more pleasant horizon than the vista he couldn't see for real, but which had occupied his mind for the past few minutes. To the left of the road was a broken scarp, to the right, level farmland where cattle grazed.

"That's Odin's Hill," Seb informed, referring to the distinctive hill that standing at just over one thousand feet, and separate as if broken off from the scarp stretching to the far side of Luxborough, is emblematic of the area, appearing on the promotional literature of a wide range of local businesses.

"And who was Odin?" Shirley asked.

"Odin was a pagan god of war and death... though looking on the bright side he also dabbled in wisdom and poetry. It was probably the Vikings that gave the hill its name. They were quite thick on the ground in this area."

"And who were the Vikings?" pressed Shirley, eager to increase what to her was far from local knowledge.

Even though she did have some small inkling, some vague recollection of a period in British history touched upon in school, that in the dim and distant past the Vikings were a fierce lot infamous for rape and pillage, she had no idea from whence they came.

"You've not heard of the Vikings?" questioned Seb, more than a little surprised.

"Have you heard of the Mende or Temne?" rejoined Miss Margai pointedly.

Once over the railway bridge and on the straight stretch leading into Yatton seen for the first time against an impressive backdrop of hills to the south, Seb took his right hand off the steering wheel and slapped the back of the left hand steering the car: a punishment he truly deserved.

"This is the village where Neffie and I live," he said as he drove into the centre, where, two minutes later, having found the only space then available, he parked the car.

Chapter Five
A Likely Story

Like two people of more or less equal height and weight going up and down on a see-saw, two aspects of Sebastian Forrest's life were mutually compatible. The first of these he had mastered when young and therefore took for granted, and since those first teetering steps into his mother's waiting, outstretched arms, he had travelled far on Shanks's pony. He loved to walk. On the basis that practice makes perfect he had become quite good at it. At the age of three he had set off from home with the intention of climbing Luxborough Hill, a distance of three miles from his parents' home in a suburb of Ferrousby, rounded off with an ascent of eight hundred feet to the top of the scarp. Then he would have to make his way back. Tempted, after two miles, to knock on the door of a house in the last row before the fields, the house where his aunt lived, on that occasion he didn't make it, but succumbed instead to lemonade and cake, and his aunt's prohibition when it came to his furthering that day's perambulatory ambition.

Since then, having grown much stronger and a little wiser, he had trekked over eighty miles across the moors in a walking time of just over thirty hours. In the company of Neffie he had trekked across England and raised £1,000 for the National Health Service; trekking across Scotland they had endured being eaten alive by the midge, millions of them; they had walked several long-distance paths in France; they had traversed the Pyrenees and then turned right at Pamplona to trek five hundred miles across Spain, Seb burdened by a full pack and tent for the entire way. Before meeting Neffie, and whilst in the army, he had walked in deep snow wearing snow shoes, and had kept a wary eye open for arachnids and snakes as he stepped out in Kenya and Belize. For not having been bitten by either he hadn't been deterred from practising one of life's simple pleasures.

The second aspect, the one compatible with the first, was Seb's great reluctance to pay for parking, a disdain which usually compelled him to park his car up to a mile away from his destination whenever he went into Ferrousby on business, the fact of the matter being that in the town centre parking was of short duration if free, whereas in some quiet, out-of-the-way cul-de-sac away from the centre there were likely to be no restrictions whatsoever.

Such measures weren't usually necessary in Yatton. An attractive and salubrious enough village for people to want to visit in large numbers during the summer, it was hardly a motorist's paradise when it came to parking, but it was usually possible to find a space within a few hundred yards of the centre, and Seb didn't think himself particularly fortunate in being able to switch off the engine within thirty yards of the restaurant he had in mind. If it had been a perfect summer's day then the situation would have been different, for people come to Yatton for the day to picnic on one of the two village greens, to eat ice-cream and feed the ducks, and watch their children paddle almost naked in the shallows of the gently flowing river. On such days parking is at a premium, and though it was hypocritical of him, he complained bitterly whenever he turned into the little road where he and Neffie lived to discover a car he hadn't seen before parked in front of the house.

The significance of this rather mundane aspect of daily living becomes greater when the people involved are disabled or not as steady on their legs as they once were. In the short distance that Seb and Shirley had to walk, the man couldn't help but notice that the woman walked with a limp, an infirmity which he had failed to notice previously. Only after Seb had taken a few leisurely steps, and realised that Miss Margai couldn't keep up, did he become aware of the difficulty she was experiencing walking. The first thought to cross the newspaper man's mind was that Shirley was mocking the fact that as recently as the other day he had limped downstairs wearing only one slipper. One thought followed another as Forrest asked himself how was it possible that a woman whom he had known for no more than half an hour knew about his unintentional comedy act on the stairs. It was indicative of his somewhat paranoid mindset that he hit upon the notion that he had been observed by the people living in the house directly opposite his. It was

72

certainly true that if one of the adults, or either of their two teenage daughters, living there were to look out of the larger of the two upstairs windows it would be possible to see through the transparent, semi-circular pane of glass above his and Neffie's front door. That was it Seb concluded. There could be no other explanation for a man so self-absorbed. The people living across the road, though in all respects helpful, friendly neighbours, for a reason he had yet to fathom were in collusion with the spy from Sierra Leone.

Fortunately for the continuance of his amiable disposition no sooner had Seb come to the conclusion he had than he dismissed it. The idea was absurd. He knew, because he had had to contend with such wayward thoughts on numerous occasions, and delusions even more sinister, that they represented the mentality of a sane man confronting a moment of madness. Sebastian was well-practised in analysing his own cognitive processes. By his reckoning true madness is when such delusions become the norm and as a consequence the subject becomes an emotional wreck. He had been an emotional wreck, but as a believer in the maxim that that which doesn't kill you makes you stronger, his outlook on life was that the future would be better than the past, and in his opinion the best way of remaining on the level, as it were, was to solve the puzzle of false perspectives by having the courage to ask the right questions.

"Have you hurt your leg?" Seb enquired, stopping and half-turning as he waited for his companion to catch up with him.

"Is it that obvious?" Shirley replied.

"How did you do it?" Seb interrogated as they continued on their way together.

"It's a long story," Shirley replied. "I'll tell you over lunch. Is this the place you were going to take me for lunch?"

She nodded in the direction of the glass door which happened to be the entrance and exit of the restaurant wherein Seb had intended they would eat. A sign on the inside of the door stated, 'CLOSED FOR RENOVATIONS FOLLOWING A FIRE'.

Up until this moment of disappointment Seb had been wondering whether to assist Miss Margai by offering his arm as support. He had hesitated in so doing because he didn't want to be thought overly familiar, and though he was pleased to be distracted from one quandary, he was displeased at the emergence of another. In fact he could have kicked himself, especially since he had known about the fire in question since the afternoon following the morning when it had happened. Despite his forgetfulness the Yatton man wasn't fazed completely. In this village attractive to visitors there were several alternative venues. Bearing in mind Miss Margai's difficulty, for being the nearest eating establishment on the High Street was the Captain Cook Inn, an eighteenth-century coaching inn which had changed its name in honour of the great explorer as recently as a year ago. Realising, as she followed Seb's pointing finger with her eyes, that the distance which they had farther to walk wasn't that much greater than the ground they had covered on foot since leaving the car, Shirley readily acceded to the suggestion. Upon entering the watering-hole where the drink least likely to be served is water, neither of the media stars was surprised to find that initially they were objects of curiosity to patrons and staff alike. The length of time they remained under scrutiny was longer than Seb would have expected under normal circumstances, say in the company of Neffie, or his brother.

Seb believed that he was witnessing a fundamental aspect of human nature in the curiosity of people keen to know who has just entered their enclosed domain. He pondered over the idea that perhaps upon hearing a door being pulled ajar by as yet an unseen hand, whether for those already having their lunch it occurs between the starter and the main course, or the main course and the pudding, a little piquancy is added to the dish. He also hypothesised that the observers chewing their cud, as it were, are more often than not disappointed to discover that the new arrival is as ordinary as themselves and not Donald Trump or Vladimir Putin.

There were faces in the L-shaped room which Seb recognised, although he didn't know a single fact about the people in question. He had seen them often enough to believe that they were local, and sensed from the looks they gave him that in a similar way he was familiar to them. It was to be expected. In a village of five thousand souls, no matter how gregarious an individual it would be impossible to get to know everyone personally. In addition to the majority, seated and nameless, propping up the bar were a few acquaintances with whom Seb was accustomed to exchanging banter, and these he acknowledged either with a friendly smile or a just as friendly vocal greeting.

With regard to the lingering looks of the simply curious Seb couldn't decide whether the prolonged interest was the result of his putting in an appearance at his local pub in the company of a female other than Neffie, or whether it was because the woman he was with was black. At the onset of the last decade of the twentieth century it was unlikely that the people enjoying lunch, hadn't seen a black person before, but this being a rural backwater it obviously wasn't Brixton, and to see a black face in Yatton was as yet a rare event.

Gradually the gapers lost interest and returned to the serious business of sating a primal need, just as the two objects of the curiosity were about to do. Shirley made herself comfortable at a table for two by the fireplace. No fire had burned in the grate since the beginning of June. Hanging on the chimney-breast was a painting of a fox-hunting scene. The picture's focal point was the scarlet jacket the master was wearing. He was leaning forward in the saddle as his doughty steed, a dappled grey with a wild, exhilarated look in its eye, was immortalised in the act of leaping a hedgerow.

"A typical English country scene I would say," said Shirley as she rested her elbows on the table and cradled her chin in the palms of her hands. Seated with her back to the window gazing up at the picture she appeared to be perfectly at ease.

For the first time in his life, though he had probably seen this dynamic representation of equine and manly courage a hundred times without having given it a second thought, Seb perused the painting intently. To his way of thinking the talent involved in creating the picture was way above anything he could do, yet his admission of artistic inferiority was unlikely to enhance the painting's value: it was the sort of thing one could pick up in a charity shop for a couple of pounds. It wasn't surprising that, coming from where she did, Miss Margai should perceive the depiction as being typical of English country life. Hovering like a waiter about to take an order, but minus pad and pen, Sebastian stood.

"Don't you think it's unfair that so many dogs are chasing one little fox?" inquired Shirley, eager to gain an insight into a pursuit she thought arcane. She was referring to the pack of fox-hounds in the foreground, canines which looked as if they were about to vacate the space where the horse's front hoofs were about to land.

"They're called hounds," informed Seb, relinquishing his self-appointed status as a waiter for the moment by turning his attention back to the picture. "They're not called dogs... they're called hounds... and as for your suggestion that fox-hunting goes against the spirit of fair play... an ideal for which we in this country have a reputation I believe... well, I have to admit many would agree with you."

"But what's your opinion?" enquired Miss Margai with journalistic incisiveness. "Do you think the sport... if you can call a pack of dogs ripping an animal apart a sport... goes against the spirit of fair play as you put it?"

For having previously given the matter some thought, and for having responded to a number of similar questions over the years, Sebastian didn't need to think long and hard about his answer. "It's not something I feel strongly about either way," he said. Feeling it necessary to justify his fence-sitting he continued matter-of-factly, "I was born and brought up in one of the less salubrious areas of Ferrousby, a town once renowned throughout the country for its heavy industry, and not for country pursuits... though I did once get into trouble for wandering too far from home. I was three years old at the time and my little legs made it to the farm fields at the foot of the hills. I was lucky, or adventurous, or both. I should think there are people in town that didn't see a cow or a sheep... other than on television perhaps... until they were well up in years. So you see, I don't have a fox-hunting background, but that said I wouldn't rail against it in respect of the people that do enjoy the local meet. Foxes can cause carnage in a chicken coop."

At this point, in the belief that he had answered Miss Margai's question more than adequately, Seb kept quiet. Surprised that she didn't appear to have been flummoxed by the ambiguity in the sound of the word he had used for a gathering, and searching for a sign that he had answered her question satisfactorily, his eyes focused upon each of hers in turn.

"Your ambivalence seems like a cop out to me," retorted Miss Margai bluntly. "You're sitting on the fence because hunting is something which doesn't directly concern you. If you were to take that attitude on…"

"Perhaps it is a cop out," interposed Forrest emphatically, "but that's what I think," he concluded, equally bluntly, hoping to have the final word on the subject. Intent on changing it, the subject that is, after moments of embarrassing silence, he asked, "What would you like to drink?"

"I'd like a glass of water."

The omission of the word he had been brought up to use as much as thank you reverberated like a silent shock wave in Sebastian's ear drum. "Water!" he exclaimed.

Seb intended his retort to be a mock expression of shock and horror, rather than the real thing, but Miss Margai wasn't so sure. Consequently her demeanour became a little sheepish, and with a look that implored forgiveness she changed her mind and said, "Perhaps I'll have a fruit juice instead. Will that be all right?"

It was. Once the minutiae necessary for the ordering of drinks and lunch had been discussed and put into effect, in the interval between their taking the first sip of liquid refreshment and their food arriving, Seb went on the offensive. The reason as to why his guest walked with a limp had begun to gnaw at him.

There were two elements to Seb's curiosity. First, and undoubtedly foremost in the sense of it being the most important to him personally, was that what he was about to hear could have some bearing on Neffie's safety. If that were to be the case, however, his problem then would be how to communicate his concerns to his partner with the speed necessary to make the warning effective. That she had chosen not to take a lap-top or mobile phone with her didn't help in this regard. The second motivation for Seb wanting to know was that he entertained the possibility that Miss Margai's story may be the making of him as a hack. If his head was filling with ambitious thoughts at that moment, they didn't take up so much room that he was prevented from making a tangible input by sipping a mouthful of ale.

After licking his lips and placing the glass from which he had drunk firmly down onto a beer mat advertising the brew he had just savoured, he posed a question in earnest. "So is the injury to your leg so serious that you'll be stuck with a limp for the rest of your life, or do you expect that in time you'll be able to walk on an even keel again, if you catch my drift?"

Seb had intended to be tactful, but he didn't think that it had sounded like it.

"Do you mean will I be able to walk properly again?" enquired Shirley, not quite catching the drift of Seb's nautical metaphors.

"Yes," Seb confirmed.

"That won't be possible without surgery, and I'm not just talking about re-setting a bone that has knitted together badly. I was told by my doctor in Freetown that the surgery I need, to have at least a chance of walking properly again… requires expertise of a kind that currently isn't available in Sierra Leone, or in any of the neighbouring countries."

"I assume that the expertise you speak of is readily available in this country," said Seb, not expecting to be contradicted.

The young man gulped another mouthful of beer. Prior to responding to his comment Shirley sipped demurely from her glass. "Mmm…" she hummed approvingly, before adding, "I quite like this. It tastes of apples." Then, with hardly a pause, she returned to the more serious topic. "I'm not eligible for treatment in an NHS hospital, and a private operation would be prohibitively expensive." Seb recognised his cue. "It tastes of apples because that's what it is… apple juice." In the same way that Shirley had made a gustatory preamble to more serious concerns, Seb imitated her example. "By how much would it be prohibitive?"

"I haven't looked into the figures in detail, but I'm sure that the fees involved would be way above anything I could afford. The wages in Sierra Leone, if you can call them that, are a pittance compared to how much people in similar occupations are paid in this country. It took all my savings to make the trip to Britain to see my mother, and she paid half my fare."

Seb realised that his guest was more hard-up than he was. Ordered in a quiet interval food arrived to cause a hiatus in their discussion. The waitress who attended to their needs was tall, elegant. Her blond hair was tied back to reveal in full her fine features and fresh complexion. She was dressed in funereal black save for the white pinafore signalling her occupation. Her manner was as pleasant as any top-notch restaurant guest could wish for, and she smiled at each of the pub's diners in turn as steadily and methodically she performed her duties.

When the serving wench fortunate enough to be endowed with a ballerina's looks and figure was halfway to the labyrinth wherein the kitchen was located, Miss Margai once again deviated from talking about herself by making an observation. "You wouldn't find me working as a waitress if I looked like she does."

Like a student who reads the same passage twice to make sure that he or she fully understands the author's gist, following Shirley's lingering look over his right shoulder, Seb turned his head to look over the same shoulder just in time to see the blond sylph disappear through a door marked 'STAFF ONLY'. "She's probably a student working to earn a few pounds during the holidays," he said, turning back to give Shirley his full attention.

He was surprised, and amused, to discover that with the aid of her fork Miss Margai was holding up a Yorkshire pudding the size of a man's clenched fist. To Seb, in acceding to Shirley's request for a traditional dish, roast beef and Yorkshire pudding had seemed a good choice of fare.

"So is this a good example of the world-famous Yorkshire pudding?" enquired Shirley, somewhat disdainfully.

"It certainly is," Seb replied as he tucked into his food, "though there's also a two-legged variety." It was Miss Margai's turn to be amused.

Chapter Six
Her Terrible Ordeal

During the course of the next couple of hours, as the Captain Cook Inn's lunchtime patrons vacated the hostelry in dribs and drabs to make for a quieter and more spacious room, the conversation between the two journalists fluctuated between matters trivial and matters of grave concern. The periods of time spent in light-hearted exchanges however, were shorter than the preponderance spent in serious discussion. One of the lighter topics involved Shirley's inability to imagine the tactile quality of snow, what it felt like to be hit in the face by a snowball, or to walk through deep drifts wearing inadequate shoes. When discussing a topic of greater gravitas Sebastian learned a great deal about life in Sierra Leone, and in particular about his guest's recent personal, and undoubtedly traumatic, history.

A big change in Shirley's life had come about when her mother divorced her father in order to live with, and eventually marry, an Englishman. In response to becoming apprised of this fact Sebastian was about to make a facetious comment, but under the influence of the controlling mind which told him it was better to be tactful than tactless, he dismissed the idea. It wasn't the right moment for levity. Even though the white man and the black woman had met and lived in Koidu, the main centre of population in Kono District, the wedding ceremony took place over two hundred miles and a five hour drive away in Freetown. The fifth anniversary of their nuptials would be this September. There were two reasons for the couple choosing to get married in Freetown, one practical, the other sentimental. The practical consideration was that the majority of the bride's relations lived in the capital, and still do. The sentimental reason, the motivation inspired by an amazing historical event, was that both parties felt it would reflect the spirit of the age if they were to be wed in St John's Maroon Church, a church founded by the first freed slaves soon after their arrival from the plantations of Jamaica early in the nineteenth century. Notwithstanding its colourful name, and contrary to the expectations of the uninitiated, the diminutive chapel is white.

The man who became Shirley's stepfather upon his marriage to her mother was Brian Cannisman, a fifty-six years old mining engineer who hailed originally from Luxborough. Fifty years ago he could have been riding his bicycle along the same stretch of road as the lad who had tested Sebastian's alertness earlier that day. At the time of his first meeting the woman who was then Mrs Margai, Cannisman had been working in one of the diamond mines that are so much in evidence in Kono District. According to Shirley an affair which had begun surreptitiously soon became the worst kept secret in Koidu. By all accounts Mr Margai hadn't taken much persuading to bow out of the scene gracefully. To all but the two male protagonists the means of persuasion brought to bear remain open to conjecture, but Shirley and her mother suspected from the outset that a sum of money had changed hands. If that were the case, the amount involved was likely to have been considerable to a labourer earning local wages; less so to a mining engineer whose monthly salary was paid into an offshore bank account.

From the moment when the radio journalist first began to speak in earnest about her personal circumstances, and the circumstances of the people whose lives were, or had been, closely linked with hers, her audience of one sat as if mesmerised.

A key fact Forrest learned about Cannisman was that he had been paranoid about security, and had acted accordingly by turning the house he had bought in the most desirable part of Koidu into a fortress. Concerns for his family's safety and the physical integrity of his home stemmed mainly from the deteriorating political situation in that part of the country. The writing on many a wall warned of a slide into anarchy which the forces of law and order would be powerless to prevent. Around the time when Cannisman was completing the purchase of the property the level of violence had been low and therefore not so threatening as to be off-putting to a man with considerable experience of working in Africa. Eventually however, being a man of intelligence and foresight, but unfortunately not so much foresight that he was able to predict how bad things were going to get, Cannisman came to believe that he had made a wrong move in choosing to live where he did.

Thinking that his best course of action was to protect what he had rather than try to off-load at a time when properties were becoming increasingly difficult to sell, Cannisman set to work. The work on his house cum fortress was gradual. On each of two trips he made back to Britain he returned with his suitcases laden with the heavy-metal paraphernalia necessary to keep out unwelcome visitors, and several weeks supply of English mustard. Each of the doors leading into the house in Koidu, either from the dusty main street beyond the handkerchief-sized garden at the front, or from the narrow alley leading past the bougainvillea-covered wall at the back, was fitted with a double locking system. Over time our security-conscious engineer reinforced the locks with chains and bolts. To complete the assemblage locally manufactured iron bars appeared at the windows made from shatter-proof glass.

To her friends Mrs Cannisman let it be known that since living with Brian she had gained some insight into what it must be like being in prison, particularly at night. Invariably of a morning she would hear her husband methodically going about the first task of the day — the unlocking of the doors and the retraction of the bolts. At first she used to shudder at the jangling of keys prior to Brian selecting the right one and inserting it into the keyhole, and cringe at the more emphatic clunk that accompanied the manipulation of each bolt. If it doesn't breed contempt familiarity may breed resignation and acceptance. It did so with the lady of the house in the sense that eventually, having grown accustomed to the repetition of sound as if each declaration of reduced or increased access were indeed echoes, she didn't pause in her mundane act of domestic preservation, but continued with dressing, or changing the sheets, or brushing her teeth. She may not like the idea of having to live in her own home at night like a prisoner, but she realised that her husband was acting from the best of motives, and that was fear for her safety.

For the reason that Shirley's feelings for her mother were of the warmest filial kind, and that she respected her decisions with regard to arranging her own affairs and future happiness, from the day they were introduced the step-daughter had got on well with her step-father. A consequence of this harmonious relationship was that Shirley had been given her own room in the fort, though because of having to work in

Freetown during the week, she only had recourse to it on her weekends off. She for one was glad of the security measures installed by her step-father, and had told him that she hadn't slept so soundly in her life.

In the months and years that followed Mr and Mrs Cannisman establishing their home in Koidu, the tally of killings and the number of people maimed increased. To travel by certain routes, thinking particularly of journeys to the Tingi or Loma mountains, was often a macabre experience for seeing, and smelling, a mutilated, rotting corpse lying by the side of the road. From the outlying villages of Kurako and Boroma to the north of Koidu, and Woama and Sidu to the south, people disappeared never to be seen again. Presumably some, if not all, of these individuals had been taken into the bush to be summarily executed and their bodies left as food for carnivores, be they prowlers on four legs or hook-beaked scavengers on two. In the larger towns, towns such as Yengema and Yamada, it became increasingly common to see victims of machete attacks and punishments ruminating on their past and speculating on their future. The most forlorn, and in this number, there were children as young as twelve, were the poor wretches that had lost both hands.

Upon hearing this most cruel aspect of Shirley's narrative Sebastian felt sickened. He tried to imagine a life without fingers and thumbs. Such a life would be a challenge in this country, but in a country where prosthetics are a wonder it was almost unimaginable. Nonetheless he did try to imagine tackling the normally simple tasks that people perform several times on a daily basis: getting dressed, brushing one's teeth, opening doors, eating and drinking, and then there's the messy business of going to the toilet. And to think that punishments of this kind were administered for nothing more serious than stealing a diamond. The mind recoils at the idea of such butchery, for any crime.

People began to leave places. At first they packed their meagre belongings into sacks and bags and forsook their villages for the relative safety of the towns. Then, as the rebels under the command of dispossessed tribal chiefs and warlords consolidated their hold on the eastern province, people began to drift away in their thousands. Mainly they made for the capital, or, fearing that the country would soon erupt into full-scale civil war, fled north to Guinea.

If Brian Cannisman had stayed amongst the living he would undoubtedly have been at the vanguard of this exodus, but on the morning of 27th April, 1987, Mrs Cannisman discovered his outstretched body on the kitchen floor. She knew there was something amiss prior to taking her first step to come downstairs that morning. It was the sudden cessation of familiar sounds that had forewarned her, and the fact that she had heard a noise which was ominous for being startlingly unfamiliar. Given, by this time, the amount of civil unrest and spasmodic violence, Mrs Cannisman might have been shocked, though not necessarily surprised, to have heard her husband drop down dead following a rifle shot, or a sickening slump preceded by a kerfuffle in which a knife or a machete was the instrument of murder. Fortunately for her in respect of her own safety however, no such act of callousness or savagery took place. Instead, what the lady of the house heard that morning was the key being turned to unlock the front door as usual, and then, in continuance of the daily ritual, two of the three bolts being extracted. What Mrs Cannisman didn't hear, the omission which caused her to pause in the act of fastening her blouse, was the extraction of the third bolt.

The sound which had taken its place was that of her husband becoming a dead weight. She had been able to divine in an instant what had happened, and the realisation filled her with dread. Despite trembling fingers, she had managed to finish dressing, and rather than risk injury by running down the stairs in a state of extreme agitation, she did her utmost to remain calm as she descended slowly, cautiously, one step at a time. Her legs had felt like jelly. Deep within her soul she knew that the event which she had just heard was a tragic end, and that there was no need to hurry.

In making her slow descent Mrs Cannisman was able to reflect upon her husband's recent medical history; not the history that is annotated on paper and kept in official files you understand, nor that which is able to be brought up on a computer screen in a matter of seconds; but the softly spoken history that was revealed by his waking up with chest pains in the middle of the night, and by his becoming short of breath when performing tasks which wouldn't have taxed him in the slightest when first the couple were married. It goes without saying that as a loving and

84

caring wife, just as Brian was a loving and caring husband, she did her best to persuade the complainant that he should visit the doctor. A stoic of the old school, Brian was having none of it, and attributed his pains to harmless indigestion that would pass of its own accord. Mrs Cannisman thought her husband's reluctance to visit the surgery in Koidu was based on his belief that the doctor who held vigil there was little better than a witchdoctor or a quack. He wasn't, but even mining engineers are subject to irrational thoughts on occasion. Brian had sought to allay his wife's fears by stating that he would definitely make an appointment to see a real doctor the next time he was in Freetown, or even better in the prospective patient's opinion, with his GP the next time he was in the UK. It was a promise he failed to keep.

In addition to encouraging her husband to put his faith in the medical profession, another stratagem employed by Shirley's mother in her campaign to improve her husband's health had been to hide his cigarettes. Brian was a twenty a day man on average, but on those days when the game his wife played produced a good result he smoked a lot less. Her trick was to place the packet where it wouldn't be impossible to find it, but merely more difficult than it would have been if she had left it in plain sight. The best locations in this little subterfuge were where Brian could have deposited the packet of injurious coffin-nails himself, and then forgotten about it, or where it could have ended up by accident. In this regard a few examples may be under a cushion, or behind a coffee jar, the dark recess under the bookcase wherein it could have been inadvertently kicked. Eventually Brian had begun to suspect his wife of dodgy dealings on his behalf, but in posing the question as to why she had hidden the sought after item in the ways that she did, Mrs Cannisman denied all knowledge of having done so, stating words to the effect that it was a pity that her husband was so forgetful so young. For the reason that it can sometimes be difficult to keep a straight face when there's a pantomime in play, initially Mrs Cannisman believed that her husband was happy to be complicit in her game of hide and seek, for there was rarely a second pack readily available, one to which he could have had immediate recourse.

The stakes might have been high, but even for Mrs Cannisman the game she had devised for two to play began to lose its lustre. Eventually

Mr Cannisman, having grown weary of always being the seeker without ever finding cause to reciprocate, took it upon himself to hide the cigarettes before his wife had a chance to get her hands on them. This might have proved a good idea on his part if only he hadn't demonstrated genuine forgetfulness by frequently failing to find them again, at least not until an hour of frantic searching had elapsed, and on rare occasions not at all on the day in question. This most mysterious of packets would turn up, or be stumbled upon as if by chance a week or a month later. God knows how many packs containing between one and twenty cigarettes were secreted around the house. Whenever Brian's search proved fruitless and his patience had all but expired, he would risk unlocking and unbolting the doors and leave, only to return twenty minutes later with a pack in which only eighteen cigarettes remained.

In the long run it could be argued that the Cannismans' game was counter-productive. On the occasions when he was unable to find the cigarettes that he could only point an accusing finger at himself for having hidden, the signs of stress, as evidenced by greater irritability and fractiousness, were obvious. Equally disconcerting for his wife was the fact that when Brian did eventually find the object he could have died for (and possibly did), he would smoke two or three of the fags in quick succession. All in all Mrs Cannisman realised that the stratagem she had devised and employed to improve her husband's health and longevity was likely to kill him. The sad irony was that although she was easily able to end her own participation in the game of hide and seek, her husband seemed to have become addicted to it.

All the while that Shirley was narrating this tale of sad events Sebastian sat listening as if he were all ears, as the saying goes, his attentiveness only interrupted by Shirley indicating that she would love the same again: she was referring to her drink. Fully aware that he was responsible for taking his guest back to her Luxborough home Sebastian refrained from having another beer and followed suit.

Whether the cause of Brian's sudden demise could be attributed to one cause or another is open to question. There had been other pressures in his life, not the least of which, as we know, was living where they did. Consequently a major concern for Brian was that he would be kidnapped and held for a ransom to be paid in diamonds. On the home front, but also motivated by security concerns, was the effort involved in completing his latest project. The quest for perfection when the job wasn't going as well as he had planned had told upon his health. The project in question had been the design and construction of a fire-escape leading from the back bedroom window down into the yard. The job of erecting the steel flight of steps he had undertaken and completed in his spare time; now, for him, there was no time at all.

In the tale as it was being told however, Mrs Cannisman is descending the stairs inside the house. Upon reaching the bottom step her intuition was all but confirmed when, peering through the half open door that linked the hall to the kitchen, she espied her husband's lifeless head. She had paused on the step in total silence, staring down at the only part of the body which was visible from where she stood. She had no idea how long it was that she had stood there motionless, gathering her thoughts, steadying her emotions, but she reckoned later that it must have been for over a minute.

Brian's face was turned towards her, and for a moment Mrs Cannisman was surprised that his eyes didn't move in recognition of her presence, but remained as if focused upon the lower level of the boot and shoe rack which she couldn't yet see but which she knew to be in his line of sight, if only. Other aspects of her husband's demeanour which she noted were his agonised expression and his grey, ghostly pallor. A petrified grimace told of his pain. From the skin tone Mrs Cannisman had gained the impression that the body, at least this cerebral part of it, had been drained of blood. She had seen several dead bodies in her time, but only from a distance, and certainly this was the first white person she had seen devoid of life, and to think that only an hour earlier this vital being had been seeking her amorous attention. In the telling of this part of her story Shirley didn't reveal how her mother had reacted to Brian's sexual advances. Perhaps she didn't know.

Still motionless at the point where she had first cast eyes upon Brian's lifeless head, the recent widow considered whether it would be practicable to ring Shirley in Freetown. This she could do by retracing her steps back up the stairs to the master bedroom in order to retrieve her mobile phone. She knew precisely where she had left it amid the feminine clutter strewn across one of two bedside tables, a profusion which revealed which side of the bed was hers. The upper storey was the best place to obtain a signal. A thought which deterred her from making the call was that Shirley would already be at work, no doubt busily involved in Radio Freetown's early morning news programme. It would be unprofessional, Mrs Cannisman surmised, to blight her daughter's career over a mere family matter, and because no one since Jesus Christ has been blessed with the power to resurrect the dead, there would be little Shirley could do to help that couldn't wait until her shift had ended. Resolved, therefore, to confront her husband's death full on and alone Mrs Cannisman had entered the kitchen.

Taking the last sip of juice that she was to have in the Captain Cook Inn, Shirley explained to Sebastian that she really wouldn't have minded if her mother had made the call that she had had a mind to, and neither would have her employers. She proceeded to describe the ghastly scene which had greeted her mother.

The position of Brian's body was in all respects unremarkable. The legs were almost straight, and the naked ankles were clearly visible at the end of his pyjamas. The toes of his blue carpet slippers were pointing upwards at angles which were more or less at equal variance from the perpendicular. Mrs Cannisman had stood for a while looking directly down at the body, her bare feet barely a foot from the deceased's head: it appeared upside down to her scrutiny. Noting that Brian hadn't shaved prior to rushing off to meet his maker, his widow wondered whether the omission would have bothered him — bothered Brian that is. Listening to the sounds of traffic emanating from the street, since getting over her initial shock Mrs Cannisman was surprised at how composed she felt. In the days, weeks, and months ahead this realisation would give her food for thought. In the harsh reality of the present however, she had wondered whom she should contact first. Should she first try to contact Brian's doctor, or would it be better to make a call to the police her first priority? In either instance she doubted that she would get through at the first attempt. Despite being quite sure that she ought not to touch the body, in defiance of her internal inhibitors, she had slowly lowered herself to her knees in order to reach out to her husband. Her next solemn act was to take hold and raise his head off the floor so as to be able to cradle it in her arms. She was surprised at how heavy it felt, a fact which she jocularly attributed to the weighty mass of grey matter. Gently, lovingly, she rocked back and forth. Subsequently the sensation of a tear trickling down each of her cheeks she found comforting. Half an hour later, her tears wiped out of existence, she was to leave the house to go in person to fetch the doctor.

Chapter Seven
An Invitation

Once Neffie had answered all the questions put to her by the two detectives, and they, rather reluctantly it seemed to their interviewee, had departed, she took all of ten minutes to pack her bag. After a quick check of the room to ensure that she wasn't about to leave behind any of her possessions, encumbered by her holdall she made her way down to the dining-room for breakfast. She may not have wanted to stay in the Sussex Hotel longer than was convenient, but she wasn't going to forgo a meal included in the price of her overnight stay.

Streaming in through the hotel windows to make for stark contrasts between light and shade, the morning sun's effulgence could be expected to raise the most depressed of spirits. Its cheery aspect certainly helped to dissipate further the lugubrious thoughts which Neffie had succumbed to during the night, although not to the extent of changing her mind about leaving. If there was one thing she was clear about it was that she didn't want to lie awake tonight, and the night after, and the nights after that, awaiting a repeat performance of the creepy visitation she had recently experienced. The turning of the door knob had been too unsettling for her to want to stay where there was a high risk of a similar encounter happening again.

"Good morning, Miss Goodwin, did you sleep well?" greeted and enquired Joshua from behind the reception desk as Neffie stepped off the last creaky step onto the chequered floor. She wondered why so many hotel foyer floors could double up as boards for draughts or chess.

Perhaps it was because she was still primed to have negative thoughts that she couldn't help but think that Joshua's broad smile hinted of mischief, and she wondered whether he knew more than he was letting on about recent happenings. For the reason that she intended to leave within the hour she decided not to broach the subject, but instead matched the man from the Banana Island's cheerfulness with a cheery smile of her own, before adding a little white lie for good measure. "It was probably because I was so exhausted from travelling that I went straight to sleep and didn't wake up until I had a surprise visit from two charming members of the local constabulary. I was told it was a routine procedure…"

There was a slight pause as Neffie tried to remember Joshua's name, but despite probing the nooks and crannies of her memory she couldn't bring it to mind. This was disconcerting for being unusual, for up until now she had believed that she was good at remembering names, having had lots of practice at school. Consequently she felt a little guilty, not only for answering Joshua's question before responding to his greeting, but for making that greeting more impersonal than she would have wished.

"Good morning by the way," she said apologetically. "Is breakfast through here?" she enquired despite, through a pair of glass doors, being able to see people enjoying the first meal of the day at tables which were striking to behold for having red tablecloths.

"Yes, Miss," Joshua replied, still smiling in a manner reminiscent of her little charges at school. "You are permitted to sit at any of the tables which are free."

Neffie found the tone and language of the pronouncement delightful. It was so precise, so clear, and so formal. The politeness with which Joshua granted permission didn't escape her either. Typical of the people she had met on her travels across Africa, it was remarkably different from the advice she would expect to hear in a similar situation back home. Whether uttered pleasantly, or churlishly by a sour-faced grump, in the part of Britain she came from she would more than likely be told to 'sit anywhere you like'.

Thus charmed by Joshua's words, Neffie entered the breakfast room serenely, whereupon she discovered that only two of the eight tables were occupied. A quick glance to her right, in the direction of the window, revealed a solitary white woman whose attention, for the seconds that she remained under Neffie's initial scrutiny, was devoted to the content of a book. It wasn't possible, at the distance she was from the person contravening good etiquette by reading at the table, for Neffie to make out the book's title, but she was of the opinion that the page being turned constituted genuine literature. In that same brief first look Neffie observed that the woman was casually dressed in a white, loose-fitting shirt and light blue jeans. She appeared to be about the same age as Neffie, and despite wearing her hair rather boyishly didn't look less feminine for it. Within easy reach of the reader's left hand sat a lonely cup and saucer. These objects, and the absence of any other, indicated to Neffie that the woman, whom she imagined to be Scandinavian, had already breakfasted.

Upon looking in the opposite direction the sight which greeted Neffie's gaze was less cerebral, more animated. In the far corner, seated around the table and making it look too small for their needs, were three men and a woman. Regardless of the fact that their features weren't dissimilar to members of the local Mende or Temne tribes, they gave Neffie the distinct impression that they were foreigners visiting Sierra Leone. In the accumulation of those small perceptions that go to make the whole picture, this was apparent in their dress sense and in their assertiveness. Without doubt, however, the main reason for Neffie jumping to the conclusion she did was the distinctive and unmistakeable accents she heard. She was certain of their origin because she had spent a year in the States on an education exchange scheme teaching mainly black kids in leafy Tuscaloosa, Alabama. Neffie's discernment in this regard wasn't precise enough for her to say for certain that the speaker came from the same town where she had taught: he could, as far as she could tell for being English, just as easily come from Mississippi or Georgia.

Miss Goodwin had nothing against American accents in general, and indeed was quite taken with those she had heard in the south. The strident tones she was hearing presently, however, repulsed her. The main culprit was a gargantuan individual sitting with his back to her. The offence against her sensibility stemmed from his berating the waitress for having taken so long to come and take his and his companions' orders. He accused her of being dilatory, a word which the poor girl was unlikely to know the meaning of, and said that she wouldn't last five minutes doing the same job back home. Perhaps the tirade wouldn't have offended Neffie so much if the waitress hadn't resembled one of her former Tuscaloosa students.

Instantly upon becoming aware of the newcomer's presence, the girl — she couldn't have been older than thirteen — glanced apologetically at Neffie. It was obvious that the erstwhile schoolgirl wasn't apologising for anything which she as a waitress had done, but for the boorishness and intolerance demonstrated by the man still ranting on at her. Like any good teacher observing a student having to face a difficult situation, one which, for the sake of the experience gained, it would be better to face up to alone, Neffie smiled reassuringly at the girl but didn't intervene. Instead she sat down at the table which was closest to the door, positioning herself in such a way that she was able to observe every person in the room simply by glancing either to left or right. Looking in the direction of the lone woman seated by the window, Neffie managed to catch her eye. The women smiled at each other warmly, possibly in recognition of the fact that they perceived each other to be fellow travellers on an uncertain journey. Whether it was because they were too shy to speak in a volume loud enough to be heard across the room, or simply because neither party could think of an opening gambit, as yet no words were exchanged between them. Consequently the blonde woman returned to her book.

Neffie extracted a small red notebook and a pen from an easily accessible pocket of her bag, her intention being to write up her journal, a diary of events which would eventually form the basis of a major part of this story. It was the first time, in a literary sense, that she had put pen to paper since her arrival in Sierra Leone. Thinking about meeting Samuel at the airport, the lorry breaking down on the ferry, the journey across the river, the unwelcome intruder in her room that was the cockroach, and the scary visitation which came to nought, and all this happening in her first eighteen hours in the country, prompted Neffie to think that she ought to have brought a bigger journal.

Meanwhile the obstreperous man, an individual who gave the impression that in his time he had breakfasted on more pancakes dripping with maple syrup than had been good for him, ordered bacon and eggs. He wanted his eggs griddled sunny side up and his bacon crispy. Despite his having made the order more in hope than expectation, he was, upon being told that there was no bacon to be had, given the excuse he needed to express further dissatisfaction. In addition to yet more verbal expressions of disbelief he raised his eyes to the ceiling as if there, among its innocuous cracks and alarming fissures, his gaze would be greeted sympathetically by the God he feared and worshipped. Meekly but calmly the waitress informed that guests could choose between omelette and yebe.

The woman sitting to the obstreperous man's left, she could have been his wife, or she could have been his secretary, picked up the Bible which he had recently relinquished: she didn't want him to start thumping it over breakfast. She sought to bring harmony to a discordant situation by enquiring about the composition of yebe, a dish she hadn't tasted.

At this point Neffie, ever eager to learn about local ways and local delicacies, stopped writing about how much she struggled with the high humidity and listened intently. Upon learning of what exactly yebe consisted she decided that when asked she would opt for an omelette. A potato and cassava stew was more than she could face at that time of day.

Evidently neither dish appealed to the stroppy American, for with a great deal of exertion he rose to his feet, held out his hand for the return of his Bible, and, after pushing back his chair with greater force than was necessary or warranted, with the Good Book in hand proceeded towards the exit. He was followed by his flock.

The young waitress also followed, but only for the few strides that after a deviation brought her to the table where Miss Goodwin was seated. Standing with pencil and pad at the ready, as if taking the order for one, and for one of two dishes, were too complicated to be consigned to memory, the girl shrugged her shoulders as if to say, "It takes all kinds."

The one thing an impartial witness could have no doubt about was that in this instance the mundane business of taking an order for food was in marked contrast to the hotel employee's recent experience. The present verbal exchange couldn't have been more cordial.

No sooner had the waitress departed, the pad she carried still blank, because the ink in her pen, if there was any, had refused to flow, than the woman who had been reading at the table by the window closed and put down her book. She then ventured across the room to stand where the waitress had stood.

Neffie looked up at her expectantly. The bibliophile's features were set in a frown, as if it mattered to her that Neffie's day might have been spoiled unnecessarily. That look of concern was matched by the tone of her voice as she spoke. "I hope you don't mind my disturbing you, but I feel as if I must apologise for the behaviour of my fellow countrymen. We're not all like him you know."

The accent told Neffie that the speaker's country of origin was a state along the eastern seaboard, one much farther north than indicated by the English she had heard spoken earlier.

"That's all right," responded Neffie. "He's probably been bitten by something nasty during the night and he's out of sorts because of it," she added magnanimously. "Besides, I'm not the person he was rude to, so you don't need to apologise to me on his behalf. If anyone deserves an apology it's this young lady," Neffie added just as the waitress arrived bearing a tray laden with breakfast — a yellow mound on an oval plate, a cafetiere, a jug of milk. The smile she gave each of the white women in turn signalled that she was tougher than she looked. "Could you fetch another cup?" Neffie's request caused the waitress to stop in her tracks before turning to acknowledge that she had heard, and having heard would comply.

It seemed, as the American woman changed the subject, that nothing more need be said of the matter which had served as an excuse for her to approach and introduce herself.

"From the way you speak you can't be from anywhere other than the British Isles."

She held out her hand for Neffie to shake, a gesture to which the Briton responded gladly. Like psychic magnets drawn irresistibly towards each other, both ladies were keen to establish friendly relations, and it was for this reason that Neffie, demonstrating vatic anticipation, had requested the bringing of a second cup. Neffie half rose out of her chair to grasp the proffered hand. The fingers and thumb that grasped hers were long and slender: the palm cool.

"Do you mind if I join you?" enquired the bibliophile, already sensing, so obvious was the empathy between them, that the answer would be 'yes'.

"Please do," responded Neffie, gesticulating with open palm for her new-found friend to take a seat.

Aware that she hadn't completed the first paragraph of her journal, Miss Goodwin returned her pen and all but blank writing book to her bag. The bibliophile sat down directly opposite and encouraged Neffie to eat. "It tastes better than it looks," she advised, referring to the yellow mound that was a mushroom omelette. Neffie took her first mouthful and by means of a polite mumble agreed.

"It's very good," she confirmed after swallowing. "Would you like some coffee? Now where is that girl with the cup I asked for?" she added, looking past the American woman at the entrance through which she expected the waitress to appear.

"Thanks, but no thanks," the American replied. "I've had my caffeine fix for this morning."

She continued the conversation by introducing herself. Her name was, and possibly still is, though only she and the people she's in touch with presently would know for certain, Diane Fussey. Too far back in time to remember exactly when, Di, as she liked to be called, had made a resolution not to follow up stating her name with the predictable comment that although she was Fussey by name she wasn't fussy by nature. She had made this pact with her seemingly wayward vocal chords because she felt that the conditioned reflex of Fussey not being fussy was undermining her self-image: she had begun to doubt that she was an intelligent, resourceful human-being. From the day of her pact till now the automaton had kept silent. Not so today though, for it blurted the cliché without inhibition, so that it was as if the self-discipline she had demonstrated thus far had come to nought. The consequences may not be as dangerous, but in this regard she was like someone who has given up smoking cigarettes for a lengthy period, but who then succumbs to temptation in an unguarded moment, a moment of weakness. Fortunately for Miss Fussey, however, she wasn't the sort of person given to chastising herself for long, and in the instant following her faux-pas she made a second resolution; but only in her head.

"When I first set eyes on you I formed the impression that you were from one of the Nordic countries," said Neffie.

"My great grandparents were Dutch farmers who came originally from Friesland, so I suppose that goes a long way towards explaining my appearance. It was before their time even, but do you know that New York used to be called New Amsterdam until 1664?"

"I didn't know the year when the change of name took place," Neffie replied, before posing the question the answer to which was destined to have a considerable bearing on the English woman's stay in the country. "So what are you doing in Sierra Leone?"

"I volunteered to spend two years working with Peace Corps," said Di. "It's a volunteer organisation. It was inaugurated by President Kennedy. It exists to enable young Americans to develop certain aspects of their character by providing practical assistance wherever it's needed and welcomed. That usually means volunteers being sent to relatively undeveloped countries... countries like Sierra Leone. The individual benefits by learning about cultures different from her own. I'm just over halfway through my sentence."

Neffie wasn't sure whether the association with prison was meant to be taken seriously. Miss Fussey certainly didn't give the impression that she was enduring a two-year stint of hard labour.

She went on to explain that her allotted task in the country was to organise and assist with the planting of trees in and around Kalangba, a village a few miles to the south of Gbinti, which in turn is approximately forty miles to the north east of Freetown.

The reason for Miss Fussey being in Freetown was that she had flown in from a trip home on leave which had commenced a fortnight earlier. She had made the trip in order to visit her mother in Lakewood, New Jersey. Under normal circumstances this would have been a vacation which she would have looked forward to with pleasure, and if everything had gone according to plan, and by that she meant her plan, enjoyed immensely. The circumstance and motivation for her most recent 'escape', however, were hardly what she would have wished, for the sole reason for the journey was to attend to her ailing mother: Mrs Fussey had succumbed to a stroke. Fortunately for all concerned, upon arriving home Di discovered that her mother's illness wasn't as severe as the younger lady had been led to believe, the patient having all but made a full recovery. She intimated to Neffie that she wasn't sure which was worse, spending a fortnight attending to her mother's whims following her amazing return to good health, or returning to the tree-planting project. Most off-putting about the maternal influence was the fact that Mrs Fussey had been keen for her daughter to take them to the beach to indulge in a little talent-spotting, and if an amorous relationship were to follow as a consequence, so much the better. For a woman who had been divorced ten years back it was hardly surprising that she would want to find love and companionship with a member of the opposite sex, but accompanying her on her predatory manoeuvres hadn't appealed to Di in the slightest.

The tale Di imparted to Neffie about Mrs Fussey's antics was told with wry humour, causing Neffie to chuckle out loud between sips of coffee. The English woman had reached the conclusion that if Di had been filled with enthusiasm at the time of her first visit to Sierra Leone, time had taken its toll, so that it was considerably dulled by now.

For the time of her furlough Di had been embarrassed by her mother on only two occasions, but they were enough to make her think that her life apart from the voluntary work she was determined to see through to the end of her tour of duty, perhaps wasn't so bad after all. She explained to Neffie that what she disliked most about working in Sierra Leone, particularly at this time of year, was the sensation of being constantly coated in the salty secretions exuding through her pores; that and, with the onset of the rainy season, daily downpours.

At least Di's trip home had given her time to think, to analyse why it was that she had become so disillusioned with the project which was the reason for her being in Sierra Leone. In the early days, shortly after she had arrived in the country, her head filled with missionary zeal for a secular task, she had indeed tried to infect the residents of Kalangba with her enthusiasm. Her youthful zeal had failed to have the desired effect, and having met with indifference almost at every turn, she had, several months back, ceased to work with that energy and enthusiasm which she had demonstrated on arrival and in the early days. It was as if the ambiance of lassitude that prevailed in her corner of Africa had sapped her strength and drained her spirit: certainly where arboriculture was concerned.

It was Di's determination to be a good volunteer that got her out of bed each day. Together with a handful of locals, also volunteers, whose willingness to help was the exception to the otherwise general apathy her project inspired, she had continued to grow and transplant the saplings which one day, if they managed to survive the ravages of animal and insect jaws, would grow into magnificent trees producing cashew apples and nuts, or palm trees producing oil. At that time the natural product that is palm oil was considered a boon to an impoverished country and not the problem to the environment that it's perceived to be today. She also planted saplings that would grow into the flat-topped acacias which, as Neffie pointed out, many an avenue in Britain is named after. Di's modus operandi at work was languid for being quite insouciant. Such was the life she was going back to resume, and as the summation of an analysis undertaken at a distance of several thousand miles, she didn't mind that she was, and she wouldn't have minded if she weren't.

More than any other aspect of their conversation, the reason for Di staying overnight in the Sussex Hotel proved to be of the greatest value to Neffie; not that the teacher was seeking to capitalise on her acquaintance with the American volunteer from the outset, but a woman who is travelling independently would be foolish not to take advantage of any favourable circumstance which may present itself. It was, therefore, fortuitous that upon having imbibed the last of the coffee, and hard upon having been introduced to the nutritional benefits of cashew apples, fruit amazing for the fact that each specimen contains five times as much vitamin c as an orange, Miss Goodwin learned that the Peace Corps has its own accommodation block in Freetown. She also learned that the previous night, because of a changeover of personnel, all the beds had been taken. Consequently there had been no room at that particular 'inn' for Miss Fussey. For the coming night, however, and for the foreseeable future, Diane envisaged that availability at the Peace Corps hotel wouldn't be a problem, primarily because the cynics on completion of their sentence would have left the country, and their naively enthusiastic replacements would have been escorted into the interior by their mentors. Di advised Neffie that the block would be almost empty.

It was a prognostication which prompted Neffie to say, "What a pity I'm not American. It sounds as if your Peace Corps accommodation would be my kind of place."

Even to her own ears her accent sounded less distinctly English, more transatlantic. The significance of Neffie's comment wasn't lost on the American, her thinking being that there wouldn't be a problem, given the number of rooms likely to be available, for an English woman to take up residence, particularly someone prepared to do voluntary work independently.

Exhibiting the kind of enthusiasm she hadn't experienced in months, Di said, "Say! I've got a great idea. I'm planning to be in Freetown for a few more days, so why not come and stay at the Peace House. I know the name makes it sound as if it's the kind of place where a bunch of hippies would hang out, but that's what we call it. You might even take a liking to one of the guys. I think Sam's really cute, and Dave's not bad looking either. Dave writes poetry and plays the guitar... though I should warn you that he already has a girlfriend... in the Bahamas of all places."

"I'm sure they are... cute that is... but I already have a partner back home in the UK thanks very much," Neffie informed, making it absolutely clear from the outset that she hadn't come to Sierra Leone in search of a romantic entanglement or sex.

Realising that she had presumed too much, in her mind Di discarded the attractiveness or otherwise of her male colleagues as a line of inducement, but it didn't sound that way when she said, "Well, for as long as you're in Freetown I think it would be a great place for you to stay, and there's bound to be a few of the guys around."

Thinking that her comment about being in a serious relationship had fallen on deaf ears, Neffie looked puzzled. Instead of repeating herself however, she made a terse request for greater clarity by saying, "Your point being?"

"Oh, I see," rejoined Di. "I didn't mean that the guys being around would be a temptation to stray. What I meant was that at least you'll know you'll be safe."

"I'm not so sure about that," said Neffie impishly, but mindful of the previous night's unsettling experience, it was a thankful Miss Goodwin who accepted the generous offer without more ado. "It's very kind of you to take me under your wing in this way. I feel fortunate to have met you."

"Don't mention it," dismissed Di, reinforcing her polite command with an appropriate hand gesture. "How long do you intend to stay in Freetown?"

"Another two nights at the most," replied Neffie confidently.

"Where do you intend to go after that?"

"I've got a letter of introduction to the priest who runs the Catholic Mission in Koidu. The problem is that I can't quite make out whether he's called Father Dalby or Father Daley from his…"

"You mean to say that you intend to travel to Koidu alone?" Di interjected, an expression of disbelief writ large upon her face.

"…signature," said Neffie, a little irritated at having been cut off before she had said all that she had wanted to say. "So you think I would be foolish to travel to Koidu alone?" she asked. It was an unnecessary question.

"About as foolish as it gets," said Di categorically. "I know I wouldn't risk it. I would only go there embedded in a platoon of marines."

Neffie couldn't help but smile at the thought, and that's what she told Miss Fussey she would do, give the matter some thought. At this point the ladies' conversation was interrupted by the arrival of Samuel Massequoi in the hotel foyer. Neffie recognised his voice as he enquired of the man from the Banana Islands as to the whereabouts of Miss Nefertiti Goodwin.

"I'm in here, Samuel," Neffie called as she hastily rose to her feet, advanced towards and peered round the dining-room door, her timely intervention making it unnecessary for the hotel employee to give directions. "I'm with an American friend… come and join us," she added.

Neffie was heartened to see the acquaintance of the night before appear as a friend this morning, and delighted to see his broad smile acknowledge her bidding. Samuel had brought along his brother a fellow teacher called James. Regardless of Di's earlier comment about having had her caffeine fix for the day, Neffie instructed the man from the Banana Islands to organise more coffee, and three extra cups seeing as the waitress had yet to be forthcoming with Neffie's original request, that vessel's non-appearance being attributed to prescience rather than forgetfulness. For the present, in the round of introductions, the dangers of travelling to Koidu were forgotten.

Chapter Eight
Getting Acclimatised

A singular outcome of the chance meeting at breakfast was that Neffie and Di checked out of the Sussex Hotel together. Half an hour later, after saying goodbye to James and Samuel for the present, but not before they had arranged to meet them again for a sight-seeing tour that afternoon, in Di's company Neffie effectively checked in at the Peace Corps 'palace'.

The building, which by no stretch of the imagination could be considered palatial, was a single block, two-storey structure set in its own compound on the outskirts of Freetown. The white walls formed three sides of an oblong. The most impressive features to greet the eye upon arrival were the four-wheel drive vehicles parked out front and the sign at the gate advertising the building's purpose. Somewhat disconcertingly for Neffie a sentence at about her head height read, 'For the sole use of American Peace Corps Personnel'. Towering over the corrugated roof, at a distance not far removed, was a lush-covered peak. Neffie estimated its height to be three hundred feet. Casting the shadow of its crown upon the roof, a single palm tree stood directly behind the building, so that over half the tree's trunk was presently hidden from view.

The procedure for checking in couldn't have been less formal, and despite their different nationalities, was the same for both women. No signatures were required at reception, nor was there a need for either party to show a passport or any other official document, and that was because there was no reception desk or receptionist to speak of. It turned out that the only requirement for Neffie to be able to stay for as long as she liked, and free of charge to boot, was for Di to say, "Hi, guys, I'm back," a greeting which she quickly followed up with, "and this is my friend Neffie from England. I've invited her to come and stay with us for a while, any objections?"

True to Miss Fussey's prediction there were few residents. A trio representing seventy-five per cent of resident Peace Corps personnel were to be found in the common-room which also served as the kitchen when the women arrived. They comprised the two handsome devils Di had mentioned at breakfast. A third young man belied the maturity of his twenty plus years by giving the impression, more by his appearance than by his behaviour, that he should still be at school. The bronze demigod who was Sam was dressed only in shorts and sandals. In response to Di's searching question he merely shrugged his shoulders and said, "It sounds fine by me." His hands immersed in soap suds, he didn't break off from washing a couple of t-shirts in the sink. The guy Neffie had surmised was Dave before she knew for certain was reading a guitar magazine whilst eating cereals. Twice he raised the bowl from its resting-place on the Formica-topped table in order to be better able to get at the flakes within. The reason for hurrying his meal was so that he could greet Di with greater enthusiasm than had been demonstrated hitherto. He was still chewing as he approached Di to embrace her, and so as not to be exclusive, he also gave Neffie a hug. "That's great… that's absolutely great," he said to the newcomer. Once the ebullient guitarist's effervescence had evaporated a little, the 'schoolboy' who happened to resemble the Milky Bar Kid, merely raised his right hand as if he was about to give testimony in court and said, "Hi!" Then he returned his attention to the letter he had been writing home to his parents.

After a quick inspection of the room wherein, and the bed whereupon, she would be sleeping, Neffie felt that she had made the right choice in taking up Di's offer. The room was furnished simply, the furnishings consisting of two single beds, a couple of two-drawer cabinets and bedside lamps, a lone chair and a dresser. Remarkably for hostel accommodation thought Neffie, the room even had en suite facilities. In making comparisons between her present room and the room she had vacated at the Sussex Hotel the obvious difference was that here she would be sharing. Di was going to be her room-mate. Neffie hadn't previously shared a room with anyone other than her elder sister and the close friend she had made at boarding school. The anticipated twinning with a relative stranger would make for a pleasant change for being sociable. Neffie looked under the bed and found the floor there to be just as spotless as the floor beneath her feet. A reassuring odour of lemon-scented disinfectant entered her nostrils. There wasn't a cockroach in sight and the ceiling fan worked.

Di had remained in the common-room discussing Peace Corps matters with her male colleagues whilst Neffie was carrying out her inspection. It should be noted that the good feeling she had about the place had nothing to do with the paragons of youthful American masculinity she had met and with whom she would now be able to associate — nothing whatsoever.

In the forty-eight hours following her relocation Miss Goodwin began to get a feel for her new environment, first for the friendly space that was the Peace House, and then for the circumjacent districts that made up part of Freetown. Her greater sense of personal security enabled her to feel relaxed, so that she felt no less safe than if she were walking through the streets of Luxborough or Ferrousby.

On the afternoon of Neffie's first full day in Freetown, as promised Samuel and James turned up to show her the sights. If two's company and three's a crowd, Miss Fussey must have thought that four was a multitude, so perhaps for that reason, and because she would have been bored to tears traipsing around sights she was familiar with, she declined the invitation.

Top of the list on the tourist itinerary was the cotton tree, a magnificent specimen of Ceiba Pentandra that has come to be regarded as a powerful symbol of the city. The legend Samuel narrated to Neffie, fluently apart from one brief interruption from his brother, was that a group of former slaves, people that had gained their freedom after fighting for the British in the American War of Independence, landed in Sierra Leone as settlers, and upon landing walked up to a giant tree standing prominently above the bay. In the welcome shade provided by the tree's leafy canopies they held a service of thanksgiving for having arrived safely in the 'promised land'. The problem was that at that time it was a land where they were likely to succumb to a number of diseases, lassa fever and bilharzia to name but two.

If the two male teachers had imagined that their female counterpart would be moved by the story to the extent that she could envisage that early congregation kneeling like Covenanters in solemn prayer, or raising their voices to sing hymns of praise, they were mistaken. Being a person whose natural inclination was to respect the religious beliefs of others whilst keeping them at a safe distance from self, in the absence of imaginary choirs she saw but a tree. It was an impressive tree undoubtedly, but in her eyes nothing more than that.

By believing as she did that all living creatures are numinous, the god Miss Goodwin worshipped was life, though not in all its multifarious forms. Questions such as how the universe came into being and how life on earth erupted and developed into the multifarious forms that exist today were, for her, too big to consider to any significant degree. Consequently, when asked to state her religion to officialdom, either orally or in writing, Miss Goodwin was perfectly willing to inform that she belonged to the Church of England, but it was an affiliation which counted for little in the course of her day to day life. After thanking Samuel and James for showing her the cotton tree, she suggested where they should go next.

Neffie loved what to western eyes can best be described as exotic markets. She loved the cacophonous hubbub familiar for being English, or less familiar for being in another language. In the vicinity of the stalls where fast food was being prepared, the like of which she might not have tasted, she loved the smells that permeated the air, enticing her to come and eat by tempting the olfactory sense. She loved the vibrant colours more often than not seen in the agglomerations of unusual fruit and vegetables arrayed before the prospective buyer, and in the attire of stall-holders and shoppers alike.

Was there such a market nearby? Indeed there was, and acquiescing to the lady's wish, Samuel led the way along Wallace Johnson Street in the direction of King Jimmy's market. It was, he informed Neffie, the best place in Freetown for buying fresh produce, whether it had been grown on the land or caught in the sea.

For covering no great distance their journey on foot should have taken no more than ten minutes, but took longer than anticipated for being interrupted by what for this time of year was a typical downpour. The trio sought shelter. Their place of refuge was a bar serving coffee, soft drinks and bottles of the locally brewed ale. Thinking that they would keep her company in drinking a little alcoholic refreshment,

Neffie offered to buy her guides a beer each. They declined, opting for a non- alcoholic fizzy concoction instead. For a short while at least the rain hammered upon the tin-sheet roof surely with the same intensity as the rain that fell to float Noah's Ark. Lasting for as long as the drinks lasted, the noise of the deluge made conversation difficult. Once the beating of the myriad liquid 'hammers' abated, however, James led the way back onto the street. Samuel brought up the rear. In the rays of the sun recently emerged from behind clouds no longer threatening for moving on, the scene which greeted the trio was steamy. It was as if Wallace Johnson Street had taken on the aspect of an open-air Turkish bath.

The street began to fill with other pedestrians that had sought to stay dry during the downpour. People with money to spend had found it convenient to part with a few Leones, whilst those that were impecunious had made use of whatever canopies had been available. A small number of young men and youths, and about an equal number of children, looked like drowned rats, but smiling irrepressibly they didn't seem to mind. The profusion of puddles, some large, some small, some relatively deep, some relatively shallow, created a new hazard, specifically the discomfort of being drenched by spray as taxi-drivers, they were the worst culprits, sped to Lumley Beach or Pirate Bay to pick up their next fare. To Neffie it was wonderful. This was the shambolic, far from sterile, world she had craved to be part of: a scene she now relished.

When the three teachers eventually arrived at King Jimmy's Market Neffie took it upon herself to lead the way, ambling between the stalls, surveying the wares and produce and smiling serenely at each stall-holder in turn. For about half an hour she mooched along leading her entourage. She had yet to buy anything, but such leisurely insouciance in passing many a hopeful vendor by was entirely in keeping with her character. It was a trait which Sebastian had grown accustomed to long ago, though he never failed to be embarrassed by his partner's reluctance to make a spontaneous purchase but rather continue with her window-shopping. This embarrassment only ever manifested itself when there weren't any windows for Sebastian to hide behind.

Likewise Samuel and James were surprised by Neffie's reluctance to spend. What is the point of going to a market if one isn't going to buy anything they wondered? They knew for certain that they weren't going to put their hands in their pockets, but this was because, as teachers on the payroll of a government which didn't always have the means to pay them, they were stony broke. It was only when they reached the end of their perambulation that Neffie brought a smile engendered by the anticipation of making a profit to one fruit vendor's face. She bought a bag of grapefruits. She wanted the luscious, sharp-tasting 'grepfruts' to slake her thirst, and in the tropics it's never a bad idea to buy food contained in its own natural packaging.

The tour of King Jimmy's Market over, after thanking her guides Neffie informed that she could make her own way back to the Peace House, but before parting company she accepted their offer to take her to the beach on the morrow. "It's too far to walk," said James, referring to the following day's excursion, "so I'll bring my car."

From the look on his face there was no mistaking the pride he felt in being able to make such an announcement.

"What day is it tomorrow?" enquired Neffie, and before either of her companions was able to reply she proved the question rhetorical by supplying the answer. "It's Wednesday," she announced thoughtfully, "which means that after tomorrow's trip my sightseeing days in Freetown are over. I want to take the bus to Koidu."

"You'll need to buy your ticket in advance," advised Samuel, making no attempt to dissuade Neffie from taking such a rash course of action as travelling to Koidu alone. "I'll come to the Peace House and escort you to the bus-station," he said. "You may think that buying a bus ticket would be a simple matter, but it's not always the case... believe me."

Prepared to believe, Neffie saw no reason not to accept Samuel's offer, and having made the necessary arrangements regarding where and when — all being well — certain events were going to happen, she made her lone way back to the Peace House. She thought about the brothers who were being so generous with their time, and considered how her colleagues in Britain would react if they were to be asked to teach for no pay. She also reflected on how often over recent years she had complained about her job, and decided that unless she were subjected to extreme provocation she wouldn't do so in the future. Deep down, however, she also knew that once she was back in the thick of it, at the chalk face as it were, this resolution was bound to fail.

Meandering through the streets like a person who has all the time in the world, Neffie found her way back to the Peace House without difficulty. Upon arrival, feeling weary from the effort of walking in heat, she decided to rest for an hour. In the event she slept for an hour and a half, and would have stayed longer in repose if Di hadn't come to wake her. Even then it took two goes at manipulating the shoulder beneath her hand back and forth for Neffie to open her eyes and recognise the friendly face staring down at her. The hint of anxiety in the more wakeful of the two countenances prompted Neffie to enquire if there was anything wrong. Fortunately there wasn't. Di's slight trepidation stemmed from the uncertainty that she may be about to annoy sleeping beauty by waking her with a view to inviting her out for a meal. It was a relief for the American to discover that she needn't have worried, a fact which became readily apparent when Neffie, acting totally out of character to anyone who had known her for more than a week let's say, leapt from the bed with all the alacrity of a person who has just felt a scorpion crawl over her body.

In preference to dining in on fried spam or dried pasta, and the clearing away that such acts of self-preservation necessitate, Freetown-based Peace Corps personnel frequented a 'chop house' about five minutes walk away. It was to this venue that the four Americans invited Neffie, and where dining on 'chop' a pleasant evening was had by all.

'Chop' is the staple diet of Sierra Leone and in its simplest form comprises a bowl of rice splashed with palm oil. Always made welcome by the owner, the gathering of familiar white faces seated at a veranda table had requested that some dry fish be added to their 'chop', and this filling and sustaining dish they washed down with copious amounts of palm wine. With each boy and girl trying to benefit mankind in their own way, yet at the same time not wanting to be perceived as the naive do-gooders that most people thought they were, during the meal, and for some considerable time after, the conversation fluctuated between humorous banter and serious political debate. Laughter gave way to more sober expressions, and they in turn gave way to carefree laughter.

Everyone became a little merry, but not to the extent of being hopelessly 'chak', which in krio means drunk.

Notwithstanding the extended nap that she had taken earlier, Neffie slept well that night, so deeply that as far as she was aware come the morning, she hadn't dreamt or turned in her sleep at all. She awoke to find Di's bed already vacated. For the Peace Corps volunteers it was a working day, whereas for Neffie a trip to the beach was in the offing. In contrast to her energised leap out of bed the previous evening, however, on this occasion she released herself from the arms of Somnos slowly, reasoning that there were at least twenty minutes before the Massequoi brothers were due to call.

The brothers kept their promise, and thirty minutes after getting out of bed, having taken with her a bag she had borrowed containing a hat, bottled water and her camera, Neffie was sitting in the back seat of James' far from roadworthy Morris Oxford. For the back-seat passenger the experience was nostalgic for being undertaken in the same make of car that her dad used to drive twenty years earlier, but there the similarities ended. James' car was a veritable rust-bucket, and the once plush seats were scarred by rips in the fabric.

James let it be known that they wouldn't be able to go anywhere until they put some petrol in the tank. Ever alert to the prospect of being taken for a ride, literally as well as metaphorically, Neffie usually managed not to be fleeced unwittingly. Knowing that on this occasion the request couched as a statement was based on genuine need, she didn't hesitate in offering to pay for a few gallons of petrol. Her willingness to make a financial contribution towards today's trip to the beach, and in all probability towards a number of James' journeys in the future, journeys which wouldn't involve her, was, she felt, the least she could do to help alleviate the plight of her fellow teachers.

The price per gallon determined how much fuel Neffie was prepared to buy. Upon checking the gauge immediately after refuelling she noted that the tank was just over half full. This made for an interesting observation seeing as the beach they were heading for turned out to be only a few miles out of town, and though the financial implications of the short excursion weren't a disappointment to Neffie, the destination certainly was.

Miss Goodwin had had few preconceptions as to what she would find at the end of the dirt track which made for a bumpy ride approaching the beach, but she had imagined that the vista upon arrival would be more inviting for being more spectacular than it was. The proliferation of litter, mainly in the form of discarded drinks cans, along the approach road was a good harbinger of things to come. The leaden sky didn't help much either, but along the shore conspired with the reflective quality of the sea to make the overall scene doleful, grey. Miss Goodwin's first impression as James pulled on to hard-standing the size of half a tennis-court, was that somehow she had been transported to a beach she was familiar with back home, a dune-backed bay situated close to the steel works and patrolled mainly by lone dog-walkers. At least at home the sand was golden. Here it was fuscous.

Getting out of the car and looking beyond the rusty sign standing at a drunken angle to the perpendicular, a sign which, if the writing on it were in any way legible, might possibly have designated the ground they were on as an official car-park, Neffie put on her let's be positive face, and by so doing managed, she believed, to hide her disappointment. At least here there was no industrial eyesore to spoil the view. Obviously the energy-sapping heat and humidity were other major differences, but Neffie was of the opinion that it was better to be uncomfortably warm than perishing cold.

"It must be great to be able to come down here to chill out at weekends," said Neffie, positively, as she scanned the shoreline.

"And for a lot of people at any other time," responded Samuel, pointedly.

Neffie suggested that they walk along the beach in the direction of an enclave of buildings partially hidden by palms growing on a low promontory about a mile and a half away. She learned from James that the buildings in question were hotels owned by French companies. They had been built to accommodate mainly French tourists. Along the way, spaced at irregular intervals and appearing like skeletal remains, the last vestiges of shacks which had once been bars serving refreshments to bathers caught Miss Goodwin's eye. Midway between two of these dilapidated structures a sailing-boat lay high and dry, its single mast pointing to the sky and away from the ocean at an angle of forty-five degrees. A single spar crossed the mast to present, for any Christian who happened to be passing, a configuration of religious significance.

To enliven things and make their time together more memorable Neffie said that she would like to take a few photographs. Eyeing a number of crates strewn in the sand around the boat's stern, crates that, like the boat, to her surprise had been left unattended, she had the idea that when placed one on top of the other they would make the perfect platform on which to stand her camera.

Photography was an important creative endeavour to Neffie, and having taken her camera with her on all her travels of note, she had compiled a pictorial record that she would be able to peruse with great affection, though perhaps also rather wistfully, in her dotage. The work Miss Goodwin had produced to date, and which hung framed on the living-room wall at home, was of a quality likely to convince the viewer that it was more art than hobby. Needless to say she wasn't much taken with the idea of taking holiday snaps.

There being no one other than her two companions within a couple of hundred yards, Neffie's plan initially was to set the timer so that after making the necessary adjustments to the camera she could hurry back and be in time to say 'cheese' along with her friends. From the perspective of being a great source of humour her first attempt was highly successful, but not in any other regard. From the practical consideration of being able to get into position between the two men and adopting a relaxed, photogenic pose, the ten seconds she had allowed proved insufficient. At the first attempt she didn't get halfway before the shutter opened and closed automatically, and she had no doubt that had she been able to show the image taken, as she would have been able to do if her camera had been state of the art, the exhibition that was her rear end would have been the cause of even greater hilarity.

At the second attempt, by standing in front of the camera at the moment of depressing the timer Neffie gained an additional two seconds in which to complete her sprint, but over any distance sand isn't the best of surfaces for attempting to break a record for running, and so, slipping as she turned, yet again she failed to achieve her aim. On this occasion she made it so far as to be able to place her hand on James' shoulder as she attempted to run around the back of him. She nearly flattened him. It would have tested his composure if she had done because, other than for the soles of their highly polished shoes, it was obvious that neither James nor Samuel wanted any part of his smart-casual attire to be sullied. At the third attempt Neffie put an end to the comedy by increasing the time delay to fifteen seconds, an obvious decision which enabled her to crouch down and face the lens just in time. She took another two shots in this way and then, breathing heavily, put away the camera.

The next game on the unwritten agenda was open to all-comers, but as it turned out only the brothers chose to take part. The men took it in turns to show off by competing with each other to see who could throw a pebble farthest out to sea. Even the most intellectual minds need to play. Watching others exert themselves allowed Neffie to brush off the sand from her jeans and catch her breath. Of course, for the reason that each splash indicating where a stone had entered the water was bound to prove ephemeral, there was no accurate way of measuring and recording the aqueous eruptions consigned to memory. Eventually, their throwing arms beginning to tire, Samuel acceded to James' claim that it was one of his throws that had made its tell-tale plop the farthest; but that didn't mean to say he had conceded victory. Samuel's counter-claim was that his brother, having taken a longer run-up, had been ankle-deep in the Atlantic Ocean before letting go the pebble in question. This was undoubtedly an exaggeration on Samuel's part, but the point he was keen to make was that his best effort, for having been launched from dry land, had achieved the greater distance. James scoffed at what he considered to be a pathetic attempt on the part of his brother to get one over on him, and to settle the matter once and for all he asked Neffie to be the final arbiter.

An impracticable if not entirely impossible consideration, by way of gaining an insight into Miss Goodwin's likely response, James couldn't have done better than speak with Sebastian. On several occasions Seb had spoken, he believed with authority, about his partner being totally devoid of competitive spirit when it came to participating in sport or games, activities in respect of which he believed the sole purpose was to try to win. To play tennis with Neffie was never a dull affair as long as he remained mindful that the purpose of the game was to achieve the longest rally possible.

Point-scoring between them was never an issue because there was none to be won. Presently, on a dreary beach a few miles from Freetown, Neffie's far from dog-eat-dog attitude was about to hold sway yet again. Her judgement, one which would have exasperated Sebastian, was that both parties had done their best to earn a highly commendable draw. Unsurprisingly it was a ruling which didn't entirely satisfy James, but he was too polite not to accept the referee's decision as final.

Time passed leisurely as the trio indulged in a number of hedonistic pursuits appropriate to holiday beaches the world over. At the only cabin within sight that was intact and operating as a beach bar Neffie bought cream sodas all round. It was a good thing she wasn't feeling peckish because neither of the eatables on offer was tempting. For being by the sea unsurprisingly one of the dishes consisted of dried fish, or 'bonga' as it was described to Neffie by the lady whose enterprise it was. This woman of considerable girth and a voluminous chest trying to burst forth from a dazzling orange and yellow dress looked as if she was really in need of, as soon as she had finished serving, the one and only stool to be found in the vicinity. Meanwhile her customers had to make do with leaning against the rickety bar. There was some doubt that it would be able to withstand their combined weight, so at Neffie's behest an impromptu rota system was instigated, no more than two bodies being supported at any given time. The other dish available which Neffie hadn't taken a fancy to was 'akara', a cake made from rice and bananas. A great favourite of James and Samuel, they didn't even try to resist temptation, and at Neffie's expense each devoured a sizeable piece.

"Now there's something you could do to make for a really memorable day," said Samuel as soon as he had finished eating.

He was about to walk off in the direction of the activity he was referring to, but because James was still eating his portion, Neffie encouraged him to be more considerate of his brother and wait a while. Matters of etiquette didn't prevent her from enquiring as to what Samuel had in mind.

"And what might that be?" she said, looking in the direction in which Samuel had been looking.

Appearing as if from nowhere a few hundred yards along the beach, in the direction of the French hotels, it appeared that a number of small boats were about to be launched.

"A boat trip," he answered, "out into the Atlantic."

It was James who, having consumed his light repast, led the way towards the anticipated nautical activity. Neffie pondered over the proposal which had been put to her, and the prospect of partaking in an adventure which she hadn't bargained for didn't readily appeal, and the more she thought about it the more reluctant she became to be carried off by one of Samuel's whims. The expression on her face reflected her disquiet, for although Neffie had been brought up within a stone's throw of the sea, she had no love for the briny, or for messing about in boats upon it. Too many people had lost their lives within the distance that same stone could be thrown from shore. Furthermore, unlike at home, here there was no lifeboat station in sight.

"Where's the lifeboat station?" enquired Neffie as the teachers drew ever closer to the action.

"Why would you want a lifeboat to be standing by when the ocean is like it is... as calm as the..." Samuel searched for a suitable comparison in the near empty repository available to him at that moment,

"...as calm as the Sea of Tranquillity," he said at last, feeling somewhat pleased with himself for having pulled, as it were, such a splendid specimen of a rabbit from out of his hat.

"That's true," confirmed James. "It's as calm as it will ever be."

It appeared that there were three boats in total, just as there were three pedagogic pairs of eyes focused on the simple craft and the barefoot young men dressed in shorts manhandling them to the water's edge. It became apparent that Lumley Beach's most dynamic human activity was also being closely watched by a host of terns perched on a rock half-submerged. Furthermore, at least a dozen of the West African crested specie could be observed diving for fish about half a mile from shore. After observing avian antics for a minute or more Neffie's attention returned to human endeavour: the men she could see were stowing nets, and they could be for only one purpose. She noted also that one of the boats was decked out more ostentatiously than the others for flying the flags of more than one nation from its prow and stern.

"I think I'll give your idea about going out to sea a miss for the time being," Neffie informed Samuel suddenly, and without having given the boats the close scrutiny that she had said she would do. "I really don't fancy getting drenched for the sake of a few fish, and what's more I don't like to see them thrashing about on deck as they struggle to breathe. If either or both of you want to go and enjoy yourselves however... assuming that these fishermen don't mind your taking up room on their boat... I would be happy to record the occasion for posterity, and to take a few photographs."

The brothers were surprised at Miss Goodwin's lack of enthusiasm for their idea to make the day memorable, but as they were just as reluctant to get their feet wet, perhaps they shouldn't have been, and it certainly didn't surprise Miss Goodwin when they too opted to remain on dry land. Not to be missed, however, was the opportunity to take pictures of an activity which has been performed by people living by the shores of oceans, seas, lakes and rivers since time immemorial, and with camera-eye ready to depict this most fundamental of human endeavours Neffie set to work.

Whatever Sebastian had said in the past about photography not being art, because in his opinion, and in this instance, the act of creation involved nothing more than pressing a button, it didn't prevent Neffie from trying to obtain a perfect composition. Aware presently that her efforts to resurrect her belief in the diversity of pictorial art were being observed intently by the men who hadn't been subjected to, and tainted by, her partner's uncompromising logic, kneeling one moment and standing the next, Neffie changed her position several times as she zoomed in and out in her quest to obtain pictures of artistic merit. Inevitably her subject matter was the small groups of partially clothed men going about their piscatorial business. She tried to capture their facial expressions, most of which revealed the pleasure to be gained from purposeful physical exertion, also the pleasure to be gained from working as a team. The majority couldn't care less about being photographed and carried on working regardless, but a couple of individuals, perhaps because they had seen film stars pose in a certain way, stopped what they were doing to smile at the camera.

While all this was going on Samuel and James had no choice but to become acquainted with a phenomenon with which Sebastian was all too familiar, and which he would have gladly forewarned the brothers about if it had been possible for him to pass on this frustrating aspect of his experience.

He would have told them that it was necessary to develop the patience of a saint when taking a stroll with someone intent on taking photographs, especially when the camera in question is a relatively bulky single lens reflex job which the photographer insists needs to be put in the camera bag after each sequence of shots. Initially the two male teachers had observed Neffie's attempts to turn the sinuous exertions of others into art with interest, but after twenty minutes had elapsed that interest had begun to wane. After a further twenty minutes had passed, they began to kick their heels, so to speak, in frustration.

In the absence of any facilities close by, when Samuel needed to answer a call of nature he made his way across the sand to disappear into the scrub and bush beyond the beach, there to do what was necessary as discreetly as possible. By this time Neffie had run out of new ideas when it came to this particular scene representing life as art. She had taken thirty-seven shots — a number which included those of her gang she had taken earlier — of a roll which advertised thirty-six available. By carefully removing the exposed roll and depositing it in its little plastic tub, and not reloading, she effectively called a halt to picture-taking for the day. By this time the three boats were all at sea.

The fishermen aboard the craft farthest from shore had already shipped their makeshift oars and were preparing to cast their net. For a fleeting moment Neffie regretted having used up all her film, but the feeling didn't surprise her. For the reason that there were always more pictures to take she invariably felt this way.

"Where's Samuel got to?" Neffie enquired as she looked about her upon completion of the most important task, only just realising for being so preoccupied that Mr Massequoi was nowhere in sight.

"He's gone to spend a pound," said James. His answer made Neffie laugh.

Visibly embarrassed by the thought that he might have used the wrong expression James sought clarification. "Isn't that what you say in England? Did I say something stupid?"

"I am sorry," said Neffie, her countenance somehow able to mirror the apology and implied request for forgiveness at the same time as being able to convey repressed mirth.

Her contrition didn't stop there. Acting not unlike a mother eager to soothe a distressed child, in seeking to reassure James more demonstratively than by simply apologising, Neffie wasted no time in taking hold of his nearest hand and, in an act of physicality aimed at providing reassurance, for several seconds held it between both of hers.

"I wasn't laughing because you said something really stupid... far from it," Neffie began to explain. "If anything, I was laughing because what you said was very clever."

"What did you hear to make you think that?" James enquired, looking somewhat puzzled.

"Well... in Britain it's not uncommon for people to say, 'I've got to go and spend a penny', but I doubt anyone does these days... not literally. What you said will probably catch on in a big way for having taken account of inflation, so it wasn't just clever, it was brilliant... absolutely brilliant!"

"You wouldn't like to have dinner with me tonight would you?" James blurted.

The younger brother's mindset had evidently been persuaded that he was on to a good thing. His sudden outpouring of words quickly spoken could have been influenced by Cassius' famous speech in Shakespeare's Julius Caesar: "There is a tide in the affairs of men, which, taken at the flood, leads on to fortune. Omitted, all the voyage of their life is bound in shallows and in miseries." If he had been privy to this conversation perhaps even Sebastian would have admired James' 'who dares wins' attitude rather than taken offence enough to kill him. It was perhaps unfortunate that the negativity inherent in James' rushed request revealed his diffidence. In an attempt to improve on his powers of persuasion he spoke with greater confidence when he backed up his initial sally by informing that, "They may not be up to the standard you're used to, but there are one or two restaurants in Freetown that serve dishes other than chop."

If the invitation surprised Miss Goodwin, strange as it may seem it surprised James even more. It wasn't the distracting business of mulling over the idea in his mind that was so startling — he had been doing that ever since he had witnessed Neffie's lighter side in running to take up her position to be photographed — it was the fact that he had dared to give expression to his hope. The apparent encouragement which Neffie had shown had provided James with the perfect opportunity to relieve the pressure on his simmering psyche. Unbeknown to anyone but himself, however, a fact which made his bold invitation even more remarkable, even more courageous than it might have at first appeared, was that at the time of asking he didn't have enough money to pay for one meal at either of the restaurants he had in mind, never mind two.

Neffie's initial response was instinctive: she let go James' hand, folded her arms, and took a step back. Even though her considered opinion was that James had been really sweet to have made such an offer, she took the view that she had sent the wrong signal by being too tactile. On another occasion, on the basis that going out to dinner is usually a pleasant sociable event, and needn't have other connotations, she might have agreed to the assignation. Presently, however, she wasn't intending to go anywhere special other than to Koidu in the morning. She knew that as the day progressed her thoughts would become increasingly focused on getting up early to catch the bus. Therefore, this evening of all evenings, the idea of being wined and dined didn't appeal. Rather she was keen to have a good night's sleep. Consequently Miss Goodwin's only practical course was to let James down gently and decline his invitation as graciously as possible. In so doing she was sure she identified a look of relief illuminate the face on which she would have expected to observe dejection born of rejection. She wasn't bewildered for long though, for out of the corner of one eye she espied Samuel approaching nonchalantly across the sand. In the opinion of Neffie and James alike his imminent arrival couldn't have been better timed.

At a distance considerably greater than Neffie would normally begin a conversation she said, "James was just telling me how many good restaurants there are in Freetown."

At first Samuel was at a loss as to how he should respond to this statement. It had come out of the blue, and several seconds passed before he determined how best to reply. Eventually, as he drew near, he said, "Knowing my younger brother as I do, he's probably hoping that you'll let him take you to one of them. Be warned though, if just for the pleasure of his company he'll expect you to pick up the bill."

Samuel's comment was unkind and not altogether true. If Neffie had accepted his invitation James would have made every effort to borrow the requisite money from somewhere. This thought had occurred to him as soon as he heard Samuel's jibe. A likely source would have been the most affluent member of the family, cousin Mariana. No matter, as things stood the ways and means of obtaining money to pay for a special meal were no longer relevant, seeing as tonight James would be eating 'chop' as usual.

Acting out of hurt pride however, he couldn't let Samuel's barbed comment pass without protest, and in response to the calumny he said, "You have no idea how much I've got stashed away, big brother."

No matter how small the sum James had in mind, this statement was undoubtedly true.

"You're obviously worth more than I had imagined, so why don't you go ahead and tell us. I'm sure Miss Goodwin will be impressed."

"It's more than enough to take a lady to dinner," James replied, defensively. This statement was undoubtedly false.

The fact that no one was laughing, or smiling for that matter, indicated that a certain amount of acerbity had crept into the exchange. Neffie, sensing that the tropical heat would increase by several degrees if the bickering were allowed to continue unabated, interrupted the discussion. "I think it's time we made our way back to the car," she said, her reference to the vehicle reminding her that it was she who had paid for the fuel that had enabled them to come to the beach in the first place.

In conciliatory fashion Neffie placed her left hand between Samuel's right arm and ribs. In a similar manner she thrust her right hand between James' left arm and his body. Thus linked she proceeded to steer her guides in the right direction. This cosy threesome didn't last for long though, for in the next instant, having taken no more than a couple of strides, James broke free of Neffie's grip. The woman in the middle no longer, at first Neffie thought the chum to her right was being petulant. She was relieved to discover, however, that James' bid for freedom was for an entirely practical reason, which soon became apparent as he more or less followed in Samuel's footsteps towards the scrub and the impromptu convenience. Meanwhile, Neffie felt somewhat ill at ease to have been left holding the elder brother's arm. In the light of the saying that two's company and three's a crowd, she much preferred linking when there had been a crowd. Consequently, she let go of Samuel's arm, and at an amicable but less intimate distance from each other they ambled back along the beach towards the car. More that of a turtle than a tortoise, their pace was slow. Unable to go anywhere far without him, their procrastination was designed to let James catch up with them.

Neffie in particular hoped that he wouldn't be long. Even though she had perspired profusely when taking photographs, she was beginning to feel the pressure of the soda she had drunk building up in her bladder. She believed that if they weren't too dilatory she could hold on till they got back to town. Neffie's thoughts in respect of her physical needs were interrupted when Samuel spoke.

"Seeing as my little brother has brought up the subject of going out to a restaurant, do you have any plans for what is likely to be your last night in Freetown for some considerable time?"

Neffie was impressed by the confident subtlety of Samuel's approach. "That's an easy one, Samuel," Miss Goodwin replied as she turned to look over her shoulder for James. "I aim to get a good night's rest so that I can get up bright and early and be ready for when you come and collect me, and as far as eating is concerned, I'm not French."

Samuel pondered over this enigma before seeking clarification. "British people have to eat don't they?"

"They do, but the saying goes that we eat to live whereas the French live to eat. What it means in practice is that I'll probably prepare a snack for myself at the Peace House and make do with that."

If Samuel was disappointed to learn of the British attitude to food compared to the French, mainly for the reason that the cultural divergence had effectively scuppered his plans, he didn't show it. If he was disappointed by Neffie's unwillingness to perceive and go along with any ulterior motive he might have had, he didn't show it. His sangfroid remained intact. To all appearances his ego hadn't taken a knock in the slightest.

When James at last joined his brother and Neffie, the trio walked back towards the car at a normal pace and without sharing much by way of conversation. It was as if the dark clouds which had recently dissipated to reveal tracts of blue had forsaken the sky to enter their souls. It was as if for the present each wanted to spend some time in his or her own secret world. The journey back to town was no less introspective.

Chapter Nine
Mariana Pays a Visit

Mariana Koromah was a woman who commanded respect. She was able to do so for two main reasons. Foremost, because if it had not been for her innate qualities and attributes she might not have developed the other, was her impressive appearance. Standing six feet tall without shoes, she towered over the rest of the women in her family and most of the men. She was certainly more linear than curvaceous. Providing barely any cleavage, her bosom was hardly worthy of the name. In combination Mariana's remarkable height, her nearly flat chest and strong facial features, gave her the appearance of an Amazon. No legendary female Scythian warrior could have looked more formidable.

Mariana's head deserved to be painted, but so far had only been photographed, many times. A long, slender neck led to a face which was striking for revealing high, prominent cheekbones framing dark, scolding eyes. Her mouth was a feast for being eminently kissable, her lips offering sensual delight of the most alluring and dangerous kind, the kind that for a passionate male is maddening to resist even if he were gifted with the foresight that hard upon his rapture he would be eaten alive.

The hair topping this beauteous whole Mariana brushed back and up to form a shape reminiscent of the 'beehive', a style fashionable in Britain when the Beatles first took to the stage. A rather severe demarcation between black hair and ebony skin was maintained, usually, by an intricately patterned headscarf. Miss Koromah tied this item of apparel at the back of her head, and from there it hung down as low as to touch the base of her spine. Being the owner of a plethora of headscarves that were differentiated only by colour and pattern, more often than not the one she chose to wear on any given day matched her dress.

Looking like a darker version of Queen Nefertiti, Mariana could have graced the catwalks of London, New York, Paris or Rome, but perhaps working on the basis that it is better to rule in hell than serve in heaven, as the saying goes, she was focused on building up her empire in Sierra Leone. This empire consisted of a bar in Congo Town — a district of Freetown bordering Whiteman's Bay — and another on the main street in Kalangba Junction. In the medium to long term Mariana wanted to become ten times richer than she was, and the way she envisaged being able to achieve that goal was to own ten times as many establishment as she did. For the present, however, her ambition was to consolidate her position as a respectable business woman, and she was happy to travel to and fro between her businesses in a rugged four-wheel drive vehicle rather than, as one might expect of a successful fashion model, motor along the Champs-Elysées in a more prestigious car.

How their cousin had acquired the funds to set herself up in business in the first place was a question which the Massequoi brothers had asked themselves more than once. Strange as it may seem neither had mentioned his ruminations to the other, and neither had broached the subject directly with his cousin. It had been rumoured that she had become involved in smuggling diamonds, a suspicion which had been aroused by her having often been seen in the company of gentlemen of Lebanese origin, all of whom were known to the authorities. Of course, the relationship between Miss Koromah and certain members of Freetown's Arab community might have been above board in every respect, and had involved nothing more egregious than negotiations about the repayment terms of Mariana's business loans, if indeed she had any. On the other hand, a thought which James found difficult to dispel was that his cousin had been selling her favours to rich men. It was a thought which for obvious reasons he kept to himself. Whatever the origins of Mariana's success, they were in the distant past, and the majority of family, friends and associates held her in high regard for her business acumen.

"Mohin-o," Mariana greeted as she breezed in through the insect-deterring beads that hung down from above the open door separating Samuel's dwelling from the street.

The voice that had rasped 'good morning' in Krio surprised the only occupant, causing him to spill a little of the mango juice he had been pouring as part of his breakfast. The spillage pooled on the table around the base of the plastic beaker from which he was intending to drink.

Samuel wasted no time in setting about clearing up the mess, but even so two flies that had found a gap beat him to the nectar until such time as they sensed danger and took flight. From a human perspective it was folly to leave food or sweet sticky substances, viscous or liquid, lying around for any length of time.

It was a little after seven and Samuel wondered why his cousin had called to see him, particularly at such an early hour. The slight mishap she had caused didn't cause Samuel to be uncivil, and he bid his cousin, "Kushe-o," (greetings).

In keeping with the other two rooms in the tin-roofed, single-storey house, the kitchen in which the cousins stood facing each other was basic. The furniture therein consisted of a three-ringed cooker which glowed red occasionally, when switched on, and a fridge which whirred into life as if it had been deliberately synchronised to work when the cooker did: their ability to function was, of course, dependent upon the intermittent electricity supply. There was a large sink fed by two cold taps. The sink was prone to blocking. More reliable for serving a lesser purpose was the square table which Samuel had wiped, two accompanying chairs and a cupboard, whose width was twice that of its height. Painted pale blue, as were the table and chairs, this repository for miscellaneous items of crockery, cutlery and pans was also Samuel's larder. Most of the ironmongery had seen better days, but that didn't preclude Samuel from taking pride in his meagre household possessions. His pride was also evidenced by the fact that he had made it a rule of his domestic life to wash and clear away the dishes and cooking utensils he had used in the preparation and serving of his evening meal almost as soon as he had finished eating. There was barely enough room to swing a rat by its tail in Sam's kitchen, but it was clean and tidy, and as far as Samuel was aware, it was rat-free.

Mariana laughed and said, "You look as if you've seen a ghost, or did you think... as I was about to enter your little hideaway... this putative literary lion's den... that I was a former girlfriend intent on getting her own back, or a creditor impatient for his money perhaps?"

She looked about her with a disdainful, supercilious expression.

"What do you expect when you walk through the door without a by your leave at this time of morning? I don't see you for months at a time and then suddenly you turn up out of the blue like a…" Samuel struggled to find an appropriate simile.

"Like a guardian angel," said Mariana helpfully, "that's it, a guardian angel, one who's always ready to give my clever cousin sound advice."

"If you say so," rejoined Samuel.

"I do say so." The stern look on Mariana's face as she sought to get the better of her cousin in this particular exchange went a long way towards contradicting her self-proclaimed status of being his guardian angel. It was a look which Samuel couldn't fail to notice, but he made a conscious decision not to let it bother him. He was well aware that Mariana owned a property in Kalangba Junction which was much more substantial than anything he would be able to afford on his erratic teacher's pay, but so what? His cousin may be richer, but he was better educated. Consequently it was he who had the greater understanding of the world, its history, its geography, its politics, and its people. When it came to literature there was no competition. Armed with this considerable bank of knowledge he countered Miss Koromah's materialistically based sense of superiority by not taking umbrage.

"I thought you would have realised by now, Mariana, that I'm not like you, and don't wish to be. I don't borrow money so I don't have any creditors, and I always sleep well at night. Why are you here anyway?"

"If you pour me a glass of that mango juice and make me a cup of coffee I'll tell you," said Mariana, in a more conciliatory tone. "If you don't have any… coffee I mean… I can go and get some for you."

Once again Samuel did his best not to let his irritation show. It seemed that his cousin couldn't open her mouth without making a comment which had a ring of condescension about it. He hoped that the jar he took from the cupboard had at least two spoonfuls of the brown finely ground powder remaining. Doing his best to comply with Mariana's request he poured mango juice into a plastic beaker similar to the one he had yet to drink from, and proceeded to boil water in a pan for the coffee. Realising that he had been remiss in not offering his cousin a chair, he sought to make amends. In so doing, however, he inadvertently drew attention to his relatively impoverished state by forgetting that the slats which formed the back of the wooden contraption he was about to offer Mariana had come unstuck. It fell apart with a clatter.

"I'll have to get some glue to stick that," Samuel muttered, more to himself than for Mariana's benefit; but even so, despite his apparent nonchalance, he couldn't help but feel a little awkward with regard to this sudden turn of events.

Initially Mariana looked on with amusement, but sensitive to her cousin's feelings at last she quickly adopted a reassuring tone. "I know I'm telling you what you know already when I say it's the climate," said Miss Koromah sympathetically. "Nothing lasts for long in this humidity."

Despite the banality of stating the obvious Mariana believed that her comment would be appreciated. After all, who would rather be mocked than soothed? Samuel took the broken chair for himself and passed the chipped, stained, but unbroken one to his cousin. Prior to sitting down at the table the host remove a small pile of books from out of harm's way. Classics all, the paperbacks comprised *The Mill on the Floss*, *Jude the Obscure*, and *Mrs Dalloway*. It was from these sources and others like them, that Samuel had largely formed his impression of Britain, though he wasn't so ingenuous in this regard that he didn't make allowances for the fact that many of the books he had read had been written in the previous century. Notwithstanding their poor condition, the tattered tomes that made for a pathetic library were his most treasured possessions. In affluent Britain, where people complain about the weather concomitant with a cool-temperate climate, the patches of mould that tarnished the covers of Samuel's treasure would have precluded the books being offered for sale in a charity shop, or for 50p on a market stall. In Sierra Leone, however, at the time of Neffie's visit books were hard to come by and hard to keep. In Samuel's opinion his treasure was worth more than Mariana's gold.

"So to what do I owe this pleasure?" enquired Samuel, sounding like a character from one of his novels as he reiterated the gist if not the actual words of the question he had posed earlier. "I don't have much time to entertain you this morning. I said to Miss Goodwin... she's a teacher from Britain I've met and am showing around... that I would pick her up around eight, and I don't want to be late. You know what English ladies are like for being punctual," he added, though immediately upon making this comment he realised that he wasn't really in a position to judge what constituted such an interesting specimen of humanity, his conceptions in this regard, as already intimated, having been mainly derived from fiction. A flash of insight it might have been, but it didn't deter him from further speculation, and he said, "And I should think teachers are more punctual than most." His local knowledge of the pedagogic breed and their habits made it obvious that he was referring to the British variety.

"Well to tell you the truth, cousin, she's the reason I've come to see you this morning," said Mariana.

Her expression was one of protective familial concern. Whenever Samuel heard the expression, 'To tell you the truth... ' he scowled, and with good reason. To his way of thinking it was as if everything said hitherto by the person emphasising the truth of their present pronouncement had been, at best, dubious. The discomfiture caused by his sensitivity to language quickly overcome, Samuel continued to scrutinise his cousin warily nonetheless, as if he wasn't sure that he wanted to hear her message.

"Oh! There's no need to look so worried," Mariana advised solicitously. "I haven't come to spoil things for you, but being the nosey bitch that I am, I would like you to tell me about this new girlfriend of yours."

Samuel's wary look remained, and because Mariana had failed to dispel it, she knew that Samuel knew her little game, that she was being deliberately provocative in setting a trap with words to lure her relation into revealing his true feelings for Miss Goodwin. It wouldn't have perturbed Mariana, however, if her cousin had been able to read her thoughts as clearly as a page in one of his books, because what she was counting on was his inability to resist the lure regardless. Samuel's reaction was to be defensive, but it was in a hollow, rather disingenuous kind of way, a way which indicated that he wasn't really displeased to be associated romantically with Miss Nefertiti Goodwin.

"I don't know where you get your information from," began Samuel, "but believe me when I tell you there's nothing for you to worry about, or be enthusiastic about for that matter, regarding our relationship. We've only been going out... I mean seeing each other since the day before yesterday, and today she's going to Koidu. Who was it who told you about us anyway? Come on, tell me."

Grinning broadly Miss Koromah raised her hand to her face. The index finger protruding from a tightly curled fist of digits she pushed against the side of her nose. Her message was clear. "No names, cousin," she added, "but you know as well as anyone that you can't keep something like this secret for very long in this city. It's all over Congo Town."

"You've been talking to James haven't you?" said Samuel, leaning forward suddenly so that his face was no more than a foot distant from that of his cousin's, a gesture which served to add even greater emphasis to the question he had enunciated with all the intensity of a detective interrogating a suspect.

"Now that's hardly surprising is it, seeing as I'm just as much his cousin as I am yours?" replied Miss Koromah feigning innocence, and as she spoke she leaned back in her chair, her instinct being to maintain a sociable distance between them rather than the present gap.

Samuel looked at his watch and was relieved to discover that time was getting on towards the hour when he would have to go. The spinning top that is planet earth had turned faster than he had surmised, which in turn made him think that he would soon be able to free himself of his cousin's company without appearing inordinately rude.

"I'm sorry, Marri," began Samuel, addressing his cousin by the sobriquet he used when wanting to be friendly, "but I really must be going. You're welcome to stay and make yourself at home till I get back. Why not make yourself another cup of coffee, or some breakfast if you wish? I'm sorry I can't be a better host, but as you can imagine my thoughts are elsewhere at present."

The significance one could attach to Samuel's thoughts being elsewhere wasn't unintentional on his part, and neither was that statement's ambiguity. Other than frowning with disdain at the prospect of eating in an environment which she considered to be less than ideal, Miss Koromah offered no resistance to this line of reasoning. Her go-getting personality was such that more often than not she was assertive in a selfish way rather than considerate of others in a selfless way. On this occasion, however, she was perfectly able to accept 'where her cousin was coming from'. Moreover, she had just identified an opportunity which she hadn't previously considered.

"Thank you, Sammy," Mariana said, mimicking her cousin's familiar style. "Yes, of course I would love to meet Miss Goodwin. After you've introduced us and we've got to know each other to the extent that we would be able to stop and chat in the street the next time we meet, I'm going on to Kalangba. Seeing as the place where the Peace Corps people hang out is on my way, you wouldn't be putting me out in the slightest."

In stately fashion Miss Koromah arose from her chair, and without another word, and without even noticing the look of horror on the poor man's face gazing up at her, she exited through the strings of beads like a dominatrix who expects to be obeyed. Samuel, realising that he had just lost the first battle in a war which he hadn't been expecting, followed his cousin submissively.

The short walk from his modest abode to the front passenger door of Mariana's all-terrain vehicle was distance enough for the teacher to be able to reflect on why he had wanted to create a false impression regarding his relationship with Miss Goodwin. The first plausible reason that came to mind was that he had deliberately wanted to lead Mariana up the jungle track, just for the fun of it. He quickly dispelled this notion however, and for the best of reasons: it simply wasn't true. If one is to analyse the motivation for one's actions or pronouncements, Samuel reasoned, there's no point in making a conscious effort to delude oneself. No; the only possible motivation for his wanting to make his cousin believe that he was romantically involved with Miss Goodwin was vanity: in truth he liked the idea even though the reality was somewhat different. In having reached the correct conclusion he decided to put an end to the charade.

Samuel wasn't at all sheepish or embarrassed at the prospect of setting things straight with Mariana, primarily because he knew that she had been a willing participant in their little game, so much so that it was Samuel's steadfast belief that if he had indeed created the wrong impression in his cousin's imagination it had largely been as a consequence of her encouragement. No; he wouldn't be embarrassed in the slightest to put a line under their little joke, and as for the rumours that were supposed to be circulating around Freetown, it was easy for Samuel to convince himself that they probably weren't as rife as he had been led to believe, especially when the thought struck home that Mariana had probably instigated them.

Samuel eased his way through a group of half a dozen boys gathered around the vehicle waiting with its engine running. Mariana was in the driver's seat. The smallest for being the youngest member of the gang showed that what he lacked in feet and inches he more than made up for in impudence by standing on the rear bumper, a strategy which served to make him appear taller than the rest. By staying put when Mr Massequoi initially encouraged him to go and pester someone else, he seemed determined on hitching a ride. Four of the boys the teacher recognised as his former pupils, and needless to say the same number of friendly, smiling faces recognised him.

"I mean it... get down from there this instant," ordered Samuel vehemently.

Indeed, so sharp and stentorian was his command on this occasion that a woman several yards away with her back to the group around the car visibly jumped, and she wasn't the only person to turn and look for the source of the noisy disturbance. Obviously the order given on health and safety grounds was directed at the bumper boy, who this time jumped to the ground as if his life depended on it. He then ran for cover behind his friends.

"Can we come for a ride in your jeep, please, sir?" pleaded one of the boys known to Mr Massequoi, a boy named Joseph.

"Another time perhaps," the teacher replied as he opened the door wide enough for himself, and no one else, to be able to squeeze through the gap. The last thing he wanted was for one of the rascals, and he had a likely culprit in mind, to climb in, either before or after him. Only when he was comfortably seated and had buckled his safety belt did Mr Massequoi consider providing these young fellows with a parting thought. Upon opening the side window to speak, his first communication was to shake his head at the request for money implied by the grubby palms, fingers and thumbs pointing towards him. On the basis that it was always worth making the effort even if they received, as on this occasion, nothing for it, the boys weren't overly disappointed.

"You should be studying rather than getting up to mischief, that's if you want to own a jeep like this when you're older," was Samuel's valedictory advice, and without waiting to see how his comment was received, like a commanding officer in complete control he turned to Mariana and said, "Let's go."

After first checking over her shoulder to ensure that none of the boys was behaving like a monkey, Miss Koromah pulled out into the road, driving, so as to avoid hitting insouciant pedestrians, about as fast as a man in a hurry might walk.

"But it's not your jeep is it?" shouted one of the boys as soon as he thought he was safe to express himself freely without fear of reprisal.

"I suppose what you told those 'pikins' is right," said Mariana as, the road having become less congested, she engaged third gear, "though even a high-minded person like you has to admit that it's not always the kids that work hard at school, and work just as hard as adults, that get the finer things in life. A little animal cunning doesn't go amiss."

Samuel considered the significance of his cousin's words, but thinking that it would be a complete waste of time to try to refute her logic, said nothing to encourage her further. Instead, seeking as quickly as possible to clear his mind of his cousin's dubious philosophy, and in keeping with the intention he had formed earlier, he rejoined, "You know as well as I that there's no truth in the rumour that Miss Goodwin and I are in a relationship. I was asked to meet her at the airport and make sure she got settled in all right, and that's what I did. Once I had performed that duty it didn't seem right to say goodbye without offering my services, to provide further assistance… if you see what I mean."

Mariana's silent sideways glance indicated that she had fathomed perfectly the depth of the hole her cousin was digging.

"So it shouldn't have caused tongues to wag that I ended up showing Miss Goodwin around this fair city of ours," continued Samuel, clambering at last towards the light of an unambiguous truth. "The arrangement this morning was, and still is, to make sure that she gets a ticket and catches the bus to Koidu. You know the kind of chaos there can be at the bus-station first thing in the morning."

It had been a long time since Mariana had travelled on public transport and having done so rarely in her youth such memories weren't exactly vivid. She dropped down a gear as once again the road ahead became congested with early morning shoppers and people on bicycles. It wasn't unknown for one of the latter to wobble and fall off into the path of a vehicle about to overtake. The vibrant colours worn contrasted with the leaden sky as usual at this time of year, but from Samuel's and Mariana's perspective they also contrasted with the black fumes emitted by a bus in front of them. When the air-polluting omnibus stopped to let passengers disembark, Mariana had no option but to pull up behind it. The diesel engine's noxious fumes got right up her nose.

"I'll be very pleased to leave Freetown behind this morning," Mariana said as the unwelcome particles caused her to screw up her face. The contortion didn't make it appear any less attractive. Her thoughts, once she had driven the trials and tribulations of urban life, particularly driving, out of mind, returned to their former topic of conversation. Adopting a serious tone she said, "That's where you're wrong, cousin. I really thought there was something going on between you and the Englishwoman — what's her name again — Miss Nefertiti Goodwin?"

The fumes from the engine at the rear of the bus were no less noxious to Samuel, but dealing with the unpleasantness more stoically than Mariana, he showed no signs of aggravation. "Are you disappointed that there isn't?" he enquired, the focus of his gaze and attention having settled on the faces of the small congregation of former bus passengers waiting for a gap in the traffic that would allow them to cross the road. Samuel didn't recognise anyone.

"Well you can't stay single forever," advised Mariana, which was strange advice coming from a woman who in respect of her own circumstances had no plans to tie the knot any time soon. She let the bus get some distance ahead before letting out the clutch. "But what I will say is that you don't want to be giving all your time to that woman for nothing in return. Is she rich?"

The question shocked Samuel out of a state of mind near to reverie, and it was a highly critical eye that he turned upon his cousin.

"She's beautiful," he thought, "but wicked."

"That's probably something you've yet to find out," pre-empted Mariana, effectively answering her own question. "If there's one thing I can be certain of though, it's that she'll be better off than you. Teachers in Britain are well-paid I understand, unlike here. Here, you count yourselves lucky if you're paid anything at all. If I were you, I would try to get her to spread her wealth around, but mostly in your direction. I mean that's why they come to Africa isn't it... these do-gooders from Britain and America? To help us climb out of poverty and improve our lot? Just make sure that she pays you for your time, and your services if you know what I mean," concluded Mariana, grinning broadly as she overtook the wicked bus.

"You are so mercenary, Mariana," said Samuel, and to add emphasis to his appraisal of his cousin's character he repeated the essential point, "so mercenary."

Chapter Ten
Neffie Goes to Koidu

Citizens of a country where the trains run on time, more or less, must think themselves very fortunate. The same can be said of long-distance travel by bus. To people whose experience of life wholly pertains to the developed world, the thought of going to a bus-station four hours prior to the scheduled departure of the bus bound for the destination one has in mind must seem absurd, but this was precisely what Samuel Massequoi did for his friend Nefertiti the morning after his initial attempt to buy a ticket for her failed. Apart from the obvious reason this was a pity because, seeing as Mariana had been willing, he had intended to make the purchase in question with her assistance. Unfortunately, however, the fact that his quest had come to nought proved that there were gaps in even his local knowledge. The relevant gap, one so recently closed by experience, was that it was a forlorn hope to arrive at eight-thirty and expect to be able to obtain a ticket for the bus to Koidu scheduled to depart half an hour later. A further irritation was that it wasn't possible to buy a ticket even one day in advance. There was no alternative therefore but to apologise to Miss Goodwin for having let her down, and then, by way of softening the blow, promise her that he would be in line at five o'clock ante meridiem. Confident of success, he also told her that on the morrow there would be no problem if she were to rendezvous with him between half eight and nine.

Being the experienced traveller that she was Neffie took the news of the delay phlegmatically, and how could she be anything other than be touched to hear what Samuel was prepared to do on her behalf. She said goodbye to Mariana, a woman with whom, for the short time that they had been in each other's company, she had got on famously. Interestingly Mariana had decided that she wasn't in so great a hurry to get back to her place in Kalangba Junction not to be able to take her cousin home, but it turned out that her services as a taxi-driver weren't required. The postponement of Neffie's trip meant that the two teachers were able to spend longer in each other's company than could have been foreseen, and their decision was for Samuel to escort Neffie on her return to the Peace House on foot: he would carry her bag. Free to go where she chose and do as she pleased, Mariana might easily have felt that certain piquancy of having been rejected, but she didn't. Indeed, she was more than happy to have gained an insight into her cousin's affairs, and she was genuinely pleased to have made Miss Goodwin's acquaintance.

Furthermore in respect of the relationship which the two women had established, Miss Goodwin had reason to be grateful to Miss Koromah for an invitation to look her up if she were ever in Kalangba Junction. Samuel was equally grateful, but for a different reason: his cousin hadn't behaved as objectionably toward Miss Goodwin as he had feared; or towards himself for that matter. Whatever his disappointment at not being able to wave Neffie goodbye on the day she was originally due to depart, an act which would have been testament to his competence, had been more than offset by his not wanting the ground to open up beneath him at any time when Mariana was present. Given Miss Goodwin's phlegmatic attitude, tolerance and goodwill, he was in a good frame of mind as he escorted her back along the road by which they had come. Uncertain of his welcome, just as Neffie wasn't entirely sure of hers, they parted company at the gate to the Peace Corps compound.

Happy to discover that the bed she had vacated at the Peace House could still be hers, for another night at least, Neffie greeted her American friends with a display of affection equal to that which she had been shown earlier that morning. Once she had settled in again, an undertaking which took all of ten minutes, she passed the day reading about the politics and history of Sierra Leone whilst at the same time trying to shut out the sound of the Waterboys. Some of the facts she read she already knew, one such being that it was Sir Milton Margai who as Secretary General of Sierra Leone People's Party became, in 1961, the first prime minister of an independent country. In contrast a former lacuna filled by present study was an event known as the Sergeants Revolt, a coup in 1971 which led to Syaka Stevens breaking off all ties with Britain and declaring Sierra Leone a republic: needless to say it was he who became the country's first president. With regard to the Waterboys, they were a group whose music Neffie enjoyed, but not so much when she was trying to read. Being the guest of a friendly but foreign power, however, she felt that she had no right to turn off the ghetto-blaster, and so did her best to concentrate regardless. In addition to her studious reading the unexpected time which Neffie had on her hands offered a good opportunity to write to Sebastian.

The following morning, after going through the inevitable valedictory rituals for the second time in two days, during which she informed Miss Fussey that if time allowed she would try to visit her in Kalangba Junction to help with the renowned tree-planting project, Neffie set out for the bus-station alone. The route she had travelled on foot and by car the previous day had made an impression on her to the extent that she had no trouble finding her way. Her earnest wish as she strolled in the early morning sunshine, uplifted slightly by the sensation of warm air as it gently wafted across her face, was that Samuel had been true to his word and was, on her behalf, already waiting in line.

That Neffie had set out on her perambulation alone didn't mean that her progress continued in a like manner. Notwithstanding the early hour she frequently found herself thronged by separate groups of strangers, particularly as she made her way along Wallace Johnson Street. Tired of getting no joy one group of five or six kids and young adults would disperse prior to another forming to try its collective luck. Such pestering was tiresome, and because not for the first time she hadn't slept as well as she would have wished, Neffie believed that the cumulative effect was affecting her mood. Lurking beneath the obvious reason for her not being in good spirits however, was the reason she would have been loath to admit: that she was apprehensive about making the trip. Given that Miss Goodwin was about to venture into regions where she had been advised not to go, her trepidation was hardly surprising. For the time being there was no one by her side to provide reassurance.

That was about to change, for no sooner had she entered the single-tiered building that constituted the bus station's administrative offices than Neffie caught sight of Mr Massequoi. The sighting caused her spirits to rise considerably. True to his word of the previous day, that is to say to a degree that made any deviation irrelevant, Samuel had been standing in line since five thirty. The presence of only two people in the queue ahead of him — a middle-aged woman and a boy of about eight — was proof enough that on this occasion Samuel was determined not to fail. Confirmation was provided by the long tail, consisting of approximately fifty people, making up the queue behind.

Neffie hesitated. Not wishing to be the cause of angry protest by being perceived as a queue jumper, she paused to consider her best course of action — whether to walk brazenly along the line explaining and protesting her innocence as she went, or whether she should try to attract Samuel's attention from a position which couldn't be misconstrued and so wouldn't appear threatening. Standing at a right-angle to her friend, from a distance of several yards Neffie called out to him.

Being the reserved person she undoubtedly was, Neffie was always going to be loath to draw attention to herself in such a crowded place, but that's what she did when it seemed that almost everyone else in the queue apart from Samuel turned to look at her. Evidently her name-calling hadn't been too softly spoken for most people's ears, even though they surely couldn't all be called Samuel. She knew for certain that the Samuel whose attention she wanted to attract wasn't deaf, so what was his problem? More than a little disconcerted to be the centre of considerable attention, the vociferous white woman felt her face blush as she called out again, a little louder this time. This time she succeeded in eliciting the desired response from her fellow teacher: he appeared to have just woken up from a trance. A keen equestrian when at home, Neffie knew that horses are able to sleep standing up, and she wondered whether Samuel possessed the same ability.

No sooner had the sound of his own name penetrated Samuel's brain, dispelling the thoughts which had preoccupied him, and which had been of sufficient distraction to enable him to stand for hours as resolutely as a guardsman and as stoically as the woman and child in front, than he turned towards Neffie with a look of relief writ large across his face. One of the thoughts which had troubled his mind for so long was whether he had enough money to buy Miss Goodwin's ticket for her if she were to turn up after the ticket-office had opened. It was little wonder, therefore, that his first thought upon seeing Neffie was to dispel a nagging concern by beckoning her to approach.

"Do you have the money for your ticket?" he enquired abruptly. Of course he knew that she had, otherwise she wouldn't be going; but in order for him to be able to complete his mission he wanted her to hand over the requisite amount.

Twenty minutes after the pecuniary business had been transacted and at long last Neffie's object of desire in the shape of a ticket obtained, the bus to Koidu drew into the otherwise empty waiting area. Appearances as presently perceived in the absence of hustle and bustle can be deceptive, so it was a useful premonition which convinced Neffie that it would be unwise to tarry long before getting aboard. The bus in question, though sturdily built, looked as if it had just completed a long journey rather than it being in a state of readiness to begin one. A green strip approximately a foot wide encompassed the bus directly beneath the windows. Otherwise the livery was insipid for being pale yellow. In places it was smeared with laterite, the reddish, ferruginous clay which constitutes many of the roads in Sierra Leone and other tropical countries. The vehicle was considerably longer than the buses Neffie was accustomed to seeing on the roads in Britain, and just behind the passenger door was a ladder leading to a repository for luggage on the roof. Presently the roof-rack was empty, and because it was open to the elements, and because of the daily downpours, it was likely to remain that way. All the windows were open wide.

Not unexpectedly, prior to climbing aboard Neffie experienced a dilemma in not knowing how familiar she should be towards Samuel in expressing her gratitude for the extraordinary kindness he had shown her. She was in two minds as to whether she should give him a hug and kiss his cheek — that's what she felt he deserved — or be less effusive and merely shake him by the hand. The awkwardness she felt stemmed from her not wanting to offend by overstepping the mark. In the end caution won over reckless abandon as she held out her hand for Samuel to shake. The thought occurred to him to take the proffered hand in his and kiss it. Such behaviour would have been thought distinctly weird by his chums, but it was considered normal behaviour for a gentleman in many of the novels he had read. In the end he too chose the less demonstrative option and merely held Neffie's hand until she had promised that she wouldn't hesitate to contact him if she were to get into difficulties. In response to

Neffie's query as to how she might go about getting in touch he wrote down Mariana's telephone number, as well as the number for his school, on a scrap of paper hastily taken from his wallet. Neffie took the lifeline offered her, placing the neatly folded paper in the breast pocket of her shirt. It was the safest place she could think of without delving into the money belt tied around her waist or rummaging about in her holdall.

"You had better go and claim your seat," said Samuel, conscious of the fact that a number of passengers had squeezed past them to board the bus ahead of Neffie. "I wouldn't want the couple of hours I spent standing in line to have been a waste of time," he added, reaching down to pick up the familiar red bag.

"That would be a pity," said Neffie, "and stupid of us seeing as everything has gone so smoothly this morning." Reaching down and taking hold of her bag before Samuel could get his helpful hands on it she said, "That's okay... I can manage," and heading for the open door of the bus glanced over her shoulder to present Samuel with the warmest of smiles to show her gratitude yet again.

The seat Neffie chose looked out upon the concourse where Samuel still waited. There were, as yet, a number of window seats vacant across the gangway, and she had been tempted to take one so as not to be further encumbered with the niceties of leave taking. She didn't want to have to wave and smile, and smile and wave inanely, as the bus pulled away to begin its journey, but she realised that it would seem churlish and ungrateful to do otherwise. Now that she was definitely bound for Koidu she wanted nothing more than to be left alone with her thoughts.

For the time being she would have to be patient however, for in this limbo of departure the focus of Neffie's attention alternated between watching her fellow passengers and peering down at Samuel. Her embarrassment each time they made eye contact was greater than his. Each time she looked his way he smiled. She was glad of the distraction each time a passenger stepped aboard, showed his or her ticket to the driver, and then trundled down the aisle to occupy a seat. It meant that she didn't have to direct all her attention towards her benefactor, or simply ignore him for there being nothing of interest to focus on elsewhere.

It was uncharacteristic of Miss Goodwin, but after five to ten minutes waiting for the wheels to turn, five to ten minutes during which time the bus wheels were still perfectly still, she became a little fidgety, impatient for the chariot to depart. After all, there are only so many smiling gestures a woman can make before she begins to feel really stupid, and in any age since Adam and Eve first set foot on earth, that's not a good feeling for a woman to have.

Eventually, and it probably wasn't so long after she had taken her seat as she imagined, Neffie heard a throaty roar as the driver started the engine. The wheels were turning, there was forward motion: they were off. The engine sparking into life and life emerging from limbo prompted Neffie to wave one last time, and then her attention was diverted away from the view through the window by the presence of a young man standing in the aisle. His manner was pleasant as he asked her if she had any objection to his sitting beside her. Perhaps it was because he was such a handsome devil that she acquiesced so promptly; but then again, there was no reason whatsoever why she shouldn't respond positively. The second thing she noticed about the young man standing before her was that he was dressed impeccably in a brown suit and light-tan shiny shoes. His tie struck a slightly discordant note to Neffie's aesthetic eye, but it didn't detract from the overall impression of smartness. He looked as if he could be on his way to a job interview, or a wedding perhaps, or to meet for the first time his girlfriend's parents. If Samuel was expecting to receive one last parting gesture from Neffie he would have been disappointed. She was otherwise distracted as the bus pulled out of the station.

No sooner had Miss Goodwin's fellow passenger become ensconced in the seat beside her than she learned that he was a footballer. In turn the footballer learned that his fellow passenger was from England. The gist of this initial exchange, undertaken as the vehicle motored along East Street, was of greater interest to the young man — he can't have been out of his teens — than it was to Neffie. She happened to be one of those women whose interest in the beautiful game is nil and if her interest were to compete with her knowledge of the said game, the result would be a nil each draw.

The footballer's name was Jeremy. His delight in learning Neffie's country of origin was because he was an ardent follower of Tottenham Hotspur. In his opinion Spurs were the best team playing in the best league; a sentiment no doubt echoed in many a North London household near to White Hart Lane. Jeremy was somewhat disappointed to learn that his travelling companion had little interest for the game he loved, and for the time being the conversation between the pair was put on hold. This silent pause allowed Neffie to look out of the window in order to gain some strong, first-hand impressions of Freetown's bustling streets, an activity to which she applied herself with enthusiasm of an introverted kind. In this regard she was like a girl of quiet disposition on her first school trip.

The bus stopped twice prior to leaving the city limits, and each time nobody got off and more people got on, so that eventually all the seats were taken. The tarmac thoroughfares which had led them out of the centre and towards the suburbs were superseded by the clay road which led into the interior. About as riveting as talk about football, the natural scenery at the outset of the journey wasn't sufficiently spectacular to hold Neffie's interest, so she began to daydream. There were a number of reasons for letting her thoughts turn inwards, for superimposing images of home, of Sebastian stripped to the waist as he turned the soil at the allotment, on to the verdure passing beyond the now closed window. Foremost for making the reality of the present uninspiring was the lugubrious light. The sky hereabouts was overcast, and in observing the lack of contrast in the vast tracts of verdure interspersed here and there by the bungalows which formed the more substantial part of many a village, Neffie was put in mind of Vincent van Gogh heading south to set up his studio in Arles. She understood perfectly why it was that he had gone in search of the light.

In terms of visual interest another factor adding to the dullness of the journey was that for long stretches the vegetation formed a dense, impenetrable screen either side of the road, thwarting any chance of gaining greater perspective, and creating a sensation approaching claustrophobia. The unevenness of the road caused the traveller in a trance-like state to hit her head against the window-frame more than once.

The occasional involuntary head banging didn't prevent Neffie from drifting off to sleep. She only realised that she had succumbed to that unconscious state when she awoke, and initially she had no idea whether her time in the land of nod had been minutes or hours. The vegetation that hurried by was steaming. Evidently it had rained recently, but there was no precipitation at present. There was a distant view of densely forested hills. Their summits formed from undulations seemed to diminish in height as the eye followed their course towards the horizon.

Neffie's first act upon waking was to straighten her posture. "How long did I sleep for?" she enquired at the same time as attempting to eliminate the pain emanating from a tendon in the back of her neck: she did so by applying gentle massage.

"About thirty-seven minutes," Jeremy replied looking at his watch.

Neffie was surprised by the precision. Not yet alert to the humour in Jeremy's answer, she was somewhat disconcerted to think that her slumber had been monitored so carefully, and she gave the footballer a searching look. Seeing that she was still in a state of bewilderment following her forty winks Jeremy sought to reassure. "I did say about thirty-seven minutes," he explained, grinning broadly. "It could have been a few minutes more, and then again it could have been a few minutes less."

Miss Goodwin was relieved to learn that the young man had been teasing her. In her opinion being teased was preferable to being watched unawares. In the next instant, however, the Englishwoman was surprised yet again as she noted the look of horrified astonishment on the footballer's handsome face. The transformation had been sudden. There was an audible buzz that matched the buzz of excitement along Neffie's and Jeremy's side of the bus. For a reason not known to Neffie as yet the bus had slowed to a crawl. The murmur of agitated voices grew steadily louder until it reached a crescendo; one that was subdued, but a crescendo of sorts nonetheless. People craned their necks to get a good look at whatever it was that had created the wave of excitement. Whilst rising to her feet, and leaning first one way and then the other in an attempt to see the object of collective curiosity for herself, Neffie couldn't help but notice the combination of horror and fear on faces that had already seen the worst, but were now turned towards her. Were they imploring her to

143

avert her eyes? Were they ashamed of what she as a guest in their country may see? Many of those people that had been seated on the side of the bus farthest from the spectacle slowly passing on the left had left their seats to stand in the aisle, simply to get a better view.

When Neffie saw the cause of the commotion she was sickened. It was only a fleeting glimpse that she caught, but the image she beheld was no less searing for that. Vanishing from view almost in the instant that she saw him was a man with two arms. Hardly an unusual occurrence you may say, and under normal circumstances not one to shock and horrify teachers and footballers alike.

The reader aspiring to omniscience however, will already be aware that the seemingly unremarkable entity that is a man in possession of two arms has been described as such for effect. What was truly remarkable about the sight which Neffie and her fellow passengers beheld was that the man was carrying his right arm in the hand of the limb which hadn't been severed. His only attire was a pair of blue shorts that had a white stripe down the side. Presumably both sides were the same, though for the reason that only one and the same stripe was ever visible to Neffie and her fellow passengers, in their eyes the existence of the other must remain supposition. To hell with fashion statements however, when it is a tale of arms and the man I tell.

Above the ragged flesh and near to the shoulder of the severed arm a blood-stained bandage served as a tourniquet. An image so horribly surreal, so grotesque, couldn't fail to scorch Miss Goodwin's psyche, and there can be no doubt that of all the sinister events she had witnessed to date, no sighting so quickly lost from view could have left its mark so indelibly. Her soul had been scarred, and she knew that she would be haunted by the image for the rest of her life. For the present however, her visceral response was to feel nausea in the pit of her stomach and jellified weakness in her legs. The two sensations combined compelled her to collapse into her seat. She espied two soldiers, one carrying a first-aid kit emblazoned with the trusted symbol of the red-cross on a white disc, the other carrying a rifle, run in and out of her field of vision. Neffie naturally presumed that they were running to attend to the injured man.

"He's collapsed," a young woman shouted from the back of the bus. She looked to be in her twenties. Evidently she had assumed the responsibility of keeping her fellow passengers informed, whether they wanted to be or not. There was some irony in the fact that the person keeping a close watch on proceedings and reporting back on what she saw was wearing a patch over her left eye. "He's lying in the road," she continued. "He looks like a dying animal."

Two morbidly curious passengers made their way towards the back of the bus to see what they could before it was too late.

"The soldiers have reached him. They're helping him to his feet," imparted an older woman sitting next to the person who had first briefed passengers on the man's condition. Neffie suspected that the two women were mother and daughter.

"I can hardly believe what I've just witnessed," she said, turning to look at Jeremy.

He had remained standing in the aisle, one hand holding on to the top of his own seat, the other, the better to maintain his balance, holding on to the back of the seat in front. The focus of his attention was still on what he could see, over a number of heads and shoulders, of the scene gradually receding through the back window.

"They've just injected him with something," said Jeremy, looking down at Neffie as he spoke. He didn't look into her eyes for long. "One of the soldiers is speaking into his mobile phone," he added, assuming that Neffie was hanging onto his every word.

She was, until the reporting came to an abrupt end when from her seat near the back a tall woman with a broad back suddenly emerged to block Jeremy's view completely. He sat down as the bus came to a halt.

Whether sitting or standing, passengers at the back of the bus didn't have to wait long to become as enlightened as the driver and passengers at the front regarding the cause of the hold-up. The driver was responding to an external command when he flicked the switch to open the door.

He remained seated as the door opened and a soldier with a rifle stepped aboard. After inquiring and being told of the bus's destination, the soldier made his way towards the rear where he ordered the only passenger still standing — the woman who had blocked Jeremy's view — to sit.

After peering through the rear window to check that nothing was about to explode in that direction, or simply to see what all the fuss had been about, the soldier turned about to keep a watchful eye on the majority of passengers. Evidently he didn't consider the people sitting on the back row behind him to be a threat. Its barrel pointing along the aisle, he held the rifle at the ready. Neffie assumed that it would be loaded and ready to fire. A short time after the first soldier established control, reinforcements arrived. They comprised an officer, and a second soldier armed with a rifle. The officer was armed with a pistol which he kept in its holster.

What struck Neffie most about the military men in their midst, was the lack of uniformity in their uniforms. The camouflage jacket and trousers worn by the soldier who had first boarded made him highly conspicuous in his present environment. The soft, broad brimmed hat he was wearing was patterned similarly. It gave the impression that the wearer believed his head less likely to be shot at than that of his comrade, who was wearing a steel helmet. The second soldier's garb was drab for being olive green throughout. Of the three it was the officer who looked least ready to fight a battle for wearing smart khaki shirt and trousers, and on his head a scarlet and black forage cap edged with gold. An audible hush, so to speak, could be heard ever since the military had assumed control.

The presence of the soldiers prompted Neffie to think of Sebastian, for the obvious reason that he had been a soldier, and although she fleetingly wondered what he would be up to at that moment, of greater consideration was whether he had performed a similar duty when serving Queen and country in Northern Ireland, and if he had, how he would have appeared to people travelling from Belfast to Armagh, or Fermanagh, or Londonderry

It was then that Neffie's ruminations were interrupted by a military manoeuvre which lightened her mood considerably. It's a widely held belief that the words 'military' and 'efficiency' are naturally contiguous just as 'forlorn' and 'hope' or 'dismal' and 'failure'. It so happens therefore, that when an event occurs contrary to the expectation to which the pairing of words refers, the effect created is likely, at the very least, to be one of surprise, and may even engender a reaction which is quite effusive. Imagine all the soldiers in the 'forlorn-hope' surviving the frontal assault, and it's not difficult to imagine a 'magnificent failure'.

The little fiasco that humoured Neffie involved the officer turning in the aisle too abruptly. The idea which had seemingly just occurred to him was to interrogate the driver, that is to say, for the sake of making his intention appear less Draconian, ask him a few questions prior to retracing his steps in order to scrutinise each passenger's face. The comical aspect of this hardly complex military operation was that upon turning, the officer inadvertently bumped into the soldier who, as escort, had been following hard on his heels. For a few unmilitary moments they became entangled — a same sex pair, looking as if they were about to dance. Naturally the officer rebuked the hapless individual. The soldier several ranks below him had failed to anticipate his sudden about turn. Once free to move of his own accord, in order to let his superior pass the soldier stepped aside as best he could.

A dark thought had occurred to Neffie whilst watching the military two-step, a possible consequence of which, were she to act on its purport, would be the break-up of her relationship with Sebastian. Some thoughts, those that are never expressed, are destined to remain a mystery.

For the main the passengers continued to sit in silence, as if a spell had been cast over them. That spell was undoubtedly a collective disinclination to provoke the men with guns. Of course, everyone knew that the men confronting them were soldiers, and everyone knows that soldiers adhere to a strict code of conduct, but evidently the general consensus, one that to all intents and purposes had been communicated telepathically, was that it was better to be safe than sorry. The exceptions to the widespread hush were the cries of a baby demanding to be fed, and a man trying but failing to suppress a cough.

After giving an order for his erstwhile dancing partner to take up a position adjacent to the driver and keep watch from there, the officer made his way down the aisle alone. His progress was slow. His face was expressionless. His large brown eyes missed nothing as they scanned to left and right in keeping with a gentle sideways motion of his head. Scrutinising the faces he looked down upon, literally if not metaphorically, his actions formed a sequence repeated several times over.

Prior to his arrival at where Neffie and Jeremy were sitting bolt upright in the hope of being given a pat on the head for good behaviour,

147

the officer stopped only to talk to the mother of the crying baby. "Why don't you feed your child?" he said, in a tone which implied that she wasn't being a very good mother.

"I shall," the mother replied, "just as soon as we are left in peace."

Reassured that the baby wasn't going to starve, the officer moved on without challenging the mother further. For being the only white person on the bus Neffie had a premonition that she was going to be singled out for some attention — just how much she was about to discover. In the event, sensing that the officer was about to address her, Neffie took the initiative. "Good afternoon," she said, unaffectedly.

The greeting elicited a mute response, its reciprocation being nothing more than a barely perceptible nod of the head. Neffie noticed, as the officer leaned forward slightly, that there were three stars on each of his epaulettes, though not being an expert in military insignia meant that she could only guess at the rank they designated. She also couldn't help but notice, following her pronouncement, the faces that had turned to look in her direction.

"What is your name?" enquired the officer, in a tone no less overbearing than that which he had used when questioning the mother.

"My name is Nefertiti Goodwin," she answered, "Miss Nefertiti Goodwin."

"You are British?" said the captain, intoning his words in such a way that they couldn't fail to be construed as a question.

"I am indeed," replied Neffie.

For the reason that her own antecedents and those of her fellow countrymen were responsible for colonising much of the planet, and aware that not everyone in the colonised territories had thought it a good idea, Neffie considered apologising there and then for the legacy she had inherited. Her attitude in this regard was in marked contrast to that voiced by Sebastian, whose pride in his country's achievements was, he believed, instrumental in forming his own character. It was a contentious issue between them, one which Neffie dealt with on the basis that Seb was entitled to his opinion and she was entitled to hers; yet though he was thousands of miles away his influence must have been at work when she chose not to be in any way self-deprecatory, and not to apologise for the sins of the fathers. She decided that the staccato questioning was best responded to in a similar vein.

"You have your passport?"

"Yes; would you like to see it?" said Neffie sharply.

The question escaped her as if of its own volition. Contemporaneously her hand made a move to undo the left breast pocket of the denim shirt she was wearing. She didn't complete the action.

"That will not be necessary," said the captain upon seeing the Englishwoman's positive reaction. "I would like to know what your mission is in Koidu."

"My mission!" exclaimed Neffie, astonished to hear her trip described as such.

The thought that her intentions in the country were perceived rather differently in certain quarters from the aims she had in mind alarmed her more than a little. She envisaged being arrested as a spy and having to spend the foreseeable future in prison. Needless to say the prospect didn't appeal.

"Yes; what is your mission? Why have you come to Koidu?"

Neffie glanced at a passenger's face turned to look over her shoulder at her, but if the teacher was looking for moral support she found only a blank expression. Miss Goodwin took a deep breath as she gave some thought as to how she should reply.

"I am a teacher by profession," she began calmly, "and I've come to Sierra Leone to offer my expertise in whatever way would be most useful." Evidently the time of quick-fire questions and answers had ended. "I'm not here on a mission as such, at least not as I understand the word. I just want to help people the best way I can, and I've come to Koidu specifically because I have a letter of introduction to Father O'Brien. He runs the Catholic Mission there. Do you know him?"

At this point Jeremy piped up, thereby adding a third dimension to the conversation. "I know Father O'Brien," he interjected. "I've known him since I was knee high to a monkey. Everybody in Koidu knows Father O'Brien."

Jeremy's youthful input served to lighten the atmosphere. The army officer's previously uncompromising expression softened a little. Unfortunately the transformation proved transient.

"Koidu isn't such a peaceful place at present. You would be wise to return to Freetown at the earliest opportunity," advised the captain strongly.

They were the last words Neffie heard him speak. After signalling to his men that the bus was clear, the soldiers made to disembark, the officer pausing only to exchange a few words with the driver. The driver turned to stare at Neffie for a time, giving her good cause to think that she had been the subject of the officer's parting comments.

Miss Goodwin's valedictory words, though uttered loudly enough for Jeremy to hear, were meant to be a short soliloquy.

"From what I've seen already you're probably right," she said, and then again more softly, "you're probably right."

Chapter Eleven
Miss Margai's Misadventure

It's not science fiction to state that time slows down or speeds up depending on how fast one body moves relative to another. According to Einstein's special theory of relativity a twin travelling at a speed approaching the speed of light would age more slowly than the alter ego who hadn't left his or her house that morning. The pudding is proved digestible by highly accurate chronometers aboard satellites orbiting earth, the timepieces gaining thirty-eight micro-seconds per day. If such a startling effect can occur to a physical entity hurtling through space, it hardly makes for a revelation to appreciate that in the noetic sphere writers and readers often achieve a similar effect, and in the comfort of home to boot. It is certainly thus in the tale of Miss Nefertiti Goodwin's adventures relative to Miss Shirley Margai's, and of Samuel Massequoi's participation relative to Sebastian's.

In marked contrast, therefore, to the days that have passed in Neffie's African odyssey, hours have slipped by since Shirley and Sebastian first entered the Captain Cook Inn. Between sips of coffee the journalist first pondered over and then summarised events as told to him by Miss Margai so far.

"So after a great deal of hassle you and your mother managed to bring back Brian's body for a funeral in Luxborough, but that still doesn't explain how you came to be injured, to end up walking with a limp."

By now most of the lunchtime patrons had departed, leaving behind the acceptable detritus that is scraps of food on otherwise empty plates and the last dregs of drink in otherwise empty glasses. There was an air of closing-time at hand as a couple of members of staff set about clearing things away. In point of fact the doors of the Captain Cook Inn wouldn't be locked for at least another nine hours; that would be around midnight. The present effort being put into making things ship-shape again was a tried and tested procedure, one that made good use of a quiet interlude prior to the next numerous influxes of customers, around six o'clock.

"What a weird affair that was," said Shirley, "the funeral I mean. For Brian's friends and family it all passed quite smoothly as far as I could tell, but what made it feel strange for Mother and me was that neither of us had been amongst so many white people before, and to be the focus of so much attention when we were already feeling overwhelmed with grief... well it was difficult for being so strange, do you know what I mean?"

"I can imagine. Were people nasty to you?"

For knowing the stamp of Luxborough people he felt that Shirley and her mother's recent funereal experience wouldn't have been daunting because of blatant prejudice; surely not in this day and age, and given the circumstances. That said, he had asked the question because he couldn't be absolutely certain that there wasn't an ignoramus or two in the town.

"People couldn't have been more helpful," announced Shirley emphatically. "To cut a long story short, and this gives you some idea as to just how helpful and friendly people were, my mother decided to stay."

"I'm guessing that Brian left your mother well provided for," said Seb, well aware that the distribution of a deceased person's estate can lead to bitter inter-familial arguments which in some cases, to the detriment of everyone concerned, are never resolved. In dealing with an estate of substance the absence of a last will and testament makes that unwished-for outcome all the more likely. Furthermore in this context, as a cause of jealousy Seb wondered whether the racial element had raised its ugly head.

"She was fortunate in that she was the beneficiary of my stepfather's will, which was only right and proper, and as far as I'm aware nobody raised any objections. In addition to my mother being entitled to receive half his company pension there was a life assurance policy. We're not talking huge amounts here, enough to ensure that my mother can keep a roof over her head, pay the bills, not go hungry in her old age."

"I'm glad to hear it," said Sebastian, accompanying his words with a slight nod of approval. Then he added, "All this sounds great as far as your mother is concerned, assuming that by this time she had come to terms with the suddenness of Brian's death, but what I really want to know is how has what happened to your mother following the bereavement impacted upon you?"

"That's just what I was coming to," rejoined Shirley, somewhat tersely. "In addition to the cash sum my mother received, most of which she spent on furnishings for the house here, and to the income she's guaranteed, there's also the house in Koidu. After much discussion we decided that it should be for my benefit. She didn't make a fuss about it, it's not her style, but she believes, as do I, that eventually the killings and maiming will cease, and then the fort, that's what we call it, would make an ideal home for my husband and I, to raise a family."

"But I thought…"

"Not that I have a husband you understand," resumed Miss Margai, correctly anticipating the gist of Sebastian's interruption, "and there aren't any contenders, not in Sierra Leone," she added, significantly.

Sebastian's response to this intelligence was to remain silent, and to try to see the future — his future — in the dregs that remained in the bottom of his cup. Finding that nothing was revealed he could draw no conclusions. Evidently coffee was no substitute for the real thing — tea-leaves — when it came to fortune-telling. If Miss Margai had wanted Sebastian to communicate the effect of her recent pronouncement upon his psyche, she had to be frustrated by his choosing to remain obstinately mute. It was left to her to resume the conversation.

"Where was I?" she mused as the raucous voices of teenage boys alighting from the school bus only yards from where the pair were seated momentarily disturbed the speaker's train of thought. "Ah yes… I was telling you about the house in Koidu. It was where I lived when I wasn't working and living in Freetown. It so happened that I was staying at the fort when there was a particularly nasty outbreak of violence. The rebels tried to take over the town, and there was lots of shooting. Some of my friends and neighbours were killed. For me the nightmare, except it wasn't a nightmare because it was real, for me the horror began when the fighting came to our street. Can you imagine it, people you have shared a meal or a drink with being shot dead outside your front door?"

"It's not the sort of thing I would expect to see in Yatton," Seb responded glibly, "although the village does have its moments."

He was thinking of the time when a couple of crooks raided the post office and the village subsequently became the focus of police activity as they whizzed about in their cars. No shots were fired. Mainly the 'moments' Seb was referring to involved the rowdiness of lads returning home from a session in the pub on a Friday or Saturday night. If these young men of eighteen or nineteen were intent on committing murder it was invariably with regard to what they could do to a song 'sung' out of tune at the top of their voices. Any assault, therefore, was upon the ears; the only resulting deaths were an end to many a dream.

"The short answer is I really can't," said Seb laconically.

"Can't really what?" enquired Miss Margai curtly.

"I can't really imagine anyone being shot dead outside my front door."

"Are these finished with?" asked the strikingly attractive waitress, reaching for the rim of the saucer that supported Seb's empty cup as she spoke.

"Not yet," said Shirley, instinctively she moved her hand as if to create a defensive barrier against any attempt to remove the cup which had yet to touch her lips.

Evidently as a stimulus to conversation the coffee that was Miss Margai's post-prandial beverage wasn't a necessity. Indeed, up until the time that she became alert to the possibility that her cup was about to be taken away, she had quite forgotten it was there. For her part the waitress, feeling that she had interrupted a conversation of some importance, retired gracefully, one cup and one saucer held in one hand.

"Well I'm sure you can imagine that if people can see that your house resembles a fort and is able, therefore, to provide a much greater degree of security than any other building nearby, in turbulent times they're going to want to come and stay."

"I can," said Sebastian.

"You can what?" enquired Shirley.

"I can imagine that they would want to be where they feel safest," Seb replied.

"It's only natural," Miss Margai confirmed, "and so when the shooting came to our street my house became a safe haven for at least a dozen of my neighbours as well as myself…"

"An instance of thirteen being a lucky number I hope," Seb interrupted.

"At least that was the idea, but the house didn't feel much like a fortress given the furore going on outside," Miss Margai resumed, choosing to ignore Seb's interruption, "and that's despite the numerous locks and bolts. Thank goodness we had them though. We spent what seemed like hours listening to sporadic bursts of gunfire... sometimes quite distant, at other times seemingly coming from as close as I am to you right now but with the wall of the house between us. There was also lots of shouting, harsh, male voices directing fire towards a target or warning of where they could expect shots to be fired at them. At the height of the gun-battle we sat quite still trying to work out whether it was going to end any time soon."

"Where were you hiding... inside the house I mean?"

"In the living-room. It's the largest room and seemed the safest place, particularly after we had used the furniture to make a kind of inner sanctum. All thirteen of us cowered together in a little enclave formed by a few chairs, a wooden chest and a couple of bookcases. We thought that the books would provide good protection against stray bullets that might come our way." Shirley pondered for a while before giving voice to a maxim she had just thought of. "If the pen is mightier than the sword," she said, "the book may be armour against the bullet."

"I like that," said Sebastian. "That's really clever. It has an Oxford Book of Quotations ring about it. I'll make sure I put it in when I come to do my piece, that's if you've no objection of course."

"Of course not," said Shirley prior to resuming her story. "We had closed the window shutters, and because there was no electricity we sat or lay in near darkness. I think for the entire time my eyes were focused on a crack in the shutters which let in light. It was no more than a millimetre wide, but I became fixated on the idea that it would lead to our whereabouts being discovered."

Shirley paused to moisten her mouth. She did so by taking her first and last sip of the coffee that had nearly been taken away. The liquid proved efficacious, but being stone-cold she reacted to the taste with disgust prior to pushing the saucer and the cup she had put back in place to one side.

"It was obviously a terrifying experience," Seb commented, stating the obvious.

"The really scary moments were when the rebels tried to enter the house. Not surprisingly, just as any civilised person would (the irony wasn't lost on Seb), they tried the front door. When they discovered that it wouldn't open, and that despite their demands we weren't going to open it for them, they shot at the lock with an automatic weapon. They still didn't manage to gain entry — praise be to Brian."

"How many of them were there?" Sebastian enquired, the article he was thinking of writing uppermost in mind.

"I can't say for certain, but I had an idea that there were four or five intent on breaking in. That's the impression I got from the amount of noise they were making. For a time they either kicked at the door or used something as a battering ram, but still it held. Thwarted in that ambition, they next set about smashing in the windows and shutters. That was when panic took hold amongst our group. One of the women, a close friend of mine as it happens, screamed at the sight of a rifle butt shattering the shutter. That was replaced by an even more sinister sight, the gun barrel. Rather than remain in hiding where we were, my friend, still screaming, ran towards the stairs. I expected her to be shot, but luckily for her she wasn't. I don't think that my friend had a plan in mind when she ran up the stairs, or had any conscious idea of what she was doing for that matter. The others followed. It's amazing how quickly it can spread, panic that is. It's as if everyone, or nearly everyone, succumbs at more or less at the same time to a contagion that undermines completely their ability to act rationally. In extreme cases…, like that of my friend, it develops into wild hysteria. I must admit I felt the urge to run, to be with the others. You may think I'm deluding myself when I say that although I did run to join them, in the end, I didn't panic. I was the last person to leave our hiding place. The simple fact is I didn't want to be left alone."

At this point in the proceedings the door leading from the street opened, rather tentatively it seemed, causing Shirley once again to stop speaking as she focused her attention on who was about to enter. Sebastian's attention was similarly diverted. It intrigued the two journalists that for seemingly an age, at least twenty seconds, nobody appeared. The pair seated within continued to watch and wait. Eventually

156

the reason for the delay became apparent as a little girl with an angelic face entered alone, a young adventurer making an early journey of discovery. After deftly closing the door behind her she stepped into the centre of the room to get her bearings. She responded to Shirley's and Sebastian's quizzical look with a mischievous peal of laughter. Whether the no doubt anxious mother had heard and recognised this expression of her daughter's mirth the journalists wouldn't ever know for certain. They presumed such an eventuality likely when, before the child had stopped giggling, the door opened once again to reveal a woman who in a scolding manner said, "Come out of there this minute, Jessica." Jessica did as she was told.

The charming interlude over, to become a mundane memory in four people's lives, Shirley returned to recounting her tale of horror, but only after the journalists smiled at each other in silent recognition of how they thought life ought to be lived. That silent exchange contained an entire philosophy which had to do with our time on earth proving to be worthwhile for being a continuum of pleasing experiences rather than a series of dramatic and needlessly tragic martyrdoms.

"Just as there's sometimes method in madness it turned out that there was method in our panic," continued Miss Margai, "because by fleeing upstairs we would be able to exit the house by the fire escape… another of Brian's innovations."

"All praise to Brian," Seb interrupted.

"All praise indeed," said Shirley. "As far as we knew the rebels hadn't made their way round to the back."

The existence of the fire-escape prompted Sebastian's next comment. "I'm surprised they didn't try to smoke you out," he said.

Shirley opened her eyes wide in acknowledgement of her interlocutor's percipience. "It was the smell of petrol that really got us moving, that and the warning that if we didn't give ourselves up within two minutes, they would burn down the house. I think they must have poured petrol through the window with the smashed in shutter. We took them at their word, and because no one wanted to be incinerated, we didn't need to hold a discussion about what to do next."

"Don't tell me," said Seb, "you left by the fire-escape."

Seb would be the first to admit that there were times when he liked to hear the sound of his own voice, usually when there was little chance of his being contradicted. It was a characteristic which often led, as exemplified by his most recent pronouncement, to his stating the obvious.

"We left in more or less an orderly manner by the fire-escape," said Shirley, determined to continue her tale as she wished to tell it. "I was the last to leave. It wasn't that I wanted to show how brave I was, I don't think I am, but I did feel responsible for making sure that nobody was left behind, which is understandable seeing as it was effectively my house we were escaping from."

"You had taken on a mantel similar to that of a sea-captain, when in the course of duty he is last to leave his sinking ship."

This comment was hardly predictable, and it was far from obvious, but it served to confirm a certain characteristic: even to Sebastian's ears it sounded pompous.

"Absolutely," Shirley responded, feeling pleasantly flattered by the comparison.

"So what happened next?" Seb enquired earnestly, sensing that the climax of the story was drawing near.

"Everyone trooped into the courtyard. I know that sounds posh, but it's quite a large space at the back of the house and attractive for being nicely appointed. There's a yard door leading into an alley. Fortunately, though I accept that it could be seen as a bad oversight, it wasn't locked. Everyone exited through it, everyone except me that is. I stopped in my tracks at the foot of the fire-escape when I heard a rebel fighter cock his weapon. That's what you have to do before pulling the trigger isn't it?" Shirley didn't give Seb a chance to reply. "Then I heard him say, and it struck me as strange that he didn't raise his voice at all, I heard him say, 'Stop or I'll shoot'. His voice sounded familiar. I couldn't see him and he couldn't see me, but through the open doorway I saw a few of the others put up their hands to surrender."

"Did anyone manage to get away?"

"My friend did. It's ironic isn't it that the person who was first to panic when we were hiding behind the bookcases should be the one to get away?"

"So what did you do?" said Seb, emphasising the pronoun.

"Thinking quickly, as I had to, there seemed only two practicable options open to me. The first and the easiest would have been to follow in the footsteps of the others and surrender myself to the mercy of the rebels. It might have been the easiest course of action, but I had no idea as to how well or badly I would be treated by my captors, or what fate awaited the others. My second option, the one I chose, was to climb over the side wall which separated my mother's property from the house next door and hope that I wouldn't be noticed."

"And were you... noticed I mean?"

"It was a good idea in principle, but it turned out badly for me in practice. When I look back it all seems so pathetic. After climbing up onto the wall — being nine feet high that took all my strength — I jumped. If it had been soil or grass on the other side it wouldn't have been so bad, but it was concrete, and I landed so hard that I couldn't prevent myself from letting out a whelp of pain, and as if that wasn't enough by way of advertising my presence, I clattered into a box of empty beer bottles. That was when I fell to the ground after losing my balance on landing. I suppose I was fortunate in that none of them smashed and cut me to shreds."

"And when you tried to get to your feet you found that you weren't the same person that you were prior to making your leap of faith?" questioned Seb, instilling into the conversation a slant with which he had some affinity.

"I didn't move for quite some time. I just lay there, listening all the while, not sure yet whether the noise I had made was inevitably going to lead to my downfall."

"I thought that that was something you had accomplished already," Seb joked.

Miss Margai's sense of effrontery was momentary in that it lasted only until she realised that Seb's comment was an example of British humour.

"It seemed a foregone conclusion that it would," Shirley responded unabashed. "After what seemed like an age in which nothing happened, one of the rebels peered into the yard and saw me lying on the ground. By this time I was in considerable pain. He approached with caution, as if I was still capable of pulling out a weapon that I had kept hidden and blowing his head off. Eventually he must have made up his mind that I was nothing more dangerous than a poor defenceless woman who posed no threat to him whatsoever. That was when he threw caution to the wind, that's an expression I heard for the first time only last week, when I was telling this story to one of my mother's friends, he threw caution to the wind and came straight towards me, his rifle no longer aimed directly at my head. The point of aim moved less menacingly to about the centre of my chest. Judging by the expression on his face we recognised each other more or less in the same instant. It was the light of knowing that lit up his face, and no doubt a similar radiance emanated from mine. Unless my memory was playing tricks on me, I identified my captor as a, how shall I put it, let's say a friendly acquaintance whom I hadn't seen in years. The last time we had been in each other's company was in the village to the east of Koidu where we used to live. That must have been six or seven years ago. Anyway, I'm as convinced as I can be that it was our recognition of each other as former friends that saved my bacon. That's another expression I've just learned, saved my bacon. Funny, isn't it?" The fact that she moved swiftly on made for another rhetorical question. "Gesticulating with his gun barrel he urged me to get to my feet. I tried to do just that, but as soon as I put any weight on my injured leg it collapsed beneath me. The pain was excruciating. My captor looked on sympathetically. Then he made himself useful by searching for a suitable stick for me to use as support. The improvised crutch which came to hand was an old yard brush. Its head was almost devoid of bristles. In order to help me to my feet he grasped my arm, and for a few seconds I felt as if I was in the company of a lifelong friend rather than a man who, only moments before, had threatened to shoot me. When he saw that I was able to make some headway he ordered me to go. 'Go! Go away and hide' he urged, to which I responded, 'Go where?' His reply was no help at all."

"What did he say?" questioned Seb, for no other reason than to allow Shirley to catch her breath.

These memories being relived were evidently still raw, and the combination of pain and fear Shirley experienced at the time were manifesting themselves as post-traumatic stress disorder in the present, as evidenced by the tenseness in her body and the speed at which latterly she spoke.

"He said, 'Go anywhere, just get away from here as quick as you can,' and then, as if I was in need of encouragement, he warned, 'I don't want to have to shoot you.'"

"So what did you do next... where did you go?"

"I hobbled off into the bush, sat down under a tree and cried. I cried because I didn't want the rebels to destroy my mother's house to leave me without a home. I cried because of the gnawing pain in my leg and my inability to walk. I cried because I didn't know what had happened to my friends and neighbours and I didn't want them to come to harm. But mainly I cried because of what was happening in my country, for the fact that it was being torn apart."

"You had a lot to contend with," said Seb in a sympathetic tone. "I'm not surprised that you had a good cry... all that fear and emotion had to be released somehow."

He hadn't recognised that he had made a distinction between the specific and the general where none existed.

"Eventually I began to see things in a positive light," said Shirley, her demeanour relaxing a little as she responded to the inner illumination of her words. "Come on Shirley,' I said to myself, 'you can't sit here all day.' I reasoned that I was really rather fortunate in that I hadn't been killed or badly wounded. I hadn't been raped. My friends and neighbours might have been released without harm, and as far as I knew my house was still standing. Using arms, crutch and a handy branch as much as my legs, slowly, painfully, I got back on my feet. Levering myself forward I became quite adept at walking without the foot of my injured leg touching the ground. I was making for the nearest road, but I was picked up by an army patrol, so I got a free ride back into town. They had regained control by this time, which meant that things had quietened down."

It suddenly appeared as if Miss Margai had grown tired of talking when she looked at her watch and exclaimed at the lateness of the hour. For the present her tale of adventure, injury, and salvation as told to

Sebastian had come to an end, and he followed her example as she made moves to leave the Captain Cook Inn. Rising to his feet Sebastian thought, "What a hell of a story!" It undoubtedly was.

Chapter Twelve
At the Catholic Mission

It was a tired and apprehensive Miss Goodwin who knocked at the arch-shaped door of the Catholic Mission. Behind its secretive walls was where she had planned to stay and work, for most of the time she was to spend in Sierra Leone. Everything depended upon the spiritual leader in charge, be he a bishop near the top, or a humble father lighting the way from a lower rung of the ecclesiastical ladder, being amenable to the itinerant teacher's aims and wishes. Presently Neffie was in two minds as to whether she should stay or leave the next day.

Who could blame her when the sight she had witnessed on the way had been far more extreme in its horror than she had been expecting, this notwithstanding the warnings she had been given prior to leaving Freetown? The images implanted in her psyche were having a profoundly adverse effect on her spirits. In addition to the obvious horror of seeing an amputee carrying his amputated limb were the sights which were merely unsightly. In this regard were the numerous tracts of land spoiled completely, the legacy of redundant diamond mines replete with stagnant pools and rusting bits of machinery.

Taking it in turns to occupy Neffie's mind, the two unsettling images vied for supremacy, not only for the remainder of the time spent on the bus after she had observed that which she wished she hadn't, as well as that which she merely would rather not, but also during the journey by taxi from the centre of town to the Mission. For being just over a mile and devoid of hold-ups, the final leg of that day's travelling had taken only a few minutes. On any other occasion, given the short distance involved, Miss Goodwin would have probably opted to walk, but because she was encumbered with her bag, and because she didn't feel completely safe and was obviously unfamiliar with the route, she was glad of the ride. Furthermore, she hadn't objected to being accompanied in the taxi by Jeremy, Koidu's star footballer.

Waiting patiently for her first sequence of knocks to be answered, Neffie's attention turned towards the taxi. In the darkness the vehicle's presence was mainly revealed by only one working headlight. In compliance with Neffie's instructions, its engine running, the taxi also waited. Miss Goodwin had thought it a wise precaution not to chance being left stranded in what to her was the middle of nowhere. Standing a yard behind Neffie, like a faithful escort whose only wish is to see the lady he is escorting safely ensconced, Jeremy also waited.

After an interval which seemed like an age, but which in reality was no more than half a minute, half a minute in which Neffie's anxiety became almost tangible, the suspicion entered her head that the Mission was deserted. Naturally she knocked again, demonstrating greater determination for her knuckled raps to be heard. In the event her second summons was hardly necessary. Neffie had just lowered her hand when she heard from within a bolt being withdrawn. Seconds later, the large heavy door having been cagily opened — and who but a fearless man of faith would have dared to test the darkness? — Neffie was astonished to find that standing before her was a famous actor, or so she at first thought. Light from the paraffin lamp the Father was holding only partially illuminated his face. Holding the lamp in his right hand it was that side of his body which could be seen more clearly. The other side of his thin, wiry frame wasn't in complete darkness however, for at the extremity of its illumination the taxi's headlight revealed something of the seemingly frail and under-nourished man who was getting on in years. This diminutive figure was also back lit by candles burning, more or less steadily, in the room set back ten yards from which he had emerged.

"Father O'Brien?" enquired Neffie above the noise of the taxi's idling engine.

"Yes..." came the tentative reply, and then, after a short pause to allow, so to speak, the penny to drop, he added, "Ah yes, you must be the young lady from England who wrote to me a while ago stating that you intended to come to Koidu to put your skills as a teacher to good use. Miss..."

The Father's memory failed him as he tried hard to remember the name printed above the signature at the foot of the letter in question, the letter indubitably written by the woman standing before him.

"Miss Nefertiti Goodwin, though everyone calls me Neffie," the teacher informed, at the same time as she offered her hand to the man who, to judge by his accent, couldn't have hailed from anywhere but the Emerald Isle.

"Yes... yes... that's it... Miss Nefertiti Goodwin," Father O'Brien responded prior, in order to complete the introductions, to passing the lantern from his right hand to his left. "You'll have to excuse me for not being able to bring your name readily to mind... my memory is still the well-oiled machine it once was, it just doesn't work as well as it once did." He chuckled at a bibulous thought. "I remember thinking at the time... when I first read your letter... what an unusual name. I was put in mind of the pyramids and the death mask of Tutankhamun."

"I've grown to like it," said Neffie, "it gives me a feeling of longevity."

The ageing Irish missionary and the young British teacher shook hands. It was a gentle handshake, Father O'Brien being mindful of Neffie's femininity whilst she was mindful of his ageing bones.

"And here's Jeremy, whom I believe you know," said Neffie, suddenly remembering that she wasn't alone and, upon relinquishing Father O'Brien's hand, turning to bring her friendly footballer into the frame, doing so by a sweeping motion of her arm from behind his back.

"Oh! Everybody in Koidu knows Jeremy," said Father O'Brien, advancing to give the young man a friendly punch on the upper arm. "I've known you since you were this high, haven't I, Jeremy?" To show just how high, Father O'Brien held his free hand palm down at a level midway between his knee and his hip. "Have you still got hopes of playing for Manchester United?" the Irishman teased, in full knowledge of the footballer's true allegiance.

"He knows that the team I most earnestly wish to play for is not Manchester United," said Jeremy, charming Neffie with the pompous innocence of his denial. Indeed, she was so charmed that the horrors of the journey were temporarily expunged from her mind.

"And to think that I always considered you to be a bright young man," said Father O'Brien, continuing the vein of playful banter.

These cordial exchanges were rudely interrupted when the taxi driver tooted his horn. Evidently his patience had expired. Every face gathered at the Mission gate turned to look at the driver whose face, hidden in darkness behind the glare of the solitary headlamp, couldn't be discerned, and every face other than the driver's revealed a frown of disapproval. Nobody was in any doubt that he wanted to be on his way; but first he wanted payment for work done.

It was Miss Goodwin who took command of the situation. "If you tell the driver where you want to go, I'll settle the fare," said Neffie to Jeremy, fully expecting to pay the equivalent of a journey back to Freetown for a trip which in reality would be a couple of miles.

In the event Neffie subverted the exaggerated distance she had envisaged having to pay for by handing the driver a note of relatively high denomination while at the same time instructing him to keep the change.

After watching the car with one passenger and one working tail-light drive off in the direction of town, Father O'Brien made a move to pick up the single item of luggage which Neffie had earlier placed on the ground, but he put on such a display of creaking mobility as he reached down for the bag that Neffie felt compelled to beat him to it. To do so she moved at a speed she rarely aspired to, and therefore rarely achieved, whether it be in the numbing cold of a British winter or in Sierra Leone's tropical heat. Despite starting second, however, Neffie's hand closed around the floppy fabric that formed the handle ahead of her rival. It was a race which Father O'Brien was pleased to lose, and having lost it, upon straightening his back he seemed to regain some youthful suppleness. No sooner had the car exhaust fumes dissipated than the air regained its tropical fragrance, and before the sound of the taxi's engine had all but faded, a familiar chorus of cicadas could be heard.

"You really have chosen to come at a difficult time," said the Father as he led the way into the Mission grounds.

"So it would seem," said Neffie, thinking of the numerous warnings she had been given and that it would probably have been a wise move to have taken greater heed of them. "I would like you to tell me just how bad things are."

"In the morning will be soon enough," the Father responded, "but I will say here and now that you ought to give some serious thought as to the wisdom of staying in Koidu. I thought of writing to you," the Father

166

continued, stepping aside to let his guest into the sanctuary prior to closing the heavy door behind her.

"I think I already know what you would have written," the teacher said. "You would have tried to put me off coming wouldn't you?"

"Sorry... what did you say?" asked Father O'Brien absent-mindedly, his faculties suddenly focused elsewhere.

In the action of stooping to push home the lower of two bolts Father O'Brien had paused to listen. At first Neffie thought he was merely demonstrating the inflexibility of his ageing bones and muscles, but then she too identified a sound similar to that which had distracted her host for being out of the ordinary, and menacing to boot.

"That was a shot wasn't it... a shot from a gun?" Miss Goodwin enquired.

Several more shots rang out spasmodically. The sequence of percussions had originated at some considerable distance, and for that reason neither Neffie nor Father O'Brien would have described them as bangs. It was intriguing to note that the sound of distant gunfire produced a more anxious expression on the Father's face, a face yet illuminated by the lantern, than it did on the countenance of his guest. Consequently Neffie, in the belief that Father O'Brien had some inkling, waited for him to reveal what the shots may portend.

"They could have been," he replied, initially providing his interlocutor with the explanation he believed to be true, but then, perhaps for wanting to allay any fear such an eventuality may cause, he added, "but it could just as easily have been that old taxi back-firing."

In an attempt to instil peace of mind, to convey the message that although there may be much cause for concern there was no point in worrying, the priest smiled at his guest. Even in the dim light cast by the lamp Neffie was able to discern that the smile was forced. The Father turned and led the way across a few yards of open ground before he stepped up onto a sheltered walkway the like of which Neffie had seen on many a western film on television. Several of the boards creaked as she stepped on them, but none proved so rotten that it broke beneath her weight. Her eyes were focused mainly on the heels of Father O'Brien's trainers and the frayed hems of his light-blue jeans. She couldn't be absolutely certain, but she thought his shirt to be of similar hue. Miss

Goodwin had formed the opinion that her holy host was dressed casually because he hadn't been expecting visitors, and that he had been taking time off from liaising with God. Ultimately this last thought struck her as being silly when she reasoned that a man, or woman for that matter, doesn't need a cassock or mitre to commune with the Almighty.

A surprising aspect of the domain she had just entered was that thus far Neffie hadn't noticed a single artefact or icon which typically symbolised the Catholic Faith. When travelling extensively in southern Europe she had found it unsettling to come upon, by the side of the road, a weeping Madonna or an agonised figure representing the crucified Christ. Upon entering buildings other than churches she had found their presence morbidly funereal. In her present surroundings, however, she perceived nothing of the kind. There were the candles of course, but in a domicile without electricity the purpose they served was more practical than votive. For the reason that the combined light from candles and lantern wasn't all-illuminating, it didn't pass Neffie by that she might have missed seeing a solemn crucifix lurking in the shadows here, or a kneeling Madonna there.

Neffie's first impression of her new residence was that it was a place of austere simplicity. Most prominent among her shadowy visualisations were a dozen or so huts built around a quadrangle. To judge from the little she could clearly perceive, and the dark silhouettes discernible against the lighter sky, there was little uniformity in the design of the buildings. Holding the lamp as high as he could in order for the light emitted to be more widely spread, Father O'Brien led his guest across the quadrangle to one of the huts. Here and there clumps of grass had sprung out of the compressed earth. Miss Goodwin's accommodation for the foreseeable future appeared to be in the smallest of the huts, but because the guest room she was shown was more or less equal to the building's surface area, the space available to her was more than adequate. It was greater than would have been available elsewhere, for in none of the other huts were there less than two rooms. Neffie was reminded of a scene from her childhood, specifically the bathing huts along the sea front close to home, one of which her parents used to hire for the summer months. This one-room chalet faced the Mission's main entrance. The fact that there was no lock on the door obviated the need for a key. There wasn't even a keyhole. Security was provided by the simplest fastening imaginable: a four-inch by half an inch piece of wood which had been screwed into the inside of the door in such a way that it was able to pivot. When this latch of sorts was in the vertical position the door could be opened and closed without hindrance. For thinking that even when the latch was in the horizontal position a child of ten could have forced the door open with a determined shove, Neffie didn't find this particular security measure reassuring.

But she was reassured to observe that the double-bed was protected by a mosquito-net suspended from the ceiling. Dimly visible in the far corner of the room the presence of a toilet minus its seat and a wash basin also served to uplift her spirits. Their sanitary state was yet to be discerned, but because she had faith in Father O'Brien, Neffie didn't doubt that when she needed to go, she wouldn't have to wander about in the dark in search of facilities, or a convenient bush. The teacher concluded that the accommodation was the best she could have hoped for under the circumstances, and she smiled appreciatively at the priest as she stepped over the threshold.

Remaining without, in turn Father O'Brien handed her the lamp. Glad to be rid of the burden which is any weight held aloft for long, whilst massaging his energy-depleted arm he said simply, "Goodnight, Miss Nefertiti Goodwin."

"Goodnight, Father O'Brien," Miss Goodwin responded.

Chapter Thirteen
A Town too Dangerous

Neffie was awakened the next morning by a knock on her door. This was followed by the sound of a voice which never had been, and never would be, the slightest bit deferential. It was a woman's voice and in no-nonsense tones it informed Neffie, though not by name, that if she wanted to eat breakfast then she had better come and get it now, this instant, without a minute's delay. The same summons for chop Miss Goodwin heard twice more. From what was effectively a diminishing echo she deduced that Father O'Brien had other guests.

Contrary to expectation when first she pulled the solitary sheet over her, the Mission's new arrival had slept well. She attributed her restoration mainly to the sense of security provided by the pristine mosquito net, though she fully appreciated that being utterly exhausted after the journey to Koidu, as well as being emotionally drained, were also contributory factors. The teacher was surprised and pleased that she had no recollection of having had nightmares as a consequence of the gruesome event which she had witnessed, one which now seemed totally surreal.

After opening shutters one stride away from the foot of the bed Miss Goodwin was disappointed to discover that her view was hardly panoramic. Just out of reach beyond the aperture devoid of glass was an adobe wall. Standing at least two feet taller than Neffie, it formed one side of the wall surrounding the Mission. Its light-restricting proximity caused Neffie to feel hemmed-in, quite claustrophobic in fact. She poked her head through the opening where the shutters had been, looked up and then down, then to right and left. What she could see of the sky resembled an elevated pathway, an impression enhanced by the pavement of cloud looking so dark, so grey. It foretold precipitation. There was nothing surprising in that, but the prospect of another wet day deflated Neffie's spirits nonetheless. She remonstrated with herself for having been so unreasonably optimistic on waking.

Covered to a large extent by lichen, the wall was predominantly green. A few yards to the left it had crumbled away to leave a jagged-edged more or less V-shaped gap, the inverted apex of which plunged to approximately two feet above the ground. An intruder seeking entry into the Mission would merely have to step through the gap over some fallen rubble.

In making her structural survey of the wall Neffie was astonished to see, on a patch of grass between the wall and the left hand corner of her hut as she was looking, a snake. It was curled up like a particularly large ring of Cumberland sausage. The thought crossed Neffie's mind that Father O'Brien wouldn't need to have the wall rebuilt if a venomous snake were on permanent guard duty. Regarding the species of snake Neffie could only guess, with not much chance of being right. A lack of knowledge about snakes and the configuration of the reptile's body made identification difficult.

Neffie stared at the presumably deadly creature for at least a minute, willing it to move, preferably in the direction which would increase the distance between her and it. A bead of perspiration dripped from the teacher's brow onto a leaf directly below. Having observed the globule fall and splatter she watched the leaf quiver. The snake remained as if lifeless. Its apparent inertia prompted Neffie to think that perhaps it really was lifeless, but she wasn't of a mind to find out for certain by being provocative. Instead, thinking that she ought to get a move on if she didn't want to risk going hungry, she turned to complete her ablutions and dress with all the more alacrity for having been delayed by her own curiosity. She made a mental note to inform Father O'Brien of her latest discovery.

Upon emerging from her room Neffie was greeted by a scene which was reminiscent of a picnic in a public park back home. The four picnic tables and their integral benches were identical not only to each other, but were familiar to Neffie for being the same as she would expect to find at many a beauty spot in Britain. Positioned in a row, the tables were occupied by what appeared to be two distinct family groups: men, women, and children of both sexes ranging in age and size from toddlers to teenagers. There being considerable interaction between the tables, and more than one incidence of a youngster making a bid to escape parental control, Neffie didn't attempt to make a head count, but instead made a quick visual estimation that there were at least fifteen fellow guests at Koidu's Catholic Mission.

She wasn't wrong. The three men, four women and eight children were at various stages of enjoying their breakfast of chop. Some of the children had finished completely. At first, there being no vacant space at any of the tables, Miss Goodwin was at a loss as to what she should do. Father O'Brien was as yet nowhere in sight. Upon observing her obvious predicament however, the man sitting nearest to where the white woman stood looking perplexed, got to his feet, picked up his bowl, and with a generous gesture of his free hand offered Neffie his place. She accepted the invitation gratefully, and sat down next to a man who turned out to be the brother of the kind man now standing behind Neffie's left shoulder.

Before she could utter a word with regard to what she would or would not like to eat, a woman, Neffie presumed it to be the same person who had earlier rapped on her door, unceremoniously plonked a spoon and fork down in front of her. The items of cutlery were quickly followed by a blue and white striped plastic bowl two-thirds filled with chop.

Leaning to his right in order to be closer, and using his hand to partially cover his mouth, an act designed to prevent a single syllable of what he was about to say being overheard by the person he was about to comment upon, Neffie's neighbour said to her, "She's in a bad mood this morning because Father O'Brien has just threatened to sack her as the Mission cook."

"Is her cooking that bad?" Neffie questioned as she inspected the food which had been placed before her: she then raised her head and smiled at the smiling faces of the boy sitting directly, and the girl sitting not so directly, opposite.

"Her cooking's fine, as you are about to find out, I trust," said Neffie's informant. "It's her attitude towards people that annoys Father O'Brien and the other priests."

"I didn't think that Father O'Brien ran this place alone, but without any evidence to the contrary…" Neffie suspended that line of thought to ask, "Who are the others? And where are they for that matter?"

"The other two fathers are attending a conference in Freetown," Neffie's neighbour replied before he too went off on a different tangent. "Her name is Millie by the way… the cook's name is Millie."

"I suppose that's short for Millicent," said Neffie, pleased to contribute to the conversation even if her contribution sounded banal.

Now that her newest confidant was no longer leaning up close to impart his information of a confidential nature, Neffie was able to get a better look at the face turned towards her as she spoke. In this instance to say that he had a long face doesn't mean that he was moping and that at an indeterminate time in the future he would become less dispirited and his face not so long. The visage belonging to Neffie's amenable neighbour was an inherited feature and was, therefore, more or less permanent; although the hollow cheeks and the readily apparent thinness of the man's upper body were revealing of factors involved other than inherited traits. The well-fed Englishwoman's impression was that she was speaking to a man who knew what it was to go hungry.

"To my knowledge she is just Millie," the man replied, and though he imparted this innocuous information in a normal voice, it so happened that these words were uttered during a brief period of otherwise total silence, and so were easily heard.

"Who's talking about me behind my back?" enquired the woman called Millie upon emerging from the kitchen doorway.

Standing on the walkway armed with a wooden spatula Millie appeared no less formidable to the gathering than Mr Bumble did to Oliver Twist and his confederates, though apart from Miss Goodwin no one present was likely to have known that. The comparison certainly came to Neffie's mind. Like chastened children the people at the tables maintained their silence, staring with apologetic, puppy-dog eyes at the ogre standing before them. Miss Goodwin felt no less intimidated, and not a little guilty for being party to the discourse which had effectively summoned the termagant. She felt inclined to say, 'Please Miss it was him'; but fortunately for the man whom she had considered blaming she managed to resist the urge. The ogre returned to her dark hole.

It transpired, as Neffie learned from the conversation which followed, that the people with whom she was breakfasting had fled from the misery of conflict in Guinea. Whatever their official status, in Father O'Brien's eyes these people were refugees to be given succour, and on that basis they could stay for as long as they wished. Neffie's overriding thought on learning of their flight on foot across the border, given what she had already seen and heard during her short time in Koidu district, was that things must be really bad in Guinea for them to consider this town a place of refuge. She expressed as much to her new acquaintance. Her thin-faced interlocutor simply nodded in recognition that there was more than a grain of truth in what she said.

"You should eat your breakfast before it starts to rain," advised the boy who was sitting opposite. His instruction made the teacher chuckle at the role reversal, and then she did as she was told.

Neffie had almost finished eating when the door into the Mission compound opened and Father O'Brien appeared. She watched his every move as he closed the door behind him. She sensed that he carried a weight on his shoulders that she hadn't previously seen. He was wearing the jeans she had seen him in the night before, but he had changed his shirt. This short-sleeved garment was remarkable for being brilliant white and having a collar, epaulettes and breast pockets. It gave the wearer, jeans notwithstanding, a look of official authority rather than its spiritual counterpart. Neffie presumed that the Father continued to wear 'civilian' clothes because his colleagues, who were perhaps also his superiors, were away. Then again all three fathers may be somewhat casual in their attire when not in church administering one or other of the seven sacraments. This latter thought prompted Neffie to look around the compound and its clusters of bungalows in search of one building in particular. Its location wasn't immediately apparent.

"This being a Catholic Mission I would expect there to be a church in evidence, or am I so out of touch with the way things are in this part of Africa?" said Neffie, her head tilting in the direction of her friendly and informative neighbour.

"You're only out of touch in not knowing that the church was burnt to the ground two weeks ago. All that remains are a few charred timbers. It used to stand behind the bungalow in which the Fathers live. Its destruction was no great loss to architecture, and it wasn't very big. Everyone you see here would have probably filled it, but when it's all you've got the loss is felt more keenly. It's sad for the Fathers. They work so hard to make everyone feel welcome."

"How did it happen?" Neffie quizzed: she was eager to know. "Was it an accident? Lighted candles are so dangerous, and I've seen a few of them since I've been here. Was anybody hurt?"

Miss Goodwin's questions prompted the man who had vacated his seat for her to join in the conversation. He was still standing behind her when he spoke. "Nobody was hurt thank God," said the brother without a seat, "but it was deliberate, arson I believe it's called, when a person deliberately sets fire to property, it's a crime. The rebels did it. They sneaked in through a gap in the back wall, near to the hut in which you stayed last night. They set it well and truly alight with petrol and then fired their guns in the air to celebrate. Once they were sure it was a blazing inferno they ran off, leaving through the same gap in the wall they had come in by."

"So much for the snake being a deterrent," said Neffie.

Her reference to the coiled serpent she had observed was meant to be rhetorical. "What's that about a snake you say?" questioned her neighbour.

"Just a passing thought," replied Neffie. "Forgive the distraction. Please continue."

"There was nothing anybody could do to save it," said Neffie's seated neighbour. "The reason the other two fathers are in Freetown is to petition the bishop, and no doubt members of the government, to provide the means to build a new one. I hope they succeed."

"We all do," added his brother.

"I'll help to build it," beamed the boy sitting opposite Neffie.

"Can I help build God's building as well?" enquired the girl sitting next to him, addressing her question to Neffie, as if the teacher were destined to be in charge of the work details.

Father O'Brien approached, and as he did so he kept his focus on the two eyes that kept their focus on him. Miss Goodwin, being the person in Father O'Brien's line of sight, smiled in an attempt to elicit the same. On this occasion however, in respect of obtaining the desired response, this natural and normally so effective expression of our shared humanity failed. It failed miserably, for it was the Father's sullen mien which was to have the greater influence, transforming the teacher's demeanour completely.

Neffie wasn't alone in sensing that all was not right with the world outside the Mission gate. She wasn't alone in divining that Father O'Brien was about to impart unwelcome news. The atmosphere amongst the throng darkened with dreadful expectation, so that once again, only this time for an easily identifiable reason, the children could be seen but not heard. Unaware that her boss was the cause of what to her was a sudden and initially unaccountable hush, Millie the overbearing cook reappeared from her dark domain. Even though she was seeking enlightenment she didn't at first notice that Father O'Brien had returned.

"The trouble with you people is that you don't appreciate good food when it's put in front of you," the cook bellowed defensively, though she had no reason to be.

Following her unwarranted outburst, only when heads turned from looking in her direction did Millie realise that the cause of the sudden hush had nothing to do with her cooking, and everything to do with Father O'Brien's sombre approach. For not being in his good books Millie didn't wait to find out why he was looking so downcast. Instead, she stepped back into the shadows muttering, "How was I to know that old goat..."

Nobody outside heard what she had said and she didn't finish the sentence. Father O'Brien came directly to where Neffie was sitting, but first he greeted the man standing just behind her. Far from being a cheery hello, it was the sort of greeting bestowed upon a relative one hasn't seen for years: a relative who has turned up to pay his respects at a funeral.

When the Father turned his attention to Neffie the face she perceived was morose but saintly. "The expression suits him," Neffie thought as she gazed up into those saintly, wistful eyes.

She noted the broad, sun-tanned forehead, the size of which was considerably increased by the receding hairline. Her eyes also took in the wiry grey hair that grew on the top of his head and framed his face, and the straight moustache of darker hue which ran parallel to the two thin lines that were his lips. For the moments they came into sharp focus the

176

latter remained tightly zipped. In a flash Neffie made the assumption that the nose was more bulbous than it had been in the Father's younger years, the consequence of his predilection for whiskey no doubt, from wherever it came.

"And how are you this morning, my child?" the Father enquired of Neffie, whilst at the same time placing a hand on the head of each of the children sitting opposite her.

Overcoming the resistance they met, the children glanced at each other and grinned as if they had just been anointed with a great beneficence. Neither of them thought of breaking free. Neffie was impressed at the Father's ability to take an interest in her well-being when it was obvious that he was masking a greater concern.

"I'm very well thank you, Father," Neffie replied, wondering at the irony of a mature woman, and a teacher to boot, being so addressed.

The Father's solicitous greeting made her feel a little strange, as if she were an actress playing the part of Miss Nefertiti Goodwin in a film for which she had yet to learn the script; so different was her present role from the life she normally lead. Not having been addressed as 'my child' before, not even by her parents, she half expected to be told to 'go in peace' as an anthem composed for strings and a choir of angelic voices led her towards the gates of paradise.

Those illusory gates disappeared in an instant when the priest next spoke. "I think you should leave Koidu at the earliest opportunity, and by that I don't mean tomorrow... I mean today," said Father O'Brien, unable to resist the dark significance of the news he was soon to impart from bursting forth: like molten steel soon to harden.

"Why, what on earth has happened?" enquired Neffie, the transformation of her face matching her anxiety.

"Those bangs we heard last night hadn't anything to do with a car backfiring. They were gunshots. The taxi in which your friend... my friend... Jeremy had set off back to town was ambushed just down the road. I'm afraid Jeremy won't be playing for Manchester United, his beloved Spurs, or even Koidu ever..."

"Are his injuries that serious?" interrupted Neffie, hoping that the worst she was about to hear involved a wounding.

"...ever again," Father O'Brien continued, "either in his imagination or on the field of play. He's gone to a better place, my child."

Father O'Brien removed his hands from each child's head and clasped them together in front of his chest as instinctively he assumed an attitude of prayer. The children were told to run along and play: they needed no further encouragement.

It would be incredible for a person of even average intelligence to think that 'a better place' involved a transfer to Freetown or Lagos. The bad news was that someone who had sat beside Neffie for the greater part of the journey to Koidu, and who had been so enthusiastic, so optimistic, and so helpful, was dead. For a few moments there was complete silence as the impact of Father O'Brien's words hit home, adding to feelings of insecurity and fear in many of the people gathered. Neffie couldn't help but shed a tear: it was a mark of respect for the young life lost.

"There are bad people everywhere," said Neffie's neighbour in a tone, not surprisingly, morose.

"There are soldiers patrolling the streets, but any extra security now is too late for those two. The taxi driver was also killed."

"Can I get you something to eat, Father?" called Millie from the kitchen doorway, unawares, because 'nobody told her anything', of the awful magnitude of the event being discussed.

"No thank you, Millie," the Father replied succinctly, and without turning to look at his questioner.

"Who were the people responsible?" Neffie inquired, more from a desire to say something to the point rather than to discover whether the murders had been perpetrated for financial gain or if they were politically motivated: for her to know the reason why was an irrelevance when either way the result was so tragic.

"I did say that you had come at a bad time," said the Father, though he took no pride in the fact that the recent tragedy had gone a long way towards proving him right. "The bus to Freetown leaves in just under an hour. I think..."

"What about something to drink?" hailed Millie, determined to prove her worth, and hoping thereby to remove one of Damocles' swords from above her head.

"A cup of tea would be nice," the priest replied, turning to bestow upon Millie a beneficent look. Turning his attention back to Neffie he echoed the gist of his cook's kind offer. "Can we get you something?"

Perhaps because she was feeling so shocked the Father's kind offer received no reply. Instead, Miss Goodwin was moved to say, "It's all very well for you to say get on the bus and leave, but what about these people and others like them, they're going to have to contend with the violence if they stay in Koidu. It's probably as bad here as it was for them in Guinea."

"They can't pick and choose like you can, Miss Goodwin," responded the priest, indicating by the use of Neffie's surname that he no longer considered her to be his child. "They don't have the freedom to choose that money provides. If I were you I would think myself fortunate that you are able to leave so soon, before the situation deteriorates even further. Who knows what will happen tomorrow or the day after?"

Displaying unaccustomed deference the cook appeared. She placed a mug embossed with a youthful image of the queen and Prince Philip on the table, commenting, "There you are, Father, just how you like it... flavoured with a drop of whiskey instead of milk."

Clearing his throat before speaking the Father muttered his thanks. The man sitting adjacent to Neffie spoke in support of Father O'Brien more or less insisting that Neffie should leave Koidu at the earliest opportunity. The seated man's brother nodded his agreement.

"I'll go and get my things," said Neffie as she rose to her feet. On the way to her room Miss Goodwin remembered what it was that she had meant to tell the Father prior to his spoiling her day. Stopping in her tracks as the first drops of rain fell from the darkening sky, harbingers of heavier precipitation to follow, she said, "I almost forgot to say, but there's a snake coiled up outside my window."

"There often is," Father O'Brien replied.

Chapter Fourteen
Revelation and Reward

Sebastian Forrest had a number of reasons to be grateful for the caring ministrations he had received at the hands of the National Health Service. If it hadn't been for the skill of that organisation's orthopaedic surgeons he would have been left crippled and deformed as a result of having broken several bones. The consequence of playing competitive sport too zealously rather than any inherent brittleness, the injuries to his wrist, fibula, patella, ankle and thumb had been sustained on five separate occasions.

His first big break occurred in a goal-mouth melee when he was just thirteen years of age. The boy had had hopes of being signed by Leeds United, so obviously it wasn't the sort of break he was looking for. On top of the sudden curtailment to his playing career, and the two-month hiatus to allow the bone set in plaster to mend, the pain he had endured in the hours immediately following the accident — several players had landed on top of him — had been excruciating. It wasn't the kind of experience he was keen to repeat, and he wouldn't have been able to if the surgeons hadn't done such good work initially, and then each time after that, thereby allowing him to return unabashed to the field of play, fully intending not to do himself further harm demonstrating his prowess, or lack of it, at football, cricket, and a few games of rugby.

Fortunately given the number of times that Seb's body was pinned and plastered, he didn't suffer any impairment to his mobility, and although it suffered in other ways, neither did his bank balance for having to pay for treatment, which, as we all know, is free at the point of delivery. Thinking along the lines of cause and effect, in the long view he attributed his good fortune in both regards to the organisational skills and social conscience of his forbears: the people led by Clement Attlee.

For Shirley Margai such provision was sadly lacking, and though she was aware that an operation to enable her to walk properly again was feasible, there wasn't the relevant expertise available in Sierra Leone, and as a visitor to Britain she wasn't allowed to benefit from a system to which she hadn't contributed, this despite the fact that her mother was now a permanent resident. The only option available to Miss Margai was to have the operation done privately. She had been told that the cost of rebuilding the tissue and repairing the Grade 3 sprain to the anterior cruciate ligament in her right knee would be in the region of £2,000. Insofar as she couldn't access that amount of money, it seemed that undergoing private treatment wasn't really an option either.

Given her plight, and the fact that her country of origin was one of the world's impoverished states, Sebastian knew that he would have no difficulty in promulgating Shirley's story, certainly in the press, and by virtue of her profession probably on radio: he was less confident about television. He envisaged being able to get good coverage locally, and who knows what else besides? It had been to this end that the enthusiastic correspondent had arranged to meet the poor, crippled, black woman, the victim of a war which, for being in its infancy, few people in Britain were aware of. In Sebastian Forrest's opinion therefore, Miss Margai was certainly newsworthy. It was, however, perhaps indicative of his lack of imagination that in telling her story to the world he didn't foresee any likely ramifications.

In the days ahead Sebastian got to work. At that time his most efficient method of communicating with people whose faces he couldn't see was by telephone. Sensitive to the timbre of the stranger's voice at the other end of the line, his own manner was relaxed for being well-practised, and he had no difficulty in making the desired appointments. In keeping with the dates and times he had arranged, Seb accompanied the radio journalist to the offices of two local newspapers, namely the Luxborough Chronicle and the Ferrousby Times. Able to boast of a circulation sometimes above and sometimes below, but invariably close to, one hundred thousand, the 'Times' was by far the larger and generally the more influential of the two publications. That said, in this instance it would be difficult to identify which newspaper proved to be more influential in instigating the transformation to Miss Margai's life. Sebastian was well satisfied that the respective features editors conducted themselves in accordance with his expectations and wishes and published articles which were sympathetic to Shirley's recent history and present predicament. In each case the words were supported by a photograph, and in the opinion of both journalists neither image flattered.

Following the press interviews and more telephone work Sebastian escorted Shirley to the BBC studios in Ferrousby. Seeking to impress rather than denigrate the area in which he had been born and raised, Sebastian took the more attractive of several routes he could have taken into town. One of several dicta he had learned in the army is that you have only one chance to make a first impression and that impression counts. In the event he was too late. No sooner had Sebastian ascertained that Shirley had arrived in Ferrousby by train than he knew that his chance of making a good first impression had vanished and that the best he could hope for was to counter the doubtless impressionistic damage already done. After driving along the leafy lanes and well-appointed semi-detached houses that led toward the centre of town, Seb could also take some pride in the vicinity where the BBC studios were located. Overlooking the bright, modern bus-station, these were housed in a building which in its design achieved an impressive elegance and simplicity. Needless to say, in a town in the North East of England once renowned for steel-making, there were parts which Sebastian would have been reluctant to reveal to anyone from afar.

After arriving with only minutes to spare following the seemingly inevitable difficulty finding a parking space, once the introductions to the relevant presenter had been dispensed with, Seb was allowed to sit quietly in the corner of the studio whilst the red light indicating that the programme was being broadcast live remained brightly lit. Shirley was interviewed by a presenter noted for his serious and often contentious discussions. His name was 'lucky' Jim Gambol. Watching the person whom Seb now considered to be a friend put on the headphones with expert confidence and ease, and listening to her answer the probing questions put to her, he savoured the experience as one which added to his own self-worth.

Mr Forrest enjoyed a similar sense of reflected glory when on another day he escorted Miss Margai to the TV studios located on an industrial estate on the outskirts of town, but whereas he was delighted for knowing that Shirley's story had been broadcast to a potential audience of many thousands over the radio, he was disappointed to learn that Shirley's tale of woe didn't have sufficient visual content for television: there was little for one of their camera operators to film.

Overall, however, Sebastian's stratagems had proved successful. After a round of interviews which had taken the best part of a week to arrange and conduct, Shirley's story had become widely known; but still Sebastian didn't give a thought to the possibility that there may be consequences.

Perhaps Shirley thought differently because women are supposed to have intuition, and being of the feminine kind it's obviously a faculty which men sadly lack. She believed, and hoped, that there would be further developments as a result of the publicity she had obtained with Sebastian's help. Or perhaps it was because as the more experienced of the two journalists she sincerely believed in the power of the fourth estate to bring about change for the better by focusing people's minds on a situation they might not have been aware of or considered worthy of their attention.

Her hopes were vague. Existing as mere intimations and feelings rather than clearly defined thoughts, Miss Margai was in the best of moods as she and Sebastian returned in the car from yet another meeting with the media. It was the final sortie of its kind, and for the first time in a long time Shirley was completely relaxed. The difference in her manner was pleasing to behold. She was playful, and the only potential playmate of the opposite sex who was available for being in close proximity, and with whom she had a pleasing rapport, was Sebastian.

Miss Margai didn't have much faith in the loyalty of men when it came to their libidos. She believed that a man who was as young and vigorous as Sebastian could easily be tempted for having been left to his own devices, some would say vices, for more than a week, no matter how resolute his intentions might have been at the outset of his projected period of abstinence. It was, therefore, an intriguing thought which crossed Shirley's mind as once again she expressed her gratitude for all that Sebastian had done to help her thus far. She considered placing her hand upon his thigh. In the psychology of making the first move she calculated that if such a gambit were to be frowned upon she could defend her action as being just her way of demonstrating her gratitude palpably. Then any sexual connotation relating to where she had placed her hand would exist only in the poor deluded boy's mind. On the other hand if such a gesture were to meet with approval who knows what may happen? Thoughts which were undoubtedly wily were also fleeting, for the young lady came to the conclusion that it would be better for being safer if she were to keep her hands to herself, certainly while Sebastian was responsible for their safety when they were travelling at the speed they were.

Only when the journey along busy arterial roads was behind them, and the steam and smoke rising from the industrial skyline that had been in plain view along the way no longer offended the eye, did Shirley make a foray into uncharted territory, though once again the move she made was ambiguous in that it could easily be misconstrued. Her test of Sebastian's fidelity to the woman who would be out of sight for several weeks if not out of mind was put into effect when Seb and she were making their way from the car towards the front door of her Luxborough home. Sebastian was supporting the invalid in his care when she tripped and stumbled. Fortunately she fell, as she had planned, into his waiting arms. For Sebastian not to have arrested her fall in the assured way that he did would have been negligent of him to say the least. Being the gentleman that he was he naturally assumed that the incident which had resulted in their most intimate physical contact to date to have been an unintended accident.

Whether it appeared as a genuine accident or a deliberate ploy, the scene was witnessed by Mrs Cannisman through the net curtains that shielded her living-room from the prying eyes of passers-by. It didn't matter that the passers-by were few: this was a woman who was jealous of her privacy.

She was about to return to the book she had been reading and let events in the street take their course when the telephone rang. She had no inkling as to who would be trying to contact her at the time of day it was, and therefore half-expected the caller to have got the wrong number. Even more irritating would be someone trying to sell her something in a voice she could barely understand. She had no time for double-glazing or people trying to give her grants for loft insulation. Regarding wrong numbers and sales pitches both were wide of the mark. Able to understand perfectly what was being said to her, Mrs Cannisman was no less pleased to discover that the call was for her daughter. For having observed Shirley's somewhat unsteady approach Mrs Cannisman was able to inform the caller that the person he wished to speak with was about to come through the door, and that he should 'hang on'.

Mrs Cannisman reached and opened the front door seconds before her daughter, and just in time to see Sebastian let go of Shirley's arm. Aware of her injury and the support she sometimes needed, the mother thought nothing of Sebastian's sudden withdrawal.

"Hello Mrs Cannisman, I was just…" Sebastian wasn't allowed to finish the sentence he had begun.

"There's a telephone call for you, Shirley," Mrs Cannisman interjected, thereby overruling all other considerations. Without saying a word, Shirley squeezed past her mother to disappear from Seb's view into the house.

"Would you like to come in and wait? I'm sure she'll not be long," offered the woman whose substantial bulk effectively blocked the doorway.

"Thanks, but I think that I better be on my way," Seb responded, his body half turned in the direction of his car. Raising his hand palm open in a final valedictory gesture, peremptorily he added, "Tell Shirley that I'll be in touch."

After turning his back on the woman to walk off, he hadn't taken his second step before he heard the door close emphatically.

Chapter Fifteen
Zimmi Town is Now Fred!

The title of this short chapter is a direct quotation taken from a newspaper called 'The National' dated August 23rd — 26th, 1991. At first I assumed that 'Fred' should have been 'Free'. That may be the case. On the other hand it could be that the writer sought to demonstrate his linguistic skill by using the word for peace in three of the Scandinavian languages. The article which appeared on the front page reads as follows:

Zimmi Town in the Mapkele Chiefdom, which has been one of the strongholds of Charles' NPFL rebels has been liberated by combined troops under the banner of Sierra Leone Military Forces.

After long and protracted battles, our gallant soldiers routed the rebels completely inflicting heavy casualties on them. There were only two wounded on the side of the combined forces. They are now heading towards the border.

A blast from a hand grenade resulted in the loss of two lives with sixteen people sustaining injuries in Kenema. Police investigations in the township revealed that the grenade exploded in the hands of a Liberian soldier, Anthony Koroma during a night patrol.

The two deceased, seven-year-old Sampha Kamara and sixteen-years-old Thomas Njavombo, a volunteer in the civil defence unit in a mark of solidarity to their dead colleagues marched through the township.

In words of consolation to the relatives and sympathisers, the SDO, Kenema Mr Ernest Surrur said, 'Thomas will be remembered in the history of this country as one of the patriotic citizens whose efforts to defend this nation had cost him his life'.

Prior to the capture of Zimmi from the rebels, fourteen rebels including a Sierra Leonean, Brima Jenge Koroma who is reported to have confessed to the Bo Police that he led rebels to Tai Village, Bontho

District on April12 this year to behead Paramount Chief Mahuloi Farma commonly known as Bonie Fine'.

Jenge was arrested last Saturday by Chief Inspector David Sesay of the SSD with the help of Inspector Brima a prosecutor attached to the Bo Magistrate Court.

Before his arrest at Shellmingo Section, Bo, Jenge was deputy rebel commando.

He is reported to have contested the last Paramount Chief election with late Chief Farma which the latter won.

Koroma told the police in Bo that on the day of their attack at the village, Chief Farma was met lying in his hammock where he was shot by one of the NPFL rebels in the leg. He further said that the chief pleaded with them to spare his life but he Jenge told the late chief that all he was after was his head.

With all the pleas he explained to the police, he ordered the NPFL rebels to strip the chief naked and was then taken to the centre of the village where he, Jenge used his knife he was carrying to cut off the chiefs head.

Chapter Sixteen
Neffie Goes to Kalangba Junction

Three days after she had learned from Father O'Brien that Jeremy and the taxi-driver had met an untimely and tragic end, Miss Nefertiti Goodwin was setting out on another bus journey. That she wasn't heading for the airport to take the next flight home surprised even her, but she had decided to stay in Sierra Leone for the time she had allotted on the basis that she was presently a long way from Koidu, that place of danger beyond the Nimini Hills. It wasn't the same vehicle on which she had travelled back and forth previously, but it looked similar. She couldn't exactly remember the number on the registration plate of the Koidu bus, but she could see that the one on the front and back of the bus about to take her to Kalangba Junction was different. She had been assured that Kalangba Junction was safe.

Nonetheless it perhaps wasn't surprising that Neffie chose to sit as far away as possible from the seat she had sat in on her initial bus journey, its location on this occasion being the same as that chosen on the journey back to Freetown: directly behind the driver. Sitting beside Neffie was her friend Samuel Massequoi. His presence at least meant that she wouldn't have to be magnanimous in her conversation by talking about football. Ostensibly Samuel was travelling to Kalangba Junction to visit his cousin Mariana, but, as he had so ergonomically put it when telling Neffie of his decision to accompany her, 'there's no harm in killing two birds with one stone' if he were able to keep her out of trouble. Miss Goodwin doubted that the two birds in question would agree with Samuel's claim, but the prospect of their being stoned to death, metaphorically speaking, didn't prevent her from being gladdened by his company.

Sitting by the window seat on the half empty bus Neffie's thoughts wandered back in time; but no farther back than the morning on which she had first intended to take her leave of Father O'Brien and leave the

Catholic Mission. By her reckoning she had arrived at the bus-stop five minutes early, but that had been too late to prevent the fully laden bus to Freetown from leaving without her. She had stamped her foot on the lateritic road, behaving not unlike a spoilt child that hasn't got its way. No sooner had her anger subsided than the realisation that there could easily be adverse consequences for having missed the bus made her feel dejected. Her spirits hadn't been lifted any by the sight of so many gun-toting soldiers ambling here and there or assembled in small groups at irregular intervals along both sides of the main street. In Neffie's estimation they had outnumbered the civilians by approximately two to one. There had been no recourse for her but to return to the Mission. In this intent she had been assisted by an army officer in charge of an open-topped Land Rover. Despite being a little crestfallen on her return, after thanking the military Neffie calmly explained what everyone with an interest in her reappearance had already surmised. On the understanding that she should leave in good time to catch the bus on the morrow, by simply saying, "Don't worry, my child," Father O'Brien had welcomed Neffie back into the fold.

On the day when Miss Goodwin was travelling to Kalangba Junction she smiled at the thought, at the image she had conjured of Father O'Brien's kindly face. A subsequent memory engendered a more serious expression. For on the day that Miss Goodwin had spent mainly within the Mission walls, to the drumming of raindrops on corrugated roofs she had discussed the situation across the border in Guinea with the refugees that had recently come from there, and had learned that in the camps people were going hungry simply because there was a lack of organisation; or, to put the problem another way, too much organisation of the bureaucratic kind. A less emotionally demanding way of passing the time had involved Father O'Brien introducing Neffie to his short-wave radio. It was the means by which he was able to communicate with his family in Ireland and listen to the news on the BBC. He was also, Neffie had learned, able to keep in touch with other friendly call- signs around the country, and consequently was able to obtain a patchy picture of what the rebels and government forces were doing. In the Father's opinion it was possible that being privy to such information may one day save not only his life, but the lives of everyone at the Mission.

Her Mission memories in mind, Neffie didn't regret having spent over an hour listening to the news from the BBC. She had soon come to realise that events which she considered grave in the extreme, and therefore worthy of being revealed to the world, didn't necessarily carry the same weight with journalists and editors in London. Not surprisingly she had been disappointed when the woes of the country she was in failed to get a mention. What she had learned, however, was that there had been demonstrations in Russia in support of Mikhail Gorbachev following his ousting in a coup. Along with President George Bush, Prime Minister John Major, Chancellor Helmut Kohl, and President Francois Mitterrand, Neffie had welcomed the news that stability had returned to a country which in the opinion of the five monitors mentioned is such an important player on the world's political stage. Her initial thought had been that with Gorbachev's reinstatement there was hope for world peace. Sitting on the bus bound for Kalangba Junction she wasn't so optimistic.

In addition to having learned certain items of news regarding events in the political sphere, Neffie had also learned that Tottenham Hotspur had won their most recent match. It had been a poignant snippet, so much so that she had felt that she was being singled out by the presenter, as if the BBC were trying to communicate with her by special code.

Miss Goodwin's goodbyes the next day had been brief. Goodbyes don't appeal to her, and to have to go through the rigmarole twice in two days had been tedious, a formality best kept as short as possible no matter how appreciative she was of the people whom in all probability she wouldn't meet again.

She had caught the bus without difficulty. Compared to the journey from Freetown, the journey back had been relatively uneventful, the vehicle having been routinely stopped and searched without further incident on two occasions. The first search had been conducted by the army just outside Yengema, the second by the police in Maslaka. Each halt had lasted about twenty minutes. Apart from these distractions Neffie had gazed out the window for the entire journey, saying barely a word to the stony-faced woman who had occupied the seat next to her ever since Makeni. Disembarking at the exact same spot where two days previously she had set out on her big adventure to Koidu, what a relief it had been for her to arrive amid the colourful hustle and bustle of the capital.

Almost immediately Neffie had set about making contact with 'old' friends, namely Di and Samuel. The teacher had only been able to meet up with her Sierra Leonean colleague, but that didn't prevent her from formulating a new plan of campaign, her revised schedule being to spend the remainder of her time in Sierra Leone assisting Miss Fussey with her tree-planting project. The arrangements Neffie had been able to make to this end had only been possible as a result of the radio link between Kalangba and the Peace House established by technicians from the American Embassy. It had been set up for Di's benefit, for her safety mainly, on the direct orders of the ambassador. In fact so concerned was he for the young woman's safety that he had told Di that he was considering sending a marine to Kalangba Junction to watch over her. In combination with a shortage of manpower, however, Miss Fussey's insistence that such a course of action wasn't necessary had deterred the imposition of a military deterrent. No doubt a twenty-first century incumbent of the post held by Di, if such a position still exists, would rely on a mobile phone for communication, but in the dim and distant past that was the last quarter of the twentieth century the radio link proved invaluable.

Details of the plan which had been hastily arranged in the strange jargon that people use when speaking over the radio, jargon such as 'do you copy?' and 'over and out', were that Neffie would take the bus to Makeni the next day, where Di would meet her in Jake's Bar on Main Street. The conversation between the two women had been succinct and to the point. Her mind flustered at hearing and then imitating the strange expressions that make for radio procedure, Neffie had been happy not to chat, though it was only after her interlocutor with the almost unrecognisable voice had signed off that Neffie had been able to think of a number of questions she would have liked to have asked.

One aspect of the plan which they couldn't possibly have discussed, for the reason that it had yet to be arranged with the third party involved, was that Neffie wouldn't be travelling alone. That particular plan was finalised more or less at the last minute and on the basis that Samuel would visit his cousin 'on spec', so to speak, and although Mariana wouldn't know that he would be arriving on her doorstep unexpectedly, he had no doubt that she would provide him with a bed for a few nights. Loath to take anyone's generosity for granted, Neffie was yet hopeful that Di would be able and willing to transport her and Sam from Makeni to Kalangba Junction, a distance of approximately twenty miles.

Such were the circumstances leading up to Samuel and Neffie sitting together shortly after one o' clock in the afternoon as the bus taking them to Makeni pulled into Makari, the last settlement on the road before their final destination, final in respect of public transport that is. A village typical of this part of Sierra Leone, and one which Samuel had passed through several times, Makari held no particular interest for him, and for the entire time that they were in the village precincts he didn't look up from the book he was reading. It was 'Love in the Time of Cholera' by Gabriel Garcia Marquez. A rather tattered copy by this time, it was the one book which Neffie had brought with her, and, having finished reading it the previous evening, she had given it to Samuel. To delve into the world within its pages was something of a new adventure for Mr Massequoi, bearing in mind that hitherto he had mainly concentrated on British authors, though with an occasional foray into American literature. This being Samuel's first venture into the Hispanic mind, albeit in translation, he was captivated by it, though he did manage to tear himself away from the printed pages to express his delight at the characters of Florentino Ariza and Fermina Data. He also apologised to Neffie for being such a poor travelling companion. In turn she insisted that no such apology was necessary, and that on the contrary she was pleased to have been able to expand her friend's literary horizons. She didn't say as much, but she felt that Samuel's enjoyment of a book which she considered to be one of her favourite novels strengthened the bond between them. She was happy to leave him to his silent occupation.

Scenes which were commonplace to Samuel, and to his way of thinking unimpressive for being so primitive, were of considerable interest to Neffie. In contrast to the villages she had observed through the window of the bus on previous journeys, she was presently enthralled by the circular, thatched-roofed dwellings that were so basic and therefore so very different from the mishmash of structures in Freetown, and elsewhere. Without being blind to the poverty of the villagers, she nonetheless took delight in observing people, women and children mainly, living seemingly uncomplicated lives. Such simplicity was evident in the sparsity of material possessions, and that included clothing. The young children were running around naked. The older boys were wearing shorts, the girls either shorts and t-shirts or simple dresses. Whether performing domestic tasks or standing idle but for their gossip, some of the women were naked from the waist up. The tasks being performed appeared to be routine, the ambiance peaceful. Then the bus left Makari behind.

About a mile from the village, exhibiting a high degree of urgency for not wanting the image to escape Samuel's notice, Neffie posed the question, "What type of bird is that?"

Neffie's sudden quest for knowledge had made her careless of propriety as she sought to emphasise her words with spontaneous action of a tactile kind. She gripped Samuel's near leg just behind the kneecap. In truth her excitement had caused a momentary misapprehension as to who was sitting next to her. She had momentarily been under the illusion that it was Sebastian's leg she had grabbed hold of, and though upon realising her mistake she withdrew her hand in an instant, it was perhaps revealing that she didn't follow up with an apology.

Samuel's response to the friendly assault upon his person was impressively insouciant in that rather than respond immediately to Miss Goodwin's verbal and physical importuning, he chose to finish the paragraph he was reading.

"Then she lay for a moment on top of him, gasping for breath, and she ceased to exist in the darkness," he muttered aloud, though for not wanting to cause a general disturbance, not loudly.

There wasn't meant to be any interpersonal suggestiveness in the sentence he enunciated. The quotation from the book by Marquez was amatory without doubt, but it also just happened to be the extract that he, Samuel, had just read. Not surprisingly, by the time he raised and turned his head to look over his shoulder, searching for the ornithological specimen in the direction he thought most likely, the bird was nowhere in sight.

"Too slow!" said Neffie with affected disdain.

"What did it look like?" Samuel enquired.

In turning to face Samuel and answer his question Neffie noted that the young woman sitting in the seat across the aisle had unbuttoned her blouse so as to feed the babe cradled in her arms. For Miss Goodwin, in contrast to the many sights which had given her cause to despair, the spectacle was uplifting. In that image of the infant suckling at its mother's breast she saw great hope for the future of the former British colony. Not letting sentiment get in the way of science, however, she proceeded to describe the bird she had seen on the ground, where for a few moments it had been looking up at her as if she, like it, were an object of curiosity.

"Well..." began Neffie, "it was a big bird. It had a yellow head with quite a prominent black circle on the side. It had a black back and tail. Its back was also..."

"Did it have a white breast?" interrupted Samuel, letting his eyes rest for a while on that part of a woman's anatomy which is so alluring to men and, for an essential reason, to hungry babes.

"Yes it did," Neffie confirmed.

Her instinctive reaction upon becoming aware that she was being ogled was to fold her arms. It was her defensive response to a look, it was no more than a glance, which she didn't really object to for thinking it perfectly natural.

"So come on, prove to me that you're not just a bookworm," Neffie ordered. "What's its generic name?" she questioned in a jocular manner, unfolding her arms as Samuel's eyes found hers.

"The bird you have just described is a rockfowl... a white-breasted rockfowl to be precise," said Samuel.

Subsequently he turned his head and let his eyes follow Neffie's alternative line of sight to the focal point she perused intermittently. The spectacle of a woman breast-feeding he had seen many times on many buses, and in numerous other locations. There being no other distractions in the offing, the man from Freetown returned to his book, searching for the place at which he had left off reading. The journey from Makari to Makeni took half an hour, time which passed uneventfully.

At the onset of the last decade of the twentieth century the city of Makeni had a population of approximately eighty thousand souls. A settlement which has spread outward rather than upward, the fourth largest city in Sierra Leone is also the capital and administrative centre of Northern Province. Where in this low-rise, thriving metropolis Jake's Bar was located in relation to the route taken by Neffie's and Samuel's bus through the western 'suburbs', neither passenger had any idea; nor did the driver, nor any of the passengers that responded to Neffie's outspoken request for information. They had already travelled a mile along the city's main thoroughfare, a mile along which, under brightly coloured umbrellas, were numerous stalls selling local crafts and produce, as well as a plethora of signs advertising the presence of more substantial and permanent businesses set back from the road. Several of these enterprises were hotels and bars, more often than not nestled in their own decay and dripping verdure. Miss Goodwin, concerned that they might already have passed the venue they were looking for, encouraged Samuel to get up from his seat and go instruct the driver to stop the bus, at once, forthwith, no ifs or buts. The driver did as he was bid and let his two lost sheep off at the earliest practicable opportunity.

Placing her red, canvas holdall on the asphalt surface as she watched the bus move off and gradually diminish until it eventually disappeared from view, Neffie was in a dilemma. She wondered whether it would be wiser to proceed in the direction the bus had taken and make enquiries along the way as to the whereabout of the bar where they were to meet Miss Fussey, or turnabout and go in the opposite direction, back towards the city limits. The latter course would ensure that they hadn't already passed the place they were looking for, and if they had to double back the distance wouldn't be great. Such was Neffie's way of thinking, but to ensure that she wasn't being irrational she sought the opinion of the man whose knowledge was more local than hers.

At the same time as he readjusted the position of the white canvas bag that was slung from his shoulder Samuel gave the matter some thought. Whilst he was occupied weighing up the pros and cons of taking one course of action in preference to the other Neffie took in the sights and sound. She knew that her olfactory sense was working perfectly when she detected a combination of fried plantain and rain. It wasn't raining presently, so the aqueous fragrance had to have been rain that had recently fallen, or, somewhat mystically, rain yet to fall. In one direction lay the preponderance of the city bustling with traffic and people; in the opposite direction was the quieter stretch of road along which they had come. Beyond the suburbs spreading towards their slopes on the far side of the city towered two solidly impressive hills. Comparing these twins, as it were, to the hills which overlooked the towns and villages she was most familiar with back home, Neffie estimated the height of both to be about eight hundred feet. She was just imagining herself standing atop what appeared to be the nearer of the two summits enjoying a panoramic view of Makeni when Samuel interrupted her reverie.

"Well..." he said, in a tone which, prior to any further comment, suggested that he had resolved the problem, "... you were looking out for Jake's Bar when we were on the bus, and didn't see it in that direction..." (he nodded in the direction from which the bus had come) "... so I suggest that we head for the city centre and make some enquiries along the way."

It was out of character for Miss Goodwin to be passive, but as she had sought Samuel's opinion she decided to go along with it, even though it was contrary to her previous inclination. "Perhaps we should have stayed on the bus until we reached the centre of town, and then caught a taxi," Neffie commented as she stooped to pick up the bag containing all the belongings that she had with her in Sierra Leone. It seemed much heavier now that she was faced with the prospect of carrying it some distance. "Surely a taxi-driver would know the whereabouts of Jake's Bar," she announced. Her voice was plaintive.

"It's obviously too late to do anything about the bus, but we could still flag down a taxi if you want," said Samuel, more than a little tempted by the idea. The prospect of having to walk any distance greater than a mile was anathema to him: as far as he was concerned walking for pleasure was an alien concept, and walking to maintain fitness and good health an aberration demeaning to one's self-esteem. "If a taxi does come along I shall flag it down," said Samuel, taking it as fact that Neffie would be willing to pay.

For the time that they were striding towards the centre of town only one taxi passed them by, and though the driver was the only occupant, at the moment of the cavalier's closest proximity to the perspiring pedestrians Samuel's eyes had been focused on Miss Goodwin's heels. The pink patches of skin visible above the platforms provided by her sandals attracted because of their steady, alternating rhythm. The effect was hypnotic, mesmerising, and Samuel only looked up to see the taxi that he could have stopped but didn't when Neffie drew his attention to it, by which time it was too late.

"I thought you were supposed to be keeping an eye open for a cab," Miss Goodwin said, quite loudly for not wishing to expend more energy than she needed to by turning around to face Samuel. Her voice was matter-of-fact and served to make the import of her words seem highly critical. Whenever the circumstances warranted such a disapproving tone she certainly had no compunction about making people aware of their failure, and Samuel was no exception.

"Sorry!" Samuel responded, his apology giving no indication of the scowling face he pulled behind Neffie's back. "I'm surprised that he didn't stop and ask us if we wanted a ride into town," he added, a little pointedly in an effort to deflect some of the blame, and channel some responsibility for the taxi not stopping, "seeing as you have to be a rich westerner struggling with a heavy bag, and therefore likely to be good for a tip once you had been relieved of your burden."

"The bag's not that heavy," said Neffie, a bead of perspiration trickling down the nape of her neck. In keeping with the natural way the human body tries to keep cool, other beads in other parts of her body were exuding from her pores.

"Perhaps he was on his way to pick up a fare. Who knows?"

Who cares?" she questioned, evidently a little exasperated. "It's not us."

A woman carrying a bundle of material on her head approached. She was followed a few yards behind by a boy of seven or eight years of age. Neffie assumed, despite there being no obvious sign of familial affinity, that the pair were mother and son. The distance of approximately eighty yards at which Neffie had first noticed the pair gradually diminished as the parties advanced towards each other. Obviously Miss Goodwin had no idea as to the language spoken by the woman, but she could think of no better option than to make her initial enquiry regarding the location of Jake's Bar in English. If that were to be met with a blank look of incomprehension she would call upon Samuel, with his knowledge of local dialects, to assist.

In the event Neffie uttered not a word to the woman but let her pass by unhindered. It wasn't that in the simple task of asking directions of a stranger Neffie's resolve had weakened. It was just that moments before it would have been opportune to pose her question she caught sight of two male figures on the opposite side of the road, men whose faces were familiar to her even though at first she had been at a loss to place them. It took a moment for the penny to drop, so to speak, but when it did the thought which was bound to cross her mind as a consequence was that there could be no better person to ask the way of than a policeman, and within hailing distance there were two of a kind across the road.

Neffie recognised the officers as being Detective Constables Charles Conteh and Julius Kallon. Without a word of warning to Samuel following hard on her heels Neffie turned ninety degrees to the left and crossed the road, presumably after first checking that she wasn't likely to become the victim of a road traffic accident. Startled, and initially puzzled by Neffie's sudden change of direction, Samuel stopped in his tracks. His assessment of the situation was that Neffie was already acquainted with the two Africans, and he wondered how that could be. As with Neffie there was something in the men's appearance which wasn't unfamiliar to the teacher from Freetown, but with Samuel the proverbial penny remained resolutely free from the influence of gravity when it came to his trying to determine where and when he might have seen the two men previously.

It's often said that you can wait for a bus for an hour, and then two come along one behind the other. Making no attempt to keep to a route or maintain a schedule, chance as perceived by Miss Nefertiti Goodwin appeared to be operating to a similar principle as eccentric bus arrivals when a white pick-up truck pulled up behind her, and she, upon turning her head to ascertain who was behind the wheel and, if possible, why the truck had stopped, discovered that the driver was none other than Di. It was a case of one serendipitous event having followed another.

For having been preoccupied with looking at mopeds through a showroom window the two policemen weren't to know that as direction-finders they had served their purpose admirably. Still blind to her presence for having their backs to her they entered the premises. No longer having a need for their services Neffie let them go without making a claim on their time. She now focused all her attention on the pick-up's driver.

"Jump in," Di commanded.

Di had kept the engine running. She smiled warmly at Neffie through the open window. She was clearly pleased to have found her friend.

"I've brought someone with me," responded Miss Goodwin, peering over the vehicle's bonnet in the direction of where Samuel was watching events from across the road. His continued existence was made momentarily doubtful by a truck heading out of town. "He's here to visit his cousin in Kalangba," added Neffie as Samuel reappeared.

"That's OK," said Miss Fussey, "there's plenty of room for three up front… though you had better chuck your bags in the back."

Neffie beckoned to Samuel to join her, and he, being as averse to walking as he was, needed no further encouragement. After disposing of her luggage as advised, in the process of which Neffie couldn't help but notice the trappings of her American friend's arboreal endeavours, specifically a number of slatted wooden boxes and an assortment of plastic plant pots, Miss Goodwin first heard and then saw the two policemen emerge from the building they had so recently entered.

She called out to them as if they were long lost friends. "What are you two doing in Makeni?" the teacher enquired, and then, without waiting for an answer, she added, "I was going to ask for your help, but as you can see now there's no need."

Neither of the policemen dressed in plain clothes said anything in reply, though both grinned at Neffie as if to them she were a figure of amusement. Feeling a little nonplussed at their silent response, without more ado she climbed into the pick-up. She was working on the basis that as the smaller of the two passengers she should sit in the middle. She left the door ajar for Samuel to follow, which he duly did. Impervious to Miss Fussey's advice and Miss Goodwin's example Mr Massequoi chose not to relinquish his bag, but kept it on his lap like a treasured possession, or a mundane receptacle for the treasured possessions it held. Appearing like one of three wise monkeys Di gently accelerated away from the watching policemen.

"Whatever became of our plan to meet up at Jake's Bar, wherever it may be?" enquired Neffie as they picked up speed heading out of town the way they had come.

The fact that she was in another part of the country, a region which was meant to be safe compared to Koidu District, had allowed Neffie to develop a sense of security which she didn't expect to be proved so false so soon. Di's answer to her question therefore, was all the more shocking for being unexpected.

"Jake... and I should point out that I had only met the guy once... was found dumped by the side of the road two nights ago, at least what was left of him was."

"You mean dead?" said Neffie naively. It distressed her to think that she was experiencing déjà vu of the most horrific kind.

"I mean dead," said Di laconically. "I heard tell that the dogs had got to him before his remains were retrieved. Anyway, the place formerly known as Jake's Bar is now known as Mike's Madhouse, and I thought the change of name might confuse you, so I came looking. It looks like I saved you guys a walk."

Samuel leaned forward and turning towards Di gave her a big smile to show his appreciation.

"Do you think your man Jake was killed by the rebels," enquired Neffie in a solemn tone as she reached out with one hand to grasp hold of an integral part of the vehicle.

Di had caused the vehicle to swerve in order to avoid hitting a cyclist riding his bicycle none too skilfully. The erratic manoeuvring of the man on two wheels was hardly surprising given that he was trying to pedal whilst balancing a sack of something, it could have been rice, or sweet potatoes, or plantains, or some such produce, slung over the handlebars.

"It could have been," Di replied, "but my impression is that it was more a case of good old- fashioned criminality, possibly involving diamonds, but it could just as easily have been to do with drugs."

"Perhaps that's why those two detectives are here in Makeni," Neffie suggested.

"You mean those two smooth-looking operators you were speaking to back there?" interrogated Di.

200

"The very same," said Neffie. "Those were the guys who came to my room to check me out the morning after I had landed," she added, "so seeing as how they're both detectives they may be in Makeni to investigate Jake's murder."

"They could be," Di responded, "but then again perhaps they're in Makeni because you're here, they may be keeping watch on you. Perhaps they think you're a spy working for the British Secret Service."

Whilst listening to the two women converse Samuel realised that a subtle change had occurred in Miss Goodwin's speech: it had assumed a transatlantic quality. For having remained silent for too long his ego now sought expression.

"Now I know where I've seen those two suspicious-looking characters before," he interjected.

Neffie's memory was also proving to be defective when she introduced the people sitting either side of her to each other. "By the way this is Samuel… Samuel this is Di," said Neffie, unnecessarily in that it wasn't the first time the two had met.

Di leaned forward a little and turned her head askance to get a better look at Samuel. She wanted to make sure that the person sitting one place removed was the same individual she had met in the Sussex Hotel back in Freetown.

"We met over coffee at your hotel if you cast your mind back," she reminded Neffie prior to greeting Samuel. "Hi, Sam, how are things?"

"They would be better if the country had greater stability," answered Samuel. It was typical of him to respond in terms of the wider political situation rather than with regard to aspects of his personal life, though there was undoubtedly a correlation between the two. "The administration of Sierra Leone needs a good shake up from top to bottom so that corruption and nepotism are eliminated for good, because if they aren't, and the situation continues to deteriorate, then it won't be long before the streets of towns like Makeni will run red with blood and then there'll be a clamour in some quarters for the return of our colonial masters."

"Heaven forbid!" Neffie exclaimed.

"Heaven forbid!" echoed Samuel.

Neither of the women was expecting to hear a diatribe on the political situation in the country, and with raised eyebrows they looked at each other as if each knew what the other was thinking.

"Do you have to be so cheerful?" questioned Di, thinking that now wasn't the time and the cab of her pick-up wasn't the place for serious discussion.

Soon after leaving the last of Makeni's dwellings behind the peace corps volunteer turned right onto a road which was sign-posted Manke three miles, and Rundong seven. Even though the road surface was made from laterite she was able to maintain a speed similar to that averaged on the major metal road; for the time being at least.

"This isn't the most direct route to Kalangba, but it should be quicker because it saves us having to go through the centre of town and getting snarled up in crowds, and maybe traffic," Di informed.

"I have not been by this route to Kalangba Junction ever before in my life," said Samuel. "Thank you for showing me more of my beautiful country." His tone was light. He was evidently intent on being cheerful.

Peering at the dense bush encroaching upon the road to right and left, all beneath a leaden sky, Miss Fussey was inclined to say, "You know where you can stick it," but the words she spoke instead were, "Glad to be of service."

"I hope the rain keeps off until we reach Kalangba," said Neffie, keen to maintain the air of civility. "I don't want my bag to get soaked."

"I don't think you need worry," said Di, confident that they would reach their destination before the heavens opened.

A period of silence ensued, and the mood in the cab only became animated again when Miss Fussey turned right onto the narrow track which leads from Manke to Kunshu. The fact that the village of Kunshu hadn't been signposted previously confirmed its insignificance to all but those that live there. Barely the width of one vehicle the route proved to be a daunting proposition, primarily because of the deep ruts filled with the rain water that fell and then partially steamed away on a daily basis. The two passengers wondered if their driver had brought them this way in order to provide an adventure; but even the redoubtable Miss Fussey questioned her own judgement when they arrived at a stream in full flow. She had last driven through it in the dry season, when the flow had been barely a trickle. Now, after already having driven a mile or so through squelching mud, mud which would have held them fast were it not for four-wheel drive, the stream was at least ten yards wide, and there was no telling yet how deep. Moreover, the track on the far side seemed to have disappeared, the opposite bank having collapsed and become completely overgrown.

Di stopped a few yards from the water's edge. She wanted to assess the situation before committing the pick-up irrevocably. Despite the road being wider at this point, she realised that any attempt to drive through the stream at speed would be reckless: a large boulder and a fallen tree appeared to block the way. In reality, however, these objects formed a natural chicane, the gap between them being just wide enough for the pick-up to be driven through with care. Getting the angle of approach right was paramount.

"What do you think?" asked Di as she stared fixedly at the current: she wondered whether it was strong enough to send the pick-up and its people on a journey they didn't want to make.

"Are there likely to be crocodiles?" queried Neffie, alerting her fellow travellers to her overriding fear with regard to pushing ahead. "I won't be responsible for my actions if we get stuck in the middle and become surrounded by crocs," she added, her levity clearly emphasising how much she would dread such a prospect.

"I can't see any," said Di. She too didn't much fancy being dragged under and becoming a meal for such, in her opinion, a hideous creature.

"Did you know that some people believe that crocodiles weep when they're devouring their prey?" posed Samuel: he had a didactic mien.

"You're kidding," Neffie retorted.

"Hence the expression crocodile tears," said Samuel, rounding off his linguistic lesson prior to benefiting the others with his knowledge of reptilian natural history. "It looks the perfect spot for crocs, as you call them, to gather," the male teacher informed, "and just because you can't see them doesn't mean they're not there, lurking menacingly below the surface. That's why I'm for turning around and going back through town."

There was a stubborn streak to Miss Fussey. It was a trait which was more likely to become apparent when being advised, but more often than not dictated to, by a man. The consequence of Mr Massequoi having advised caution therefore was that the wilful American made up her mind to venture onward, citing the motto of an elite British Army regiment as she impelled the vehicle gently forward.

Contrary to her inclination to be contrary when it came to men giving her advice, it's doubtful that Di would have turned the vehicle around if Samuel had suggested they should attempt to cross the stream regardless of its real or imagined subaqueous dangers. For his part Samuel harrumphed loudly in response to his recommendation having been disregarded. Between the two Miss Goodwin sat in pensive silence.

Di negotiated the obstacle course with consummate skill. Then, after straightening the wheels, she drove forward to enter the water. At this point the views to left and right up and downstream were as good as they were going to get in respect of how much of the stream was visible, and to the relief of Miss Goodwin in particular there wasn't a slender-snouted crocodile in sight, nor any other breed of reptilian for that matter.

The pick-up lurched forward over the uneven ground that was the stream bed. Di and Samuel each wound down the window closest to them to observe how deeply submerged the front wheels became. Progress was slow and far from steady, but it was progress. Fortunately the stream proved not to be as deep as those aboard the pick-up had feared. From halfway across, the closer the pick-up drew to the terra firma of the approaching shore, the way ahead became more easily discernible, and when the individuals concerned were able to observe that the front wheels were a tyre's width of being completely exposed, their relief was considerable.

No sooner was the pick-up free of hazards, of being swept away or becoming well and truly stuck, than Di let out a loud whoop of triumph in the way that Americans often do when greeting success. "I knew we could do it," she said as she drove through the foliage covering the bank at their crossing point prior to heading along the track revealed thereafter. Relatively speaking the track in question was welcoming to behold and a pleasure to drive along.

It didn't take them long to reach the village of Kunshu, where they turned north onto the main road heading to Pendembu, though their ultimate destination was approximately halfway between the two. The mood in the cab was buoyant. It remained so until journey's end.

Half an hour after the day's main adventure that was the swollen river crossing, upon pulling up outside the house that belonged to his cousin, Samuel said, "I always knew that you could do it. I only advised you to turn back because I knew it would spur you on to success." He spoke as if the woman behind the steering-wheel were one of his pupils.

"Is that right?" questioned Di, her tone one of disbelief.

"That's right," said Samuel as he exited the vehicle.

Moving across to the seat which was warm for having just been vacated, through the open window Neffie said, "I didn't realise that you were a psychologist as well as a teacher."

Settling his sports bag comfortably over his shoulder Samuel responded didactically. "It's impossible to be a good teacher without being able to motivate people, but I'm telling you what you already know."

"Indeed I do," said Miss Goodwin. "See you later, Sam," said Miss Fussey.

"Yes, see you later, Sam," echoed Neffie as the pick-up pulled away in the direction of the house which was the centre of Kalangba Junction's tree-planting project.

Chapter Seventeen
Letters to the Editor

The following is the text of a letter sent by Charlie W. Tucker (Jr), a student in Form V at Bonthe Secondary School, and published in an August 1991 edition of the New Shaft Newspaper.

MY NARROW ESCAPE FROM CHARLES TAYLOR'S BANDITS

Dear Sir,

Kindly allow me space in your widely read newspaper to let every reader know how I narrowly made my escape from the evil hands of bandits who attacked my village Gbap on the 11 July, 1991 before the high-sky victory of our soldiers, all Sierra Leoneans stationed in Bonthe over them the following day.

I am the son of C.W. Tucker of Nongoba Bullom Chiefdom. News of these bandits reached Bonthe the same day I left with seven military men that were posted to my village to beat back these bandits. We left Bonthe at night around eight p.m. and reached Gbap at midnight. We slept at my father's house and very early the following day we sent two villagers to go and spy the next village not far from ours where we heard the bandits were so that I would lead the soldiers to Solon, the village they had already based. The two spies could not reach Solon as they heard gunshots almost at the end of their destination. They came back and confirmed to us that the rebels were truly in the village Solon.

On hearing the report, I led the way with two soldiers an M.I.B. (Mr Bendu) and a private soldier who volunteered to go with me. We walked along the Sewa. The two soldiers advised that we return to Gbap realising that they would be overpowered as the rebels were in their hundreds. We went back for the remaining five soldiers and they all went back well-armed for the attack. I stayed behind in the village as it was already night. When the soldiers reached the village they could not meet bandits as they had already boarded boats for the chiefdom headquarter Gbap, my village. The soldiers were told that the bandits were mostly Liberians and few Sierra Leonean captives. The soldiers decided to return to Bonthe for reinforcement as they had no means of communication in the village.

That night as I was alone in the chief's house and knowing full well that if these bandits were to reach Gbap the first place to go would be the chief's compound, I left there and slept elsewhere. The soldiers came back (a few words are indecipherable here) same night and when they couldn't see me in the house they felt I had already run away to save my life. They had to walk on foot thirty-six miles to Momaya to board the launches from Mattru to Bonthe. I was now left behind alone in the village with no soldier with me.

Very early the next day at about six thirty a.m. I went to the chiefs compound to see if the soldiers returned or were still on operation at Solon. No sooner had arrived in the chief's compound, then I saw a very large crowd at the jetty and not recognising the bandits I started running towards them feeling that they were our soldiers. Getting closer to them I noticed ununiformed men dressed in assorted colour ronkos made from cotton cloth with jujus hanging all around them. I took to my heels to save my life. As I was fleeing a very small boy opened the door to urinate outside their house. I grabbed him on the way and entered the house where I found all in the house women. The bandits followed me to the house and knocked at the door but nobody answered. That time the oldest of the women in the house had already hidden me under the bed putting pots before me. They forced their way into the house and asked the woman to produce the male that entered the house. The woman denied that no man entered the house and in fact that they were all women in the house except the six-year-old boy I had saved outside the house.

They entered the room I was hidden and when they saw the pots before the bed they asked why the woman had placed the pots that way. She told them she had cassava in the largest of the pots and it has been her usual practice to hide her cooking equipment under the bed. They asked for food and as one was about to take the pot of cassava the woman rushed and took it for them to the parlour to eat. She gave them soup and water and sat with them. Whilst they were eating they made their plan for the village. Another civilian one Eddie Kamara who had once been a prisoner in the Bonthe prisons for several years and a native of the town came in who had been made commando since he knew the town better. He told them that the soldiers were in the chief's compound and that I, the chief's son brought them. They left to search for me and soldiers.

As they left for the chief's compound the woman who had saved my life told me it was better if I made my escape as soon as possible. I ran into the bush but the vegetation of the place is some sort of savannah grass land with only few dwarf trees. I was therefore in a place of seeing the bandits making their way to the chief's compound led by their new commando Eddie Kamara who incidentally was my own uncle. When they found no one at the chief's compound they went to the government house 'The State House' and no one was found there also. I could still see them from my hiding place. They came back to the chief's house and burnt it down and they started looting civilians' property and killing those whom they caught. My uncle told them that I was in the house they first went and my head was all he wanted from them. They came back to the house. For the whole of that day gun shots became a household sound in my village. Other houses of prominent people including the court Barri were put ablaze.

At this point of time I left my place of hiding and continued to make my escape crawling on the ground since I could be seen running away. I made a successful escape into a very big forest where I stayed for three days till three speed boats came from Bonthe with soldiers. The bandits were met at sea returning to their bases where our soldiers had a high-sky victory over them with no return of bullet from the bandits. A grenade was first thrown into each of their three boats which destroyed the boats and all the bandits went into the river and bullets were rained on them from G.P.M.G. and anti-aircraft machine guns with no survivor amongst the bandits except the commando who was asked to stay in Gbap as they promised coming back the next day when the soldiers would have gone. He was later captured and taking down to Bonthe with some of the ronkos they left and so many single-barrel shotguns they left with him. He was paid back in his own coin before thousands of jubilating Bontonians for our victorious Sierra Leonean soldiers. (Yours faithfully... etc.).

The following is the text of the letter from Kpang Kepetewa, Section Chief — Panguma, published in *The Nation* in August 1991.

REFERENDUM?

Dear Sir,

The decision of the A.P.C. Government to go ahead with the referendum on the multi-party constitution on 23rd August, is a very sad mistake.

I wonder whether the Freetown people suspect that something horrible is happening in the Eastern part of the country — Sierra Leone. The entire Pujehun and Kailahun District, part of Kenema and Kone District are seriously perturbed by this rebel incursion. In fact there are more than 120,000 refugees in Guinea and 91,000 displaced. How will Government expect these people to vote? Late Siaka Steven said, "We can never put our house in order when the enemy is at the back door." The most urgent thing to do now is to drive these rebels out of the country before thinking of any general election on the multi-party basis.

But sadly enough, some of the Sierra Leone soldiers, I.S.U. and Liberian soldiers who are fighting against the rebel are no better than the rebels themselves. They have terrorised our people in a way that many of them will be too afraid to come forward to express their right to vote in this coming election. For example in the Lower Bambara Chiefdom, in the Kenema District, the military personnel stationed in Foindu do pay a frequent visit to the surrounding villages like Dandabu asking the poor village people to pay Le2,000 and a goat for protecting their lives. At the check points on the road from Kenema to Panguma-Tongo, soldiers are harassing passengers for identity cards. At the check point in Mano Junction, I showed my driving license to one illiterate I.S.U. who told me, "Me not to traffic police. Either you show me your I.D. card or you give me Le200.00." Is this the type of security personnel we are going to entrust our country for the future elections?

It is now an open secret that some of these soldiers were involved in looted properties in the war zone. I have seen some of these soldiers selling drums of palm oil in Bo, and Kenema. Most of the properties looted in Bunumbu Teachers' College were not looted by the rebels alone. Some of our army personnel were involved.

Even though some of them are working hard to bring this rebel incursion to an end, some of the soldiers will take this rebel crisis to continue so that they will enrich themselves more and more. We are now fed up and tired of feeding them. Let Government do something about these irresponsible soldiers who do not know their duty: otherwise it will be too late. (Yours sincerely… etc.).

Chapter Eighteen
A Conversation

Three days after her arrival in Kalangba Junction, in the fading natural light Miss Nefertiti Goodwin was sitting on the veranda of the house in which she was staying as Miss Diane Fussey's guest. The previous night she had enjoyed — in the later stages endured — a late-night drinking session in Mariana's Bar situated on the far side of the village. Presently, therefore, it was pleasant to be sitting quietly listening to the natural sonority of a tropical evening. The dwelling in question was a bungalow. Like many buildings in Sierra Leone it had a corrugated tin-sheet roof. The drumming of the rain, though as heavy and as insistent as ever, no longer disquieted the Englishwoman. She had become habituated to it. At a right angle to the Peace Corps bungalow stood a more traditional thatched-roof dwelling. This was occupied by a local family whose members assisted Di in her work.

The sun was sinking fast behind a line of spindly palms, and as if it were a window for a far-sighted person to be able to observe the movement of the spheres, the only gap visible in an otherwise ubiquitous blanket of cloud tempted the human spirit to look upon where it lingered in the western sky. The window on the cosmos shaped by the cloud was a soft-edged, rather lop-sided parallelogram. The fact that the lengths of the top and bottom were so much greater than the sides gave it a squashed appearance. Plumb in the middle appeared a segment of that giant orange which in the tropics is often the image the sun presents. The segment grew larger with each minute that passed. More than once Neffie looked up from the book of literary criticism she was reading, a book chosen following a cursory inspection of the titles lining the two shelves of books that formed Miss Fussey's library, and each time she became a captive to the spectacle long enough to lose her place. Her attention oscillated between words aspiring to create pictures in the mind and the purest form of kinetic art.

Having observed the sun's lower rim appear, on the second occasion she looked up she saw the mass of the star minus its upper and lower segments; on the third the upper rim about to disappear. She watched transfixed as the final sliver sank from view, and the most stunning effect of its setting was the way in which the lower edge of the gap in the clouds reflected the sun's effulgence with molten intensity.

There was, by this time, insufficient natural light to read by, and for the last time that day Neffie closed her book, and having done so she consciously tuned in to the music of the forest as the chirring of the cicadas, and numerous other creatures, grew louder for becoming more prolific. Neffie thought the evening serenade enchanting; romantic. In keeping with the ambiance of the concert hall when the audience listens as if spellbound, demonstrating quiet solemnity she placed the book on the table beside her. This and two chairs constituted the only items of furniture on the veranda. In expecting Di to have emerged from the bungalow half an hour since Neffie hadn't expected the other chair to be still unoccupied. She began to wonder if her American friend was ever going to appear. It wasn't that Neffie was in any way worried. Indeed, she had been perfectly content to pass the time alone, in the presence of so many natural wonders.

Enveloped by darkness but for that patch of clear sky now turned turquoise to the west, a patch which presently adhered to no geometric shape in particular, Neffie's thoughts turned towards home and Sebastian. She was only too aware that he hadn't been in her thoughts much over recent days. This was hardly surprising insofar as the pattern which was so familiar to her had been established over years of travel. The pattern was always the same. She would miss him terribly at first, and then, as the spirit of her new environment and the personalities she met within it became more deeply embedded in her psyche as a consequence of her greater depth of knowledge, of it, of them, and of herself in the midst of both, thoughts of home and the tentacles of commitment which tied her to it gradually became more desultory. The longing which she had felt at first — on the ferry crossing from the airport, her one and only night in the Sussex Hotel — had lessened, and she knew that with regard to her love for Seb she would be able to see out her time in the country with a quiescent mind. It goes without saying that this recently acquired serenity didn't preclude the possibility that she would have to contend with further traumas extraneous to her love life, the emotional fall-out from distressing incidents geographically closer than home.

Neffie wasn't selfish when it came to thinking about her relationship with Seb. She knew that in at least one way their time apart was worse for him than it was for her. She would have had a heart of stone if she hadn't been aware of the sudden sense of loss she caused whenever she walked out of the door at the height of summer not to be seen again for over a month. He had likened the feeling to bereavement. Whereas she was heading for new experiences, new adventures, Seb had to contend with life alone, life which they had grown accustomed to leading together. In every one of the several discussions they had had on the subject he had expressed the view that his longing was greater than hers: it didn't take a genius of psychology to appreciate the implication of such a statement. Neffie had said nothing to contradict her partner in his view, and Sebastian was keen to aver that he made no apologies if by this often repeated belief she were to think him pathetic.

"He's probably been going to the pub every night and come home tiddly," said Neffie aloud. She was under the apprehension that the only ears in which her words were audible were hers.

"Who has?" inquired Di as she appeared in the doorway.

The wooden door had been left wide open, but to cross the threshold it was necessary to pull apart the magnets which held the fine mesh of a fly screen together. It was through this screen that Di heard her friend's short soliloquy. Following hard on the heels of her question Miss Fussey used her free hand to prize the screen apart and emerge onto the veranda. In her left hand she carried a lighted oil lamp. After making sure that the flimsy but effective defence against marauding insects was closed behind her, Di strode a few paces along the veranda to where she knew there to be a handy nail. Protruding for half its length, the nail had been put in place for the sole purpose of enabling the lady of the lamp to hang her means of illumination from it. Already a multitude of apparently crazy moths and other insects were flying and buzzing around the luminescence. It was to serve a dual purpose that Di had hung the lamp at some distance from where she intended to sit and from where Neffie was sitting.

"I'll be right back," said Di prior to re-entering the house.

Either from carelessness or for a reason which only she knew, Di omitted to close the fly screen behind her.

She wasn't out of Neffie's sight for long however, and returned with four bottles of beer in one hand and a bottle opener in the other. One after the other she placed the bottles on the table so that they were standing upright in the shape of a diamond. Neffie took it upon herself to secure the fly screen and for good measure closed the door. In the meantime Di removed the first bottle top and plonked the bottle intended for her friend back down on the table next to Neffie's book. Upon opening the second bottle Di took a swig and then wiped the froth from her mouth. She had no inhibition in using her shirt sleeve. Notwithstanding that their faces and necks were exposed to those insects not tempted and possibly driven to distraction by the lamp, for the fact that each of the women was wearing a long-sleeved shirt and full-length jeans, they were evidently sensibly dressed for spending an hour or two in the open at night. They sat down together.

"Thanks," said Neffie referring to the beer. "I was thinking out loud," she added prior to raising the bottle to her lips, but pausing in this action she made what for her was a mordant comment, "I didn't realise you were creeping about behind me."

This remark wasn't meant to be as cutting as it sounded, and it certainly wasn't meant to be taken to heart.

"You were thinking about Sebastian?" rejoined Di interrogatively, seeking to get to the nub of her friend's former pensiveness.

"That's right," Neffie replied after mirroring Di's performance in wiping away the froth. Evidently it was difficult to take the first gulp from the bottle without creating some excess which didn't go where it was intended.

"Are you missing him?" said Di, posing the question which sounded trite to her ears for being obvious.

"When I say yes and no don't get me wrong. I missed him terribly at first, and I was certainly thinking of him just now, before you came onto the veranda, but once the pain of being apart has become less acute and I no longer have the urge to catch the next flight home... then I can look forward to our reunion positively, and once that... how should I say... once that optimistic outlook has developed and become established, then I can begin to live in and enjoy the present, providing the murder, rape and pillage is kept to a minimum."

A tendency to speak lightly about serious matters was a trait she had picked up by dint of living with Sebastian. She thought it a useful stratagem in that it kept the horrors of life at a safe distance.

"I mean let's face it... to be six weeks apart is hardly a lifetime," Neffie continued prior to taking a sip of beer, and having done so she expounded further, "before we lived together our relationship was rather furtive, and that was because Seb was already engaged to be married. Most if not all the arrangements for the wedding had been made. A considerable sum of money had already been spent. His fiancée was from La Rochelle in the Vendée would you believe?"

If asked Neffie wouldn't have been able to give a reason as to why she had concluded her last sentence so sceptically, but the tone of incredulity had a particular resonance for her listener, prompting Di to surmise that Sebastian's decision to forsake his betrothed had come as a complete surprise to Neffie, and consequently it was at least possible that she had had to make a commitment which in other circumstances she might not have chosen to make. This was mere speculation on Miss Fussey's part, and because she considered her friend's question to have been rhetorical she continued to be silently attentive.

"Anyway, a number of years ago I decided that I was going to fulfil what at the time was my life's ambition, which was to travel to those parts of the world I had no direct knowledge of, at least as many as I could manage in a year. To that end I booked my place on an expedition organised by a company called Overland Odysseys — you might have heard of them."

"Not till a few seconds ago," said Di as she made herself comfortable in the chair she had manoeuvred a little closer to Neffie's. The light from the lamp illuminated the right side of her face, the side facing Neffie, and gave her features a haunting look, a look redolent of reflected moonlight.

"People like me," resumed Neffie, "pay to travel hundreds, if not thousands, of miles in the back of a Bedford truck, usually a British Army cast-off, across Africa and Asia. It was a big decision to go because it meant having to give up my job, but the way I felt on coming home from school after having handed in my notice told me I had done the right thing: I felt quite elated. There could be no chickening out after that. When it came to deciding which trip I wanted to go on I opted for Africa and the more southerly countries of Asia."

"Why was that?" Di interposed.

"Well I had already travelled across your patch from coast to coast, picking up a boyfriend along the way I may add, and then I took a trip to South America, sampling most of its countries before journey's end in Argentina. I have yet to go to Canada and visit the countries of Central America, but I think I've done reasonably well to explore what I have of the Americas in the time I had available."

"I'll say," Di affirmed emphatically. "You've certainly seen more of the world than I have," she added.

A hypothetical third party listening to this conversation might have noted that there were occasions when the American woman's accent sounded more northern British than was wont. In the next instant Miss Goodwin's confidante made a lightning fast movement of her hand, slapping the side of her neck as she sought to end the life of a blood-sucking insect. The sudden movement startled Neffie, but she soon regained her composure once she realised that Di wasn't trying to do herself harm.

"It doesn't end there," said Neffie. "Australia I had been to a couple of times, and then there was my trip to China, and I mustn't forget my journey by train all the way across Russia and Siberia from Moscow to Vladivostok. I suppose that journey really began when I stepped outside my front door in Yatton to catch the bus into Ferrousby. That was my greatest worry, dashing the fifty yards to the end of the road and turning the corner to see the number twenty-nine bus pulling away from the bus-stop, on its way to town without me. You see I'm terrible at getting up in the mornings, always have been, and if I had missed the bus I would have missed my first train and then my entire schedule would have gone to pot."

216

"Gone to pot?" Di questioned, seeking clarification regarding a phrase which wasn't familiar, though inevitably her recollection of parties and people smoking a recreational drug came to mind.

"Yes, gone to pot. It's an expression we use in England meaning…" Neffie paused as she considered how best to translate the phrase in question into less idiomatic language. "…it means gone awry, you know, when all your plans are in a mess."

She wasn't completely satisfied with her explanation, but on the basis that it was the best she could do on the spur of the moment Neffie continued with her revelations. Given that she would have described herself as a naturally reticent person her loquacity in this regard surprised even her, so much so that at one point she eyed her ghostly lit host suspiciously, as if the latter had some mystical power that compelled confession.

"The point I'm trying to make is that Seb made his move of his own free will knowing perfectly well the sort of person I am — a person who loves to travel. I also love horses but that's another story. I'm sure I don't need to tell you that when I speak of travelling I don't mean in a tourist sense, but in the sense of really getting to know the country I'm in and its people. If I hadn't taken up teaching I would have loved to have become an anthropologist."

"And this man of yours… Sebastian… waited for a whole year while you were away enjoying yourself?" Di's tone gave the impression that she found it astonishing that any man would be prepared to put up with such a lengthy absence by his prospective partner, particularly when that absence had been instigated as a matter of choice, and for reasons which many would consider hedonistic. In truth she found Neffie's willingness to subject Sebastian to such a test impressive, and Sebastian's resilience in passing it no less so.

"Don't imagine that I go travelling merely to enjoy myself," Neffie insisted, "though it would be a silly thing to do if I weren't to gain a great deal of enjoyment from it. If there was no pleasure in it I wouldn't do it," Neffie explained with feminine logic. "I think of travelling as a means of developing myself as a person and becoming a wiser human being I hope. You know the old cliche about travel broadening the mind."

"This Sebastian of yours sounds quite a guy," proclaimed Di prior to tilting back her head to drain the bottle of its content.

Not wishing to hog the conversation when it came to making revelations of a romantic nature, insofar as there appeared to be a natural break in the proceedings Neffie took the opportunity to change the viewpoint.

"What about you… has there ever been anyone in your life who came close to tempting you to settle down?" Before Di had a chance to answer Neffie added, "Or perhaps was the real reason for your taking off into the forest?"

Di's startled response was to splutter beer uncontrollably. Upon regaining her composure, she said, "What… don't you think that I believe wholeheartedly in this tree-planting project? Don't you believe that I'm doing what I do for the benefit of the people living hereabouts as opposed to subjecting myself to a kind of penance for an ill-fated love affair?" Smiling as she spoke, Miss Fussey's demeanour was at best confusing, at worst beguiling.

"I was only asking," said Miss Goodwin, a little diffidently for thinking that despite her friend's amicable expression revealing the contrary, she might have irked her sensibility somewhat. The thought occurred to Neffie that personal relationships weren't a topic of discussion which Di found comfortable, and that by posing the questions she had she really had got beneath her skin, so to speak. Neffie felt that by effectively unsettling her friend's air of self-confidence and self-control, in an emotional sense she had opened up a previously hidden wound. "If you would prefer to discuss politics, or religion, or anything that may be less provocative, it's all right by me," Miss Goodwin added, trying to be helpful by providing an escape route of sorts.

"He was called Doug," said Di, solemnly as if speaking about someone who had been close to her but who had died.

This solemnity of tone gave Neffie the impression that Di had suddenly determined to expunge the pain of her lost love by speaking freely about it, and where better to open one's heart than in Kalangba Junction on a balmy tropical night, and who better to enrol as a therapist to help alleviate hidden pain than a British primary school teacher who had more pluck than most. There was no one likely to be more considerate, more understanding.

"He was considerably older than me," began Di as she opened the two full bottles of beer, depositing the first one opened in front of Neffie. "He had just turned fifty when we met. I didn't think the difference in our ages was going to be a problem at the time, and it wasn't, at least not as far as our compatibility was concerned." Her story was gaining in fluency and momentum. "He was quite a lot taller than me as well. He would have made a good basketball player, even though I don't believe he ever played the game. Cricket and tennis were his sporting metiers."

"Cricket?" interrupted Neffie. She had had it in mind that this erstwhile man in Di Fussey's life was either an American or a guy from Sierra Leone, neither of whom she would have expected to play cricket.

"He was from Adelaide, and you know what Australians are like… sport mad. I met him in Freetown when I first arrived in the country. He was very protective of me at first, which I thought was sweet of him. It didn't take long for me to stop thinking of him as a kind, father figure and see him as the sexy bronze Adonis that he was. But it wasn't just sex. Gradually our feelings for each other deepened. Come to think of it," Di blurted latterly in a voice changed from the confessional to a tone vibrant with the excitement of discovery, "our meeting was perhaps not so different to your meeting Samuel at the airport and then becoming…"

"Mr Massequoi," interjected Neffie abruptly, "is nothing more to me than a friend." Evidently she was keen to assert the differences rather than the similarities in the relationships being compared. "And what's more I know of at least one Australian who isn't the least bit interested in sport, not even tiddly-winks."

It was Neffie's turn to gulp the last of the beer from the first bottle, and having done so she wasted no time in disposing of that bottle and picking up the second. The smooth glass her fingers were curled around added to her sense of security.

"What was Doug doing in Sierra Leone?"

"Trying to bring power to the people," Miss Fussey replied.

It didn't take Neffie longer than a moment to realise that rather than being an activist for a left-wing political party, Doug was more likely to be involved in generating power of the kind that runs along cables to make everyday items such as ceiling fans and refrigerators work, a conclusion which was confirmed when Miss Fussey made reference to the King Tom Power Plant.

"I take it that Doug is an engineer of some sort?" Neffie questioned.

"He was," Di replied, emphasising the verb to ensure that there could be no doubt that the past was different from the present, and because her friend had been somewhat woolly when it came to describing her former lover's occupation, less demonstratively she informed, "He was an electrical engineer."

"What happened to him? Did he give up being an engineer to become a professional sportsman? Or did he drop down dead after being hit on the head by a cricket ball? What happened?"

"That's just what he did do… die that is. We were playing tennis at the Lagonda Hotel, just the two of us. You may know it. If you don't, I can tell you that it's a rather grand complex overlooking Man of War Bay. It boasts a night club which is popular with Freetown's more affluent boys and girls. It used to be popular with French tourists, but that was in less troubled times when there were such people. Anyway, we were well into the second set if I remember correctly, when suddenly he dropped his racket after sprinting from the base line to return a cross court volley close to the net. It was a Saturday in February and the temperature on court must have been over thirty degrees. In the next instant I saw him raise his hands to his chest. I thought what game is this: the gesture made him look like an opera singer expressing his undying love. I almost burst out laughing. I'm sure glad I didn't because the expression on his face as he dropped to his knees told a different story. He was obviously in agony. Then he crumpled into a lifeless heap onto the clay. It all happened so quickly. I was still too far away to know for certain that he had died of a heart attack there and then, but I sensed that he had. My stomach felt queasy and I went weak at the knees. Fortunately I was able to remain standing. For what seemed like an age I was transfixed to the spot, unable to move."

"How tragic," croaked Neffie for want of something sympathetic to say, though of course she realised that whatever she might have said wouldn't have adequately expressed the shock that Di had experienced.

"You must have been devastated. What did do you do once you got over the initial shock?"

"For the first few seconds, seconds that seemed like an eternity, I just stood there in stupefied silence, tennis racket held limply in one hand, my free hand raised to my mouth as if about to suppress a scream. I distinctly remember saying to myself you're not going to... scream that is... and I didn't. Once I had gotten over my initial shock, as you say, I shouted for help. At the first attempt I could barely get the word out of my mouth, and I thought that was pathetic. My second attempt was better for being several decibels louder, and it was evidently effective for whilst kneeling at Doug's side, and this was only a few seconds after I had called for assistance, from over my shoulder I heard a man speaking in French. Without a by your leave he pushed me out of the way and set about trying to resuscitate Doug by applying pressure to his chest. He kept up a steady rhythm, but it was no use. The patient failed to respond. At some point in the proceedings Doctor Michelet — it was an hour or so later that I learned his name and that he was indeed a medical doctor — checked Doug's wrist and neck for signs of a pulse, but I'm not sure if that was before or after he had set to work on trying to bring Doug back to life. If only there had been a defibrillator to hand, things might have been so different."

"I'm so sorry," said Neffie.

"So am I," said Di, trying to force a smile but finding it easier to shed a tear.

Demonstrating a desire to provide emotional support by tactile means, Neffie reached out with her hand across the table. From the midst of nearby trees a bird shrieked its presence; a soulful sound followed by a rapid beating of wings. For not wanting to appear weak Di didn't respond to Neffie's gesture. Instead, demonstrating greater resolve, she wiped away a tear and said, "Life goes on. I'm going to have another beer. Can I get you one?"

Up until a quarter of an hour ago Neffie would have declined a third, but now, under the circumstances, how could she refuse.

Chapter Nineteen
A Man Alone

When not fully awake, but occupying instead that far from distinct isthmus that links dream and reality, it wasn't unusual for Sebastian to reach out with the palm of his hand for that surface which is somehow soft yet, paradoxically, firm to a man's touch. The cool tautness of Neffie's naked thigh or buttock was reassuring at whatever time of night or early morning he sought its smoothness, and this morning upon making the transition from sleep to wakefulness he acted in good faith by doing that which had become instinctive, habitual.

We were correct to surmise that Sebastian's barely conscious anticipation was bound to meet with disappointment, there being no gentle contours of flesh, no resistance until his hand came down flat upon the sheet covering the unyielding mattress. Only then did reality, like the sun or moon suddenly emerging from behind a cloud to shine in all their glory, break through sleep's tenuous hold to ruffle his psyche. Only then did Sebastian fully realise that the space beside him remained as it had been when he had switched off the light he read by shortly before midnight. Now fully alert he reached across to Neffie's normally cluttered, now strangely tidy, bedside table to check his watch. There had to be a reason as to why he had put it on her side of the bed, but he hadn't probed his mind to find it. Perhaps it had to do with his being master of the master bedroom completely. Or, abstrusely, perhaps it had to do with a longing to share time with his departed lover.

The sun's effulgence filtering through the thin, translucent curtains heralded a fine summer's day. It was earlier than Seb had anticipated, and if he had been able to choose he would have preferred to have remained dead to the world for another hour. It was 5.50 a.m. For Seb this meant that the morning was sufficiently advanced for him not to be able to get back to sleep. Personality traits preventing further repose were compounded externally by happenings in the street, and internally by a rather pressing physical need. In the street, between the whir of arrival and the whir of departure that was the sound of his electric float, the milkman could be heard clinking bottles and stacking crates. These sounds, though familiar, were responsible for disturbing Sebastian's sleep more than any other.

Seb's sensitivity in this regard was in marked contrast to Neffie's near total deafness when she was in the land of nod. Owl hoots, dogs barking, cats wailing like babies suffering torture, drunks returning from the pub after a lock-in and singing at the top of their voices, she could be oblivious to them all. If Sebastian hadn't told her, and she hadn't seen the evidence on the doorsteps of the houses across the street, she wouldn't have been aware that there was still such an occupation as milkman or milk-woman. Whenever Seb enquired sotto voce, "Are you awake?" to ascertain if she could hear the owl, the dog, the drunk or the pussy-cat, there was rarely a response.

Five minutes after the milk float was out of his earshot Seb was eavesdropping on a conversation being conducted without regard for the somnolent peace of the neighbourhood. A volume which wouldn't have been excessive at midday, or even two or three hours hence, sounded particularly loud at six in the morning — to one wide-awake listener at least. It was as if the two women holding forth were of a mindset which believed that if they had to be awake at such an ungodly hour then so should everybody else. This morning's discussion in public about a third party's fraught relationship with her husband not surprisingly grew to a crescendo when the confabulating pair passed directly beneath Seb's window, and gradually faded as no doubt a crescendo was reached farther along the street.

Seb had heard these voices many times, but he hadn't ever been sufficiently curious to jump out of bed with the intention of identifying the speakers, or, failing that, at least putting faces to the voices. He imagined them to be cleaners on their way to restore cleanliness and order to the bar of the Captain Cook Inn, and if not there then to the counters and shelves of the newsagent's shop also located in the centre of the village. The next sound to assail Sebastian Forrest's ears was the throaty roar of a diesel engine, one which, Seb was sure, powered a bus passing the junction at the end of the road. His auricular sense also led him to deduce that the bus was heading out of Yatton on its way to either Ferrousby or Luxborough, the route and destination being determined by the number displayed above the driver's window. This was the last significant noise that Sebastian heard before he threw back the covers and leapt out of bed.

He was in a good mood. Notwithstanding Neffie's absence two factors contributed to his positive frame of mind and benign emotional state, more or less in equal measure. These were that it was the first day of his weekend off and that the weather forecast for the two days was good. In the light of these considerations it could be said that Seb's cheerfulness had been enhanced rather than soured by his waking early. He certainly wasn't going to succumb to self-pity as a consequence of Neffie having gone off on one of her jaunts for the summer. No; for the reason his mind was presently functioning at a superficial level, life was far from being doom and gloom, particularly as he now had the sole use of the car they shared and could, within reason, travel to wherever he chose. The only arbiters were the requirement to get back in time for work on Monday morning, and how much money he had in the bank. But whatever the hours ahead had in store Seb's immediate recourse was to go to the bathroom to relieve the pressure on his bladder. Subsequently, whilst washing his hands, he decided that the next thing he would do was to go down to the kitchen and make a cup of tea. He considered the first cup of the day to be the perfect stimulus. Then, to gain clarity of thought, he would savour it in bed.

Prior to negotiating the stairs Seb searched for his dressing-gown. He was unable to find it for the reason that he had forgotten where he had put it the day before, forgotten that it was hanging from the washing-line in the back yard, where, in addition to several pairs of underpants and socks, it had been gathering dew for having been left out all night. Upon giving up his search he went downstairs naked; not such a big deal seeing as there was little chance of his being seen by passers-by or neighbours, although he undoubtedly felt more vulnerable, and therefore took considerable care, when pouring the boiled water into the cup.

Nine minutes after he had forsaken what is arguably the most seductive place in the house, any house, Seb was back beneath the covers staring up at the ceiling. The clarity of thought he sought in returning to

224

the warm comfort of bed was in respect of which far-flung corner of Britain he was going to explore. His brain was two sips of tea to the good when the prospective traveller allowed his eyes, and consequently his thoughts, to focus on a crack which ran from the centre, where its point of origin was hidden from his view by a lampshade in the style of a Chinese lantern, halfway across the room. There it came to an abrupt end like the lines on a map representing roads that stop in the middle of nowhere, like those venturing into the Lammermoor Hills for example, or probing the Forest of Bowland.

For a time both these parts of the country tempted. Burdened by their rucksacks Neffie and he had walked across the former as they had approached the end of the Southern Upland Way, the trek of two hundred miles across the Borders Region of Scotland. The Forest of Bowland he had yet to visit, even though its rugged, treeless hills weren't that far. Thinking that he perhaps should travel farther afield alternative destinations came to mind: Exeter and Lichfield to name but two. He had been tempted to visit the Staffordshire town after seeing a photograph of its twelfth-century cathedral, after being inspired by the three spires known affectionately as the ladies of the vale. A greater temptation than the city in Devon for being nearer, Lichfield had other testimonials to recommend it, the most recent being from a woman, a nurse, sitting beside him on a train travelling north from London. She had sung Lichfield's praises even though she was from Lincoln. Undoubtedly the most prestigious recommendation however, was the result of Seb having browsed through the *Oxford Dictionary of Quotations*, wherein he had read these words of George Fox, the founder of the Quaker movement. 'I espied three steeple house spires, and they struck at my life'.

Sebastian's problem was that the longer he pondered over the prospect of seeing the three spires for real, the less inspired he became, so that eventually, in favour of going elsewhere, he dismissed the idea as one to put into effect another day. He sipped more tea. The beverage-stimulated thoughts which ensued were that he should go somewhere he knew and liked for the knowing. In this regard the town which came to mind was Keswick, a contender for being his favourite destination in the entire country. Why that should be isn't difficult to understand given the natural beauty of its setting; but another consideration for Seb was that he and the Cumbrian town had history. The accumulation of pleasant memories had made them the best of friends.

In thinking of making Keswick the destination of his weekend jaunt he recalled the camping trip he had made as a schoolboy, a week's sojourn under canvas in the company of his uncle. The event which had made the trip so memorable, and which served as a strong enticement for Seb to make many such journeys across the Pennines once he had learned to drive and was in possession of a car, was the hour he and his uncle had spent on Friar's Crag.

For the reader who is unfamiliar with the topography of the Lake District, Friar's Crag is the promontory that juts into Derwentwater a mile south of Keswick town centre. From the crag's knobbly outcrop there are superb views across the lake to Catbells, Causey Pike and Grisedale Pike, and to the nearby wooded mounds of Derwent Isle and Lord's Island, and to the islands beyond as the beholder's vision is channelled by the fells toward the southern tip of the lake in Borrowdale.

On the occasion in question, on the evening when that remarkable foundation stone was laid in the youthful Sebastian Forrest's memory, the setting sun was radiant, casting its mellow light and beneficent warmth over the eastern fells and the lake. The scene was sublime in its tranquillity. Such bucolic beauty would have left a lasting impression in its own right, but the man and youth were not alone. Whereas Seb and his uncle had shifted position from sitting on tree roots protruding from the dry, compacted earth to crouching unsupported on their haunches, but only until such time as that position became too uncomfortable and they opted to sit on the tree roots again, occupying a seat which had been strategically positioned to provide the most spectacular view were a frail elderly woman and her younger female companion. To judge by the resemblance of their features beneath the lines, the many and the few, and the undoubted affection which the women had for each other, Seb had assumed that they were mother and daughter. Despite her physical frailty the old woman's voice was assured as she addressed the small gathering. She had a receptive audience.

Seb and his uncle had listened intently. The subjects of the eulogy were Coleridge and Wordsworth. The familiarity with which the old woman spoke about the poets gave all who were listening to her the impression that she had known them personally. The effect on Sebastian of such a sublime evening and the biographical account combined was long-lasting for being profound. For having been so enchanted in his youth, it was hardly surprising that whenever he thought of going away for the weekend Keswick came to mind, for to think of 'pencil' town was to picture Friar's Crag and the depth of feeling that his first evening in Cumberland had invoked.

By this time, however, the tea which had undoubtedly stimulated Sebastian's imagination had also brought a modicum of reason to bear. In practical terms this was no bad thing. In Seb's case however, the application of more sober thought generated a dark cloud on his mental horizon, one which by subverting all thoughts of the sublime couldn't be ignored. The dark cloud was the perennial problem posed by money, or at least the lack of it in sufficient quantity for Sebastian to be carefree in his spending. Any problem there may be wouldn't be immediately apparent in the sense that even without checking his bank account he was certain of being able to fund a weekend away in Britain, but being able to fund it doesn't necessarily equate to being able to afford it. In the medium to long term he may well be depriving Peter and Paul in the guise of his creditors in order to gratify Sebastian. The question was did he really want to spend money on fuel and pay for a bed for a night or two when he didn't have to. He reckoned that a bed of his dreams away from home could be as much as £50 per night, which was a nightmare outlay compared to the pleasant reality of paying nothing for the comfort of sleeping in his bed at home. In this wiser state of mind, as a cheaper alternative he considered going camping, but because of the effort it would involve he didn't dwell on the idea for long. The thought of rummaging through cupboards for the equipment he would need — tent, stove, spare gas canister, bedroll, sleeping-bag, and so on — didn't appeal.

Perhaps it was because he was lying on his back gazing up at the ceiling that predisposed the young man not to be enthusiastic about doing anything so demanding of his organisational skills as going camping for the weekend, or perhaps it was the prospect of staying on a campsite crammed with house tents and caravans — as would undoubtedly be the case at the time of year it was — which was so off-putting. For Seb such a prospect had about the same appeal as a trip to a theme park, which was no appeal whatsoever. The imagined whoops of children running around interspersed too frequently by the shrill tones of a baby crying for no reason at all settled it for Seb, and he decided to make the most of the weekend by packing a small day-pack with food and drink for sustenance, and then drive a short distance into the country with the aim of spending the day, certainly several hours of it, navigating his way along footpaths and bridleways which were as yet either totally unfamiliar to him, or only vaguely familiar for having been their way only once or twice.

Seb was pleased with himself for having hit upon an idea, probably the one he was always going to arrive at, which was inherently wise in that his day's outing would cost next to nothing, therefore the money he would save on fuel and accommodation could be put to better use. His plan to explore near home had other advantages. By spending more time walking than sitting behind the wheel he would be getting more exercise, and that had to be good. Secondly, he would be a pathfinder for a walk which as early as this coming September Neffie and he could do together, either as a couple or as part of a larger group. Few things were more vexatious to Seb when leading others into the unknown than having to keep referring to the map whilst subjected to a plethora of comments, some helpful, others less so, from his impatient troupe. From personal experience he also knew that getting hopelessly lost could be tedious in the extreme for those being led. By plotting and then reconnoitring a circumambulation not too demanding in respect of length and ruggedness, and which was scenically attractive, would ensure that he remained, assuming that he was there already, in Neffie's good books, at an as yet indeterminate future date. His plan thus formed, Seb leapt out of bed with purpose.

Preparations relating to his day of active leisure need no description for being too commonplace to mention. Suffice it to say that an hour and a half after he had made up his mind what he was going to do and where he was going to do it, Seb was adjusting his pack for comfort as he made his way along the narrow road which led into Ferndale. The road was a car's width, though two-way traffic could proceed with care in view of the fact that there were numerous passing places.

A quick look over his shoulder confirmed to Seb's satisfaction that he had parked his car where it was unlikely to be a hindrance to other motorists. A day which had begun with the intrepid traveller giving serious consideration to driving hundreds of miles to Exeter, and on which the distances had diminished as alternative destinations were considered, had, in driving terms, resulted in his driving all of three miles from home in less than ten minutes.

The road he trod led steeply up the hill, and he felt good for feeling the strain on his calf muscles. Later it would descend less steeply into Ferndale. A means of vehicles being able to access a few isolated farms and a single but nonetheless solidly impressive row of dwellings known as Ferndale Abbey, it was a road which few had cause to use, and this was reflected in its poor state of repair. It was evidently of low priority on the council's list of things to do. Adversely affected by the previous winter's frost and ice coupled with subsidence, in places the surface was severely cracked or broken to such an extent that jagged sections pointed to the sky, albeit at an elevation slightly closer to the horizontal than the perpendicular; and then there were the numerous potholes.

The condition of the road had come as no surprise to Seb. A sign warned all that came this way on four wheels not to expect a smooth ride. Furthermore, the warning in bold, black letters on a bright yellow background hadn't deterred him a few weeks previously when he had driven to the Abbey whose religious significance exists in name only. This morning it was a case of once bitten twice shy, meaning Seb was pleased to have parked the car where he had, for it goes without saying that the upheavals which presented such serious problems for drivers presented few difficulties for a sighted person on foot.

Seb's planned journey of discovery would begin when he reached the end of the paved road he was on. The distance to that point he estimated to be over a mile. Familiarity didn't make the walking tedious. That would have been close to impossible when the magnificent vistas to the west gradually became more expansive, and therefore more impressive, the higher he climbed. Thus far Seb was acting in accordance with the plan formulated at home, but because there wasn't another person in the whole wide world to whom he had to justify his itinerancy, that plan could be altered or abandoned at a whim — his whim. In a mind free to roam where it would a thought occurred that if he were to deviate from his intended route he would merely be complying with Neffie's wish that he shouldn't be so set in his ways, and that it would be no bad thing if he were to demonstrate a greater flexibility of mind. She hadn't called him a robot as such, but she had exhorted him to be more spontaneous. This bout of self-analysis as he walked into Ferndale was redolent of the life he and Neffie shared, and the image of her holding forth as they sat down for supper at the little round wooden table tucked into a corner of their back room was uppermost in Seb's mind as he considered rebelling against the man he had been a few moments ago.

The path which he hadn't planned to take but which now tempted him led off to the right, and though throughout the land its very existence could be called into doubt because it wasn't marked on the map, there could be no doubting that for the first twenty yards or so it clearly existed on the ground. Any indication of its existence farther than the first twenty yards was obscured by ferns.

Map in hand Seb stood for a while surveying the terrain he would have to cover if he did decide to act in an unpremeditated manner and go off at a tangent. A vast swathe of the concave hillside was covered with the flowerless flora of ancient origin. It was difficult for Sebastian to determine their extent because of the dry-stone wall surrounding Simon's wood. The wall restricted his vision of anything growing lower than the topmost level of stone. For no reason other than that in the here and now he wanted to experience more than he had planned for when studying the map spread out on his living-room floor, Sebastian stepped out into totally unfamiliar territory.

For being comprised of the springiest kind of grass the ground which welcomed his first few steps was pleasantly enticing. Unfortunately the pleasing sensations underfoot didn't last for long, and it soon became apparent that the trail exemplifying a triumph of impromptu decision-making didn't range much farther than the short distance visible from the fissured excuse for a road. No wonder the map showed no trail, but merely open access.

The way ahead wouldn't be easy, but in contrast to the plan formulated by his conscious mind and then discarded, his present course was probably in total accord with his deeper yearnings. In view of the kind of pleasure he sought it could be said that Sebastian at this time was a masochist in search of pain, pain which would overpower, and therefore assuage, another. The self-inflicted torture Sebastian's deeper self envisaged would be relatively easy for him to deal with for being merely physical and not so painful as to cause him severe distress, whereas the pangs he needed to subdue were emotional. At this deeper level they were also chronic. In missing Neffie so much her image haunted his psyche like the Holy Ghost might trouble the mind of a man seeking penance.

It was, therefore, a physically strong but emotionally fragile young man who strode into the closest semblance of jungle he was likely to find within a hundred miles of home. There aren't many parts of the country which could be described as wilderness, and between Land's End and John O'Groats there surely isn't much in the way of impenetrable jungle to explore. Seb's motivation for getting lost in the hope of finding himself again was as yet nebulous, but by setting forth on his impromptu adventure he had the feeling that he was forming a spiritual bond with the woman who, as far as he was aware, may presently be hacking her way through the most impenetrable forest imaginable. It didn't take Seb long to realise that his quest to subvert the ache within by flirting with physical hardship was succeeding, no more than a few strides in fact.

The wide open vistas he had seen from the road were replaced by fronds taller than his head. Consequently the observable universe shrank to a patch of blue sky above him; not that he looked more than once in that direction. His attention was focused on forging ahead, and with no machete or cutting tool of any kind to hand, he pushed the ferns aside, his upper limbs making movements not unlike that of a swimmer doing breast-stroke. The going proved tougher than Seb had imagined, but to his way of thinking he had already come too far to turn back. Sweat seemed to be pouring from every pore, and as if the heat and the density of the vegetation weren't hardships enough, the unevenness of the ground beneath his feet added to his difficulties. The grass that had put a spring in his step at the outset had soon given way to rocks hidden from view by the ferns, and several times during his tortuous progress Seb had stumbled and fallen down on one knee. Thus far his left knee had taken more punishment than the right. Arguably, at least in the context of this singular quest, the pain he suffered at each impact was just what the proverbial doctor had ordered in that it occupied his mind to the exclusion of all other concerns. Fortunately, despite the hard knocks the knees in question sustained no serious injury. Another frustration for Sebastian down below was the tendency for unseen tendrils to become entwined with his boot laces, untying them with irritating frequency as these green fingers seemingly operated with a dexterity equal to that of human hands. The thought crossed his mind that John Wyndham had possibly experienced a similar phenomenon prior to writing The Day of the Triffids.

At the height of Seb's ordeal, where the ferns were at their tallest and thickest, and when he had already endured a great deal even though his first destination, the dry-stone wall this side of Simon's Wood, was still some way off, a feeling akin to panic made its first assault on his psyche. More than once prior to the present incursion Seb had managed to become lost on the moors. When still a schoolboy he had floundered in snow when the path to follow had become completely obliterated, and more recently, as a man, he had encountered the eerie solitude imposed by fog. Both these eternities of disorientation he had experienced by night. The state of mind which out of fear teeters for a while on the brink of desperation wasn't, therefore, unfamiliar to him, and in this regard above all others Seb's army training made for having no alternative but 'to get a grip', as it were, and carry on. This awareness of his mind's propensity in such circumstances, and perhaps it's the propensity of all minds, enabled Seb to do just that — carry on.

There were a number of tried and tested counter measures Seb could call on to regain total self- control. His first stratagem in this regard was to pause for thought so that he no longer stumbled like a man who has imbibed too much liquor. Merely standing still for a while enabled Seb to cool down physically as well as mentally. Being stationary also enabled him to take his bearings. Thinking that he wouldn't need a compass he hadn't brought one, so he had no alternative but to try to ascertain precisely where he was by sight. He prised apart the ferns closest to him in the hope of being able to determine the way of least resistance. Ironically given his motivation for going off piste as it were, if a path a yard wide had revealed itself at that moment he would have taken it without hesitation. Not surprisingly there was no such apparition.

Another stratagem Seb put into effect to produce a state of mind conducive to rational decision-making was to regulate his breathing. For the best part of a minute he took slow, deep breaths. He counted five of these deliberate inhalations and their corresponding exhalations. He had learned the technique from Neffie, who in turn had learned the technique in the yoga class she attended twice-weekly. In combination with Seb's other measures to counter perturbation the sequence of breaths produced the desired result, which was to slow down his thought processes and thereby allow him to realise that he didn't need to arrive anywhere in a hurry. When all was said and done this was England in the summer, so he wasn't likely to die of starvation or exposure. Heat stroke coupled with dehydration could prove to be a problem, but from his experience of suffering the same plus altitude sickness whilst training with the army in Kenya, he reckoned he was a long way from being in that physical state. The plan now was to take his time, for to all intents and purposes he had all of it that there was in the world.

This more sanguine approach to life unfurling before him, literally as well as metaphorically, proved successful in that by taking greater care with each step he took Seb was able to make better progress. The number of times he stumbled after having controlled his impulsiveness and taken stock of the situation could be counted on two fingers. This was a considerable reduction compared with the number of times he had fallen from grace previously. In each of the two subsequent instances he was able to regain his balance before his knee or some other vulnerable part of his anatomy impacted against the hard protuberances that previously were felt before they were seen. Even the creepers growing at ground level posed less of a problem now that Seb's steps were more deliberate. They continued to tug at his boot laces, but refrained from going to the former extremes of untying them completely. Half an hour after he had stopped to assess the situation and regain his composure, and ninety minutes after he had left behind the safety of tarmac and his pre-planned route, Seb reached the wall at the edge of Simon's Wood.

A ditch which ran the entire length of the wood prevented the ferns from encroaching upon the wall's solidity. The 'triffids' had stopped their advance at the very edge of the shallow trench. By standing on top of the wall Seb was able to look back and survey the hill above and below the way he had come. His trek through the jungle had made no impression on the landscape. Next he noted that a few yards from where he was standing part of the wall had toppled into the trench to lie there as a sizeable heap of stones. In a place where walkers' boots passing that way would have been a rare event indeed, Sebastian pondered over why it was that so many stones had become dislodged. The best answer he could think of was that deer had been the cause; but the more he thought on it the less likely his best answer seemed.

Seb climbed down to sit on a fallen stone. Of regular hexahedral shape and lying on the side of the wall with the better view, it looked the perfect repository for Seb's aching body. Upon winning the struggle to remove the pack from his back he placed it on the ground between his feet. At rest Sebastian had a sense of achievement, derived in the main from his belief that where he had just been no one, Neffie included, in a balanced state of mind would have willingly followed. Not surprisingly he very much doubted that he would ever retrace his steps.

It was certainly a relief for Seb to be able to see more than two steps in front of him, to gain a sense of where he was in relation to the undulations of the land beneath an expansive tract of sky. Presently the shadows cast by the trees in the wood at his back extended for several yards into the ferns. Now that the sun was past its zenith, and until such time as the effect was no longer discernible, the edge of the shadow was a line which would advance in an easterly direction with each minute that passed.

After unclipping the two straps securing his pack Seb took from it a plastic container. Through the nearly opaque lid of the box, he could just make out the food he liked to take on hikes and picnics. Cut into halves were a Scotch egg and a pork pie. He placed the box down on the ground beside him, deferring eating until he had poured himself a cup of tea from his flask, the next item he removed from his pack. He took a sip of the hot, fuscous liquid. Even though it had seemed counter-intuitive at the time, he had learned in the army that it was better to drink a hot drink in hot weather than one which was cold. Consequently, because he also took a flask of hot tea or coffee when trekking in cold weather, his pack seldom contained cans of cold beer or fizzy pop.

Sebastian bit into the piece of pie with gusto, but on a day of sweltering heat, or on any day at the height of summer for that matter, he couldn't do so without being mindful of his mother's warning about the dangers of eating pork in hot weather. Of course the young recipient of a parental warning isn't necessarily going to take heed of it, and Seb had eaten many a pork pie over many a summer without having been adversely affected. Thus far, however, he had been more concerned about the possibility of getting food poisoning as opposed to any damage he may, in the long term, be doing to his heart.

Miss Nefertiti Goodwin's views on her partner's al fresco diet were hardly encouraging. From experience Seb had no doubt that if Neffie were sitting beside him without a morsel to eat of her own chosen fare, she would decline his offer of half, or even a quarter, of pie; and the Scotch egg would no doubt be greeted with similar disdain. Seb could only hazard a guess as to how many days Neffie would have to go without food before she could be tempted. Either she would need to be ravenous or unwilling to offend. Regarding the latter Seb recollected a history of Christmas Eves, occasions when Neffie's mother placed a wedge of pork pie on her youngest daughter's plate without expecting there to be leftovers.

Presently Seb was just about to bite into a piece of pie when the filling fell out of the pastry. The content looked destined to land on the toecap of his boot, and would have done so if he hadn't already relinquished the mug of tea by placing it on the stone beside him. Demonstrating the top form reflexes of a wicket-keeper or a fielder in the slips Seb caught the plummeting dollop of meat before he was aware that his hands had moved. He returned the lump of meat to its gelatine-coated bed of pastry. Feeling pleased with himself for having moved with the speed of a Shaolin graduate, and carelessly masticating the delicacy in his mouth, Sebastian gave some thought as to why so few women eat meat pies. He had arrived at this unashamedly sexist conclusion by deductive reasoning: if the women he knew rarely ate meat pies — and they didn't — then the female population as a whole was probably equally averse.

Why was this Seb wondered as he washed the last mouthful of the first half down his oesophagus with tea? The answer he came up with was that men like him ate pies because they had gone to football matches at a time when most spectators chose to stand to watch the match rather than sit. Then the atmosphere generated by thousands of men, and considerably fewer women, standing shoulder to shoulder, made for a better match experience, particularly when to watch from a seat was relatively expensive. Then the only half-time refreshment had been a pork-pie and a cup of Bovril; and what, Seb remembered, a pleasure it had been on a Saturday afternoon in a cold, dark December to eat such ambrosia, to imbibe such nectar. The scene before Seb's eyes couldn't have contrasted more starkly with the images from his past he had brought to mind, and gradually his present perspective across land that was a combination of the rugged and the pastoral cohering into a scene of bucolic beauty set beneath a cerulean sky tinged with wispy cirrus blotted out his match-day memories.

Eventually this man alone, being of an age when time spent in contemplation and watching the light was considerably less than the active pursuit of one goal or another, felt that it was time to make a move. To this end, after scoffing a digestive biscuit he had dunked in the last few millilitres of tea in his cup and then discarding these dregs with a flick of the wrist, he returned the containers now depleted of most of their provisions to his pack. Revitalised Seb sprang to his feet and in the next instant once again became accustomed to the additional weight — noticeable rather than heavy — centred on his back and pulling at his shoulders.

For Seb to do as he intended and enter the wood would be to pass from where it was legally permissible to wander at will into a sylvan expanse which, if it didn't belong to the Forestry Commission, was no doubt owned by someone who would rather not have him traipsing through it, the upshot being that he was probably about to trespass. Undeterred by this prospect, and to some extent spurred on by the knowledge that Neffie wouldn't approve, he surmounted the problem posed by the wall with ease, making use of the weather-worn protrusions of the larger more firmly placed stones as ledges to support his boot-clad feet. He had considered breaking into the wood via where many of the stones had fallen, but the thorny creepers of a bramble bush deterred.

For Seb the task of getting down from something was invariably more problematic than getting up it, whether the ascent and subsequent descent involved a mountain, a dry-stone wall or the stairs at home. In this instance, given the height he had to contend with, approximately five feet, he decided to jump, and from a crouched position he launched himself towards mother earth. Needless to say he had selected what looked to be a soft and therefore safe plot on which to land. Fortunately appearances didn't deceive, but though the landing was painless, the unevenness of the ground caused Sebastian to lose his balance and topple over, his feet seemingly bound together.

Aware that there wasn't much chance of his being heard Seb swore out loud. Slowly he picked himself up to stand upright, and as he did so he felt the spirit of ancient trees encroaching upon his every move. It was a deciduous wood comprised mainly of oak and silver-birch trees. Far from being a lugubrious place, however, light streamed through the abundance of leaves to create dappled patterns on the forest floor, patterns which by their ceaseless motion had the power to mesmerise. On the trunks and branches the filtered light created a multitude of large and small reflectors.

Not surprisingly, bearing in mind Seb's point of entry, there was no obvious path to follow, and nor were there nearby any of the features he would normally look for on a map to orientate himself and then guide his way. Consequently the lone explorer advanced slowly, taking as much care in raising his feet as he did in placing them. He didn't want to become entangled in the rampant briars, the barbs of which could easily lacerate his ankles. For the reason that the trees and other forms of vegetation, unlike the layout of conifer forests where the pines are planted in rows and there's not much undergrowth to speak of, grew in accordance with the tenets imposed by mother nature, Seb had no choice but to thread his way through this English jungle by whichever route he considered to be least difficult; but the going wasn't easy. He had to clamber over a succession of fallen, moss-covered trees that impeded his progress, and squelch through seemingly as many quagmires doing their utmost to suck off one or other of his boots. The effort required to make any headway at all concentrated Seb's mind wonderfully, and he soon lost track of time. He also lost all sense of space beyond the arboreal enclosure in which he walked, stumbled and sometimes fell. It was as if Yatton, Ferrousby and Luxborough, the familiar towns and village he had been able to see in the valley below from as close by as where he had parked his car, were in a different country. Cities like London and Leeds might as well have been on a different planet. In a similar vein all the people he knew either as friends or acquaintances were now mere phantoms, no matter how strong their individual impressions had been on his psyche; and as for Neffie, she really was in a different country.

A thought which did occur to Sebastian at this juncture was a lesson he had learned in the army, and that was to keep off obvious tracks if you were trying to evade capture. The expression the SAS instructor had used was 'go where the shit is thickest'. In trying to escape from his own self-torment Sebastian seemed to be doing exactly that. Here in this primordial forest he could be stepping where no human-being had stepped before. No sooner had this thought entered his head than he let his mind wander on a flight of fancy. He began to plan what he would do, what evasive action he would take, were he to encounter a ferocious dinosaur. Mr Forrest was in that kind of forest, and its seemingly prehistoric aspect was enhanced all the more by a somewhat steamy atmosphere.

After a considerable length of time heading towards the centre of the forest, or so Seb hoped, he stopped to look around, and in so doing he realised how easy it would be to become completely lost, particularly on a foggy day or at night. Presently, however, although the sun's disc was more often than not hidden by leaves, the effulgence signifying its presence was always visible, and this made for a trustworthy guide. From this point onward, though Seb's intention was to head in the general direction of the sun's apparent descent, like a sailing-ship tacking when the wind is unfavourable, he was only able to do so by making a series of tangents. He hoped and believed that he would be out of the woods before the onset of darkness.

In stepping off again towards a small brightly lit clearing, in marked contrast to his earlier flight of fancy Seb concluded that what was good about playing at being an explorer in Britain, as opposed to being really adventurous and getting hopelessly lost in the Amazon rain-forest or the jungles of Borneo, was that sooner rather than later there was every prospect of the would-be explorer hitting upon a track which in turn would lead to a road leading back to civilisation. Seb had high hopes of arriving home in time to watch the televised highlights of that day's play at Trent Bridge.

He pushed onward perspiration dripping from his forehead, his strong, youthful legs growing wearier by the minute. It would have been absurd for Seb to think that he wasn't going to make it, but after yet another half hour of self-inflicted torment had passed he certainly wanted his ordeal to end, and to end soon; and lo and behold, suddenly, unexpectedly, it did.

It came as a pleasant surprise to discover that on this side of the wood he had just traversed there was no obstacle in the form of a dry-stone wall or barbed-wire fence to prevent his escape. The jungle Seb was pleased to see the back of came to an abrupt but neat end along the edge of a track made up of small stones set in dry, well-compacted earth. To be free of Simon's Wood once and for all, all Seb needed to do was to step down onto the track. In so doing he entered a world umpteen times more brilliant than the one he had left, for here in the open the sun beat down with fierce intensity.

For the reason that Seb hadn't trekked or cycled this way previously, in one sense the track was unfamiliar to him, but because he knew precisely where in the nearby village it opened onto the road, and where in the opposite direction it led up to and joined the moorland track which followed the hill's highest contour, without needing to look at the map he had a good idea where he was and where he wanted to go. Consequently, forsaking the easy option leading down into the village prior to heading back to his car by walking along the road, his morale now boosted he set off up the hill.

Midway between the upper extremity of the forest and the top of the hill the track became more deeply rutted as it deviated from the straight and not so narrow — it was wide enough for a four- wheel drive vehicle or a tractor to drive along — leading the now considerably happier wanderer between huge rocks, their majestically solid but rather sombre grey forms standing like sentinels. They served as portals to the higher reaches of the hill and the open moors. At this point the ascent was steep, causing Seb to breathe heavily and drip with sweat. But he knew that he was near the top, and he had every reason to be optimistic that soon the strain on the muscles of his legs and back would be relieved by walking on the level. He decided not to rest until he had gained the top, where he would be able to get his breath back as well as take in a view which he knew would be spectacular.

Before reaching this next goal on his journey however, Seb noticed a narrow track to his right. No more than a few inches wide it led off through the heather. At first he gave scant consideration to what he thought was merely a sheep track, of which there are many on the moors, and walked past. It was only after he had taken several strides that an inner voice compelled him to stop, turn back, and explore. Notwithstanding his weariness, Seb's curiosity had got the better of him and he set off along the relatively insignificant path with the expectation that he would be soon retracing his steps.

If the thought had occurred to Seb prior to leaving home that morning he would have brought one of several telescopic walking-sticks that Neffie and he had acquired over the years, but no such thought had entered his head. This was hardly surprising seeing as how an item of equipment which was so useful as to be indispensable on the Lake District Fells he considered to be far from necessary when walking over the gentler hills near home. Equally, if it had crossed Seb's mind to pick up a stick from off the forest floor in anticipation of the difficulties ahead, then he would have searched until he had found one which was suitable; but in the event there had been no such foresight.

Perhaps contrary to what most people would imagine, the reason Seb inwardly bemoaned not having brought a suitable stick had nothing to do with the demands of his body, and everything to do with his not wanting to step on an adder. Be it man-made or natural, be it tubular steel or oak, if Seb had been in possession of a rigid extension to his arm at that moment he would have used it to beat the ground ahead and generate sufficient vibration to cause any snake lying in wait to slither away in search of safety. He would have wanted to create what to an adder would feel like a series of earthquakes measuring nine point nine on the ophidian equivalent of the Richter scale. Seb's fear of venomous reptiles was nothing out of the ordinary, and certainly didn't amount to a phobia. By way of an alternative deterrent therefore, and indicating flexibility of mind and a willingness to make do, he determined to achieve a similar earth-shaking result by every so often stamping down hard with his boot. This stratagem, though it's impossible to say that it proved successful, as Seb hoped didn't turn out to be a failure.

The terrain the narrow path led over was undulating. Eventually Sebastian, after he had been walking with a peculiar gait for just ten minutes and had covered approximately half a mile, arrived at the top of a rocky outcrop. From its vertiginous height he was able to look down into a natural amphitheatre created on three sides by an unbroken wall of rock. For Seb to lose his balance now and topple over the edge the height he would fall would be approximately thirty feet. If not leading to his sudden demise, it was a big enough drop to cause serious injury.

Once he had put concerns about his safety into perspective Seb was able to focus on a sight which he hadn't expected to see. Standing centre stage down below was a man-made contraption. Constructed on the more or less level grassy surface of the hollow, it was made, primarily, from chicken-wire and wood. Measuring approximately eight feet square and six feet high at its highest points it was the size of a small hen-house. The chicken wire served for the walls and roof and the wood as the frame which held everything together. The structure was undoubtedly some form of trap. Further evidence for this supposition was provided by a crow behaving frantically within the confines of the cage. The bird's agitation was clearly exacerbated by its awareness of the human presence close by, and its inability to escape from the danger which that presence posed. Instead the bird flew repeatedly from the carcass-strewn floor onto a perch and then back to the ground. The perch in question was a garden cane positioned laterally a few feet above the ground. Every so often the bird changed tactics and took flight from one side of the cage to the other.

Until now Sebastian hadn't encountered an 'aviary' of this kind on any of his forays into the wilder parts of Britain, and he was perplexed as to the trap's purpose. Surely, he thought, nobody would go to such lengths merely to catch a crow. What would be the point of that he wondered? The only feasible hypothesis he could come up with was that the crow had been put in the trap as bait for a more formidable predator — a stoat or weasel perhaps.

From his vantage point Sebastian stood watching the bird's seemingly mindless antics for at least five minutes before he descended to take a closer look. Strange as it may seem, prior to leaving his perch he twice looked about him to ensure that he himself wasn't being watched. After having taken the safer, albeit longer in time and distance, of the two ways to descend available to him, from its open side Seb entered the amphitheatre at what now appeared to be ground level.

In a book about the natural history of the British Isles, our curious wayfarer had read that members of the Family Corvidae, are among the cleverest of birds, that they search boldly for all kinds of food, and will avoid traps and ignore scarecrows. They may also store food for the winter and open snails by dropping them onto a stone. This captive specimen was evidently a contradiction, the exception that proves the rule if the generic description of the bird is correct. In thinking about his own kind Seb realised that though human-beings are the most intelligent life-forms on the planet, there were a number of individuals whom he could name whom he thought were anything but — intelligent that is. He didn't consider the possibility that there may be those that would include his name in their own list of dullards. Standing only feet away from the frantic bird, by no small measure Seb burdened his intellect by making a careful study of the captive, its cage, and the cage's immediate environs. One conclusion he came to was that the design of the cage was an excellent example of human ingenuity and cunning. Upon describing his discovery at a later date it was in terms of a house, though in all probability it wasn't a dwelling in which a human-being had ever lived. The peculiarities of the structure were two six feet high walls separated by an inversion best pictured as a house on which the roof has been put on upside down. For its entire length the apex which might have been, but which now aspired to be a trough, was missing the point, because at the lowest point of this not quite triangular declination were two parallel lengths of wood the width of the cage. Between these two slats was a gap the width of a man's hand at full span. For the crow this gap represented the only possible escape route, and though to human eyes for the bird to tuck in its feathers and saunter out into the big, wide world appeared to be feasible, evidently the fraught creature was either unable to conceive of such a stratagem, or was loath to do so if it had. Seb noted that the bird was able to drink from a metal bowl half filled with water, and the carcasses of three dead rabbits strewn around the floor of the cage provided sufficient food. From the pungent smell of dried blood a blind man would have been aware that there was rotting flesh nearby: as it was the odour in combination with the purple gore of pecked at lapidary guts made Seb think that he was in animal hell; though he didn't lose sight of the fact that the scene before him was a human creation entirely. Outside the cage and near to where he was standing were two more dead rabbits. Their bodies being as yet whole, Seb presumed that they would be thrown into the trap to become the crow's dinner sometime soon.

"Well what would Neffie make of this?" Seb wondered aloud as he surveyed the carnage. He could easily imagine her disgust as he stepped around to the side of the cage where the only door was a small square constructed of the same materials as the rest of the cage with the addition of a couple of hinges. On close scrutiny it was immediately apparent that the door couldn't be opened easily, not by a casual passer-by, if there ever was such a creature other than himself. The small portal had been nailed shut. Despite his sympathy for the crow's plight Seb decided against kicking in the door. It had been many years since he had last committed a wilful act of vandalism, and he was far too mature to be wilful in that regard now; and besides, he was aware of the high probability that in letting the crow escape, in somebody's eyes he would be doing the wrong thing, even if it were for a high-minded reason.

Seb repaired to his former position, where he willed the bird to make a bid for freedom through what to his eyes was the obvious gap. His telepathic powers proved ineffectual however, for the bird continued to behave manically. Not once did it approach the linear exit that from wherever in the cage the unfortunate creature chose to settle for a moment was at most only a few feet away. Not for the first time that day Seb regretted not having brought a stick, his thought being, a rather fanciful one he realised subsequently, that if he were able to thrust a stick into the cage the crow may be tempted to hop on it and allow itself to be transported slowly, gently, through the gap.

There being no such implement to hand, however, Seb decided to give the trapped crow the benefit of the doubt, hoping that at some point it would demonstrate the intelligence for which the breed is renowned: thrice therefore he thrust and retracted his arm into and out of the trap, his intention being to show the creature the one practicable escape route, a route which to all avian intents and purposes it couldn't discern for itself. Furthermore, each time that Seb extended his arm as far into the cage as he could he wiggled his hand to attract the bird's attention. In the end though, Seb's seemingly strange but undoubtedly well-meaning antics were to no avail and he gave up, and although he didn't actually shrug his shoulders, his attitude was such that if others had been present to bear witness he would have undoubtedly shown his resignation accordingly.

By this time Sebastian's concern for the crow's welfare was also undergoing a transformation. To judge from the evidence he had been privy to Seb was beginning to think that the ornithologists, or whoever had come up with the hype he had read, were wrong and that crows were indeed dim. He also came to the conclusion that so stupid a creature deserves what's coming to it, and that his own behaviour had been somewhat foolish. He went on to imagine that in the farms and homesteads in the vicinity most people, were they to become apprised of his recent antics, would consider him to be an ignorant 'do-gooder' with mush for a brain. Such thoughts allowed Sebastian to leave the crow to its fate with no sense of guilt whatsoever.

Seb decided to retrace his steps back to the main track. For being careless about the possibility of there being snakes his gait was less peculiar than it had been previously. Upon reaching the main track he turned right onto it and continued up the hill. His plan upon reaching the top was to turn onto a track which from past exploits was very familiar to him and follow it along the edge of the scarp until he reached the road that would eventually lead him to his car. Anticipating no problems he estimated that he would cover the distance in about an hour.

For the reason that he no longer needed to give much thought as to where he should place his feet, and which direction they should take, Seb was able to ponder over his recent encounter in the hope of putting the experience into some kind of meaningful context. His motivation in this regard stemmed from his belief that there was a purpose to his existence over and above the merely sensual, though there was no denying that the awareness the senses provided was either to be savoured or endured. For the introspective wayfarer he now was the sensory aspects of human experience fed and formed part of a greater whole, an entirety which incorporated a rational and therefore moral dimension. Given Seb's view of his place in the world, and indeed the cosmos, it was hardly surprising that he considered each and every experience to be a new and valuable lesson, one which if he were to absorb it with goodwill would enable him to grow, possibly to grow a little wiser.

The thoughts which permeated Seb's mind during these moments of quiet introspection were stern in the sense that he could see how easy it would be to turn his back on the suffering of others. The plight of the crow was the starting point from which he was led to generalise about the plight of his fellow man. The captive carrion scavenger had soon disappeared from Seb's view to become a less bothersome image with each step that he took. He realised that the plight of people facing terror and starvation in parts of the world less fortunate than his own wasn't so different. All he had to do to make these troublesome, two-dimensional people disappear was switch off the television. If he needed to salve his conscience for being able to eat steak and enjoy a glass or two of wine of an evening, then he could sign a cheque to make a donation to an appropriate charity. Seb wondered how much longer the crow had to live.

At the top of the hill Seb rested for considerably longer than planned for having fallen asleep. He was surprised to realise that he had slept for twenty minutes. It was the noise of a low-flying fighter-jet engine that woke him as the aircraft roared overhead; where exactly took him several seconds to discover. The engine's roar soon dissipated as the warplane disappeared from view. Feeling like a man older than his actual years Seb got to his feet and began the trek back to his car. Gradually his legs lost their stiffness and his stride became more youthful. Upon reaching the car he took off his boots and replaced them with a pair of canvas shoes. Cheap and nasty and looking the worse for wear, his royal-blue footwear contrasted garishly with the colour of his trousers, which were green. The down-at-heel combination persuaded the wearer to go straight home rather than go for a pint of beer at the pub. Neither did he think that he was presentable enough to call in at the shop. Consequently the short journey home proved uneventful.

It was exactly four p.m. when Sebastian stepped over the threshold of his front door. He knew this without checking his watch because the grandfather clock situated in the front parlour greeted his arrival with a succession of chimes which he didn't lose count of for not listening. It felt good to be back in a house which at the height of summer is blessed for being shady and cool, and the weary homecomer's delight was doubled when he caught sight of a familiar-looking, pale-blue airmail letter lying next to a glossy publication on the coconut mat near the door. The publication was 'The Moors Messenger', a newsletter publicising the work of the authority responsible for the national park in which he had just been wandering. A consequence of the effort demanded by his recent odyssey, once again Seb moved like a man who has aged prematurely to pick up the letter which for having been dropped through every letterbox in the county had been disseminated widely, and the missive which had been written for his eyes only. He felt his back creak as he regained his full height.

Seb didn't bother to take off his shoes at the door. This would have been an act worthy of a scolding if Neffie had been there to greet him. After dropping his pack with a thud in the hall he made his way to the kitchen. He went straight to the fridge for the carton containing his refreshment of choice — cold milk. He filled a pint glass with the pure white liquid, and after slaking his thirst by gulping down a big cat's share, glass still in hand he entered the room in which Neffie and he spent most of their waking time when they were at home. He placed glass and letters on the cloth covering the round table directly beneath the window and then, having pulled out a chair from under the table, sat down to read where the natural light was best. Realising that he was in danger of tearing the letter apart if he tried to open it without making use of a letter-opener or at least a practicable substitute, Seb repaired to the kitchen to obtain a knife from the drying-rack on the kitchen sink. Upon his return he inserted the point of the knife into the epistle at one side and then sliced the folded paper along its top edge. It was a well-practised procedure, one which allowed the letter to unfurl and reveal Neffie's familiar hand on the single page.

Of course Seb wanted to read news of Neffie's exploits, but what he really needed to know, was that she still loved him. It was the reason why he often began by reading her opening words, and then her parting words, first. It was only when he had discovered that they corresponded with his wishes and expectations that he was able to digest the body of the letter with a quiet mind. On this occasion, as on every previous occasion that he had sliced open a blue envelope that had been addressed to him, the sentiment which Neffie had expressed at the outset and in conclusion was more than satisfactory for ensuring that Seb remained secure in the knowledge that he was still a wanted man.

Nevertheless, there was often at least one aspect of Neffie's letters which caused her beloved reader a certain amount of disquiet. Seb knew that the cause had more to do with him than her. Being fundamentally insecure he wanted her to be more effusive about her feelings for him than she was: it was a case of his wanting more than she was accustomed to expressing. Consequently Seb frequently found the content of his beloved's letters rather matter-of-fact. That said, however, for knowing that Neffie wasn't romantic — in the emotional, artistic sense of the words rather than the red roses on Valentine's Day sense — and having, over the years, become used to her epistolary style, he no longer found it to be as disquieting as he once had.

These days his equanimity only became sufficiently disturbed to niggle him hours later when Neffie described her exploits not in terms of a vulnerable woman travelling alone, or even in the company of one or more female companions, but in the pleasant company of an unknown male, unknown to Sebastian that is. In this instance therefore, it was undoubtedly the case that Seb read Neffie's intimations of love for himself, and her expressions of gratitude and appreciation in respect of an individual named Samuel Massequoi through distorted eyes. Of course, for his having accompanied Neffie on her preparatory meetings prior to her trip, the man left back at home in Yatton knew something of the man in Neffie's company whom he hadn't met, but this shadowy knowledge of the 'ever so helpful' stranger's circumstances served only to exacerbate Sebastian's problem: his jealousy.

No matter how deeply he was loved and missed, Sebastian's problem was that he wanted that love to be expressed more demonstrably, maybe even more poetically, and he wanted this helpful Mr Massequoi — Neffie invariably referred to her host in Sierra Leone as Mr Massequoi — to be appreciated less. In truth Sebastian was learning how not to be jealous in respect of his partner's adventures in the big, wide world, and though it was uncertain whether Neffie was consciously aware that she was the perfect teacher in this regard, for as long as she travelled in the company of men her reluctant student would continue to suffer.

After having read the letter thrice over to extract every possible nuance of meaning Sebastian took a shower. It boosted his morale to get rid of the sweat and grime generated by the strenuous effort he had put into living that day, and, Mr Massequoi's appreciation society notwithstanding, set about preparing his evening meal in good spirits, the consequence in the main of his having read Neffie's letter in the wake, as it were, of his minor feat of endurance.

Seb was a mean chef when it came to cooking meat and two veg, and the meal usually satisfied, particularly when accompanied by half to two-thirds of a bottle of red. It was perhaps significant that in sitting down to eat at the table he sat in the chair in which Neffie would normally sit. After he had eaten and washed the dishes he slumped onto a bean-bag in front of the television.

Chapter Twenty
Mariana's Advice

Miss Koromah had chosen well when she opened a bar in Kalangba Junction. It stood at the crossroads of major and minor roads, and it was this accessibility to passing trade rather than the patronage of the settlement's few hundred souls which made a success of a business which otherwise would have been mediocre.

The major road branched off the road linking Makeni and Pendembu and led up into the Katabai Hills eventually to come to a dead end at the village of Madina. About ten miles before any traveller reached Madina it was possible to turn south and make for Binkolo via the Makump ferry; for being little more than a track in places, this so called road was a hazardous route in the rainy season.

Of the two minor roads leading to and from Mariana's Bar the most important led for about twenty miles west before it too stopped abruptly. Nonetheless, it provided the only practicable means of reaching the villages of Maketi and Mawuli. The road which was less of a lifeline headed north to join up with the main road from Pendembu to Karina.

Not only had Mariana chosen well because her bar was at a convenient hub, but yet another factor in her favour was that after conducting some painstaking research in her four-wheel drive she had discovered that in none of the surrounding villages was there an establishment such as hers. She therefore possessed the only licence to serve alcohol within a radius of umpteen miles, and such was Miss Koromah's reputation that her place in the sticks frequently proved a temptation to the young bloods from the larger towns: Pendembu to the north; Makeni to the south. When it came to keeping the peace it was usually for the best that the two groups didn't turn up on the same night. When that happened an evening which was sociable at the outset often degenerated into a fracas. Fortunately for Mariana, her stock, and the fabric of her business, the trouble that there had been to date had taken place outside, and for this blessing she could thank a few locals whose sense of decorum matched their physical prowess.

In the small matter of payment for the drinks consumed on her premises Miss Koromah was easy-going for the reason that many families were supported by one or more members working away, either in the diamond mines or as far away as Freetown, and sometimes the money brought home by the remunerated family member on his or her previous visit ran out before he or she returned. There being no public transport to speak of, for people lacking private means other than Shanks's pony, a visit to the post-office in Makeni or Pendembu necessitated a long walk there and back, so in view of Mariana's flexible attitude, for the majority of the local inhabitants it was better to wait for any cash which was likely to be forthcoming to arrive by hand. It should be borne in mind however, that Mariana's pliability regarding money owed to her didn't mean that she was a soft touch, for as to who owed what her record-keeping was worthy of an accountant. Moreover, she was reputed to have a persuasive manner when it came to collecting those debts which in her opinion had been on the books too long.

At night the physical entity that was Mariana's Bar was as flamboyant as the person who owned it. Its colourful, flashing lights were powered by a reconditioned former RAF generator, a machine which had been left behind on completion of the runway at Lungi Airport. Night after night the diesel engine droned until the early hours. The array it powered could be seen for a considerable distance in either direction along the straight stretch of road that ran through the village. The ostentation on display was almost equal to that which decorated the walls and roofs of many a house in Luxborough and Ferrousby at Christmas. The people of Yatton were generally more restrained.

If on the outside the temptation to potential customers was mainly visual, on the inside it was loud music that kept people entertained and tapping their heels. Throughout the day and well into the night, from a state of the art sound system's powerful speakers an eclectic mix of music performed by artists from America, Britain, and a number of African countries could be heard. When Mariana opened up in the morning — it was usually around eleven — she liked to listen to Simon and Garfunkel. She enjoyed the freshness of their harmonies. No matter how sad a particular song was, their singing always made her feel cheerful and optimistic. Her choice of an evening was likely to be a toss-up between the Rolling Stones or the music of Mansour Seck, or Baaba Maal from Senegal. There was a direct correlation between the number of customers and the volume of the speakers, the rule of thumb as determined by Mariana being that the less people there were occupying the four bar stools and the assortment of chairs placed around the round, red-topped tables, the louder the 'vibes'. Whenever Mariana was absent from the premises and a trusted deputy was in charge the music also changed.

In addition to drinking beer, palm wine, or spirits of varying strength whilst engaged in philosophical or political debate, Mariana's patrons could also amuse themselves by playing either pin-ball or table football. The machine which enticed and generated excitement in the player as he — it was usually he — sent a ball-bearing around and between the obstacles and scoring stations to instigate a series of pings and flashing lights was tucked into the corner of the room farthest from the entrance. The more popular of the two pastimes was the apparatus operated wholly manually. The game in which those competing manipulate, quite aggressively on occasion, the rods on which rows of unlikely footballers are attached, had been allocated a more prominent and more spacious position.

No one was interested in playing either at present, and though the pin-ball machine occasionally omitted a strange noise to indicate its readiness for action, the opposing teams of pink-faced footballers, all kitted out as it were in either red or blue, faced each other in static silence.

"Do you think you could turn the music down, Mariana?" enquired Samuel from his stool at the end of the bar. He was sitting farthest from the front entrance and near to a door which led those that passed through it out back to the toilets. It was a tentative request, one made in complete ignorance of Mariana's little quirk of keeping the music loud when the place was almost empty.

Hitherto Miss Koromah had been staring fixedly at the front door, but in response to her cousin's request she turned to look at him with a gimlet-eye, as if what he had asked for was nigh on impossible for her to grant. She was standing less than an arm's length from where Samuel was sitting, and even in the light kept seductively low nothing of her expression was missed by her guest.

The fact that apart from herself and Samuel, and the barman who as part payment for stacking bottles and doing a number of other jobs was allowed to play on the pin-ball machine for free, the place was deserted would normally have put Mariana in a less than an amenable frame of mind. On the evening in question, however, she was feeling optimistic that something good was about to happen, and it didn't seem to bother her in the slightest that her house of some repute was almost empty. Uncharacteristically, therefore, she acceded to Samuel's request and instructed the barman, a boy of fifteen years of age named Moses, to reduce the decibels. From where he had been placing bottles of juice onto a shelf just above ground level Moses arose as if he were a ghost or a ghoul rising from the grave to turn the appropriate knob on the little black box pulsating behind the bar. Consequently Mick Jagger's voice became less overpowering.

"My heartfelt thanks," said Samuel mockingly, prior to taking a sip of palm wine from a glass half full, "now I can hear myself think." He raised his glass in salute to Moses, and then added, as the young man returned to his former task and the chinking of bottles resumed, "It's quiet tonight… I suppose that's because it's Tuesday."

"It's not Tuesday, it's Monday," corrected Samuel's cousin, the focus of her gaze once again directed towards the front door.

A predictable thought crossed Samuel's mind, its subject being how time takes flight when one is enjoying oneself, but because his next thought was that the previous thought was too predictable to mention he chose not to express either. Instead, he put another question to his cousin. "Are you expecting someone in particular, or just waiting for custom in whatever human shape it may take?"

There was an edge to his question: it wasn't an uncommon feature of his conversations with Mariana. The reason for this, as Samuel recognised, was that he was somewhat in awe of his cousin, and consequently often felt intimidated in her company, which in turn led to his defensive manner.

On this occasion, however, it was Mariana's turn to be defensive. "Why do you ask?" she enquired sharply, at the same time giving Samuel one of her quizzical looks. It was evident by her manner that the reason for her previously quiet optimism had suddenly come under threat.

"Why do I ask? Well, it's just that for most of the evening you've hardly taken your eyes off that door..." Samuel indicated which door with a slight nod, "...as if," he continued, "you're expecting the queen of England to walk through at any moment. I mean it's not that I come by this way that often, but for all the attention you're paying me this evening I might as well have stayed in Freetown. Perhaps it's because my conversation compares poorly with the scintillating repartee you've grown used to in Kalangba Junction."

At this point in his outburst Samuel paused to survey the room to right and left. "But I'm confident that given the chance I'll say something to spark your interest."

The sarcasm wasn't lost on Miss Koromah, and she was surprised — astonished even — at her cousin's boldness in speaking his mind. Rather than take offence she was pleased to hear him speak with such feeling. Even Moses stopped what he was doing to listen. This was also a bold move in that it could have incurred Mariana's wrath. Above the dulcet tones of 'Lady d'Arbanville' the speaker's words could be clearly heard.

"I know I'm just a humble teacher," the teacher continued, "and you're a high-powered business- woman..." Once again Samuel looked about him as if he were searching for the evidence that would justify his description of Mariana, "...but that doesn't mean I have to be seen and not heard. You never know... you may find my conversation more interesting than you could possibly have imagined, rewarding, perhaps both. For what it's worth some people think I can be quite amusing at times."

There was a pause in proceedings when Samuel had said all that he had to say for the present, a hiatus lasting all of ten seconds in which Mariana considered how best to respond to her cousin's attention-seeking as she saw it. Meanwhile Samuel's concern was that he might have overstepped the mark, and as a consequence would probably find himself back in Freetown as soon as tomorrow evening. Silence, as any sales person or interrogator knows, can be an effective tool in human discourse, a means to compel the opposing interlocutor to break the spell and lose, but as it transpired Samuel's anticipation, no way did it resemble fear, proved unfounded. Mariana had taken his tirade lightly.

"There… there," she said at last, mimicking the tone of a parent soothing an upset child. At the same time she thrice patted her cousin on the head. "Is Mariana's little boy feeling neglected?"

Judging by her grin this woman of substance was enjoying herself, yet in playing and deriving pleasure from her maternal role it wasn't her intention to humiliate Samuel. It wasn't even her intention to embarrass him. From Mariana's perspective she was simply having a little joke in the company of a family member and an employee who also happened to be a friend. Only she knew for certain that if another individual, one she wasn't on such familiar terms with, had been present, she would have behaved differently. Fortunately for everyone present Samuel took the jest in the spirit which the jester had hoped it would be taken, and responded to his cousin's playfulness with a grin which easily matched hers. He shook his head a few times as well.

"Anyway, cousin, I really don't know what you've got to complain about," said Mariana, temporarily forsaking her vantage point to squeeze past Moses and reach into the fridge for a bottle of beer. She poured the amber content into a glass which she first held up to the light to ensure its cleanliness. Upon repairing to the end of the bar to take up her former place and her statuesque stance Mariana continued, "I was under the impression that you hadn't come all this way to listen to me grumbling about what's wrong with the government… with the country… the world… and a hundred things besides."

Mariana ended her sentence on a high note, and this led Samuel to believe that she hadn't finished speaking. Consequently, after a second lengthy pause, but this time one in which both parties thought that the other was about to say something, he became flummoxed as to how best to respond. Eventually, for the reason that it gave him more time to think, he requested more information. "Why do you think I came to Kalangba if it wasn't to spend some quality time with you?"

"Well, if that really was the reason you came I'm flattered," Mariana retorted, "but I don't think you're being…"

"I've restocked the shelves as you asked… will there be anything else, boss?" enquired Moses, unconcerned that he had interrupted his employer in the middle of a sentence which she didn't finish as a consequence.

"Thank you, Moses, that will do for this evening. Come round in the morning to collect your wages."

Moses' eyes lit up with delight at the prospect, and he flashed Mariana a winning smile. Released from his duties Moses squeezed his substantial frame past Mariana and the bar. She stepped back so as not to impede his progress. He might only have been fifteen but Moses was already as tall as Samuel; and he was almost as broad.

"Goodnight," said Moses, glancing from the woman standing to the man sitting.

Prior to the young man reaching the door to exit the building they in turn echoed his simple valediction.

"Seems a good boy," commented Samuel once Moses was out of earshot. "I wish my students were as polite."

"He's a real godsend," said Mariana, particularly when it comes to doing the heavy lifting. Not that he's all brawn and no brain you understand. He wants to go to college to train to be a doctor. What this country needs is a lot more like him and not so many of the machete-wielding morons that would chop your arm off as soon as look at you."

"I'll drink to that," averred Samuel, raising his glass to take a sip, his expression upon looking up at Mariana clearly revealing the respect he thought her pronouncement deserved. "If he ever changes his mind and expresses a desire to become a teacher, try to put him off, unless he sees it as a noble calling and has a private income."

It was a familiar gripe in the ears of anyone spending more than twenty minutes in Samuel's company, that being time enough for him to direct the conversation and bemoan the dire strait of his profession. Presently that habitual tone of resentment in his voice was clearly discernible and provided Mariana with her cue to broach a subject dear to her heart, a subject to which she had first alluded in her cousin's kitchen back in Freetown. Forsaking all circumspection, she felt impelled to be direct. "Well, if you were to get yourself a rich Englishwoman your money worries would be over in the blink of a monkey's eye," said Mariana.

She couldn't have been more forthright. For the reason that he was half-expecting to hear something approaching the gist of what Mariana had said Samuel wasn't taken aback. He did think his cousin's salvo somewhat tactless. Demonstrating that he could be just as tactless Samuel yawned as if he were at the world cup yawning for Sierra Leone. "Mariana you're incorrigible," offered the teacher by way of a general character assessment.

"I'm what?" queried Miss Koromah sharply, sensitive to the possibility that she might have been insulted.

"Your attitude regarding my affairs is beyond belief," he explained.

"Well at least it shows that I have your interests at heart and that I care about you. Far be it from me to tell you how you should run your life, but it seems to me that you have the perfect opportunity to get out of the rut you're in and make something of yourself. I know… I know…" exclaimed Mariana, effectively nipping an anticipated interruption in the bud, "… you don't need to tell me that it's not your fault that you never have any money, and that the government's to blame. Go back far enough and you'll be able to get on another of your hobby-horses and blame the British for the mess the country is in. What do you call them… our colonial masters… yes, that's it, why not blame our former colonial masters for the present government not being able to pay your salary? Even if they could pay you what they're supposed to it would still be less than you deserve." Now that Mariana had got into her stride there would be no stopping her until she had finished. "It's just that when the government is incompetent or corrupt, or both, then you have to take matters in hand and create your own revolution, and I don't mean by brandishing a Kalashnikov or wielding a Machete, but by having the flexibility of mind, and the courage to alter course. Only you can bring about the change you want, and one way would be to make a good match as they say in those quaint English novels you're forever reading. You've got to admit it's not such a bad idea is it?"

Like a question mark hanging in mid-air, the rising intonation of Miss Koromah's peroration clearly indicated that, for the present, she had indeed finished speaking.

Samuel pondered over the significance of what his cousin had said. There could be no doubt that 'Marri' had spoken with passion, and thereby had been totally convincing in her concern. The strength of feeling she had expressed had been just as meaningful as her words. The two combined had left Samuel feeling numb. In fact it was more than that for it would be no exaggeration to say that he had been stunned, like a man who has just been informed that his wife and children have been taken hostage, or even murdered. The metaphorical stun grenade had exploded in his face. Samuel's initial thought — once he had recovered sufficiently to be able to think — was that much of what his cousin had had to say was true. It didn't necessarily follow, however, that he considered her proposed solution to his pecuniary problems to be right and proper. No; he hadn't spent years of study to become a gigolo or a kept man. The opinion that he had long ago formed of Mariana, and which had been reinforced when they had last met back in Freetown, hadn't changed one iota, and that was that she was more mercenary than he could ever be.

At a point in time when the silence between them could be likened to taut elastic about to snap, Samuel's response was reasonable, measured. "It sounds to me that you've read a novel or two in your time," said Samuel: he was trying to be insouciant.

In reality Samuel had no idea what Mariana had read or liked to read, and the sudden spark that had prompted him to make his comment was the rather fundamental premise that in order to be able to refer to something you first have to know about it. His ulterior motive in getting Mariana onto the subject of books was that it was a sphere in which he was certain to have the upper hand. Even though Mariana had read a chapter of Austen here, a paragraph of Dickens there, Samuel's ploy was hardly successful. His cousin wasn't going to undermine her newly acquired professional status, as she perceived it to be, by admitting to just how scant her knowledge of literature of any kind was. The acquisition of money was her metier, and therefore her favourite topic of conversation. Samuel's limp response to Mariana's impassioned exhortation demanded no reply, and because none was forthcoming, he felt that he had no choice but to remain in Mariana's world and tackle her pet subject head on.

"And who do you have in mind to bring about this change for the better in my life that you're so keen to see happen? Who do you think should feather my nest?"

For wanting his cousin's reply to be specific Samuel's questions weren't rhetorical; but of course the same answer to both questions was hardly a mystery to either party.

"Oh come off it, Sammy," gasped Mariana, raising her eyes to the ceiling in incredulity, and more than a little exasperation, that her relation could be so obtuse, at which point she noted that she had omitted to switch on the fan. It was an oversight she soon rectified. 'Jumping Jack Flash' was then accompanied by the constant whir of rapidly rotating blades. "You know as well as I do that if it hadn't been for that Englishwoman... what's her name... Neffie isn't it... you know that if it hadn't been for Neffie you wouldn't have left Freetown. She's the main reason that you've come all this way, isn't she? Come on, admit it. Before letting Samuel answer she added, "Do you want another drink, on the house?"

"I wouldn't mind," said Samuel matter-of-factly. "I'll have what you're drinking this time," and in response to this instruction Mariana repeated the procedure she had earlier carried out on her own behalf, with the exception of inspecting the glass. Unceremoniously she replaced the small glass now emptied of palm wine with one of larger volume filled with beer. After savouring a mouthful and thereby ridding his palette of the wine's sweetness Samuel was only prepared to concur with what to Mariana was the least interesting part of her analysis.

"I do admit it, but I haven't come to Kalangba for the reasons you're thinking. My intentions are..."

"You don't need to tell me that your intentions are entirely honourable, but what's dishonourable about chatting up an unmarried woman with the aim of establishing a meaningful relationship, and who knows what else later? That's what men and women have been doing since they stopped grunting and learned to speak isn't it? Call it what you like — mutual attraction, sex, love, it's what makes the world go round."

It was Mariana's turn to raise her glass to her mouth and drink. Talking made her thirsty. Samuel ran his finger around the rim of his own glass as he began to speak.

"There's nothing dishonourable in that per se, but what could be perceived as my behaving dishonourably would be if I were to poke my nose in where it's not wanted. No matter how much I enjoy being in her company, and assuming that she enjoys being in mine, the fact is that Miss Goodwin is already in a stable, long-term relationship. From what I can gather she and her partner have been living together as man and wife for years, and whatever you or I may think about the morality, or lack of it, in their living arrangements, she's unlikely to want to make big changes in her life... in her relationship, possibly in her career, for the sake of someone she hardly knows is she, even if she thought I was the best thing since fried plantain?"

"Stranger things have happened," Mariana responded unimaginatively prior to letting her imagination wander, "and it seems to me that the most significant factor in your favour is that you are here and so is she, Neffie, and your rival is over there, thousands of miles away. A few glasses of palm wine shared on the veranda as the sun sinks to a chorus of birdsong and the chirruping of a myriad insects can be very seductive, particularly to a woman who lives in a country that has such a cold, damp climate."

"Is that your idea of an ideal courtship?" probed Samuel.

"Let's just say I've fallen for it myself," Mariana replied, "not that it came to anything serious."

"The tropical idyll you describe isn't so romantic when you consider that the mosquito, the female of the species I hasten to add, causes the greatest loss of human life on the planet. And what's more, Sierra Leone is much soggier than Britain."

"That may be so," said Mariana, ignoring Samuel's salient point to concentrate instead upon the differences in precipitation between the two countries, "but at least the rain here is so warm it's almost sexy."

Saying 'sexy' must have made her feel sexy, because she proceeded to perform the actions of a sensuous woman standing in the rain and getting soaked to the skin and loving every minute of it. She could imagine her blouse clinging tightly to her, and no doubt becoming enticingly transparent. Her piece of theatre was a sign that she was on the verge of giving up on her cousin, in respect of matchmaking that is. It was a somewhat embarrassed Samuel who continued to find fault with Mariana's plans for his future.

"Neffie has sensitive skin," said Samuel, and the manner in which he made this pronouncement imbued his words with deep significance.

"That sounds promising," responded Mariana dryly, although, as she was about to discover, her thoughts were on a different track from those of her cousin.

"What I meant to say was that she isn't going to stay long in a place where she's daily going to be a source of food for bugs that could kill her."

In screwing up her face Mariana didn't attempt to hide her disappointment. "In that case perhaps she'll take you back with her," she said, believing it to be a realisable prospect.

Samuel laughed out loud at his cousin's flight of fancy. "Sebastian may have something to say about that," he chortled, "though he may just get straight to the point and kill me."

"Who's Sebastian?"

"Neffie's partner, the man she lives with, and don't think that he wouldn't know how to… kill me that is… he used to be a soldier in the British Army, the army that in former times enabled the British to become our colonial masters," Samuel informed.

"All things considered perhaps you should channel your testosterone in another direction. Hey… I know… why not try Miss Fussey, the Peace Corps worker your friend is friendly with," exclaimed Mariana with great enthusiasm for being suddenly inspired. "But then again," she continued as the balloon of her inspiration just as quickly deflated, "maybe that wouldn't be such a good idea. Being American she would probably let you wash and iron your own shirts."

That was Mariana's little joke. In her battle to persuade her relation to plan and implement a strategy the successful outcome of which would be to capture the heart of either of the two white women with whom he was acquainted, Mariana had finally exhausted her supply of ammunition. In point of fact, she had unwittingly timed the moment of defeat perfectly, for just as she uttered what turned out to be her final word on the subject of Samuel's prospective love-life, the sound of an engine grew steadily louder as the vehicle it powered approached the building. Unlike the din generated by the only other car heard that evening, the noise this vehicle made didn't reach a crescendo only for it then to diminish gradually as the driver sped by in the direction of Makeni. That had been over an hour ago. Presently, by all audible indications and, as glimpsed through partially closed blinds at the window adjacent to the front door, the play of headlights as they swung off the road, the driver had come, if not from Makeni, then certainly from that direction. The vehicle came to a standstill on a patch of open ground directly in front of the building. Prior to Mariana confirming his suspicions Samuel formed the opinion that the visitor or visitors were expected.

"Excuse me, cousin dear, I have some business to attend to," Mariana said in earnest. "It should only take a few minutes."

Her countenance, indeed her entire body language, clearly delineated her newly acquired gravitas, so that it seemed as if most of what she had said hitherto had been mere persiflage. After hastily downing the remnant of her drink Mariana stepped from behind the bar. By this time the Rolling Stones had stopped playing of their own accord. The relative quietude which followed the final note of the final song was heavy with expectation. Contrary to Samuel's expectation, rather than making for the front portal, Mariana exited via the rear exit cum entrance. The manner of her departure gave the impression that she was trying to leave the premises as surreptitiously as possible. Left to his own devices Samuel decided that his best course of action was to remain seated where he was. By doing so, he surmised, eventually his patience would be rewarded as his curiosity as to what his cousin was up to, and with whom, were satisfied. For the time being he remained somewhat perplexed, but at least he didn't feel as if he was being treated like a miscreant schoolboy. At least Mariana hadn't ordered him to go to his room.

Theoretical and particle physicists tell us that as a consequence of the electromagnetic force matter is dense, not solid, that our common-sense impression of an object as being solid is false. The idea must certainly seem counter-intuitive to a person who has just been knocked down by a bus because he or she couldn't see round the corner prior to stepping into the road, yet if we were to zoom in on one of the omnibus' atoms so that the nucleus were the size of a marble, the electrons could be thought of as currants transporting their electricity miles distant, with nothing between.

Notwithstanding that he had the curiosity of a cat that still has all his lives, Samuel's repeated attempts to see through atoms too dense to be able to observe events taking place outside inevitably proved futile. The closed blinds at the window let in light from the headlights but nothing more that could be recognised. Nonetheless the teacher frequently looked over his shoulder to face the direction in which the vehicle's engine still purred. Samuel guessed that the vehicle was a Mercedes Benz. In this part of the world it was the marque of choice for rogues and princes. The teacher who was eager to learn expected the visitors to burst through the door at any moment. If that expectation wasn't alarming enough he then imagined the room being sprayed with bullets. It was a fearful prospect, and given the state of the country, one not beyond the realm of possibility. Samuel's one overriding and reassuring thought in this regard was that surely Mariana hadn't sunk so low as to do business with rebels.

From the room directly above Samuel's head he could hear someone rummaging. He presumed that Mariana had entered the building via a fire escape and was now either hiding something, or searching for it. In the next instant, also originating from above, came the sound of a door closing. The listener below formed the opinion that the door had been closed hurriedly, slammed even. Barely had the last vibration from above diminished when the front door opened. Samuel turned to see a young man's head and upper body leaning across the threshold as he conducted a tentative reconnaissance of the premises. The stranger's reluctance to enter showed that he was ready to beat a hasty retreat if he were to sense that anything was amiss. Acute powers of perception were needed to notice the difference, but the young man's manner was cunningly wary rather than nervously diffident. Samuel possessed such powers. Indeed, in the moments that passed prior to any words being exchanged between them, he was able to glean a great deal about the individual who had come to do business with his cousin.

It was Mr Massequoi's belief that everyone is prejudiced in one way or another, and he had no doubt arrived at this conclusion after analysing his own views about certain groups of people, his former colonial masters being a case in point. By a similar process he perceived Mariana's hesitant business associate to be one of a type: a sharp-witted, sharply dressed, handsome devil whose physiognomy was of Middle Eastern origin, probably Syrian, but possibly Lebanese. What aggrieved the 'poor, down-trodden blacks' about the way these people operated, and they formed a significant minority in Sierra Leone, was their ability to manipulate the system to their own advantage. They operated on two levels, one supporting the other. The olive-skinned individual at the door wore a light-blue jacket over an open-neck plain white shirt. His hair, Samuel noted, was thick, black and wavy.

"We've come to see Miss Koromah," announced the stranger as his eyes settled at last upon the bar's only occupant.

Samuel was on the point of telling him that he didn't know Miss Koromah's whereabouts for certain when she suddenly reappeared through the door through which she had disappeared a few minutes earlier. This woman of imposing, and occasionally intimidating, presence, glanced at her relation in passing, and in that fleeting look she managed to convey the simple instruction, "Don't ask." In fact she conveyed this command so clearly that from where Samuel was sitting it was as if he were able to read 'DON'T' and 'ASK' written boldly across each of his cousin's eyeballs. Only when she had breezed past him did the teacher observe, and this was only after he had registered — not for the first time — the rounded pertness of his cousin's bottom, that she was clutching something.

At first, because her long, slender fingers completely encompassed, and therefore almost hid the object she carried, Samuel couldn't make out what it was. After a longer, though not closer, scrutiny, the teacher concluded that the barely visible faded blue cloth had to be a small bag, and if it was indeed a small bag it could quite possibly be a receptacle for diamonds. "What else would a bag like that contain?" he muttered, in a volume only he could hear.

Either for his own good in the sense that if ever the shit were to hit the fan, as it were, the less he knew the better, or hers because the more discrete she was about her business dealings the less likely they would be to come unstuck, Mariana ushered the visitor through the door from whence he came.

"Why can't you people take a woman at her word? I told Ali I would come to the car," said Miss Koromah. Her tone was clearly one of irate disapproval.

Prior to vacating the building, as if in response to an afterthought, Mariana reached to close the door behind her, leaving Samuel alone once again in a room which was silent save for the drone of a mosquito and the whir of the fan. Notwithstanding that he hadn't previously taken the liberty, Samuel didn't think that Mariana would mind if he helped himself to another beer, and that was precisely what he did. He would, of course, offer to pay for his 'purchase' at the earliest opportunity, though he quite believed that Mariana would reject his offer out of hand. His glass refilled and having regained his perch, he couldn't help but take long, lingering looks in the direction of the blind that was illumined brightly by the car headlights, and as he had experienced previously no matter how long or how hard he looked his view of the world outside remained opaque.

It is said that curiosity kills the cat, but a cat which still has nine lives, as had this pedagogic tiger as far as he was aware, could surely take a risk or two, particularly if the prize were to be worthwhile. In this instance the value of the prize was difficult to estimate, but just as the quest for knowledge is a powerful incentive to act, the desire to know this or that makes for a strong temptation, one difficult to resist. To satisfy his burning curiosity therefore, Samuel thought he would chance taking a peek. To this end, and with a prowler's caution, he began to move.

From the bottom rung of his barstool he removed his feet and lowered them until they first touched and then rested on the floor. It was so tentatively done. Moving in a manner similar to actors playing at being cat-burglars in the film fantasies he had seen of improbable heists, Samuel approached the window. For not being able to see his cousin or hear her voice Samuel quite expected her to enter her domain at any moment, and he wondered, if she were to appear suddenly and witness his strange behaviour, how she would react. Would she think that he had betrayed her trust in some way? Would his status as a privileged guest be compromised?

264

Fortunately for Samuel's belief in his own integrity the door remained firmly shut. Stealthily he approached the window from the right as he was looking at it, his aim being to secrete himself in the space that was the stucco wall between the window-frame and the door. The wall felt cool against his back, rough against the palms of his hands and the touch of his fingers and thumbs. Only when he was certain that he hadn't instigated a response from anyone on the outside did he lean forward and raise one hand to prise open a small aperture in the blind. The lower and upper edges of the two plastic strips through which he had inserted his fingers felt sharp enough to cut his skin. He resolved to check for blood later. At first, as he peered through the gap he had just created, his eyes were dazzled by the headlights shining directly at him. The intense brightness caused him to turn away in order to adjust his vision. At the second attempt to satisfy his curiosity he was able to make out more for having directed his gaze away from the obvious source of the glare. He beheld a meeting, and the people in attendance were Mariana and two men. They were standing as if at the points of an imaginary triangle. Mariana was at the apex farthest from the car, the two near doors of which, in readiness for a quick getaway perhaps, were wide open.

Samuel couldn't help but notice that Mariana towered above the two men, and even though he realised that some of her height could be accounted for by the fact that she was wearing platform shoes, he estimated that Mariana would still have been an inch taller than both were she to have been wearing sandals. The thought which flashed through Samuel's brain at that moment was that his cousin must have appeared a daunting figure to the men standing before her and having to look up at her goddess-like visage above her tall, statuesque figure. He wondered whether they weren't a little intimidated to be confronting such an Amazon.

In the event, however, it took only a few seconds for Samuel to realise that neither man was the least bit cowed by the woman looking down her nose at them. Their body language said as much. It prompted the clandestine observer to assume that one or other, or perhaps both, of the men were armed, and that the weapon of choice in either case was likely to be a pistol.

Somewhat surprised at not having missed the action, in the next instant Samuel witnessed the event which he had assumed had been the purpose of the meeting, but which he hadn't expected to see take place before his eyes. Mariana handed over the bag she had been holding on to as if her life had depended on its safe delivery. That done she stepped back half a pace and held out her hand in expectation of receiving something in return. The recompense she had bargained for was soon forthcoming, but in a way which surprised Samuel yet again. It turned out that there weren't just two men conducting business with his cousin, but possibly three. That there was a third person in the car is certain: it was just that Samuel couldn't make out whether the individual in question was man or woman. Reaching across the front passenger seat from behind the steering wheel, the person of indeterminate gender handed over a package the size of a paperback edition of *War and Peace*. For the reason that he was still dazzled to a large degree whenever he steered his vision in the direction of the vehicle, transactions taking place in close proximity to it could only be partially observed by Samuel, the consequence being that the impression he gained was a combination of what he actually saw and the product of his imagination. He believed, therefore, that the package comprised brown paper secured with tape. The brown paper he had caught a glimpse of, the tape, although it had indeed been used, he had imagined. Naturally he had no specific knowledge of what the package contained, but he would have bet his next month's salary that it was money, and that the notes were of a harder currency than the Leone. The three most likely contenders were the Deutschmark, the US dollar, and sterling.

The man who had taken the package from the driver didn't hang on to it for long, but quickly relinquished his role as man in the middle by placing it directly into Miss Koromah's eager hand. Mariana's first act was to tear the wrapping asunder, but only at one end. Evidently she didn't trust her business associates to the extent that she believed they wouldn't try to dupe her. The package remaining as yet largely intact, with her thumb she deftly flicked through the partially exposed wad of notes. She seemed to be satisfied, and was about to shake the hand of the man who had handed her the package when, in response to an exhortation emanating from the car, his attention was directed towards the window where Samuel was peeking. The hand-shake didn't happen.

Samuel had fiddled with the blind once too often for the movement not to be noticed. Alerted to being watched first one stranger's hand, and then the hand of the only other man standing, moved as if to grasp something as yet hidden in each case by his jacket. In the event no weapon was drawn, assuming that that was what each sudden movement had indicated was about to happen. That the threat of violence had, for the present, been removed was entirely due to Mariana's influence. Aware that the witness to their dubious dealings could be no one but her cousin, she assured her counterparts that her silly relation posed no threat, that he was merely playing at being a guardian angel watching over her.

Mariana's associates weren't entirely convinced, and they eyed her with suspicion. She met their visual attack with forbearance, as if to say they were getting jittery over nothing; but gradually the men relaxed their guard as the hands which had appeared to reach for shoulder-holsters returned to more natural poses.

Meanwhile Samuel in his no longer secret location strove not to move a muscle. It was as if he believed that by not drawing further attention to himself his presence would soon be discounted as a mere figment of his spotter's imagination. It was only when he witnessed parting gestures and their accompanying verbal exchanges that he dared to move. Then he carelessly let go of the blind and made for his former perch at the bar. Once he was seated he heard the unmistakeable sound of the Mercedes reversing prior to it driving off in the direction of Pendembu. The effect of the headlights swinging back and forth across the room was impressive, but not as welcome to Samuel as the distance increasing by the minute between them and him.

Moments later the front door opened and Mariana, package with torn wrapping in hand, entered. Stony-faced so that she appeared inscrutable she made for the door at the rear, but just as she was about to pass Sam by without having said a word, she caught him off-guard with a direct question. "Were you spying on me, Sammy?"

Samuel's defence in lieu of telling either the truth or a lie was to enquire in turn, "Why would I want to do anything as unconscionable as that?"

There were times when he felt empowered by the extent of his vocabulary, and this was one of them. Baffled as to the meaning of a certain word if not to the general sense, without bothering to reply Mariana once again left the room. All the while she kept her hand over the open end of the package as a deterrent against prying eyes. Her intention was to deposit the package in a secret place. No sooner was she out of sight than Samuel helped himself to another bottle of beer. He resolved not to offer to pay for either this one or the last.

Chapter Twenty-One
Good News Comes out of the Blue

Not in the twenty-nine years that Shirley Margai had lived on this earth had there been a telephone call more momentous than the one she had taken after having been dropped off by Sebastian Forrest following their visit to the television studio. Whether it's possible to predict the future is debatable, but it may be that there wouldn't be a call as equally momentous in the entirety of her life to come. The voice at the other end of the line belonged to a stranger, although the assured manner in which he had introduced himself, and the richly seductive tone in which he had spoken, almost convinced Miss Margai that she had known him for years.

The caller was an accomplished life-assurance salesman, and though it hardly seems credible he didn't reveal his occupation until much later in their acquaintance. Overcoming an understandable reticence on her behalf, the salesman had convinced Miss Margai that it would be to her advantage if they were to meet in person. Tempted by the prospect Shirley had agreed. A potent factor adding to the caller's well-practiced powers of persuasion had been the detailed information he had on her. Only after she had replaced the receiver did she realise that his revelations must have been gleaned from articles — no doubt written or instigated by Seb about her in the local press; although another source could have been the BBC.

The upshot of this first conversation between Miss Margai and the stranger — at some point he had introduced himself as Richard Hindmarsh — was that he was a man on a mission. He was speaking on behalf of a group of philanthropic Christians that wished to make a difference to the life of the young lady from Sierra Leone: it was unquestionably a mission of mercy. On the basis, therefore, that he had some great and exciting news for her he had asked if he could come with a colleague who was also a friend to visit. Notwithstanding the sincerity of his request, Mr Hindmarsh couldn't help but enact years of training and practice by helpfully providing Shirley with what is referred to in the business as an alternative close.

"Which would be more convenient… if we were to call during the day, or would an evening be more to your liking?"

For some reason Richard's voice had suddenly become slightly higher pitched than Shirley was accustomed to hearing from a male. She was by no means familiar with the accents of the British Isles, but she was certainly able to discern the difference between the way in which her telephone interlocutor spoke and the people she normally conversed with in and around Luxborough. The relevant particular that she didn't yet know about Richard Hindmarsh was that he was Welsh born and bred. The fact that he lived in a leafy suburb of Ferrousby, and had done so for the previous twenty of his fifty years as a human-being, hadn't changed his accent in the slightest. That was the opinion of Mrs Hindmarsh. Her husband thought differently.

The question designed to elicit a positive reply had proved effective in that Shirley had said that it was all the same to her, that either suggestion was convenient. Thinking in terms of his business activity throughout the week as opposed to his charitable or spiritual activities, and being mindful of how much he appreciated daytime appointments over having to go out in the evening, the former being more difficult to come by, Hindmarsh had jumped at the chance, so to speak, of calling on the following day, at three p.m.

No sooner had the appointment been made and the receiver returned to its place of rest than Shirley stood for a few moments as if spellbound. In fact she was pondering over the strangeness of the call, and wondering if she had done the right thing. Naturally she had then confided in her mother. From the moment Shirley had begun to describe to her what she had done and why she had done it, however, her bewilderment at the thought of having committed herself irrevocably had loomed ever larger. Once she had been put in the picture, as it were, Mrs Cannisman had warned to the effect that the call and its consequence sounded very suspicious, and had suggested that they pretend to be out at the appointed hour. Her subsequent thought on the matter was to trump the first when she suggested that they go out beforehand for real.

Contrary to Mrs Cannisman's advice, less than twenty-four hours later the sole occupant of the house at the time opened the door to two smartly dressed strangers. That sole occupant was Miss Margai. Perhaps for the reason that her initial advice had been ignored, Shirley's mother had thought it for the best to leave her daughter to deal with the mysterious business on her own, and had determined, therefore, to go into Luxborough to do her shopping. The destination uppermost in her mind was the butcher's on the High Street where she intended to buy a couple of pork chops for supper. After that she would be able to browse at will, until such time that the strangers were more than likely no longer her daughter's guests. Mrs Cannisman's thoughts upon leaving the house and closing the door behind her had been that she would be foolish to worry, after all, as a professional journalist who until recently had been working in a country descending into civil war, her daughter had encountered much worse than she was ever likely to do in Luxborough. Her lameness was proof enough of that.

The two men facing Miss Margai across the threshold introduced themselves individually one after the other. Not surprisingly it was the man who had made the appointment, Richard Hindmarsh, who introduced himself first. His appearance was remarkable for being the shorter of the two by a foot, though in terms of overall body mass the difference in height was more than made up for in girth. Hindmarsh's waistline was rotund, his face round and fleshy. His lank, black hair was brushed straight from side to side across his head, although a single strand had fallen out of place to lie at an angle across his barely furrowed brow. Apparently stuck in place with gel, or cream, or lacquer, the mop on top gave the man an old-fashioned, roaring-twenties look. In his right hand he carried a briefcase. It was made from tanned leather.

The taller man was Richard Gilmore. His accent, recognisable to Shirley as soon as he had said, "Good afternoon, my name is..." was South African, though he had been born in a remote part of Cumbria and brought up there for the first five years of his life. Soon after his fifth birthday Richard's parents had relocated with him to the Cape. Since then they had both died, and it had been as a young adult that their son had chosen to return to Britain. Of course none of this was known to Miss Margai. What she did know, however, was that Mr Gilmore had a much thinner face than his friend, and that his hair was grey. She was correct to assume that he was the elder of the two men. He wore glasses, and whether affectation or necessity was the cause, frequently when addressing another person he lowered his head slightly to peer over the frame. There were those that found this mannerism to be disconcerting, but fortunately for Mr Gilmore, Miss Margai wasn't one of them.

While making the acquaintance of her visitors Shirley gave the impression that she was listening intently to what they were saying when in fact she was gleaning considerably more information about them through her eyes rather than her ears. She looked each man up and down for signs that were indicative of their integrity, or lack of it. They on the other hand, well aware that they were being scrutinised closely, and that it is impossible to create a good first impression at the second attempt, did nothing to undermine their cause, and everything to enhance it. Consequently Miss Margai had no reservations whatsoever about inviting the be-suited gentlemen into her mother's house, though she continued to eye them up and down as she held the door wide open to let them pass.

"Very nice... very nice indeed," Richard Gilmore commented.

It was obvious that he was referring to a number of ornaments of apparently African pedigree adorning the mantelpiece above a gas fire aglow with artificial flames.

"Are they from Sierra Leone?" Mr Hindmarsh enquired.

"They belong to my mother so I can't say for certain, but I doubt it. We're too busy maiming and killing each other for there to be a successful tourist industry in my country. There is no point in people making ornaments if nobody comes to buy them. There's a good chance that they were acquired by Brian — my mother's deceased husband — on his travels. You'll have to ask her about them. She's out at the moment."

Hindmarsh certainly wished he hadn't asked Shirley about them. She invited the men to sit. They did so side by side on the settee. Eager to get on with the business in hand they declined an offer of refreshment.

"I think I should put you in the picture as to the purpose of our visit," said Mr Hindmarsh.

Shirley sat down on one of two armchairs positioned either side of the fireplace. Occupying the chair nearest the door she leaned forward as if to demonstrate that she was all ears, so to speak.

"Richard and I," Mr Hindmarsh continued, "are members of the Church of the True Believers."

"It's not a church I've heard of," Shirley commented.

"That's not really surprising," Mr Gilmore responded, "when I tell you that six months ago it didn't exist. Richard and I are its founding members."

After placing the briefcase on his knees Mr Hindmarsh set about turning the tiny wheels which in turn controlled the numbers that needed to be aligned so as to be able to open the case. There were two combination locks to be manipulated. Working without a hitch, following pressure applied with the inside of each thumb two clearly audible clicks indicated that the designated two sets of three numbers had been aligned correctly, and Mr Hindmarsh duly opened the lid. Looking askance Mr Gilmore saw and took note of what his friend already knew, which was that apart from a few leaflets and a brown envelope the case was empty.

"There doesn't appear to be anything in there worth stealing," said Mr Gilmore, implying that it wasn't really necessary to keep the case locked. "No crown jewels, no state secrets, no cash. Why do you keep it locked?"

"I got into the habit when I started using it to carry my sandwiches in for lunch at the office."

This answer being far from serious there were smiles all round. Then, reacting just a little defensively for the reason that he believed his judgement had been brought into question, and in front of a woman to boot, he informed his friend that he had needed to keep the case locked to ensure the safety of Miss Margai's cheque. Upon hearing this news Shirley started. A particularly observant person might have seen her prick up her ears. Mr Hindmarsh proceeded to explain that after having read about Miss Margai's plight in a certain newspaper, and after having made enquiries as to how much money would be required for her injury to be treated privately, his brethren and sisters in the church had raised just over £2,000 — £2,038.48 to be precise.

Almost incredulous Shirley was flabbergasted that such generosity could be meted to a foreigner who by her own estimation had done nothing to deserve it. Forgetting for a moment that her mother had left the house to go shopping in Luxborough, the daughter stood as if to go and fetch her from… she knew not where. Once the realisation dawned that she was the sole member of her family in the house Shirley sat down again. She had to, her legs being all aquiver. Slowly she lowered herself into the chair from which she had arisen with astonishing alacrity. Mr Hindmarsh took the liberty of removing the cheque from the envelope and handing the former to her. The payee had been left blank. It was with a trembling hand that Miss Margai accepted what could only be described as a marvellous gift from her benefactor. Subsequently she also took from him a well-produced information leaflet describing the history, as short as it was, and the raison d'être of the Church of the True Believers. Over and above the obvious reason for it having been given, the only condition attached to her cashing the cheque was that she should consider joining the church. Mr Gilmore emphasised that they asked for nothing more than her thoughtful consideration, that the gift wasn't contingent upon her joining.

Needless to say Miss Margai was extremely grateful that she had been given such a valuable gift, and said as much. She also expressed her gratitude that there were no strings attached of a kind that might have forestalled her acceptance. In the knowledge that she would be travelling back to Sierra Leone at some point in the not too distant future, when that would be to a large extent depended on how soon she would be able to have the operation on her knee, Miss Margai felt that as a short-term visitor rather than a permanent resident she had no choice but to decline the invitation there and then. In rejecting the offer of church membership she expressed herself with considerable charm, and total sincerity.

She was undoubtedly a woman of the world, but that didn't prevent Shirley's eyes from misting over and her vision becoming blurred as she tried to read the figure inscribed in the rectangular box on the near pristine, buff-coloured piece of paper she was holding in her hand. After using the sleeve of her cardigan to wipe away the tears of joy trickling from her eyes and running down her cheeks, in a deliberate manner Shirley pressed down with her hands on the chair arms and got to her feet. Her tender intent was to give each member of the Church of the True Believers in her presence a hug. In the way of such things, it was just as her daughter was about to unfurl her arms from around the neck of Mr Gilmore when Mrs Cannisman opened the front door to enter her home. Unaccustomed to witnessing her daughter entangled in such an overt display of intimacy she was taken aback, but sensing that the ambiance in her living-room was completely benign her bemused expression was devoid of parental concern. Prior to their departure five minutes later neither visitor probed Shirley's mother as to the provenance of the artefacts on the mantelpiece enquired about earlier.

Chapter Twenty-Two
A Nightmare Scenario

That Miss Nefertiti Goodwin was one of the world's most experienced travellers is fact. It's a fact as incontrovertible as her mortality, and it matters not one iota that in making this statement no allowance is made for gender. Nonetheless this undoubtedly important aspect of Miss Goodwin's life, on occasion Sebastian could be heard to grumble that to his detriment it was the most important, didn't mean that she was free from doubts and fears on her travels, even, at times, in relatively peaceful locations. She had, for example, a phobia about butterflies, and the prospect of being where they appear in numbers great enough to make a kaleidoscope of the sun as its radiance filters through colourful, translucent wings, was, as they say, anathema to her.

She had already endured the nightmare scenario of being amongst clouds of flitting Lepidoptera on the island of Rhodes in the Dodecanese, and although at the time of her visit to Kalangba Junction she didn't yet know it, in Seb's company she would experience similar torture in Mexico and Laos. It was only by putting her trust in her partner that Neffie gradually became desensitised, and eventually, in northern Laos, she showed herself to be completely insouciant of butterfly wings, even though they were often the size of her hand. It took a little longer for her not to over-react to the sensation of their feelers tickling her skin.

Her fear of those creatures which it would be foolish not to have great respect for, in particular their ability to inflict serious injury or death, and in this category the usual suspects in the shape of poisonous snakes, poisonous spiders, poisonous frogs, poisonous scorpions, big cats and crocodiles come to mind, was rational rather than phobic. In this regard she believed that her best chance of keeping out of harm's way when travelling was to take the right precautions. This common-sense approach required her to give a great deal of thought to everything she did, whether it was a matter of choosing which clothes to wear, or deciding whether or not it was safe to visit a place of interest alone. For example, to consider visiting a watering-hole unarmed, alone and on foot when lions are known to gather to slake their thirst would, in all probability, be asking for trouble.

Of course a person with little or no sense of adventure, someone with his feet on the ground and bum in a chair, would probably say that if self-preservation is the main concern, then surely it would be safer to stay within the borders of Britain, where the threat to life is hardly commonplace, rather than tempt fate by going to the tropics where a multitude of unpleasant possibilities abound, and that person would be right, though as far as human-beings go the individual making such comment would also be tiresomely bland.

In Neffie's opinion it was important to strike the right balance, whether the raison d'être of one's relatively short earthly existence is to explore the planet or to apply oneself to running a profitable business. At one extreme where she didn't wish to go were the heroes that pulled sledges across Antarctica or lugged heavy packs the length of the Amazon. Not surprisingly they were few in number. Greater in number and at the other extreme were the armchair travellers gaining pleasure of a vicarious kind by watching the exotic experiences of the few that take the risks. Between these two extremes Miss Goodwin generally considered herself to be in the middle, though even in Kalangba Junction she was inclined to think herself more cowardly than brave given the nature of her greatest fear at present.

For the reason that even in Koidu Province to suffer parts of one's body being lopped off with a machete was still the exception rather than the rule, that such an atrocity could happen to her was too horrific for Neffie to imagine, and didn't, therefore, constitute her greatest fear. What did give her kittens however was the thought of having to go to the toilet at night: her trepidation was likely to reach its peak in the early hours of the morning. Facilities at Julie's edge of the jungle bungalow were hardly state of the art, and it was she who had described them as primitive and barely tolerable.

In the absence of statistics that would inform for certain, it's possible that most people living in Britain at the beginning of the third decade of the twenty-first century would not have had cause to use anything other than the 'toilette anglaise' as the French describe it, when ridding their bodies of waste matter. The distinctly shaped bowl is familiar to all, as is the plastic or wooden seat which can be raised or lowered depending on the bodily function about to be performed and the gender of the person performing it. These days it is much less likely that a British tourist visiting countries as close culturally and geographically as France or Spain will have to contend with the 'squat' latrine. This, however, was the facility which awaited Neffie and anyone else seeking to relieve the pressure on bowel or bladder whilst visiting Miss Fussey's abode. Ordinarily Miss Goodwin was greatly in favour of squatting in order to defecate, and at some point in their nebulous past had said as much to Sebastian when in sighting the 'squat' alternative he had bemoaned the absence of the system he preferred. Presently in Kalangba Junction, however, Neffie wasn't keen to extol the virtues of squatting, and for reasons which may become nauseatingly clear.

On the night when Neffie's fear in this regard was about to become acute she heard voices. She didn't know the time precisely, but guessed that it was about two a.m. She was able to make out that the voices belonged to two men, and it sounded as if they were having a serious discussion. Neffie was to remain in the dark as to the subject being discussed, for although she was listening intently she couldn't make head nor tail of what was being said. She even spent a few minutes straining her ears, as it were, trying to make out at least one word which sounded familiar amidst the general babble, but as none was forthcoming eventually she gave up, concluding that the conversation she could hear but not understand was being conducted in a language totally alien to her.

The quandary which presented itself to Neffie now that she was no longer consciously listening, and as she observed nothing in particular, was whether the men she had overheard talking posed a threat to her nocturnal wandering, a trip to the loo necessitated by the rumbling sensation in her midriff. The more insistent the agitation in her lower body became the less audible, therefore less intrusive, therefore less threatening, were the voices. Unable to wait much longer for relief, Neffie realised that she would have to make the journey she dreaded. Given that the hut in question was at the end of a rough, unlit path leading for about thirty yards from the back of the house, Neffie's reluctance was hardly surprising, particularly when the voices she could hear sounded as if they originated in that general direction. These circumstances were off-putting enough, but when she thought of venturing into that stinking box buzzing with flies and other, less familiar, loathsome creatures, it was enough to turn her stomach. If there had been a chamber-pot to hand she would have used it. To wander off into the bush to do that which was becoming urgent was no less an alarming prospect than the thought of using the official site. There being no preferable alternative, Neffie demonstrated great resolve as she stepped gingerly along the stony path toilet roll in hand. She was feeling pleased with herself for not forgetting to take the item she would have had to double back for if she had forgotten it. The satisfaction she felt as a result of her preparedness quickly vanished as the darkness beyond the house enveloped her. It was a night heavy with cloud. The moon and stars were completely hidden. The thought that she was likely to do herself an injury entered her head just as she walked into a web constructed, she surmised, by a gigantic spider. The web was suspended from the branch of a tree growing a couple of feet above her head. She made this assessment of the arachnid's size upon raising her hands to claw the entrammelling threads away from her face. Taken by surprise by an experience she found disgusting, it took all her self-control for her not to panic. In the sultry light of day Neffie would be able to reflect on her reaction and put her present trauma into perspective. Then she would imagine a perfectly formed spider's web in part filtering, in part reflecting, early morning sunlight, and she would think it a thing of beauty, a miracle of nature. Presently, however, enmeshed by unpleasant sensations on hands and face, she had to resist an impulse to scream. Three practical considerations assisted her admirable self-restraint. First, she didn't want to make matters worse by getting a mouthful of the spider's handiwork, as it were. Secondly, being the polite, middle-class Englishwoman that she was, she didn't want to wake up her friend, or anyone else for that matter. A third consideration, thinking of the two men talking and the fact the she hadn't want to attract their attention, was soon to be disregarded.

Neffie took a step back, and after taking three or four deep breaths to calm her nerves, she proceeded to divest herself of her recently acquired but unwanted silk apparel. She did so hurriedly, primarily because the demand of nature which had brought her to this mild misfortune hadn't gone away. On the contrary, her need was more urgent by the minute. That said, however, there was now no likelihood that our fraught heroine was going to venture further down the path without a torch to light her way, no matter who may be watching her solitary progress. Focused on getting hold of the said item she retraced her steps the short distance back to the house. Neffie had a clear mental image of the torch she intended to use. It was standing on end on a shelf just inside the door. Di had put it there for the purpose Neffie had in mind. In her hour of need the teacher was almost praying that it would work: so often in her life they hadn't.

After opening the door and reaching inside Neffie grasped the cylindrical object of her desire. Lo and behold, instantly on depressing the button that was also a switch there was light, its powerful beam falling upon and illuminating the dense foliage of a distant tree. Armed now with toilet roll and torch there was no stopping Miss Goodwin as she set off towards her goal certain of her route.

In the event the flashlight proved to be a double-edged sword in that it undoubtedly helped Neffie to steer clear of cobwebs, and who knows what creatures or obstacles lying in wait were she to deviate from the path just a little, but its bright beam was also highly attractive to those mainly nocturnal members of order Lepidoptera that were anathema to her — moths. If in broad daylight Miss Goodwin's reaction to the presence of big brashly coloured butterflies had at times been hysterical, the presence of a single moth on the wrong side of the kitchen window was enough to frighten Neffie out of her wits and into the living-room. At home, whenever she saw a scary creature, whose fuscous body and wings contrasted starkly with the white surface of the bedroom ceiling, there was no sleep to be had until Sebastian had dealt with the problem by adroitly capturing the moth prior to releasing it through an open window which he then quickly closed. No matter what the other may be, in Neffie's eyes moths were the worse of two evils. Imagine her horror therefore when she beheld a host of the creatures flying as if trapped in her torch beam. It wasn't difficult for her to imagine countless more unseen specimens heading her way, and though as yet they remained hidden in the shadows, like their visible friends their sole intent would no doubt be to beat their wings manically upon the brightly illumined glass protecting the torch's bulb. The surface area in question was no bigger than the circumference of a medium-sized cup at the rim. The source of light in her hand had become a target, and by extension so had Neffie. Her immediate response was to depress the on/off button and plunge her world once more into darkness, darkness more intense for being so instant. All the while the demands of her body were becoming increasingly desperate.

Neffie counted to ten to release some of her tension. In doing so she realised that she really had no alternative but to endure the loathsome creatures beating their wings around her and crawling over her hand. Consequently she switched back on the light in order to complete her mission: it was a woman who had summoned up her residue of courage who ventured along the path she had come to detest.

Neffie stooped as she walked, arching her back and sinking her head into hunched shoulders so as to make her physical presence as small as possible. This strategy might have been effective at evading a projectile aimed at her normal head height but it did nothing to discourage the moths.

Diaphanous wings continued to caress her ear lobes and tickle the back of her hand holding the torch. Like renegades from a horror movie they appeared larger than life, their monstrous wings fleetingly looming into Neffie's field of vision before disappearing from it moments later. Their power to generate fear and delusion was immense, and soon Neffie began to see skull-like patterns as first one, and then another, and yet another, death's head hawkmoth settled on her hand. On this occasion Miss Goodwin was sure that she had let out a scream, and was puzzled that no such sound penetrated her ears. She was immensely relieved and astonished, however, when an unexpected saviour appeared.

Now whether the creature which Neffie identified as her saviour in respect of present horrors had arrived on the scene in response to her cry for help, silent or otherwise, or whether the chimpanzee had been waiting for her ever since she had first set off along the garden path, is open to question, but hairy and obviously male there he was, standing upright and shielding his eyes from the glare of the torch. With the other hand, exhibiting all the courteousness of a hotel doorman, he reached for the latch that opened the lavatory door. The primate's very presence had the beneficial effect of making the moths appear less frightening. Here, having taken their place in her psyche was a kindly faced relative whose timely appearance provided Neffie with the reassurance she needed. That she wasn't traumatised is remarkable, but perhaps it was because she had already endured so much that she wasn't in the least bit fearful. After all, a friendly chimp isn't a hungry lion.

Upon Neffie the human hominid drawing near the chimpanzee opened the door wide, and, with a graceful gesture of his lengthy arm beckoned her to enter. Miss Goodwin thought this really clever even for a chimp. She half expected the animal to speak, but in keeping with a more rational expectation it said not a word. Instead, looking in the torchlight as if it were embarrassed to be an object of scrutiny, the chimp merely grinned inanely. For his gentlemanly conduct Neffie thanked the chimp with a nod and a smile, reasoning that to a creature unable to express thoughts verbally this was a means of communication more easily understood than words. Neffie's next step was to enter where angels had feared to tread.

To Miss Goodwin's delight and astonishment she discovered that the hell-hole she had last visited late in the afternoon of the previous day had been transformed completely, and in place of the cramped, stinking, fly-infested, long-drop shit-hole she had been expecting was a suddenly brightly lit pristine facility. Reminiscent of a telephone-box in a famous television programme, the spaciousness within belied the dimensions of the structure when viewed from without. Along with the 'toilette anglaise' and its working cistern complete with chain, the tiled surfaces provided for a loo in which the gods from any pantheon you care to mention would be proud to defecate. The only fly in the ointment, as it were, was the crocodile lying in wait in the corner.

Chapter Twenty-Three
A Nightmare Scenario for Real

The crocodile lying in wait to sate its hunger for human flesh wasn't the final apparition to be created by Miss Goodwin's psyche as she slept in Di Fussey's spare bed, and strange as it may seem, neither was it the most daunting. After waking the first time to realise that she didn't really need to run a gauntlet of horrors to go to the loo, Neffie had gone on to dream of appearing on stage at the Royal Albert Hall, where her ordeal was to sing solo three verses of 'God Save the Queen' to a full house. For a person who by her own admission can't sing a single note in tune, and who even when alone in the house taking a shower or a bath, wouldn't dream of assaulting her own ears by a giving a rendition of her favourite song, the prospect was sufficiently frightful for her not to be able to get back to sleep after waking this second time in a cold sweat. None of these imaginary happenings, however, was to prove as memorable for being intensely scary as the real events in which Neffie and her friend were to become involved two nights later.

After a long but not unpleasant day transplanting saplings between occasional bouts of torrential rain, the two friends — Di and Neffie — had spent the early part of the evening doing what seemed most natural for being most enjoyable, and that was to imbibe a few beers on the veranda. The conversation had vacillated easily between the two, as it had in respect of the subjects they had discussed: those of a serious nature and those that were relatively trivial. It seemed the perfect way to round off the day.

A couple of times previously this customary binary conversation had given way to a tripartite expression of views, Samuel having walked a mile to join them on Di's veranda. Simply by being the only male present it was remarkable how the social dynamic changed, and it might have been because Samuel didn't look as if he was going to put in an appearance this evening that at times Di looked a little restless.

No longer enraptured by the natural sounds, insects mainly, of the tropical night, sounds which Neffie loved, Miss Fussey suggested to Neffie that they head for Mariana's Bar in search of some sociable excitement. To get there her first thought had been to take the pick-up, but having made no mention of it she immediately dismissed this idea on the basis that she had determined from the outset that what she wouldn't do back home for fear of breaking the law she wouldn't do here. Back home in Lakewood, New Jersey, she wouldn't consider driving under the influence of alcohol, so she wasn't going to do such a thing in and around Kalangba Junction, notwithstanding that there was little chance of being stopped by the police and breathalysed. The ladies would have to walk there and back in the dark.

Neffie's initial reaction to the proposal was hardly enthusiastic. She had convinced herself that she needed to get up early the next day and so didn't want to tempt fate by staying out late. It was often a struggle for her to get out of bed even when she did have a full eight hours' rest, so it was understandable that she didn't trust herself to wake early on, she presumed, only four to six hours sleep. Another reason for her reluctance was that she had already savoured Mariana's flesh-pot on two previous occasions, specifically on Friday and Saturday night. She couldn't say that she hadn't enjoyed being in the company of strangers, men mainly, some of whom had become friendly acquaintances, but even so, her present inclination was to enjoy another beer before bed.

"What do you mean you want to pack your bag and have an early night?" interrogated Di in response to her friend's reluctance to participate in her plan for what would be Neffie's final night in Kalangba Junction prior to their leaving for Freetown on the morrow. "It's not that you've got a bus to catch, or anything so arbitrary, seeing as I'm taking you back to Freetown in the pick-up courtesy of Uncle Sam."

"I told you that I would be more than happy to pay for the fuel," said Neffie.

The coldness in her voice hung like an icicle in the balmy air. Determined not to be browbeaten, by focusing on the financial implications of her friend's willingness to take her guest and Samuel back to the capital, Neffie hoped to put a damper on Di's pleasure-seeking spirit.

"You know that's not an issue," Di retorted dismissively. "What I mean is that there's no set time that you have to be somewhere, that having our own transport makes us masters of our own destinies... well... up to a point."

A silence followed as each woman waited for the other to speak. Simultaneously, acting as if one were the mirror image of the other, they took a swig of beer. It was Miss Fussey who broke the lull. "Aha! So the devil's got your tongue, has he?" The question was the harbinger of yet another friendly but nonetheless determined attack to break down Neffie's resistance. "You must be the first teacher I've met who's been at a loss for words..."

"Hold on a minute, who's at a loss for words?" interpolated the teacher sharply, indignantly. Thus far her defences hadn't been breached.

"You are," retorted Di. "You clammed up when I demolished your argument for not wanting to celebrate your last night in Kalangba Junction, you lucky girl. Come on, don't let's end the night here, let's go and let our hair down for once."

The pressure was too great. Sensing that further resistance would prove futile Neffie shifted position slightly in her chair. It was as if by striving to be more comfortable physically she would gain strength mentally, but it wasn't going to be enough to prevent capitulation. Neffie drank the last drops of her beer and then, like a man acting out of wounded pride, planked the empty bottle down on the table. In the next instant the teacher rose to her feet, burped, and set off alone in the direction of Mariana's Bar. One step before being consumed by darkness Miss Goodwin turned to summon her friend.

"Come on then if you're coming," she ordered, her words and the tone in which they were enunciated giving every impression that it was she, Miss Nefertiti Goodwin, who was eager for a night on the town, as it were.

Di Fussey's response was immediate and positive, and using her thumb as a stopper she ran, beer bottle in hand, part of the way to catch up with her friend turned hedonist. The distance she didn't run she walked briskly. In a spontaneous act of togetherness the pair laughed out loud as they set off along the lateritic road.

Evidently Neffie's mood had lightened. In having committed herself to going along with Miss Fussey's plan, a plan which surely only an abstemious eremite would consider outrageous, she reasoned that she may as well make the most of her last night in Kalangba Junction and enjoy whatever hedonistic pleasures Mariana's place had to offer. Following her change of heart she was now looking forward to meeting up with Samuel and his cousin, assuming that they were where they were usually to be found. For her part, being the instigator, Di didn't need to make any such mental and emotional adjustments. She had got her way, and was determined to spend the next few hours as blithely as possible. Determined to live in the present, to her way of thinking tomorrow could look after itself.

To have probed Di's psyche a little more deeply at this time however, would, at the very least, have revealed a different emphasis in respect of why she was so keen to carouse. The truth then revealed would be that tomorrow and the next day, and the day after that and so on, was where an abyss of a kind lay gaping to swallow Di whole. In a purely platonic sense she had grown attached to the usually phlegmatic Englishwoman over recent weeks and didn't much relish the prospect of having to return to her old routines. Di realised that the break-up of their friendship in the sense of being able to be in each other's company on a daily basis would leave a gap in her life which, given her lack of enthusiasm for the work she had been doing prior to Nefertiti's arrival, would make the days and weeks ahead difficult to endure. To paraphrase St. Luke, a maxim relevant to Di's earnest desire to drink into the early hours was 'eat, drink and be merry, for tomorrow we mope'.

"Shit!" exclaimed Di as she put her foot in a puddle, one of many that persisted from one downpour to the next at this time of year.

These puddles weren't easy to spot in the near total darkness, and though the women had made a wise decision to keep to the middle of the road in order to avoid the preponderance of water that had accumulated at either edge, Di, leading the way, had managed to find one of the few middle-of-the-road loiterers. She wasn't accustomed to using bad language, and might not have uttered an expletive had not the water effectively filled the ankle-deep hole into which she had stepped. To deter insect bites Di was wearing socks, but now that the sock on her right foot was uncomfortable to walk in for being completely saturated, she stopped to remove the pair, leaving them, one dry, one wet, by the roadside for someone more needy to find and make use of the next day.

"That's better," Di said when she had replaced her shoes and she was mobile once more.

"It serves you right for tempting the spirit of darkness and dragging me off against my better judgement," said Neffie.

Her words were somewhat disingenuous for the fact that they harped back to when she was disinclined to accompany Di, and now that she was in accord with the idea they were no longer a true reflection of her feelings. Just as beguiling was her tone: it was ambiguous for sounding flippant and yet mordant at the same time.

"I wouldn't invoke the spirit of darkness as an ally if I were you," rejoined Di with no ambiguity whatsoever: her seriousness was unequivocal.

Neffie's comment had stirred a previously dormant element in Di Fussey's psyche, one which had its origins in her religious upbringing. The ambiance between the two women was prone to fluctuations, as it's likely to be between any two human beings that haven't known each other long but have made a commitment to share each other's company. Consequently they walked in subdued silence. It was during this time that the cadences typical of a tropical night became more clearly audible. In the sense that Nature's performances are always ad lib the music of countless insects was more redolent of some melodic jazz than a symphony which has been carefully orchestrated. The effect was mesmeric, and simultaneously induced each woman to become introspective, so that to outward appearances they appeared to have been enchanted by a tribal witch doctor. Deep thoughts in the all-enveloping darkness didn't prevent them from trying to divine where the standing water was.

Neffie was thinking of Sebastian. In the scene unfolding inside her head he was lying naked beside her, his arm encircling her rib cage, his hand cupping her breast. They had just made love, and the moment of her reverie was that tranquil time between passionate fulfilment and blissful sleep.

Di Fussey's ruminations couldn't have been more dissimilar. The scene she had in mind was one of mountains capped with snow. She was reliving a holiday she had enjoyed as a child. Accompanied by her mom and dad when she was at an impressionable age, her trip to Colorado and Wyoming had been her most memorable and best vacation to date. Indeed, she would go so far as to say that the week she had spent honing her riding skills on the Hideout cattle ranch near to the town of Shell, followed by a few days spent camping in the Grand Teton National Park, had been the best ten days of her life. Soon after she had felt that those days of innocent pleasure couldn't ever be repeated, although she hadn't taken into account fond memories unfolding in this and, before and after, other contemplative states.

A particular memory, as already intimated, was of the high snow-capped peaks and the thrill, even in June, of being stopped by the Highway Patrol and told that the road through the pass her dad was heading for was still blocked. In the final moments of her musing for the first time in her life the young Miss Fussey put on a pair of sunglasses so dazzling was the effect of the sun reflecting on the blanched terrain. Meanwhile, back in the fully conscious here and now in the vicinity of Kalangba Junction, there was no snow to speak of, and probably never had been, not in a million years.

Their faculties becoming attuned to the physical world through which they ventured, Di probably heard the drumming at the same time as Neffie, but it was the Briton who broke the spell cast by the night and the mysteries of thought. "What's that?" Neffie enquired, her sense of hearing, having picked up the sound, trying to determine from which direction it came.

It didn't take either party long to realise that the rhythmic sound of a person or persons beating one or more drums was heading towards them. It wasn't only drumming that they heard. Carried on the gentlest fluctuations of air came the sound of chanting.

"If that's what I think it is I'm confused," said Neffie cheerfully as she stood stock-still in order to listen, just as Di had done a split second before. "I know that Mariana likes her music, but I was under the impression that her taste was more Rolling Stones than the traditional sounds of Sierra Leone I'm hearing… at least I think that's what I'm hearing."

"You're right about her taste in music, but that's not coming from Mariana's," said Di, in a tone clearly expressing her growing concern.

In the darkness Neffie was unable to read the signs of worry clouding her friend's countenance, but they were there. Moreover, in the same way that a person who is visually impaired relies more heavily on other senses grown more acute, from the warning note in Miss Fussey's voice it soon dawned on Neffie that the drumming and chanting growing steadily louder could just as easily be portents of harm rather than harbingers of good. She needed more information, and the one person presently able to provide it was duly forthcoming without needing to be asked.

"We've run into a secret society," informed Di succinctly, although as yet so secret was it that there was no visible sign of the society in question. That soon changed however, for just as Di was about to flesh out this skeletal fact, she was able to make out, through the trees about a quarter of a mile ahead, the flickering flames of the secret society's ceremonial torches. At first the white women could discern only about half a dozen, but gradually more torches came into view as, approaching from Di's and Neffie's right, more torch-bearers followed the vanguard of the column. From the watching pair's perspective one by one the tightly bound burning oil-soaked rags disappeared only to reappear again once they had passed several yards of light-impenetrable foliage. Neffie was put in mind of a train going through a tunnel. Di was of the opinion that the women — by this time she was certain that the chanting denoted the all-female Sande Society — had been performing an initiation ceremony deep in the forest. Soon she would be able to tell whether the procession was about to turn towards the two presently statuesque women and meet them head on, so to speak, or move in the direction which was a straight line from whence they had come.

"You mean to say that we've run into a group of spirit-worshippers and their witch doctors?" the teacher enquired, delighted by the prospect of encountering more of West African culture than she possibly could have envisaged upon setting out. "That's so exciting!"

"Witch doctors are usually men, and men belong to the Poro Society," informed Di tersely. "This lot, the lot we've run into for our sins, more than likely belong to the Sande Society, an organisation which exists for the benefit, or so-called benefit, of women."

"Well… we're women aren't we?" said Neffie, not as naively as her words, were they to be taken out of context, would suggest. "What I mean is that we're less likely to come to harm at the hands of women, no matter how spooky they may be, than we would be if we were to run into a bunch of spooky men. That's so, wouldn't you agree?"

A statement which had begun confidently enough had transmuted into a diffident question, one which revealed that the foundation upon which the speaker had based her supposition had suddenly begun to quake. By this time the women leading the procession had turned onto the road leading to where Di and Neffie were standing. The spooky women were heading straight for them, their relentless advance keeping pace with the now unnerving drumbeats.

"What would you say to being kidnapped, stripped, drugged or held down against your will, and having your clitoris removed with a penknife?"

The thought of being subjected to such an ordeal, of being mutilated, made Miss Goodwin cringe. The very idea mortified her. She wondered what Sebastian would say, do, if she were to come home disfigured for life and not the woman she was. Despite being quite enchanted by the oncoming torches and the luridly illumined figures carrying them, the Briton was yet able to turn away to look at her American friend intently. She was searching, hoping for some indication that Di was deliberately trying to scare the wits out of her. It would have been more than a little wicked of her if she were. It was impossible for Neffie to discern the slightest detail of her friend's facial expression, and so Miss Goodwin saw and sensed nothing to make her think that Di had spoken other than in earnest. Consequently she was prepared to believe that the excision Di had just described could happen.

"What shall we do?" enquired Neffie, calmly deferring to Miss Fussey's greater experience of what to western perceptions of right and wrong were some unacceptable practices and customs still prevalent in Sierra Leone.

The teacher turned her head and eyes to look once more at the advancing procession. By this time the tail-end of the marching column had stepped out of the forest onto the road, and to judge by the distance between the front and hindmost torch the procession stretched for about fifty yards. How many marching women there were was as yet known only to the participants, but amongst this number the onlookers were able to count fifteen torches. Even at a distance of approximately one hundred yards, a distance which was diminishing by the minute, Di and Neffie were able to make out that several women at the front of the column were wearing masks. Illuminated by torchlight they appeared to be of hideous and frightening design.

"We could run back to the house," came the reply, "but I'm not one for running away if there's a more spirited alternative."

"Is there a better alternative?" asked Neffie, communicating a distinct lack of enthusiasm for being 'spirited' away.

"We could get off the road and hide in the bush until they've passed," Di informed.

That it was a practical alternative course of action Neffie couldn't deny, nor could she deny that it was more spirited, but whether it qualified as being better was questionable.

"I'm for going back to the house," said Neffie as she attempted to peer through the impenetrable darkness into the bush. If the women in the procession were indeed devils, then the bush was the hard place.

"Quick! Get off the road and hide," ordered Di in a voice no less forceful for being barely above a whisper. Exhibiting the kind of urgency which hadn't been in evidence hitherto she disappeared into the bush fully expecting Neffie to follow.

Neffie's vote for beating a hasty retreat back to the house seemed to have fallen upon deaf ears, and no matter the course of action she had wanted the two of them to take together, no way was she going to venture down that pitch-dark road alone; and particularly not with a secret society with dubious intent hard on their heels. Without a word of protest, therefore, Miss Goodwin complied with her friend's aspirated order, but instead of following hard upon Miss Fussey's heels, Neffie forsook the familiarity of the road on the opposite side.

By nearly falling into it she quickly found a suitable place to hide, initially crouching down in what she conceived to be a small crater, the front parapet of which was at a level slightly lower than the road. Upon ascertaining that the crater, which fell away towards the rear, was free of standing water for being well-drained, Neffie adopted a more comfortable position, one she would, if need be, be able to maintain for a lengthy period. Under normal circumstances she would have bemoaned the dampness of the grass compressed beneath her, but these weren't normal circumstances. The weight of her upper body rested on her left forearm, while her lower body was supported by her hip and left thigh. Her knees were bent halfway between a foetal position and being completely straight.

Breathing heavily following this exertion, Neffie was pleased with her choice of hiding-place. From where she lay all she had to do to have an unrestricted view of the road was to raise her head slightly. Equally, she believed, all she had to do to stay hidden was to keep her head down. She thought of Sebastian, and as if by magic certain words he had used in boasting of his exploits had come to mind, words such as 'ambush' and 'cut-off group', terminology which had been darkly alien to her when it had first entered her consciousness, and which had had no practical relevance since. Nonetheless, it pleased her to think that Sebastian would be proud of her at this moment. Knowing that the feared procession was no more than fifty yards from where she lay didn't deter Neffie from checking on her friend.

"Di, are you there?" she called in a voice which wasn't meant to carry more than the distance there was likely to be between them. Neffie believed that she was safe in instigating the exchange on the basis that the most audible sounds in the ears of the marchers would be of their own creation, and they, probably until they had almost drawn level, would drown out Di's and her quiet voices.

Di responded in a similar tone, a similar volume. "Yes," she said simply. "Are you all right?"

"Yes, are you?"

"Yes; all things considered I'm really quite comfortable," informed the teacher, "although I do hope nothing comes out of the bush to bite me."

"Neffie," called Di in response to this bulletin.

"What?"

"Be quiet."

There was to be no witty riposte to this final instruction. The news blackout it effectively imposed neither party would dare to break until the danger had passed. Inevitably the procession drew near. In anticipation of its imminent arrival to within spitting distance Neffie pressed her body into the warm, damp ground, careless of the fact that the clothes she wore, and which she intended to travel in the next day, were likely to be sullied.

Di's hiding place was a similar patch of damp grass behind a nondescript bush. Judging it to be the source of the American accent, and perhaps by more numinous means, Neffie had a strong feeling that she knew exactly where her friend was hiding. This sense impression was somewhat disturbing for the reason that if she as a sophisticated westerner, a person whose senses and instincts had been dulled by easy living, were able to visualise who or what lay beyond supposedly inscrutable barriers, then what was a bevy of chanting spirit worshippers capable of? Following this thought Miss Goodwin suddenly felt vulnerable for being conspicuous; at least, she imagined, to those able to call upon mysterious powers. Consequently she lowered her head until she could lower it no farther. She did so in the naïve belief that people she couldn't see couldn't see her. Relentlessly the light from the torches crept along the road to illuminate the puddles of rainwater and the bush Di had chosen to hide behind, the latter now not as unremarkable as the Peace Corps worker would have wished.

The procession's leading ladies were now level with where the foreigners lay more or less in line with each other if that imaginary line were to create right angles in crossing the road. The chanting was at its most sinister for being so loud. Its dreary reverberations were voluble torture. Slowly, to the beat of the drum, the masked women at the forefront passed by. It wasn't until the middle section of the procession was about to pass that Neffie dared to raise her head slightly, and with it her eyes, her curiosity and increasing confidence that she wouldn't be seen getting the better of her trepidation. The first sight which greeted her was umpteen pairs of legs and their adjoining feet in striding pairs.

Most of the feet were shod in sandals of one form or another, but a small number of women were walking barefoot. Their formation was three abreast.

Raising her focal point yet higher, Neffie's gaze came to rest upon a remarkable individual in the middle file. She was attractive to the Englishwoman's scrutiny for being dressed so impressively. In Neffie's view her attire was more than a little exotic. In the main it consisted of a dress made from black raffia and a face mask carved out of wood. For several lengthy seconds Miss Goodwin's gaze became transfixed. It was as if her proclivity for anthropology was coming to the fore to make her feel more like a legitimate spectator at a well-publicised cultural event than a potential victim. The chanting resonated at a lower pitch than Neffie would have expected from a congregation made up entirely of women. From the entranced expressions on those faces that were clearly visible it was apparent that to those doing the chanting the sound was strangely hypnotic.

The mask enchanted Neffie most. The headpiece was approximately eighteen inches from top to bottom, and across its shiny black surface the reflection from the nearest torch danced and flickered. The carving at the top of the mask seemed to be that of a dead bird lying flat on its back, and Neffie was put in mind of a comedy sketch she had seen on television. The sketch in question had been about a dead parrot. The mask was broadest at the base, where a series of rings seemed to represent the fleshy neck of a rather corpulent female. Between these two extremities shone a finely carved image, the beauty depicted in an idealised woman's face. The forehead was high, the features small and delicate. Despite the fraught circumstances Neffie felt privileged to be able to witness such an exotic example of West African culture.

She must have been enthralled for all of twenty seconds when, just as the individual wearing the mask had drawn level, Neffie felt a sharp pain at the base of her Achilles tendon. A few moments earlier that part of her anatomy had, to some extent, been protected by the slip-on shoe her foot had since slipped out of. The teacher's instinctive reaction was to reach down to rub away the pain, but although her right arm involuntarily jerked an inch or two in that direction, she managed to control the impulse and resist further movement: it might have been conspicuous. She also managed to stifle the expletive which in less secretive circumstances she would have had no hesitation in expressing. The nagging irritation to her foot proved a distraction to Miss Goodwin's anthropological studies, and she spent the next minute or so wondering what had bitten or stung her. She wanted to feel for blood, but held back, at least for the time being. The distressing thought crossed her mind that she might have been poisoned, and she half-expected to be overcome with delirium at any moment. Or would there be nausea first she then wondered. By this time only the back of the woman wearing the exotic mask was visible to Neffie, but the previously clear image that she had had of her had become less distinct, something of a blur.

Regardless of the need to keep her movements to a minimum and stay hidden, Neffie slowly, and it was to be hoped inconspicuously, turned her head to look down at the source of pain. The sheen of her barely visible foot revealed nothing out of the ordinary, but because of the circumstances no inspection could have been less thorough. Just as carefully as she had turned to look down, once again Neffie looked up, only to discover that she was being scrutinised closely, certainly by one pair of beady eyes, and possibly by a second. The discovery in respect of the creature watching her for certain was nothing less than horrific, for directly in front stationary on the parapet of the shallow crater and only inches from her face was a scorpion. Its tail was raised as if about to strike. Silhouetted against the torch-lit road, from a petrified woman's perspective the creature appeared a thousand times more menacing for being so gargantuan. If there is one thing that we have come to know about Neffie it's that more than once on this trip she has had to maintain rigorous self-discipline when what she had really wanted to do was scream, or swear, but in this instance, perhaps because she had gradually become inured to terror, or perhaps because the terror she was experiencing at present surpassed anything she had encountered previously, so that the most visceral part of her being could offer no response, she felt no such compulsion. Taking into account the difference in size between the human-being and the arachnid, it was remarkable how wary of each other the two sentient beings were. A positive aspect of this encounter was that Neffie was now as still as it was possible for a human being to be without her being dead or comatose. How the confrontation was going to end remained unclear. Quite sure that her deduction was correct, Neffie had deduced that the sharp pain she had felt at the base of her Achilles heel, a pain which had since dulled to a throb, was the work of the creature presently staring at her, and because the teacher of nursery children wasn't familiar with the various species in the order Scorpiones, she was more than a little concerned that her death could be imminent. That said, however, subsequently, by applying reason drawn from a combination of personal experience and information gleaned from travellers' tales, Miss Goodwin did everything in her emotional and mental power to make the concept of her demise a prospect so remote that it wouldn't happen until long after she had begun to receive her pension. She did so by remembering that it's the lighter coloured species one should avoid being stung by, as well as the notorious fat-tailed scorpion, which is dark and one of the most venomous. The specimen in front was black, but its tail, or metasoma as it is especially known, was tapered. This feature was more than a straw for Neffie to clutch at: it was deeply reassuring.

The second pair of eyes looking in Neffie's direction belonged to one of the marchers. Perhaps in response to having glimpsed a slight movement, or having heard an unnatural sound, the woman had stopped in her tracks to watch and listen more intently. Women that had been following her footsteps had to deviate slightly to avoid a collision. She didn't appear to be concerned that if she didn't set off again soon the main body of the procession would leave her behind. Compared to the more extravagantly attired ladies her dress-sense was such that she wouldn't have looked out of place shopping for produce in the market of a provincial town. An exception to the appearance of normalcy was the gaunt severity of the woman's face. There was a not-of-this-world intensity in her countenance which to Neffie was almost as disturbing as being scrutinised close up by a scorpion. The whites of her eyes appeared disproportionately large and gave her a half-crazed look as she peered into the darkness for that which was hidden. For a time Neffie believed that the woman had divined her presence by a means other than can be attributed to one or more of the five senses, that in this instance there was a mysterious sixth sense at work.

Initially upon changing her focus from the creature in the foreground to the woman in the same line of sight five or six yards beyond, Neffie was sure that she was about to be taken prisoner, but in case she hadn't been discovered she wasn't going to do anything to precipitate such an eventuality. In the event, the longer the teacher watched and waited in the hope that one or both pairs of beady eyes would simply go away, the greater her conviction grew that the woman was staring past her, searching perhaps for a numinous presence lurking deep in the forest far from where the wounded teacher lay.

Eventually the arms, legs, body and face of the woman standing upright merged into an indistinguishable mass as she became enveloped in darkness as the light cast by the rear-most torches advanced to illuminate the road ahead; but before her facial features were obliterated completely the Englishwoman was sure that she flashed a broad grin in her direction. The question was had it been flashed solely for Neffie to see? Of course there was no replay available to confirm or negate what Neffie had either seen for real or imagined. The next thing in respect of the secret society that Miss Goodwin saw for certain as she dared to turn her head ever so slightly to look along the road was the woman whom she had been watching, and who might or might not have been watching her, take her place at the rear of the procession. At this point in time, it had advanced about fifty yards.

Then, from directly opposite could be heard a familiar, friendly voice. "Neffie, are you still there?"

Wondering how best to answer given her predicament, Miss Goodwin was slow to respond. In the end she decided that her voice wasn't going to antagonise her eight-legged captor unnecessarily, and in that voluble whisper which is the natural intonation of fugitives and conspirators said, "Yes, but I'm being held prisoner."

It wasn't the answer Di expected to hear, and consequently she was somewhat perplexed. Thinking that the coast was far from clear therefore, and that it wasn't yet safe to emerge from hiding, after a few moments deliberation, Di posed the obvious question. "Held prisoner… by who?" she said.

Neffie cringed. If there was one thing worse than a scorpion sting it was hearing bad grammar. Her concern in this regard undoubtedly had its origin in her role as a teacher of young minds, and she had lost count of the number of times she had provided the correct usage to parents and children alike upon hearing such ear-jarring expressions as 'I was sat', or 'we were stood' or 'the amount of people', solecisms she did her best to discourage.

"Shouldn't that be by whom?" enquired the teacher.

The question didn't require an answer, and Miss Fussey smiled to herself in the belief that nobody so concerned with the finer points of the English language could be in serious trouble.

"All right, have it your way," said the American prior to echoing Neffie's example, "by whom?"

"By a scorpion," Neffie replied.

Upon hearing the cause of her friend's consternation, and noting that the procession was now so far away that the chances of being seen by those marching were negligible, Di broke cover and, like the chicken that is the subject of many a poor joke, crossed the road. The Peace Corps volunteer chose to walk rather than run, and be upright rather than attempt to disguise her presence as a human-being by crouching forward like one of the more hairy primates. Relying solely on the cloak of darkness to prevent her from being seen by people she would rather not be seen by, she had stepped off with the same sense of purpose that a pedestrian crossing Fifth Avenue on Broadway would exhibit.

Neffie's eyes hadn't yet become fully accustomed to the darkness, but she could hear the sound of her friend's approach quite clearly. She knew that there was no chance of it carrying as far as the procession, where the chanting and drumming continued unabated. Perhaps because it too heard the reverberations of Di's footsteps growing steadily louder, or because it felt the vibrations of heavy footfalls through its own sensitive feet, the scorpion scuttled off in search of a quiet, less confrontational life.

"Where is the infernal creature?" questioned Di from the roadside as she peered down at where she could just make out Neffie's curled-up body. The American reached down with her hand for the Briton to grasp.

"It ran off when it heard you coming," informed Neffie, hauling herself, albeit with Di's assistance, first onto her feet and then out of the crater onto the road.

"Well, I suppose you can be thankful that it didn't sting you," said Di matter-of-factly.

Neffie took a deep breath. She couldn't help but observe, as she looked over Di's left shoulder, that the torches illuminating the procession appeared to be fewer in number. To both the chanting and its percussion accompaniment were less threatening for sounding quieter.

"It did sting me," said Neffie in a voice which was slightly tremulous. "At least I think it stung me, though I can't be absolutely certain that the scorpion I saw close up was the same creature that…"

"What did it look like?" enquired Di, her tone and the fact that she had cut off Neffie in mid-flow giving a clear indication of her concern that urgent action may be needed.

"The scorpion?" said Neffie, doing her utmost to mask her anxiety. Di's answer was a perfunctory hum.

"Well… bearing in mind that my only view of it was foreshortened, I can't be sure about its length, but judging from the size of its pincers I would say it was pretty big. What I am sure of is that the tail tapered towards the end."

"What colour was it?" Di questioned.

The intensity in her voice could be likened to that of an investigator interrogating a suspect when he or she believes that the suspect is about to crack.

"It was black… definitely black," replied Neffie prior to requesting reassurance. "That means that it's not one of the dangerous, life-threatening ones doesn't it? Please tell me that it does."

Di took a few moments to consider, moments which seemed like an eternity to Neffie. "If it was the scorpion you've just described that stung you, you should be all right, unless you have an allergic reaction. It sounds to me that you've been unfortunate, or fortunate, depending on how you want to look at it, in having upset an emperor. I wouldn't worry about it if I were you. The emperor's sting is no worse than a bee's. Back in the States people keep them as pets. I don't doubt that there are some weird types in the UK that keep them as well. Where did it get you?"

Prior to revealing the site of her wound Neffie acted more demonstrably than she would have thought herself capable of and stepped forward to give her friend a hug, so relieved was she to hear what she had just been told.

"Here on the heel," Neffie informed as soon as she had regained her sang-froid. She raised her foot so that only her toes were touching the ground. Daylight would have revealed whatever mark there was as soon as she slipped her foot out of its shoe, as she had just done. In the darkness neither woman was able to discern anything out of the ordinary.

In an attempt to determine the severity of the wound they took it in turns to touch the inflamed area, Neffie leading by example. "Ouch! Be careful," instructed Neffie as Di pressed too hard for comfort.

"There's a little swelling, but nothing to worry about," said Di with absolute confidence as she felt for the extent of the infected area. The thought crossed Miss Fussey's mind that the scorpion had stung her friend in an awkward spot, but not wanting to be negative and provide Neffie with an excuse to head for home she kept it to herself.

"Have you ever been stung by a bee?" enquired Neffie for want of something to say while she was being probed and prodded.

"Now you mention it I can't say that I have," said Di as she straightened up to her full height to indicate that the medical inspection was over. "Have you?"

"Twice," Neffie replied. "Once when Sebastian and I were hiking in France the path we were on took us close to beehives. I suppose the bee that stung me was only defending its queen, sacrificing itself in the act. It stung me on the cheek. It really hurt."

"And the second time?" prompted Di, brushing back her hair with her hand and generally adjusting her clothing: not surprisingly after her time in hiding was in some disarray.

"The second time I was sitting at the computer in our local library. We didn't have a machine at home at the time, and it was a useful facility on the odd occasion when I needed to do some research on the internet. It was a sultry day in September as I remember. I felt something land on my arm just below the shoulder. I think, bearing in mind the time of year, that the normally busy bee must have been dozy. Not realising that it was a bee at first, my instinctive reaction was to swat the annoying insect with the flat of my hand. In doing so I felt what resembled a red-hot needle enter my flesh. My response to the searing pain momentarily made me the centre of attention… not something I relish."

"I can't imagine that you swore like a trooper at the top of your voice," interrupted Di, shuffling feet impatient to be on their way. "Go on, tell me, what did you say?"

"For goodness' sake," although I nearly said far worse… something I would have regretted. That's one of the problems with being a teacher, you've always got to be… well… perhaps not on your best behaviour, but it certainly wouldn't do to be obnoxious or depraved in public. Where are you off to?"

"Mariana's of course. Come on, the beers are on me. No one is going to tell your principal if you are depraved out here."

Neffie was surprised to learn that this was still Di's intention. She gave some thought as to whether she was still prepared to go along with her friend. On the basis that she couldn't leave Di to her own devices, and neither did she want to wander back on her own, Neffie dutifully followed her host: there seemed to be no sensible alternative. She hobbled to catch up. Initially her limp was more pronounced than her injury warranted.

"I don't know if you've noticed," said Di as Neffie caught up with her, "but being depraved is not something I worry about."

Neffie laughed.

Chapter Twenty-Four
A Sensitive Subject

Literally a stone's throw from Mariana's front door the first drops of rain fell to splatter on Di's and Neffie's heads. The prospect of countless more to follow soon after prompted the pair to run the short distance remaining to their destination and the shelter it would provide. There would be no sense in getting drenched if a little exertion could prevent it. Neither by bent or build was either woman an athlete, so in consequence of their not being accustomed to running over any distance it was two out of breath but mainly dry patrons who came through the door just as the heavens opened. Prior to closing the door behind them, both women turned to observe the myriad droplets splashing on the surface of the large, light-reflecting puddle they had just run around, Di to the right, Neffie to the left. The intensity of the downpour had the power to mesmerise Neffie in particular, and she would have lingered longer if it hadn't been for her friend's impatience to get to the bar. Di wasn't desperate, but she was single-minded.

The arrival of the white women didn't cause quite the same stir as it had done on the occasions of their first and second visits to Mariana's establishment together. On her first visit Neffie had felt like a film star in the pornographic genre, so lasciviously had she been ogled. Presently their entrance generated nothing more lecherous than a few familiar smiles of welcome. In most instances these were accompanied by hand gestures intended to communicate a similar message. Judging by the expression on her face, no welcome was warmer than Mariana's, not even Samuel Massequoi's, who, by sitting on his favourite bar-stool and reading the preface to 'Heart of Darkness' appeared to be at odds with his surroundings.

When visiting a hostelry in the UK Neffie was often surprised to discover that the considerable number of cars in the car-park didn't translate into overcrowding inside the establishment, whereas in Sierra

Leone the opposite seemed to hold true. To affluent western eyes the two jalopies parked out front gave a false impression as to the numbers enjoying Mariana's hospitality. The short pause in proceedings which had greeted the white women's entrance was matched by an interlude in the general hubbub created by approximately thirty people. The air was heavy with tobacco smoke, and no doubt the smoke from other leafy substances. Neffie coughed and gave the man nearby who had just exhaled a great puff of smoke a disdainful look. A few of Mariana's customers, Samuel included, were sitting at the bar caressing their beer bottles or half-filled glasses as if they were prized possessions. It was noticeable that customers whose glasses were half empty had the more sombre expressions. The remainder, the majority, were seated at tables. The ratio of men to women was about three to one. Around three of the tables the little knots of four or five people playing cards for money were, without exception, male. The game in each case was a form of poker. Di made a beeline for the bar while Neffie sauntered behind her, surveying the room in search of a relatively smoke-free area where they could sit. All the bar stools were taken, and it was the same state of play with regard to the tables, though a man whose face looked as if it had been lived in for centuries had one all to himself. For the reason that he seemed to be indifferent to everything and everyone around him this lone elderly individual caught Miss Goodwin's attention. Every so often he spoke out loud and then chortled, the words directed at no one in particular. It was as if his life was the drama unfolding inside his head, and to the world at large the only access to it was by these outward signs.

Di approached where Neffie had latterly taken up a standing position in which she had space to breathe. The Peace Corps worker was carrying a bottle in each hand. The neck of each bottle supported a half-pint glass turned upside down. Samuel followed hard on Di's heels. He had left off reading about Mr Kurst and the difficulties involved in navigating the Congo River in favour of keeping more convivial company. Perceptive to the newcomers' predicament Mariana brought up the rear, but then veered away from the human train to steer a course towards where the old man was sitting chuckling to himself. Neffie was under the impression that Mariana intended to ask the old timer if he had any objection to their coming to join him. The thought occurred to her that his acquiescence would lead to an interesting evening. No doubt he would have many an interesting story to tell about life in the former colony under the British. Contrary to Neffie's expectations, however, Mariana did rather more than beg the old man's pardon in order to make such a request.

Instead of proceeding as Miss Goodwin had anticipated Mariana gently but firmly assisted Elijah to his feet. Then, whilst continuing to demonstrate appropriate concern for his age, the landlady guided the old man towards the door. Neffie meanwhile, her hands not yet encumbered, and because she hadn't yet realised the heartlessness of Miss Koromah's intent, stepped forward to offer what help she could. It was an offer which merely postponed, and not for long, Elijah being kicked out against his will. Di and Samuel watched with bemused expressions as the two women supported the old man, one either side.

"Come on Elijah," said Mariana, "you've been here long enough, upsetting my customers with your strange behaviour. It's time you went back to your mud hut."

"But I don't want to go to my mud hut. I like it here, and besides, my roof leaks," informed Elijah pathetically.

The simple good sense he articulated surprised Neffie.

"You don't mean to say that you're turfing him out just to make room for us," she said indignantly. "It's pouring with rain out there. He'll be soaked."

Mariana stopped in her tracks, and so did the other members of the trio, though it was only poor Elijah who had no say in the matter. The person who had instigated the suspension of movement looked perplexed. It was as if the woman she was presently looking at didn't just come from a different country, but a different planet.

"Of course it's pouring with rain. It often is. It's the rainy season you know… or didn't you know that?"

For Mariana the prospect of Elijah being drenched by rain so warm it was like taking a shower was of no consequence. It would have been an interesting question to ask, however, whether she would ever be so inconsiderate with regard to herself.

"Your concern for Elijah's well-being is admirable Miss Goodwin…" continued Mariana, her formality letting it be known that being in the tropics didn't preclude a certain frostiness developing in their relationship. She had enunciated each syllable of Neffie's surname separately, so that people overhearing the conversation might have thought that the Briton was being congratulated on the outcome of a chess match she had just won, or the horse she owned coming first at the races. "But you've only just met him. I have to put up with him every day that I'm here, often from the time that I open up in the morning until I lock up at night, although it's usually the early hours of the next morning. And does he have any money to buy a drink? Of course he doesn't. He just sits there staring into space like a zombie, or suddenly erupting into a bout of insane laughter in response to some private joke inside his head."

At this point the old man made an effort to break free of the grip maintained by the women, but his strength wasn't up to it. His only recourse was to utter a few plaintive words. "Please can I go back to my table?" he said.

"Now look," said Neffie, addressing Miss Koromah in her most rational tone, "would it make any difference if I was to buy Elijah a drink and invite him to be my guest? You would like that wouldn't you, Elijah?" Neffie enquired of the man whose arm she was holding, and for whose benefit she had raised her voice in the belief that anyone who looked as old as he did must also be hard of hearing.

"Yes, and later we have jig-a-jig," said the old man.

There was an unmistakeable glint in his eye as he spoke, a glint that must have been the precursor of many a conquest in his more lusty days. Now that he was in his dotage there was no lustiness to back up his ribald remark. He was, however, even though his smile had been toothless for years, grinning like a Kalangba cat at the thought. He boasted to the young men playing cards at a table close by.

"This friend of Queen Koromah's is plying me with drink so that she can have her wicked way with me."

To a man the card-players encouraged Elijah. A number of comments were obscure to Neffie, but she surmised that they were crude. The old man's behaviour subsequent to Miss Goodwin's intervention on his behalf took the well-meaning teacher by surprise, so that she was unsure how to respond to his bravado and the commotion he had caused.

Notwithstanding her embarrassment however, she continued to treat Elijah as her guest.

Once everyone that for the present had been going to sit was seated, it turned out to be an incongruous little group made up of four people sipping beer around the table which Elijah had previously occupied alone. No sooner had Neffie ensured that her new friend was comfortable than her mind began to wander to that part of her anatomy which had been, and was becoming once again, her greatest concern. Emanating from where she was convinced the scorpion had stung her, her Achilles heel no less, she felt sensation upon tingling sensation. Despite these worrisome distractions however, and Elijah's loud guffaws and other inappropriate outbursts, Neffie managed to narrate the most dramatic aspects of Di's and her recent history, culminating in the encounter with the scorpion. No sooner had she finished the story than they were joined by Mariana, who had left the running of the bar in the hands of her capable assistant, Moses. Being the sort who likes to be kept in the know about everything that happens in and around Kalangba Junction, it was only to be expected that Miss Koromah wanted to be brought into the loop of which the two foreigners formed a pre-eminent part. She wasn't one for mysteries in fiction, and she disliked them, at least those she hadn't instigated, in the reality she strove to control. With regard to conversations she wasn't party to, and events she wasn't apprised of, there was always the possibility that people were conspiring against her.

"Tell the nosey witch what she wants to know or she'll put a spell on you," ordered Elijah in the hope that someone would obey.

By this time Di, Neffie and Samuel had become used to Elijah's forthright comments ranging from the magnificence of his member to wanting to know why he was being kept prisoner, and their earlier, well-intended responses had given way to a collective deaf ear. No one present, and possibly no one in Kalangba Junction, was more accustomed to being the object of the old man's opprobrium than Mariana, and yet, contrary to expectation and the lapsed concern of the others, she chose not to ignore the invective Elijah directed at her. Maybe it was because she was in the company of two sophisticated foreigners that she responded the way she did, which was to glare at Elijah and tell him to shut up on pain of being turned into a toad. Evidently Elijah didn't take the threat seriously because he just laughed. His laughter soon ceased however, and his expression changed to one of horror when Mariana threatened to hand him over to the high priestess of the women that walk the night.

Following on from Neffie's description of recent events Di had felt it incumbent upon her to add a few colourful details. Mariana listened intently, and would have given the others the benefit of her local knowledge there and then if she hadn't first determined to fetch surgical spirit for Miss Goodwin's foot. After an absence of no more than two minutes, upon her return she proceeded to dab the wounded heel several times with a wad of toilet tissue. The nurse apologised for there being no cotton-wool. The initial application caused Neffie to wince with pain, but in the knowledge that Mariana's ministrations were doing her good she quite enjoyed the dabs which followed.

"There… that should do it," said Mariana, trying to see the effects of her handiwork in the dingy light.

In soft, rasping tones it was then that Chris Rea began to sing about making it home for Christmas. The song, which was Moses' choice, provided for a vocal and musical overlay to the general hubbub.

"The man singing on this record, Chris Rea, comes from near to where I live," said Neffie in response to noting that Mariana had just flashed one of her disapproving looks in Moses' direction. The barman failed to see the glaring look.

"You can't call this singing," Elijah interjected, giving everyone notice that his fear had passed and that he had regained some of his cheeky confidence. "I can sing," he added prior to giving a tuneless rendition of a Rolling Stones classic, a song which, amongst others by the same band, he had heard many times.

Even so Elijah's singing, such as it was, eventually tailed off as he struggled to remember the lyrics. In the end his contribution to the evening's entertainment was simply to hum the tune.

"You were right not to risk getting involved with the Sande," said Mariana as soon as she could hear herself speak.

"Why, what would they have done to us if we had fallen into their hands?" Neffie enquired, seeking confirmation, or otherwise, of Di's alarming statement about having one's clitoris forcibly removed.

"Who can say?" replied Mariana vaguely, "but I can tell you for certain that it was wise of you to keep out of their way. Members of the Sande, or the Zadegi, or the Bundu, as they are sometimes called, are extremely, and I mean extremely, protective of their secrecy. You were unlucky to run into them at this time of year."

Mariana's reference to the season made the women that walk in the night sound like a migrating swarm of locusts.

"I think we were lucky," asserted Neffie, before, with greater humility, adding, "seeing as how Di and I still have all our bits."

Mariana smiled at the allusion and then continued. "Normally they conduct their initiation ceremony in the dry season, which leads me to believe that tonight's gathering must have been a special event — the death of an elder perhaps."

"I take it that you're not a member," probed Samuel, who, as a citizen of the country was bound to be more knowledgeable about the secret societies than the foreigners in their midst, but who on a personal level had no idea as to whether or not his cousin was a loyal devotee.

"Like our British and American friends here, I too have all my bits," Mariana answered.

"It sounds to me that the Sande women, or whatever you want to call them, are a bunch of sadists," said Di.

"Although earlier I said that we were lucky to have come across them in the way that we did. I was referring to witnessing the spectacle, that doesn't mean that I condone what they do. From what I've heard, and the more I think about it, it does seem that these societies exist merely to inflict pain on their sisters, pain at the point of mutilation, and the lifelong pain of not being able to enjoy normal relations, and who knows what other pain besides," commented Neffie, intimating that although as an outsider she was loathe to denigrate local customs, this was a matter about which she couldn't be dispassionate. The very idea of female genital mutilation made her cringe. "It's barbaric," she adjudged.

"It's barbaric," echoed Elijah in a voice several decibels louder than the statement he imitated.

"You see, Elijah here agrees with me," said Neffie, appreciative, notwithstanding the unequivocal meaning of this pronouncement, of the elderly oracle's ability to inject a little levity into the discussion.

"There's more to these secret societies than meets the eye," said Samuel, presuming to take over from his cousin in explaining the more shadowy aspects of the country's cultural heritage.

"It's undoubtedly a more complex business than the surgery involved, if you can call it that," asserted Mariana, curtailing her cousin's male incursion abruptly, "though cutting bits off young girls forms an important part of their rituals."

Following his own flight of fancy upon hearing this intelligence, Elijah burst out laughing.

Chapter Twenty-Five
The Journey Home

Following her misadventures of the night before, Neffie wasn't much the worse for wear the next morning. For having got to bed in time to have a few hours uninterrupted sleep, and for not having drunk more than she was accustomed to drinking her head was clear. The area on her heel where she had been stung was sore, and although she didn't anticipate having to, she knew that she wouldn't be able to walk far. Surprisingly for having drunk more and gone to bed later Di was no less clear-headed.

The trip back to Freetown began as scheduled but not as envisaged. Even as late in the day as eight o'clock that morning, Di and the pair she had brought from Makeni a few weeks previously were expecting to depart Kalangba Junction in the same manner as they had arrived, that is to say sitting three abreast in the cab of the pick-up. That expectation — it couldn't be said to have been a plan — went out of the window when Josie, a friend of Di's who was heavily pregnant, pleaded for a lift to Freetown so that she could be with her mother and sister when the baby decided to come.

There was no way that the Peace Corps volunteer was going to turn down such a request, and having agreed to it, there was no way that she was going to make a woman who was almost due sit in the back. In the circumstances, though faced with the prospect of an uncomfortable, rain-drenched journey, the teachers had no hesitation in relegating themselves to the rear. Fortunately for the pair travelling alfresco however, the resourceful American came up with a number of measures to make their journey as comfortable as possible. The equipment provided was a blanket for each of the two wooden boxes that were to serve as seats and, to provide protection from the rain, a square of blue plastic equal in size to the surface area of a small room. Typically the sky was overcast as Josie said goodbye to her friends and Kalangba-based family members. It was with some difficulty that following her carefully placed basket Josie climbed into the cab. Ensconcing herself in the front passenger seat she made no attempt to fasten the seat belt. Samuel and Neffie were less meticulous with their luggage as they casually threw their bags aboard. Demonstrating youthful agility they clambered in after them.

Thus organised the infant yet to be born and four adults set off for Freetown. Once the small crowd which had gathered to see them off was out of sight Neffie's thoughts began to wander. The now familiar terrain holding no fascination for her, her thoughts were split between memories of the night before and what she would do if her wound turned septic.

She and Di had walked home from Mariana's in the rain. They had been saved a drenching by Miss Koromah's act of kindness in loaning Di an umbrella. Nonetheless, it hadn't been easy trying to keep in step of a kind whilst under the influence of even the moderate volume of alcohol which Neffie, if not Di, had imbibed. One temporary benefit was that the pain in Neffie's foot had abated, so that it seemed as if her heel had been anesthetised. In good spirits, therefore, there had been much stumbling, strong language and giggles. Perhaps it had been Mariana's influence, but it was interesting to note that immediately upon leaving the bar Neffie had proved to be less solicitous of Elijah's well-being than she had been previously. She and Di had simply left him to his fate.

If at this juncture Samuel had interrupted Neffie's train of thought to enquire as to why she was looking so disdainful he would have been told that after having been woken by a cockatoo calling from the far end of the roof above her head she had discovered that she was only half undressed and that her heel had become swollen and tender during the hours of sleep, so much so that upon getting fully dressed she was unable to wear anything on her feet other than flip-flops. The recollection of one and the constant reminder of the other served to undermine her self-esteem, hence the frowning expression that could have prompted Samuel's question. Made when they had met by the pick-up that morning, Samuel's promise to take Neffie to see a doctor as soon as they arrived back in Freetown hadn't eased the lame duck's mind completely, and she continued to inspect her heel and lower leg with a frequency which was indicative of her concern. In reliving events of the night before it was as if the images crowding her mind were competing for supremacy; but mainly she couldn't help but link their almost running into the secret society with the appearance of the scorpion. In her mind their quasi-mystical syncretism grew ever stronger.

Indeed, from the wealth of knowledge that Mariana had conveyed relating to the whys and wherefores of Sande rituals, and the significance of the features pertaining to particular masks (that a full forehead denotes wisdom; that downcast eyes are an indication of modesty; that the shiny black colour symbolises mystery; and that the carved birds perched on the masks are messengers between the spirits and humans), it was this spiritual aspect of her recent experience which fascinated Neffie most. She wondered if the women she had seen tramping along the road were indeed able to control the powers of the spirit world as Mariana had said. A scene recalled from when the queen had been holding court back in her bar, Miss Koromah had informed her audience that these spirits are prisoners of the masks, and are captured in other artefacts known as 'medicines'. Needless to say the 'medicines' in question aren't like any Neffie could expect to be prescribed at home. Eventually the effect of the pick-up bumping in and out of a pot-hole jolted Neffie's thoughts back to the present and she wondered if Josie was regretting her decision.

In Makeni Di filled up with diesel. Knowing that they were well-maintained, she encouraged Josie in particular to make use of the toilet facilities. West of Makeni, somewhere between the villages of Makari and Madina the heavens opened, impelling the pair travelling alfresco to pull the sheet of blue plastic over their heads. Perhaps if Neffie had been at the outset of her latest African adventure, and perhaps if she hadn't been so preoccupied with the effects of her scorpion sting, then she might have enjoyed being cosy with Samuel, but after having already been splashed by the spray from a truck passing in the opposite direction she was in no mood for being cosy with anyone. Neither was she in the mood for conversation, evidenced by the fact that on occasion she became conscious of pretending to listen to Samuel rather than paying full attention to what he was saying.

"I'm sure it will serve me well in the long run," said Samuel, gazing at Neffie as he spoke so that she could be in no doubt as to the seriousness of his intent.

Miss Goodwin had no doubt that 'it' would serve Samuel well, but because the aerial of her attention hadn't then found the right frequency, so engrossed had she been with her own thoughts, that she had no idea what it was that would be so beneficial. She decided, for the present, not to let on that she was completely nonplussed by Samuel's utterance, and hoped to catch the drift of what he had been telling her from any pronouncements to follow. To this end she made a determined effort to listen.

"I know it means spending a great deal of my time studying, more than I've ever done in my life I should think, but I'm prepared to put in the effort. What is it that the Americans say… no pain, no gain? No; it's not the mental effort required or the length of time I'll need to invest that worries me."

At this point Samuel paused, and the pause invited his guest to pose an obvious question. After gaining an inkling of Samuel's general drift Neffie duly complied by asking, "What is it that worries you?"

"Top of my list of concerns is the cost and availability of books," Samuel replied. "The reading list for a Masters degree in English is bound to be extensive, and you've seen what this climate does to books. On my uncertain salary they would be prohibitively expensive, yet not to be able to do the required reading would mean certain failure."

"So you're intending to study for a Master of Arts degree in English," said Neffie. Her tone was one of summation rather than discovery, when in reality the alternative was true. Using the back of her hand she wiped a trickle of rain water that had run off their improvised shelter onto her forehead.

"That's the plan," Samuel confirmed, "though it all depends on whether I can convince an organisation, or an individual, that I'm worth sponsoring."

Evidently the time he had spent in Mariana's company had resulted in some of her ideas insinuating their way into Samuel's psyche; but no matter how impoverished he may be Samuel knew that he could never be as brazen as he envisaged his cousin would be if she were in his shoes, and he was being as bold as he dare be in asking for financial assistance. Samuel waited for Neffie's response.

In the short term Miss Goodwin made no attempt to put the man sitting by her side striving to keep the rain at bay out of his misery, choosing instead to focus her attention on a rapidly approaching car. From a distance, over which it was impossible to make out even the gender of the people occupying the front seats, Neffie nonetheless had a notion that she knew who they were, and in her mind's eye, conjured up an image of the faces which in reality were hidden by the rain-spotted windscreen and its wipers going to and fro. It was only when the unmarked car drew up close behind them that Neffie's premonition was confirmed and she could see, sufficiently well if not clearly, that the two men in the front were none other than the two policemen who had entered her hotel room to check her papers, and whom she had last seen in Makeni. She struggled to remember their names, and ultimately resorted to a simple technique which Sebastian had taught her. This was to work through the alphabet until the correct initial letter provided the spark necessary to recall the name which hadn't come immediately to mind. Neffie felt considerable satisfaction whenever the stratagem succeeded, and it was by this method that she remembered the names of the two policemen in the car behind as Charles Conteh and Julius Kallon.

Beyond her requirement that any car she was driving should be reliable and economical Neffie would have been hard put to identify the make and model of the covert police car. Her best description would be to say that it was white, or at least once upon a time it had been judging by the pigment revealed through the earth-coloured particles that had splashed up to become encrusted on the vehicle's sides and bonnet. Neffie wanted to compare the state of the pick-up with that of the car behind but was prevented from conducting even a cursory inspection by the sheet of blue plastic covering her head and back. She wasn't going to get up off her seat to look, but presumed that Di's vehicle was no less besmirched.

Neffie was in two minds about giving the police officers a friendly wave. Ultimately she decided not to on the grounds that by no stretch of the imagination had the intercourse between the detectives and her been personal, and furthermore someone had once told her that policemen take exception to being waved at, perceiving friendly gestures from strangers as being tantamount to an admission of guilt. Tilting his head to see beyond the pickup's tailboard, Charles Conteh checked that the road ahead was clear and then accelerated to overtake. Lacking Miss Goodwin's inhibitions Joseph Kallon smiled as he raised his hand and then opened and shut his fingers, thereby acknowledging that he had recognised the woman in the pickup. Neffie noted the gesture when it was too late to respond to any significant effect, and besides her attention had become focused elsewhere. There was a third person in the car. Neffie couldn't be certain, but she believed that the woman was none other than Mariana. Whoever it was did her utmost to prevent being recognised. Of course for Neffie, once the police car had gone from her field of vision, there was no action replay available to confirm or negate her supposition. She turned an earnest expression towards Samuel.

"Did you see who was in that car?"

"Just a couple of guys from what I could tell," Samuel replied, averting, by staring down at Neffie's foot, the embarrassment of eye contact which was bound to be intense for being too close. "I didn't take much notice."

Not that it was a deviation from the norm, but this statement was undoubtedly true. Samuel had been preoccupied with going over in his mind all that he had said on the subject of sponsorship thus far, as well as giving a great deal of thought to what else he could do to persuade Neffie to help fund his future. Being the high-minded individual he was, he was never going to be comfortable selling his soul as he saw it. The business didn't come naturally to him. Not surprisingly he was embarrassed at the overtures he had already made, and which he was about to reinforce.

"The sooner the doctor has a look at that foot of yours the better," said Samuel upon observing that the inflamed area around where the scorpion had struck had grown. Moreover it looked 'angrier' than when he had last given the wound his full attention. No sooner had he expressed his concern for his friend's well-being, however, than he returned to the subject which was uppermost in his mind, even though his expression of concern had served to indicate otherwise. "So if you can think of a way to fund my course don't hesitate to let me know."

It had stopped raining. Neffie, after first poking out her head just to make sure, removed the sheet of blue plastic. For the reason that on one side it was soaking wet, and therefore not pleasant to handle, she settled for folding it in half, and then in half again. Whereas only moments ago the road had been almost deserted of pedestrians, now it was possible to see, coming and going in either direction, more than one woman bearing a basket or a bundle atop her head supported by one hand raised. Perhaps it was because Neffie was a teacher of small children that she noticed particularly how common it was for there to be a stoical, stony-faced child in tow.

Prior to running her fingers through her hair Neffie shook her head vigorously to get rid of a few errant droplets of rain water. Then, for the umpteenth time, she inspected her foot. "I couldn't agree more," said Neffie, referring to Samuel's comment about the desirability of getting medical attention, and soon.

"So what do you suggest?" enquired Samuel.

He was somewhat confused as to what it was that Miss Goodwin was agreeing to, although he settled for the interpretation which appealed to him most, specifically that the Englishwoman had recognised that his proposed scheme was worth supporting. Consequently, Samuel grew ever more optimistic that Neffie was intending to make him an offer he couldn't refuse.

Samuel's optimism wasn't unfounded, though he did have to contend with a minor disappointment moments before Neffie said the words which were sweet music to his ears. She didn't intend to thwart Samuel's ambition when she mentioned that his cousin could be a likely source of munificence, but her suggestion certainly dampened Samuel's spirits more effectively than a deluge from the heavens was capable of doing. In the end, believing that it wasn't inconceivable that Mariana was in police custody, it was Neffie herself who dismissed the bar owner as a possible benefactor. Indeed, in her worst-case scenario Neffie was able to imagine Mariana languishing for years in a prison cell, her property and investments, all she held dear, confiscated. When she let herself be transported on a more positive train of thought however, Miss Goodwin was able to entertain the possibility that Mariana was merely helping the police with their enquiries. In respect of either circumstance Neffie thought it wise not to tell Samuel that she had caught a fleeting glimpse of a woman who bore a strong resemblance to his cousin, for no other reason than she couldn't be absolutely certain that it was indeed his cousin. Neffie came to the conclusion that she, and only she, was in a position to help her friend achieve his worthy ambition.

"If you write to me with a list of the books you need, I'll get them for you in the UK and post them to you."

"That's great but…"

"And if you send me the course details I'll do what I can to help you out financially," said Neffie in a business-like manner, and without committing herself to a specific sum.

On the road between Makatete and Makabo Junction Samuel dared to give his sponsor a hug. It was a spontaneous demonstration of his appreciation and affection to which Neffie responded with equal warmth. The empathy he engendered by a shared cause might have discovered new depths had it not been for that impish muse Thalia at work behind the scenes, for what happened next was unscripted comedy. Seated on boxes in the back of a pickup is hardly the most convenient of places for displays of affection, and as a consequence of Di at the wheel swerving to round an obstacle in the road, Samuel fell off his perch and ended up rolling onto his back on the floor. He might have dragged Neffie down on top of him had she not reacted swiftly to brace herself as she relinquished her hold on Samuel to grasp the vehicle's side. Not wishing to be the cause of too great an upset, or cause his benefactor harm, Samuel was sufficiently mindful to relinquish his hold on her. For several seconds he lay on his back staring up at the grey mass of cloud. It was as if he was searching for inspiration as to what to do next. That inspiration came from Neffie in the sound of her laughter. It was laughter of a kind which originates around a person's midriff and ascends to make the whole body quake. It was also the laughter of someone who has suddenly, if momentarily, been released from a grave concern. Whilst holding on to the unyielding solidity of metal with her left hand, as soon as she had managed to control her convulsions Neffie held out her right hand for Samuel to grasp. Far from being embarrassed at his fall from grace, but instead laughing at his own discomfort, raising his upper body from the deck he reached out to accept Neffie's gracious offer.

The remainder of the journey back to Freetown proved uneventful for the people in the pick-up. Di's worry throughout was that Josie beside her would ask her to pull in so that she could give birth. That didn't happen. Noticeable to some extent to all, but particularly to the pair in the back as a consequence of their greater, all-round perspective, was the large number of soldiers patrolling the capital's streets. The reason for their presence would become apparent in due course.

Contrary to expectation Josie was adamant that she wanted to be dropped off at the house where her mother and sister were living and not at the hospital. In a city where even that important establishment was sometimes left without power, her reasoning along the lines of 'what can they do for me that my family can't do for me at home' didn't sound so absurd. It was certainly Josie's way of stating that pregnancy is not an illness. In response to the healthy but pregnant woman's directions the pickup's first port of call was in Sibthorpe Street, not far from the Hausa Mosque.

Declining an invitation to enter the home of Josie's relatives for some refreshment for no other reason than that they were pressed for time, a rare eventuality in Sierra Leone, and one to which Neffie had grown unaccustomed over recent weeks, the passengers who had travelled in the back climbed into the front of the pickup. Without a word at the outset as to where they were going next Di set off for the hospital she had wanted Josie to attend, but her singular mission now was to obtain expert treatment for Neffie's foot. Expressed en route, and thereby revealing their next destination, Miss Fussey's opinion in this regard was, "If you can't get treatment for a scorpion sting in the hospital of a capital city in the tropics where can you get it?" Samuel lacked faith in his country's health service being able to deliver any form of expert care, and therefore wasn't so optimistic.

"Supposing there's no anaesthetic," said Di as she drove towards the open gates topped with barbed wire that led into the compound.

Failing to catch on that Di was being facetious it was with a bewildered look on her face that Neffie responded with a question. "Why on earth would I need anaesthetic? It's not as if they're going to amputate my foot, or are they?"

If the situation at the entrance to the hospital had been normal Di would have continued with the badinage to the effect that she would have left her friend in no doubt that amputation of her foot was a distinct possibility, and yet expressing herself in such a way that Neffie, and Samuel for that matter, would soon realise that she was only jesting. The situation looked anything but normal. Upon driving into the compound the new arrivals observed a large crowd gathered around the hospital entrance. A number of individuals were sitting on log seats, while others simply stood around waiting, presumably for news of a loved one. Several women were crying inconsolably, despite attempts by friends and family to console them.

Conspicuous amid the colourful attire of the women, for being out of place soldiers in their disrupted pattern camouflage stood out almost as distinctly as poppies in a wheat field. Two of the soldiers were leaning on sandbags. Between them protruded the perforated barrel of a heavy machine-gun. The others were armed with rifles.

At this point an officer emerged from the hospital building, and, after looking around to assess the situation, proceeded to berate one of his men for not having taken up a position at the gate. The trio in the pickup weren't able to hear every word that passed between the officer and the soldier, but the gist of the exchange was transparently obvious nevertheless. The expression on each face — one angry, the other submissive — spoke volumes, as did the subsequent action of the subordinate in taking up his post at the double. If there had been any doubts as to who was in charge, the officer whose rank was signified by three stars on each epaulette had certainly re-established his authority.

He advanced towards the pickup. His expression, indeed his entire body language, gave the impression that he was quite prepared to shoot anyone who dared to cross him. The three sitting in the cab of the pickup were reassured to see that his pistol was still in its holster.

"Hi," greeted Di pleasantly as the figure of authority approached at a pace. Leaning her head out of the window and smiling, she hoped that she appeared more relaxed than she felt. This was her way of taking the heat out of the situation before it approached boiling point or a point at which there could be some kind of spontaneous combustion.

She was making a conscious effort to remain unfazed by the emotional scenes she was witnessing. She wanted to make it absolutely clear to the army officer, and before saying another word, that she wasn't going to let him intimidate her. In this regard she had considerable psychological support. This was her belief that as a US citizen she had the might of the most powerful country in the world to call upon if she got into trouble. That said, she didn't want the confidence which she undoubtedly had in her team to appear supercilious.

The officer acted as if he was deaf to any greeting, choosing instead to respond with a direct question, one which he posed abruptly. "Are you sick… injured?"

"No, but…"

"Then what are you doing here?" enquired the army officer, placing his hands on the ledge of the vehicle, the ledge just vacated by Miss Fussey's elbow, provided by its open window. The officer leaned forward as he spoke, effectively forcing Di away from the space she had occupied hitherto.

"My friend here was stung by a scorpion last night and her foot has become swollen," informed Di, noting how big the man's hands were, and how pink the skin was beneath the nails.

Prominent also on the pair of hands closer to her than she was entirely comfortable with was a wedding ring and a watch which Di thought far too big and brash to be made of precious metal, but she wasn't so confident in her judgement to be absolutely certain that it wasn't. Whatever it was made from she thought it signified an overblown ego.

"You won't get treatment today for a mere scorpion sting," said the officer, focusing his gaze upon Neffie seated in the middle.

"What has happened?" enquired Samuel with genuine concern for his fellow citizens. "Has there been a major incident?"

"Who are you?" the officer interrogated, aware that he wasn't addressing a foreigner.

"My name is Samuel Massequoi. I am a teacher here in Freetown," Samuel answered proudly.

"There has been a rebel attack in Aberdeen (a district of Freetown), sir. Three of my men have been killed, and at least twice that number seriously wounded. The wounded are being treated as we speak, along with a number of civilians. The West Side Boys, as they like to be called, were trying to capture the heliport, but they didn't succeed." For the first time in the conversation the officer smiled, flashing a gold incisor. "So unless your injury is life threatening there's no…"

Aware of the officer's gist before he had a chance to express his meaning fully, Miss Goodwin interjected, "Yes… of course… we didn't realise. We'll leave right away," she added, urging Di to restart the engine.

"Good," he said as he turned about to retrace his steps back to the hospital entrance and the families awaiting news.

After a few steps he turned and signalled to the guard at the gate to let through the pick-up which, having turned around, was now heading towards him back the way it had come.

Chapter Twenty-Six
For Di People

The following article was written by Milton A. Campbell and published in the newspaper, 'For Di People', on Tuesday, 27th August, 1991.

WIND OF POLITICAL CHANGE AND A PINCER MOVEMENT TOO

A wind of change in political attitudes is now sweeping across black Africa including Sierra Leone. The new political thinking is for a return to Multi-party System of Government.

With the emergence of independent African states beginning a little over three decades ago, came the emergence of a distinct political ideology propagated by African political leaders — the ideology of one-party rule for Africa.

The Westminster style of government with all its merits, was heavily criticised for being inconsistent with the African political culture and was dropped by newly independent states of Africa, one by one.

The contagion spread rapidly. The one-party system in East European countries was in background focus to give added weight to the arguments of that new ideology.

That system was copied naively and in travesty, ignoring the provision of social services for all which form the basis of the system and upon which it rested for its justification.

The ideology has now failed for all to see.

Those who fail to see this failure are only fit for the rubbish heap.

Today, well-meaning and patriotic Sierra Leoneans hold out hopes for a change in the circumstance for their country and their lifestyle on the impending reintroduction of pluralism in government.

Democracy has won the ideological war between East and West which we have been witnessing since the end of the Second World War and one-party rule even for East European countries seems to be doomed.

In his time Mr Nikita Kruschev, Prime Minister of the U.S.S.R. derided capitalism and western style democracy and once remarked that the political system of the coffin of capitalism.

We now know that there is yet no better system of government than that brand of democracy practised by the western world.

In one of his erudite newspaper publications in the early seventies Dr Sarif Easmon pointed out that wherever a one-party system of government had been tried, it had proved a failure.

He was making a case then for Sierra Leone not to join the one-party club. Dr Easmon is a man of vision for whom I hold the greatest respect. He did play his part for love of country.

As we enter the threshold of a new political era, let us do so with a change of heart and a change of behaviour.

A change of our sense of values and most important a change of policy. A country is what its citizens make of it.

For Sierra Leone to start moving, these changes are imperative. Our task of national reconstruction is enormous. Let us get down to business and start thinking ahead.

Our political reform should pave the way for desperate economic planning and activity for the purpose of economic rehabilitation and emancipation.

To do this, the lingering obstacle of the N.P.F.L. must first be removed.

Social instability is inconsistent with national development. The Charles Taylor's menace should be removed once and for all.

There should be no mercy in the process. We cannot act in half measures.

I was saddened by a recent statement by the President of Sierra Leone, Major General J.S. Momoh, to a group of Freemasons that the most productive foreign exchange earning areas of our country were still in rebel hands.

It is high time we got over with this rebel nightmare in order for us to settle for a new political system along with constructive economic planning.

We need to coordinate with greater efficiency our defence strategies for effective and decisive military action.

The responsibility for this is in the hands of our military planners a team to which I do not belong.

However, I am anxious to offer, with humility, the following suggestions based on my years of reading of military history and strategies, and do hope that they will be taken seriously.

Seal off the Sierra Leone border with Liberia to prevent further incursions.

Identify the enemy's basis on our soil.

Identify his lines of communication and possible retreat.

Launch well-planned attacks on those bases, throwing everything we have on them and ensuring that enemy line of retreat be cut-off.

To do this, the British and American method of military operation can be deployed. This I am sure is understood by military strategists. A pincer movement may not be a bad idea.

Show no mercy take no prisoners — this is not a conventional war.

These rebel idiots are undesirable creatures not to be counted among human beings. They have sown the wind and now must reap the whirlwind.

We must be prepared to damage part of our land, if necessary, in order to save the whole, that is a basic military option.

Let us get over with once and for all this rebel situation. It is most disturbing and worrying to concerned Sierra Leone.

The following also appeared in the 27th Aug edition of 'For Di People'.

ONKO LIMBA GIVES 16 COWS

A delegation from Tonka Limba led by their paramount Chief and Parliamentary representative presented 16 cows and Lei60 thousand to President J.S.Momoh as their contribution towards the war effort.

PC Alhaji Alimany Kande Sorie I told Momoh that although they hail from a poor area of the country, it is their duty to share the present problem with the government.

MP for Kambia East 1, Dr Thaim Kamara thanked Momoh for taking prompt action to contain the unwarranted and unprovoked aggression by the NPFL bandits.

Kamara also praised the efforts of the Nigerian, Guinean and Sierra Leonean armed forces and appreciated the moves to speedily return this nation to a mufti-party system of government.

Among other things Momoh said that one should watch the way the breeze is blowing and not be like one who digs sand, covers the head but the buttocks are out.

He said there are many people with plenty tactics but caution self-advice.

Momoh also said he will choose a running mate when the time comes and does not have anyone in mind.

Chapter Twenty-Seven
Resolve and Resolution

Sebastian Forrest considered himself to be a rational member of the human-race, one more rational than most. Not even in the most demanding of circumstances, circumstances which either to him or to others threatened danger, was he likely to panic. Indeed, at the time of Neffie's absence in Sierra Leone he would go so far as to say that the fundamentally irrational psychological state was alien to him. On the morning three days prior to Neffie's anticipated homecoming however, certain tasks which he had promised to undertake and complete in her absence, and which he had yet to start in earnest, engendered a state of mind, one could imagine, similar to that of a turkey were it to learn and appreciate the significance of the first scene being revealed on the advent calendar. What made matters worse was the realisation that if he hadn't been so dilatory and put things off till the last minute, he would have been able to spend the next three days anticipating Neffie's return with mounting pleasure rather than the trepidation he would feel if he were to fail to complete his self-appointed tasks.

On the morning in question Seb had risen early and dressed hurriedly in the near rags which were his normal garb when he was intending to transform their habitat, either decoratively or structurally. He didn't consider himself to be a practical person in the same way that a plumber or an electrician has acquired the skills necessary to do their particular job, but neither was he a nincompoop, so that his endeavours with tools around the house usually produced a satisfactory result. The jeans he had put on were pitted with soil and torn at the knee, and a piece of fabric torn from the back pocket, so that there was no longer a back pocket, hung down limply. The sweat shirt he had pulled over his head and into which he struggled to insert his arms was merely daubed with paint.

Unlike the labours of Hercules there were only two jobs on Seb's mental list. The most important, and by far the most demanding, was to replace the outhouse roof, the present canopy being on the verge of collapse. The second was to repaint the bathroom ceiling. A regular call upon his time and energy, the coats of paint he had already applied on separate occasions approximately six months apart had a propensity to flake and look, in a decorative sense, leprous. The cause was attributed to steam rising from the shower.

Over breakfast, a meal which had begun at seven and was finished by ten past, Sebastian had already applied his intellectual powers to the tasks in view. He had reasoned that because the weather-forecast was good for that day and the next, then, certainly during the hours of daylight, he should devote his time to replacing the roof. He would be able to work on the bathroom ceiling at any time of the day or night, and the weather wasn't a consideration.

Sebastian's former reluctance to work on the fulfilment of his practical promises didn't mean that he had been totally inactive in this regard. He had done much of the preparation. He had, as a temporary measure and primarily for the purpose of security, transferred the contents from within the solidly built brick-walls of the shed with the shoddy roof, two bicycles (one with a cross-bar, one without), an assortment of gardening tools old and new, a pile of slates, metal shelving from which he had removed the usual outhouse paraphernalia, to a shed on the allotment he and Neffie worked together. The trips back and forth had taken up most of one Saturday. He had also measured up and bought the materials from which to make the new roof — MDF boards, roofing-felt, pitch.

The work progressed well, and by mid-morning Seb had ripped off the old, dilapidated roof to expose the wooden beams which, being strong enough to support his weight as he clambered about, he deemed good for another decade and therefore wouldn't need to be replaced presently. Upon the completion of this first significant task the present seemed a good time to take a break, and it was with cautious rather than carefree agility that he transferred his feet from the beams to the ladders which would bring him back down to earth at a measured pace.

Throughout the morning a female blackbird had been a distraction to Seb in his elevated endeavour. Curious as to what the man was up to, time and again she had landed on this or that beam a yard or so from

327

where the amateur builder was working. Then, taking a few steps at a time, she had warily hopped towards him until, having gained his attention by her bold proximity he paused in what he was doing and did one of three things as the fancy took him. He spoke to her as if she were a long-lost friend, simply smiled, or did his best to mimic a blackbird's song. Even though the bird invariably took flight, Sebastian thought his whistling struck not only the right notes, but the right timbre, and that he had given a bravura performance. He also thought that his feathered friend was playing a game with him, one which they both found charming.

Once safely on the ladders Seb chanced to look to his left, across the concrete yard which stopped at the back door of the house. His view of the door was impeded by a shirt which he had pegged to the washing-line two days previously, but he could see the lower third. Being partially open the door provided an irresistible temptation for a certain female. Seb watched as the bird hopped across the threshold into the kitchen. She did so with all the naturalness of a house-person entering his or her domain after hanging out the washing. It was with some amazement that Sebastian completed his descent and made for the door. Wafting the shirt aside he followed the bird into the house.

After having dealt in the past with the mess created by a pair of jackdaws that had come down the chimney to emerge from the fireplace, Seb wondered what he would find. On that occasion the birds had panicked. On this occasion Seb was determined not to frighten his unexpected guest; at least not more than was necessary to ensure her safe departure.

When Seb caught sight of his visitor she was hopping across the carpet. At first, she showed no fear whatsoever, as she hopped around the room surveying the contents, paying particular interest, perhaps for seeing her own reflection, to the television screen. Sebastian followed two steps behind until eventually the blackbird took fright and flew up to the window, through which she no doubt intended to escape. Evidently unfamiliar with the deceptive transparency of glass, she didn't perceive it to be an obstacle and crashed into a pane with a sickening thud. The shock of having been suddenly impeded must have been all the greater for the reason that to her understanding there was nothing there.

Momentarily stunned, the bird soon recovered, but then began to panic, flapping her wings frenetically as she tried to break through the unrelenting force-field.

At this point Sebastian decided that the time had come to lend a hand and he attempted to catch the bird. Unfortunately, the actions of the now desperate creature combined with the restrictions imposed by certain items of furniture upon the man's freedom of movement made success unlikely, and Seb was only too aware that failure could cause injury. He decided that the best course of action was to throw in the towel, in this case literally. He side-stepped quickly into the kitchen to grab a tea-towel. By throwing it over the bird he succeeded in quelling her frantic flapping even though the act of kindness probably did little to dispel her fear. Nevertheless, now that it was possible to handle the delicate creature safely her stressful experience would soon be over. Demonstrating the care of a modern St. Francis Seb secured the little dare-devil in cupped hands. Only her head protruded. The bird grew calm. Its purpose having been served Seb discarded the towel and headed for the door. Upon stepping outside, like a high priest making a votive offering to the gods, he raised his arms to the heavens and opened his hands. Then he watched the bird fly off uninjured in the direction of the allotments.

Before she had disappeared from his sight completely the telephone summoned him to the hall. "That's a first," Sebastian muttered as he picked up the receiver whilst at the same time adopting his favourite position for holding a telephone conversation — sitting on the bottom step of the stairs.

Through the clear glass of his own front door, and through the upstairs window of the house across the road, Seb could see the woman who lived there brushing her hair. With regard to her state of dress she was perfectly decent.

"Good morning, Sebastian Forrest speaking."

"Hello, Sebastian, Shirley here… Shirley Margai," responded Miss Margai a little nervously.

If she hadn't said her name Sebastian wouldn't have had any difficulty in identifying his caller by her accent.

"Shirley… it's good to hear from you again, how are you?" Sebastian enquired enthusiastically, quickly overcoming his feeling of being irked by a phone call which could upset his plans for the day; or at the very least delay him.

"Take me out to lunch and I'll tell you," said Shirley, more confident now, "or better still, let me take you out to lunch. You deserve it after all you've done for me."

Sebastian considered the possibilities as to what he had done to merit such praise, and because he couldn't come up with a plausible alternative concluded that the invitation was merely reciprocal. Ordinarily he would have jumped at the chance of a good repast at another's expense, but given his sense of urgency in respect of the tasks in hand, he decided to decline the offer. He was tactful of course.

"Just because I bought lunch for you doesn't mean that you have to buy lunch for me, Shirley, and besides, I've got so many things to do before Neffie gets back, that even if I work from now till midnight, I'm not sure I'll be able to complete them all."

"When is Neffie due back?"

"The day after tomorrow," Sebastian replied.

The two or three seconds of silence which ensued communicated a sense of disappointment, but being the persistent type that she was Shirley boldly made a second attempt to persuade.

"I'm sorry to hear that," she said, although suspecting that her meaning had been misconstrued she quickly added, "what I mean to say is that of course I'm glad that you and Neffie will soon be reunited, but I am sorry that you can't find the time to celebrate the success of my operation with me."

Sebastian pondered over this revelation. The neighbour across the road must have been about to undress because she closed the curtains. The casual observer on the telephone felt somewhat guilty at the thought that perhaps she thought he had been prying.

"That's great news," congratulated Seb finally, and although there could only be one possible explanation as to the aim of the operation in question, seeking specific information he enquired further. "What have they done to you?"

The question produced a ripple of laughter at the other end of the line. To the ears of the radio journalist from Sierra Leone the nuance of meaning sounded incongruous. The tone of the question was such that she could imagine having been subjected to a terrible ordeal at the hands of some wicked people.

"I've had an operation to replace the ligaments in my knee, which means that soon, probably in a matter of months, I'll be able to walk unaided; and it's all thanks to you. "

"What did I do?"

If Seb really had had no idea as to what he had done to assist Miss Margai the question would have been incredibly naive. In reality however, he just wanted to hear her sing his praises.

"Well it was you who created the interest that encouraged people to raise the money that enabled me to go for treatment in a private hospital. If there hadn't been the publicity there wouldn't have been a charitable donation, and if there hadn't been a charitable donation there would have been no operation. I would have been lame... permanently."

"It is amazing how things turn out sometimes. You throw a pebble into the pond and lo and behold ripples spread out in every direction... in this case ripples of goodwill. To every action there's an opposite and equal reaction." Seb gained considerable satisfaction from citing Newton's third law of motion, which, if only in the moral sphere, he often did.

"You won't be surprised to hear that my knee's a little sore at the moment, and I'll have to wear a brace for a few weeks yet, but the important thing is I'm not going to be permanently lame. You're a miracle-worker."

"I think of myself as being more of a song and dance man actually," said Seb with a chuckle, mindful that he wasn't being original. "In fact the more I think about it I'm much more song than dance," he corrected, flippancy being the only way he knew how to respond to the accolade he had hoped Shirley would make. "So who are these people that raised the money for your treatment, and if you don't mind my asking, how much did they raise?"

"Let me think for a moment," Shirley answered, "you would think that a journalist would be good at remembering names, well this journalist isn't. I know they were both called Richard... I've got it... the names of the men who came to see me were Gilmore and Hindmarsh. They're members of a Christian fellowship in Ferrousby. Do you know them? I imagined that they were friends of yours."

"I can't say that I do," Sebastian answered, racking his brain for a face to match one or other of the names. "It sounds as if they're a firm of accountants or solicitors. How much did you say they collected?"

"Over £2,000," Shirley replied, overlooking the fact that she hadn't previously mentioned a sum. "That was more or less what the operation cost, worth every penny in my opinion. Are you sure you won't come out to lunch?"

For a few moments Sebastian wavered, but he didn't relent. He was able to maintain his resolve to complete the tasks he had set himself that morning by bringing to mind what he considered to be the negative aspects of Shirley's invitation. In addition to having to drop everything he would have to take a shower, and then press a shirt. He could also envisage the look of disappointment on Neffie's face were she to arrive home and see open sky where the new roof should have been.

"Well what about tomorrow?"

"Tomorrow's out of the question too. I know," Sebastian exclaimed as if it were a Eureka moment, "why not get in touch next week when I won't be under so much pressure. I'll introduce you to Neffie and..."

"I'm going to London to meet some people from Sierra Leone the day after tomorrow, the day your Neffie returns, and next week I'm flying to New York for a job interview."

"That beats taking me out for lunch any day of the week," Seb interjected.

"Look," said Shirley, in a tone which conveyed that she had finally taken 'no' for an answer, and exhibiting no loss of pride at her powers of persuasion having proved ineffectual followed up with, "I'm really grateful for all that you did for me, and perhaps we could meet up the next time I'm in Luxborough visiting my mother. I've no idea when that will be, but until then take care, and God bless."

Sebastian was taken aback by the religiosity of Shirley's parting comment. He found it unsettling. He was also more than a little impressed at the prospect of his friendly acquaintance globetrotting as far as the Big Apple and getting a job. On any other occasion he would have wanted to know more, but given his present state of mind he chose instead to follow Miss Margai's lead and close the conversation between them.

"I'm sorry for being so inflexible and having to let you down in this way," apologised Sebastian, "but I'm delighted to hear that you'll soon be able to walk properly again, and gosh, what a coup to get a job in New York. Good luck with it," he concluded, as if the interview were a mere formality.

"Thanks, and thanks again for everything," said Shirley.

Two days later, forty minutes before the eagerly anticipated domestic flight was due to land after having taken off from Heathrow an hour earlier, Sebastian set off for the local airport. He was doing his best to contain the excitement he felt at the prospect of meeting Neffie as she emerged from 'Arrivals'. A month and a half had passed since he had last set eyes on the woman he loved. That may not seem long to people accustomed to living independent lives miles apart, but for people like Seb, who perceived his relationship with Neffie mostly to be one of interdependent and intimate closeness, a month and a half was equal to an aeon. Yes; he had missed her terribly, but in a couple of hours, all being well, they would be reunited.

Adding to Sebastian's sense of well-being was the fact that, apart from having broken a rather expensive Dartington crystal wine glass, his conscience was clear. While stopped at a level crossing he determined to tell Neffie of the breakage as soon as they were in the car heading for home, not from fear of reprisal it should be noted, but from an earnest wish for his conscience to be absolutely clear at an early opportunity. He was also looking forward to telling his beloved, again probably on the journey home that she would be impressed at the outcomes of the promises he had made of a practical nature. For without having to work into the night on any night, to his own satisfaction he had duly completed the tasks he had set himself. He had hopes of receiving more than a pat on the head as his just reward.

Other than the five minutes delay at the railway crossing the journey to the airport was straightforward, and half an hour after Seb had set out from home he entered the airport terminal. Being a provincial airport it was a small building, and not very busy. Sebastian's first act was to study the electronic display indicating flight numbers and whether the aircraft in question had landed, was about to land, or was on the way. Illuminated between a holiday charter flight from Alicante and another from Porto were the flight details the young man was searching for. He swore under his breath. Neffie's flight was delayed by forty minutes. He thought that no one could possibly have heard him, but a woman standing a few feet to his right turned her head askance to give him a disapproving look.

"Sorry!" he said.

"Apology accepted," the woman said prior to turning her attention back to the flight information.

Once he had got used to the idea of hanging around for at least forty minutes longer than he would have wished, the update didn't cause Sebastian further consternation. In fact on thinking it over, in his experience flights in which he had had some interest had more often been subject to delay than they had been punctual. He wished that he had brought a book with him but would make do with a newspaper if he could find a vendor. He knew that whatever reading material he procured he wouldn't be able to concentrate on it fully for the reason that he would spend just as much time glancing up from the printed word to focus on the doorway through which people emerge after passing through customs and immigration controls.

In the event he picked up copy of the Daily Express which someone had left folded on a chair. Seb hoped the newspaper was there to be retrieved, by someone with time on their hands. He sat down to read the story beneath the headlines. Two soldiers from his former unit had been killed in a gruesome manner in Northern Ireland. Contrary to expectation he managed to read the entire story before first looking up to see returning holidaymakers pushing baggage-laden trolleys. Their faces tanned, some were dressed as if they were reluctant to admit that their Mediterranean holiday was over. Remarkably, no more than half a minute apart, a man and a woman appeared, each carrying a soft toy in the shape of a donkey. The donkeys could have been twins.

Gradually the number of returning holidaymakers dwindled until there was none. Sebastian, having noted the time at which Neffie's flight from London had landed, knew that his waiting would soon be over. The newspaper paragraph about which football managers and their teams were likely to succeed in the coming season he had read three times, and not because it warranted such close scrutiny. On the final occasion that he looked up from the printed page he saw Neffie approaching. At the same instant she saw him, and as their eyes met across the ten or so yards between them, a space diminishing with each step they took towards each other, there was delight to behold.

It was at this juncture that Sebastian's thoughts, though he hoped not his outward expression, became distracted, for accompanying Neffie was a man whose appearance was in contrast to that of most of the men that had obviously travelled up from London. The majority were businessmen carrying briefcases and wearing suits, whereas the young man who wasn't simply walking in close proximity to Neffie, but who in addition to carrying his own rucksack was also carrying her holdall, looked like a student, or someone who travels the world in a style similar to Neffie.

Equally disconcerting to Sebastian's eyes was the sight of his beloved walking badly. She was limping, and her peculiar and obviously painful gait meant that she could move only slowly. Her male companion, though he tried to keep to a slower pace, more than once turned to look back to ensure that the invalid in his care was still making progress. One step before she and Sebastian were bound to crash into each other, Neffie stopped to relieve her gallant of her luggage. She expressed her gratitude; but to Sebastian's considerable relief he witnessed no parting kiss or hug, not even a handshake. Evidently Neffie hadn't known her Sir Galahad for long, for she didn't think introductions necessary. She wouldn't have been able to introduce him to Sebastian even if she had wanted: she didn't know his name. The young Sir Galahad departed.

The lovers embraced, kissed, and embraced again before Sebastian held Neffie at arm's length in order to look her up and down from head to toe. "You haven't changed a bit," he said following his inspection.

"Then what do you think this is, Mr Observant?" enquired Neffie sharply as she turned around and raised her foot from the sole of her flip-flop so as to show Sebastian her heel.

Purple and swollen to an extraordinary degree, it looked tender and excruciatingly painful. "Good grief!" Seb exclaimed. "How did you get that?" he asked, taking hold of the red holdall.

"A scorpion stung me," Neffie replied. "It was just the day before yesterday when it happened, but I couldn't get treatment for it because there had been lots of shooting and people had been killed."

"I had better get you to the hospital to get it checked," said Seb decisively.

Tears welled in Neffie's eyes. They were tears of relief. She didn't learn about the broken crystal wine glass until some weeks later.

THE END